The Pledge

Life Is Eternal and So Is Love

≈≈≈≈≈≈≈≈≈≈≈

Soror Joy, Thank you for your support when I needed it the most. I hope you

Linda Everett Moyé

LEJ Poetic Expressions TM

Texas

The story in this book is a work of fiction. Any references to real people, events, establishments, organizations, or places are intended only to invoke a sense of reality and authenticity. Other names, characters, places, and incidences are the product of the author's imagination or used fictitiously.

First published by:
LEJ Poetic Expressions
PO Box 301973
Austin, Texas 78703

Printed in the United States of America
First Trade Printing: 2008

ISBN: 1-893719-08-1

Book cover design by Robert R. Jones of Austin, Texas

Author's Website: www.lindamoye.com

≈≈≈≈≈≈≈≈≈≈≈≈≈≈≈≈≈≈≈≈≈≈

"This is a story that will make your face smile, touch your heart, send chills down your spine, and bring tears to your eyes. If you believe that true love never dies, you must read Moyé's new book, *The Pledge, Life Is Eternal and So Is Love.*"

Arnitria Karen Shaw, Peoria, IL
Author of *Don't Tell ME to Just Get Over Him* and
Founder of *AfraVictoria Magazine*

"If you've ever wondered if the past and present are connected, then this love story is for you. Moyé tells the story of two people whose love and spiritual connection truly spand the sands of time. Their experiences will leave you to second-guess your own experiences—passing glances; deja-vu's; and feeling that you have met someone, somewhere before."

Briant D. Ennis, Psy.D., Houston, TX
Psychologist

"*The Pledge* is a love story that will keep you up all night reading. It makes you want to believe in love at its highest form: a soul mate. Read it—it is a story that will linger in your heart."

Laura Simpson, Detroit, MI
Supply Chain Consultant and Avid Reader

"The Pledge is a very real and honest love story. Anyone who believes they have loved *and lost* their soul mate will be captivated as the story of Tom and Tish draws from their own hearts the memories of a love not forgotten."

Lorrie Moore - Oklahoma City, OK
Avid Reader

≈≈≈≈≈≈≈≈≈≈≈

Acknowledgements

There are many people to thank and acknowledge for helping me to get this story in final print. My editors, Lissa Woodson and Marilyn Weisman, worked diligently with my writing style and created a much improved fiction writer than how they found me. I appreciate their honesty and recommendations as well as the proofreading John Eric Randolph and Deborah Tinsley Pledger provided in the final edits. Thanks to Liz and Curry Zeno for being the models for the cover. The artist, Robert R. Jones, created the awesome cover art and I thank him for his patience with me. He understood what I saw in my mind's eye and was able to bring it to the canvass. That's just amazing.

There are others who showed continued faith and encouraged me to complete the book. Some read and commented on the first drafts, many purchased advanced copies, and others who knew about the story continued to ask, "When is it going to be in print?" As promised, I've done my best and I didn't quit. Because of your gifts of love and support, I acknowledge you now for giving me what I needed, even for the occasional nudge to remind me that you still wanted your copy.

Profound appreciation goes to: Donald Moyé, Midori Branch, Monique Miles Bruner, Bianca Centofanti, Alyx Chavis, Briant and Stacey Ennis, Antoinette Franklin, Cassie Levy, Lorrie Moore, Arnitria Karen Shaw, Laura Simpson, Jamie Spencer, Alfred Chaney, Sheryl Womble, Tracie Jae, Layle O'Neil McKelvey, Susan Luke, Brenda Dillard, Shirley Bell, Hector Grant, Sr., Rita Sutton, Barbara Aldave, Anna Marie Alkin, Occie Hudson Carlisle, Sathedia Bush, Mary Moore, Patricia Grant, Madora Brown, Lenny and Barbara Lawrence, Stacy Foushee, Lavon Clark, Richard Crews, Jacqueline Newton, Rosette Holmes, James Tedford, Harold and Gertrude Batiste, Tammy Jenkins, L. Gates Black, Gloria Ray, Karyne Jones, Alicia Butler, Adrian Ward, Wendi Barra, Veda Stanley, Rhonda Mitchell, Jason Butler, Deborah Stanton Burke, Elsie Daniels, Jay and Lovie Fisher, LaTonya Davis, Marvin Parker, Teresa Love, Jacquelyn Alexander, Marie Alford, Joan Ratner, Julius and Jackie Gordon, Zeff Spears, Linda and Eugene Hightower, Trevy McDonald,

Ernell Everett Skeeter, Felecia Ross, Candace and Larry Vaughn, Patsy Newborn, Wanda Hammond, Gina Allen Thomas, Timothy Netters, Marvette Thomas, Sibyl Avery Jackson, Michelle Ricoma, Sylvia Fernandez, Brendolyn Cunningham, Mary Etlinger, Rececca Trevino, Darrylyn Swift, Barbara Felix, Shauna Hardin, Alice Rose Kennedy, Tonia McGaffie, Krystle Oshon, Lisa Johnson, Vickie Richmond, Mary Taylor, Sabrina Elliott, and LaToya Abdullah.

Finally, I want to thank Sid, Michelle, Bryan and Sheryl Johnson for being the wonderful people they are. They waited patently, nudged loving, and stood proudly with me as I worked through this process. I am so fortunate and truly blessed to be their mother.

Thank all of you from the bottom of my heart. Enjoy the journey…

Linda

≈≈≈≈≈≈≈≈≈≈≈

The Pledge

Life Is Eternal and So Is Love

≈≈≈≈≈≈≈≈≈≈≈

Love that is ancient
does not ever fade away
it can never die.

Life Is Eternal and So Is Love

How many times have I been in this nowhere place?
Waiting in time to move forward
and away from this darkened space?
When will I return and who will I be?
Will my soul mate know who I am
or search until he finds me?
Alone I wait in this nowhere space
hoping the next time I will know his face.
My life's journey through the eternity of time
holds lessons to learn and rewards to find.
Each time better, each life improved –
Each time, bad deeds through Karma removed.
No more rejection or walking away,
the next time we will both know
that with each other is where we have to stay.
No longer being denied a love that is in the light
we are destined to come back until we get that part right.
He has been my lover, my brother,
my protector and my King,
Let the next time he knows me as his wife and
he allows others to see
I am his Queen.

≈≈≈≈≈≈≈≈≈≈

One

We were here before,
many times in love before.
Please find me again.

Tom stood alone, one hand in the pocket of his professionally pressed blue jeans, silently sipping an ice-cold beer at his fraternity's "Back-to-School Jam" in the Fort Sam Houston's NCO Club. He rocked and bobbed his head to the tempo of the upbeat music as he cautiously gazed at the most beautiful woman he'd seen since his military move to San Antonio. He watched her in the middle of the dance floor, laughing as her partner whispered in her ear. He noticed her every move.

He slid his hand out of his pocket and thoughtfully rubbed his chest as he admired the way the ruby red sundress with a long, full skirt draped her tall, voluptuous frame. Two tiny straps that started at the shoulders and crossed her back to her waist revealed skin the color of heavily creamed coffee. She had long, dark brown, wavy hair and the most stunning smile Tom had ever seen. He was mesmerized.

As Deborah Cox's soulful voice sang "Nobody's Supposed to Be Here," the woman glanced at Tom over her dance partner's shoulder.

Their eyes met and a slight chill ran down Tom's strong, masculine arms. "Oh, damn," he whispered as he dropped his head and walked toward the hors d'oeuvres table covered with a white tablecloth.

He piled hot wings, corn chips and queso sauce on his plate and found a new spot where he could keep his eye on the lady in red as more people arrived. *Will I ever meet this woman?*

He scanned the large room decorated with western art and earth-toned colors, now barely noticeable because of the dimmed lights and a couple hundred bodies on the dance floor.

Iceman, the DJ, had one of the best sound systems Tom had heard. His strategically positioned strobe lights helped bring some focus to the details of the mostly African-American couples as they danced, talked, and laughed. Enticing aromas from meat simmering in Mexican spices on the taco bar drifted across the room.

Iceman selected another one of Tom's favorite songs, but still he hesitated to ask the lady to dance. He feared that she might be one of those cute women, so cute that she'd tell him no. He judged from the complexion of her partner's skin that she was one of those "high-yella girls" who liked her men that same hue. Tom glanced down at his ebony hand and whispered, "No."

He looked toward the dance floor and noticed that a fraternity brother, one who looked more like him, had cut in and was dancing with her. He saw her laugh again; he had a feeling that if given the chance he'd make her smile too and if he could, he'd always keep her that happy.

Suddenly she left the dance floor, walked toward him, and turned her dark brown eyes directly into his for a quick and unanticipated moment.

He was embarrassed when he realized he was holding his breath. As she passed him, he almost reached out to place his slightly trembling hand on her exposed back.

"Okay, old schoolers, that's it for this year," Iceman announced with a strong Texas twang. Someone gradually turned the dimmer switch up on the lights as the music faded. "We'll see y'all in 'oh-three, same time, same place. Have a good evening and drive home safely, now, ya hear?"

The sound of glasses clinking together as waitresses cleared the tables rang amidst the soft roar of voices saying "Goodnight," "Where's the after party," and "Baby, what's your number?"

Tom didn't move. He wanted the party to last longer so that he could at least speak to this mystery woman. He scanned the room to see if he could find her.

"Hey, Tom. Looking for me?" Sable, a fellow Army sergeant who'd attended a leadership class with him the past four days, stood beside him looking toward the exit.

Surprised by her abrupt appearance, he smiled nervously when he realized who'd just spoken to him. He hadn't seen her in anything other than her military uniform. She looked more like Janet Jackson than the no-makeup sergeant with her hair pinned up and away from her shoulders.

"Wow, Sable! You look great! I didn't know you were here tonight. Where've you been?"

"I guess not close enough to you to get even one dance, huh? What's a girl to do? Now the party's over and it's time to go home. So who're you looking for anyway?"

Just as she asked the question, he saw Aaron, an old Army buddy, and his wife, Dee, standing near the door talking with the woman from the dance floor.

"Hey, Tom. Come over here," Dee said, waving him over. "I want you to meet my sorority sister, LaTisha Edwards."

"Excuse me, Sable. It's good seeing you out tonight." Tom gave her a quick, gentle hug and walked toward his friends.

She watched him saunter away, placed her hands on her hips, tilted her head, and tapped her foot as she contemplated her next move.

Tom grinned shyly at the woman he'd been watching all evening. "She's a Delta?"

"Through and through," Dee said with a twinkle in her eye.

He lifted his eyebrows and smiled broadly as he glanced at Dee. "As an Omega man, you know I love my Delta sisters."

"You'd better," she said, elbowing him in the ribs before the lady in red had a chance to speak.

A thunderstorm had rumbled through earlier that evening bringing with it a significant drop in temperature for the first weekend in September. A cool breeze blew gently through the open door.

"Thomas Manning, this is LaTisha, or Tish; she's a newcomer like you." Aaron's thick lips spread into a wide grin, totally aware of his friend's discomfort. "Tom, are you free tomorrow? Dee makes a mean Sunday dinner and I know how you *love* to eat."

Some nerve, Tom thought. *Aaron never missed a meal or an opportunity for seconds!* His purple V-neck sweater stretched tight around his pudgy frame; his boyish round face with its oily, olive brown skin reflected the results of years of fried foods.

"Why don't you guys come over about four?" Aaron continued with a sly lift of his eyebrow. "We can all catch up with what's going on and you two can get acquainted."

"You know me, man. I never turn down a good home-cooked meal. I'm there. I'll call and get your address and directions." He looked at Dee's perfect ten figure and wondered again what she saw in Aaron.

"Great. Tish, you can bring the kids, too. They can play with Little Aaron while we talk," Dee said in her sweet, soft voice.

"Hi, nice to meet you," Tish said as she politely extended her hand to Tom. She smiled at him as their eyes met again.

He felt a mild shock wave move up his arm as their hands met. He took a deep breath, reluctantly released her hand, cleared his throat, and adjusted his collar as he felt the temperature of his body rise in spite of the cool night air. No one had ever had such an effect on him.

Damn! he thought as he continued to admire her. He wished the night could be still young and he had time to learn more about her.

Tish lowered her eyes and quickly reached for her small black purse. "Hold this," she said as she handed it to Dee and reached for her light jacket. Tom noticed that her hands were shaking as he reached out to help her.

"So, girl, are you coming over tomorrow, too? You know you like my cooking."

"That sounds good," she answered as she started to leave.

Just as Tom was about to offer Tish a ride, David, his fraternity brother, walked up to her, gave Tom a once over and asked her, "Are you ready to go?"

"Nice meeting you, Tish." Tom reluctantly walked toward his car. He looked back over his shoulder and watched briefly as she glided into the passenger seat of David's shiny black Maxima.

Oh well, she's got a brother already interested in her. So much for that. Tom drove out of the parking lot with an image of Tish firmly in his mind. He pressed his lips and shook his head. *Maybe tomorrow I'll get to know more about her and see what that feeling was all about.*

He got as far as the first stop sign when his cell phone rang. "Hello?" Surprised that anyone would call him this late, he waited for a response.

"Hey, it's me, Sable. Where you headed?"

"What you mean where am I headed? I'm going home." He could hear other female voices in the background. "Where are you?"

"Right behind you! My girls and I are going to an after party over on Willowwood Boulevard. Wanna go?"

Tom didn't want to call it a night yet and wanted even less to go home alone. "Sure. I'll follow you because I don't know where that is." He opened the car window and waved Sable around him. She passed his car and hit the gas with no mercy.

He didn't know Sable that well, but he knew that she was single and thought she'd missed her calling. Instead of wearing an Army uniform she should be modeling designer clothes on a runway.

What would she be like on a date? She obviously enjoys the party scene. Maybe she's more than just a serious, career-mined sergeant who wears that uniform better than any other woman I know. Tom grinned. *She kept my number with her and she called. Maybe if I play my cards right…*

Two

I have been your life;
you are now the breath I breathe.
Touch my soul again.

Tish rode in silence as David drove in light traffic along Loop 410 past the ubiquitous hotels, chain restaurants and strip malls. Michael Ward's jazz CD created a relaxing mood as sexy drifts of his violin flowed through each song.

David grasped the steering wheel firmly and tapped his thumbs to the rhythm of the bass player as he drove west through the heart of the city's north side. As they approached the airport exit Tish directed him to head north on U.S. Highway 281. The clear, deep indigo sky, punctuated with hundreds of stars created a perfect backdrop for the bright, full moon.

She replayed the strange, mysterious feelings she'd experienced when she'd met Tom. Amazing how a simple introduction had evolved into a dinner invitation that included a man she knew hardly anything about, except his name and the those feelings.

Tall, dark and handsome? A definite understatement! More than that, Tish felt touched by the way his chestnut brown eyes had reached out to her. When their eyes met, she felt her chest heave. A jolt of electricity flowed from the top of her head to the bottom of her feet when she shook his hand. Embarrassed that even the slightest physical contact with him had left her insides churning and her hands shaking uncontrollably, she had tried to brush it off as quickly as she could. She hoped no one noticed.

She hadn't snatched up Aaron's dinner invitation right away; she had her eye on David and wanted to get to know him better. She'd met him at a party a couple weeks before. Tonight he'd kept her on the dance floor most of the evening and had offered to take her home. This would provide a quiet opportunity to discover if she really liked him.

Something about David attracted her, but so far the attraction was primarily on the physical package—that bodybuilder physique. She admired the way he handled himself on the dance floor and wanted to know what was hiding behind that handsome face.

Since her children were home with a babysitter, she had a built-in excuse to not invite him in. She was as horny as any grown woman with two kids who hasn't had sex in almost two years, but she knew taking this relationship in that direction wasn't an option at the moment; not for her anyway.

"Tell me about yourself," she said, in an effort to keep her mind from wondering back to Tom.

"I'm an army brat originally from upstate New York. My family lived all over the place. I attended the Air Force Academy and served my country for twenty years. I retired a couple years ago as a lieutenant colonel. Now I'm a third-year law student at St. Mary's University."

Before Tish could say anything he jumped into a detailed, one-sided description of how he had just come out of a horrible marriage and an equally bad divorce. The moment he mentioned his ex-wife, his grip tightened on the wheel. "She took my children away from me. I'll never trust or love another woman. All women are the same; they don't listen."

The more he talked, the more he reminded her of the not-so-pleasant times in her own marriage; red flags were everywhere. *Oh no, not another woman hater!* He'd been hurt and she feared he wanted to hurt someone in return.

She'd divorced the same type of man, the father of her two beautiful children. Marcus hated her for leaving him and continued to try to make her life miserable. She'd been in therapy for the past six months to rebuild her self-esteem that had been tossed down and trampled by her ex; she wasn't about to let another man do that do her.

They rode the rest of the way in silence until Tish directed him to her subdivision and gave him a code to open the gate.

As they pulled up to her place she retrieved the keys from her purse and took a deep breath. "David, I'm sorry you're hurting, but I won't be around to pay the price for your anger or disappointment."

"Hey, I didn't mean upset you. That stuff just came out." He took his hands off the steering wheel and nervously rubbed them together. Then he lowered the tone of his voice and spoke slower. "I guess it's all still so new and I haven't gotten used to the idea that my kids don't live with me anymore. And, yeah, I'm still angry about it. But that doesn't have to mess up things between us, does it?" he asked. He got out and came around to her side of the car.

"There isn't anything between us, is there? We're just getting to know each other, right?" Tish answered as David walked her to her front door. "You have to deal with your feelings about women. Thanks for the ride home."

Once inside Tish leaned against the front door and reflected on how foreign the dating concept had become. For the first time in nearly twelve years she was without a man in her life. She hadn't dated anyone since her divorce eighteen months ago. As much as she wanted to get on with her life, this dating thing made her nervous. *What if David is the best I can come up with? Great! Just great!*

Her friends encouraged her to socialize more and get involved in volunteer work to meet more people, especially men. The only people Tish knew during her marriage to Marcus were co-workers and neighbors. None were close friends; she hesitated to allow anyone to get more than a glimpse of her life.

Who'd have ever thought that a man who appeared to have so much going on would be so insecure that he had to control everything? He'd concealed that trait until they got married. Once the vows were said the real Marcus came on down. Some days he seemed totally possessed by some evil being intent on devouring her soul.

Now, David did her a big favor by lashing out. *I won't be wasting my time on him.*

Tish entered the foyer and turned off the Tiffany lamp on her grandmother's antique mahogany table. She saw a light coming from the den and heard the television playing. She peeked in to check on Cathy, her babysitter, she found curled up on the sofa. Tish turned off the TV, and covered the slender girl with a blanket knowing it would be okay to let her spend the night. She gave Cathy's mother, Joyce, a quick call so she wouldn't worry.

Tish thought about the night Dee and Aaron took her for a first solo night out at a club and taught her how to order her own drink. They encouraged her to get out on the dance floor and assured her they would be her safety-shield if any of the guys got out of line.

Where were they tonight when David decided to unleash his venom?

She checked on her children before she went to her own room. Simon, her eight-year-old, with his dark brown, curly hair, looked more like her than anybody she knew. He'd fallen asleep on top of his covers as usual. She rolled him over and moved the covers from under him, rolled him back, covered him, and kissed his forehead.

Melanie had fallen asleep with her Annie doll. They were both tucked under the covers with nothing visible but two heads of red curls on one pillow. She looked at her ten year-old daughter's freckled face and realized just how much she looked like her former mother-in-law. "You sure got your Grandma's genes," Tish whispered, then she kissed Melanie's cheek, and closed the door.

She fell on her bed and thought about how different her life had become since the divorce. She had to admit getting back into the sorority/fraternity scene even at her age made her feel years younger and gave her renewed energy. She could once again enjoy dancing until she perspired just like in her college days without fear that her husband would not only object, but also take it out on her once they were behind closed doors.

Thanks to her ex's example, Tish hoped she'd learned to ask questions that would help her recognize a control nut at the get-go and vowed not to go down that road again.

She rolled over and checked her clock. *Wow, it's almost 2:30. I'd better get up from here.* She undressed and removed her makeup. Looking into the mirror she smiled, pleased that she had pledged Delta. Having women like Dee in her life who were more than friends because of the special bond that comes automatically with being "Sorors," short for sorority sisters, proved to be one of the best experiences in her life.

She'd long awaited the opportunity to be like her old self again and it felt wonderful.

David was forgotten as she turned her thoughts to Tom. Something different about him impressed her, something she'd never expected to feel; it made her very curious. *Did he feel it too, or was it just me?*

Three

Coming together
has always been more than fate.
Again, it is so.

The adults sat at the dining room table after they'd finished the Sunday dinner Dee had prepared as well as any southern chef. The children played on the jungle gym in the backyard enjoying the bright sunshine of a pleasant fall Texas day.

"Girl, you sho' know how to cook! If I ate like that everyday, I'd need a whole new set of uniforms." Tom leaned back in the chair and rubbed his chest. "It's a good thing I'm not around you all the time. I'd be in big trouble—literally!" He grinned as he reached over and tapped Aaron's stomach.

"Ah, man!" Aaron pushed Tom's hand away. "You just jealous, that's all."

"*Right*. Jealous. You know, we could use some of that good cooking on Saturday when we finish our public service project at the Food Bank." Tom turned his wide, begging eyes to Dee, batting his long lashes. "You know, sorting food can build up an appetite. I can't think of anywhere I'd rather eat after a long day like that than right here. What'cha say, huh, Dee? Can you help a brotha' out?"

"Will I be cooking for just you or for all your troops?" she asked wondering what she was getting herself into.

"Oh, no, just me and Aaron. We won't tell the rest of the guys. I wouldn't do you like that!" he replied, as he took her hand and kissed her fingers. "I *cherish* our friendship!"

"Okay. I just needed to know what to expect," she told him in a soft, silky voice. She sat back in her chair and shifted the conversation to another subject. "Tom, have you had a chance to visit the River Walk since you moved to San Antonio? It's really pretty down there. I enjoy walking along the river eating a big ice cream cone with my family in the evening."

She turned to her girlfriend and with a smart grin, placed her elbow on the table then planted her chin squarely in her palm. "I know you've been there dozens of times, Tish. Why don't you take Tom to the River Walk? I'm sure he won't go there alone.

You know men—all work and no simple pleasures." Dee grinned at Tom and gave him a gentle nudge.

Tish looked over at him and noticed he was slightly flushed. "That would be great, Tom, if you're interested. I'm not quite as . . . *pushy* as my friend over there." She looked at Dee and rolled her eyes. "I do love the River Walk and would like to show you that part of the city. How about next Saturday? The kids will be with their dad for the weekend and I don't have anything on my calendar."

Nothing like the present to find out if he's interested in getting to know me. She trusted Dee and Aaron enough to believe that Tom must be a nice person since they were now encouraging her to spend some time with him, knowing how picky she'd become about men. Scared about men, was more like it. But she'd drive her car and meet him there just in case things didn't work up to her friends' expectations.

"Sure, sounds good. How 'bout around noon?" Tom asked, his luscious lips spreading into a big smile. "I have a morning meeting that should be over about eleven. My evening's booked too, but I'm free in the middle of the day. Would that work?"

Tish took a deep breath feeling her face flush as she looked directly at him. *What a beautiful smile this man has.* She'd seen him laugh during their conversations but had failed to pay attention to his facial features. There was something very inviting about his smoldering eyes; his lingering look at her that was even more endearing.

This could be dangerous. Her weakness for an attractive, dark chocolate man with a deep, sweet voice, perfect white teeth, and such a beautiful smile, made her knees buckle and her heart skip beats.

"Here's my number." Tish handed him a slip of paper before he had a chance to offer to pick her up or get away without her phone number. "Call me Saturday when you leave the Army Post and I'll meet you near the parking garage for the River Walk around noon." She smelled his intoxicating cologne that invited all her senses to get even closer. Her voice became softer and sexier. "We can begin our walk from there."

"Okay, fine. I'll do that." Tom folded the note and placed it in his shirt pocket. He turned to Dee. "I've enjoyed the meal and company, but must leave you good people. I still have unpacking to do and my room is screaming for order. Thanks again for a great dinner," he said as he walked over and gave Dee a Texas-sized hug.

"You're welcome…anytime."

Then he turned to Tish and gave her a hug. "I'll call you on Saturday."

"Oh, be sure to wear comfortable walking shoes. The surface of the sidewalk down there isn't always the smoothest."

He looked at Aaron who had migrated to the couch in the living room. "I'll be talking with you, my brother."

After Tom backed his purple Neon out of the driveway, Dee turned to Tish. "Okay, girl. What do you think? Is he fine or what?"

Tish picked up her glass of water, took a drink, and thought for a moment. She blushed slightly. "Well, he's nice looking. He has a pleasant personality. I just love his smile and he *smells so good.*"

Dee looked out the back window of the dining room to check on the children. "Looks like someone's coming in for a mommy check."

Simon walked into the kitchen door with a frown. He wiped a tear and yelled, "Mommy! Where are you?"

Tish met him in the kitchen. "I'm right here, baby. What's the matter?"

"I hurt my finger on the slide. I think it might be broken. Can you fix it?"

"Lemme see." She got down on her knees and examined the thumb, bending it slightly. She gently kissed it and gave him a bigger kiss on his cheek. "Oh, baby, it's not broken, but I can see why it hurts. It's a little swollen." She put some ice cubes in a baggie and placed it on Simon's thumb. "Hold the ice right there until the swelling goes down. You can sit in Auntie Dee's den and watch a movie while it gets better, okay?"

"Okay, Mommy."

She walked into the den with him and started "The Three Musketeers" movie before returning to the dining room. "I think he'll live."

"Good," Dee said.

Tish sat at the table with her friend. "So tell me about Tom. I mean, you know…single I assume, ever married, divorced, kids? Is he cool, mean, angry, got issues, in therapy, crazy, religious fanatic, controlling or in control of his feelings? I can see he's fine. But I had fine, remember? I need *sane!* And I don't want another man with power and control issues nor do I want to pay for a guy's bad relationship with a woman who was a drama queen, either."

"Aaron has known Tom longer than I have but he seems to be a really nice brother. He was married once, has a son, and is recently divorced. When stationed at Fort Hood, he and Aaron became good friends. When we moved to Fort Bliss, he moved there, too. That's where I met him."

Dee paused and frowned slightly. "I knew his wife too and didn't like her much. Stuck up heifer. She never wanted to attend any of the military family functions or just have dinner together. Her main purpose in life was shopping."

"Shopping?"

"Yeah, and I heard her closet stored a shoe collection that would put Imelda Marcos to shame! I don't know how she did it, though. She has the biggest feet I'd ever seen on any woman." Dee laughed and drank the last of her wine. "Want some more wine? This stuff's really good."

Tish shook her head.

Dee poured herself another glass. "I watched Tom care for his son like I've seen no other man care for a baby, including my own husband. He cares deeply about the people in his life and tries to do what it takes to keep them happy. I think his wife took advantage of his giving spirit until he felt all used up."

Not exactly what Tish wanted to hear; she doubted that a relationship with him would go anywhere but she decided to keep going. "So, who divorced who? Where is she now? Does he have the reckless ex drama?"

"He divorced her." Dee gathered the dishes and stacked them on the table. "Katrina lives in El Paso, which is where she grew up and where her parents still live. I'm sure she'll take her time learning how to be nice in this situation. And it's a shame, because they have a wonderful son. I hope he doesn't get damaged in all this. You know how it is when folks just don't want to let go and move on."

"Girl, you don't have to tell me about people staying mad. My ex still can't get over the fact that I divorced his trifling tail. He tries to upset me every time he comes around or calls about the kids. Sometimes I just hang up or walk away from the fool. Especially when he starts telling me how to live my life. I hope Tom's situation isn't as bad as mine." Tish shook her head.

She moved a plate with the last slice of sweet potato pie from the end of the table and began to break off small pieces with her fork. "I know. This is my third slice, but it's the bomb! You sure put your foot in this pie."

Tish took a bite before she continued. "That's why I've decided to stay the hell single and raise my children the best way I can. I can't afford the risk of falling into a new relationship with another crazy man."

"I hear you and agree that you don't deserve to be abused again," Dee replied. "You're entitled to have a good man in your life, one who can learn to love you for the beautiful person you are. You should have someone you can call, someone to talk to and share your feelings."

She reached over and took a piece of Tish's pie. "That *is* good. I'll have to give you the recipe. It's been in the family for years. Now as I was saying…it's okay for that person to be a man. I don't know if Tom is the one or not, but I do know he's a good man. I'd never try to set you up with him if I didn't know him well enough to trust him. So lower your shields, give him a chance, and decide for yourself."

"Fair enough. I can do that. What could it hurt, anyway?" Tish replied before quickly adding, "I'm not looking for a husband, though. I don't want one and will make that clear to any man I date. I don't need a man in my life that badly. But it'd be nice for a change to have a decent, positive thinking one around when I want a male's perspective on things; someone I could talk to about anything. Even to cry on his shoulders if I needed to. One who wouldn't become scared if I fell apart every now and then would be nice. I really want that. Is that asking for too much?"

"Sounds to me like *you need a man* in your life," Aaron whispered as he walked by, carrying wineglasses to the kitchen. He closed the door quickly behind him.

"Who asked *you* anyway?" Tish called after him before she turned back to Dee. "You know, maybe he's right. It's been a long time. I wasn't really expecting this strong surge of sexual energy my mother warned me about. Working out at the gym helps to burn it off. That's great and safe but it's getting pretty old. I've dropped thirty pounds and I know I look better than I have in a very long time."

"Girl, your body is tight. I see how the men look at you when we go out. You should feel great that at thirty-five years old, twenty-year-old men turn their heads when you walk by."

"Yeah, sure. That's flattering, but I really do need more." She paused and stared at the dessert. She pushed the plate toward Dee.

"Okay, so you gonna let me finish this pie, huh? I see what you're doing." She laughed. "What about David? How'd that go last night? You haven't even mentioned him."

"You know what our mamas always said, 'What looks good to you ain't always good for you.' And he's one good lookin' caramel-sweet, butter-cream, green-eyed, curly-haired brother who can't be good for me. Not now, maybe not ever." Tish tapped the table. "Sometimes I think I'm better off not trying to be in a relationship. Men can be so complicated. Or maybe it's that they complicate things that can be so simple. Anyway, I'm not liking this dating thing."

"I guess we can say David didn't make a good first impression, huh?" Dee took a deep breath and placed the pie plate on the stack with the others. "Look, you can't let him ruin how you see other men. You have to decide to have a life, my sister. And there are some good men out there. Unfortunately, we've all had to kiss a few toads before we found the prince."

"Yeah, yeah, I know. I'm really scared but I'm sure my needs aren't going to just go away by working things out at the gym." She paused and looked down at her fingers. "And I know if I give up completely on all men, my ex wins. I can't let him continue to control my life." She stared out the window, briefly mesmerized by the tiny hummingbird sipping nectar from a yellow hibiscus bloom on the patio.

"We aren't encouraging you to take Tom to bed next Saturday or anything, but give him a chance to get to know you and vice versa," Dee replied as she headed for the kitchen with the dirty dishes. "Take your time and when you feel comfortable enough, go for it. What can it hurt? Well, use a condom—then, what can it hurt? You're a grown woman with needs, my dear. It's okay to take care of them with a willing partner. But don't wait too long; we don't want you to hurt the boy!"

Four

You and I will see
what our hearts feel and what our
souls have known before.

"I can't believe how fast the week has passed." Tish walked into her bedroom wearing only a white, plush Egyptian cotton bathrobe, with a red portable phone in one hand and brushing her hair with the other. "No, I haven't talked to David all week. He's called a couple of times, but I haven't returned his messages. Maybe he'll just go away."

"Not likely," Dee said like somebody's mama dishing out free telephone advice. "He's interested in you and he's obviously persistent. You're gonna have to tell him to bug off if that's what you want."

"I'm sure you're right, but not today. Right now I need to get ready to meet Tom." She laid out different outfits on her bed as she decided what to wear. "Remember, you set up this date at the River Walk. I haven't heard from him all week, so I'm not so sure it's even going to happen."

"Get ready anyway, 'cause I bet he'll call. I saw how he looked at you during dinner. I'm pretty sure he likes you. How could he not? You're smart, beautiful, successful, and a lot of fun to be around. Any man would be very blessed to have a woman like you."

"Yeah, sure." Tish put the brush on the dresser then moved a pair of jeans to the foot of the bed. She sat on the cleared spot of the soft, white down filled comforter. With her free hand, she smoothed out the lines that formed ripples beside her hips. Her voice softened as she slipped her feet in and out of her fuzzy lavender slippers. "That is, if he isn't intimidated by me because of all that. Plus, I'm an independent woman, remember? A lot of our men don't care for that additional spice. It all sounds good to you and me but we aren't trying to date each other!"

"That's true." Dee chuckled. "But get ready 'cause he's going to call. Just wait and see. Now find those tight, butt-fitting jeans so he can see your nice figure. This ain't no time for modesty."

"Yes, Dear Abby. Thanks for the advice. Gotta go."

"Have a good date."

Tish walked through the patio door and stepped down to the wood deck outside of her bedroom and checked the temperature again. Two startled jackrabbits playing in her backyard scrambled to attention, ears perked straight up, and quickly disappeared in the nearest flowerbed. She admired the way her gardener arranged the red and yellow blooming hibiscus plants and the golden hues of the mums around an angel limestone water fountain.

She chose the blue jeans that fit perfectly, a plain red T-shirt and white tennis shoes. She didn't intend to make a statement or to be a tease, she just wanted to feel comfortable and look cute.

The sudden ring of her telephone startled her.

"Hello?"

"Hey there. This's Tom. How ya' doing?"

"Oh, I'm doing great. How about you?"

"Pretty good, pretty good. Just calling to see if we're still on for the River Walk."

"My plans haven't changed."

"Good. I'm tying my shoelaces as we speak and will be heading that way in about ten minutes. Where exactly do you want to meet?"

"Park in the Crockett Street garage of the Rivercenter Mall." She kicked off her slippers and untied her bathrobe. "Take the elevator to the street level and I'll meet you just outside the elevator."

"See you in a few."

"Okay, bye." *At least he remembered.*

After she dressed, she slid into her brand new, crystal white Lexus RX300, buckled herself in the beige, leather seat, and backed out of the garage. She drove south on U.S. Highway 281 toward downtown and turned up the surround sound of her radio. The slower version of "Nobody's Supposed to Be Here," flowed through the speakers carrying the sultry voice of Deborah Cox.

We'll just see how this thing goes. I won't get my hopes up. He is, after all, just another man.

Tish drove into the Rivercenter garage and parked in the first space she found. She took the elevator up and stood in the hall waiting and watching as the elevator opened and closed for ten minutes. Frustration started to set in. *Maybe he won't come at all.*

Just then Tom walked out and headed toward her. She took a deep breath to calm her jangling nerves.

"Hi. Guess my directions were okay."

"Yes, they were actually very easy to follow." He reached for her shoulder and placed a soft kiss on her cheek. "Parking, however, was interesting. Somehow I got behind some really slow driver who couldn't decide whether to park or leave the garage. Sorry if you've been waiting long."

"Not a problem." Surprised by his kiss and how warm that small gesture had suddenly made her face, she tried to compose herself. "I only just got here myself a couple minutes ago."

Tish smiled at him as she scanned his loose-fitting jeans and the purple shirt that covered his broad chest. Purple always drew her attention almost as much as red, her favorite color. Purple reminded her of good times in college, of hot young passion, and of experiencing her first real love.

Her eyes met his and she felt uncomfortable. It seemed almost as if he tried to draw her into him. She'd never felt that before from anyone else. "Well, are you ready to walk?"

"Yes, ma'am. I'm ready to experience the famous San Antonio River Walk. Let's do it," Tom replied, smiling brightly as he walked beside her.

"So, where're you from?"

"I was born in Hampton, Virginia, but my father was in the Army and so we traveled and lived in many different places. I guess I call Hampton home because that's where my grandparents, aunts, uncles and most of my cousins live." He followed her on the down escalator. "And, my mother moved back there after my father died."

Tish looked at him over her shoulder. "I lived on the East Coast, too. We both grew up around great rivers. In your case it was the James River and a few others. Part of my life I lived near the Potomac. No one warned me about the size of the San Antonio River so I was disappointed the first time I saw it. We'd call it a big ditch where we're from. So when you see it, look beyond its size; look at its potential, its charm, and the great care it's been given to create such an enchanting place in the middle of this large city."

"Thanks for the warning. Let's go see this big ditch," Tom said with that big smile Tish already loved. They stepped off the escalator and walked through the Food Court then through a set of double doors that ushered them directly onto the River Walk.

Five

Walk with me and share
your time, dreams and memories.
Help me to know you.

Tom noticed the array of restaurants as they entered the lagoon area of the River Walk. An all-male, South American Indian band played in front of an ice cream shop. About one hundred people seated on the off-white, stone steps and wrought-iron chairs with tables shaded by brightly colored umbrellas listened attentively to the ancient woodwind instruments and drums.

As Tish walked beside him, Tom experienced a whole new level of contentment and happiness. He was glad that he'd followed Dee's prodding to spend some time with her. Yet, something about Tish struck him in a strange, but good way. It happened every time he'd seen her and now that they were alone it felt much stronger.

He wasn't looking for a committed relationship. Because he'd gotten married so young, he hadn't had a real chance to date many women. Now that he was single and in a new city he intended to change that. He planned to explore possibilities, not get into a serious relationship with the first good-looking woman he met.

According to Aaron, Tish had no desire to rush into a serious relationship either. She'd been in an abusive marriage with a cheating husband and went through a nasty divorce. *So maybe it'd be okay. Maybe she could be a friend and we can just hang out together sometimes.*

Tom wasn't sure if he was trying to talk himself into or out of something. Being with her made him feel different inside. It began to make him experience an edgy, almost nervous sensation but it didn't keep him from wanting to know everything about her.

She asked him to tell her about himself and his eagerness to oblige shocked him. He'd never before shared much of his life on a first date. "I dropped out of college right after I pledged Omega during my junior year at Virginia State because my girlfriend got pregnant. We got married. Then I worked as a department manager for a men's clothing store. Later, I joined the

Army to make sure the medical bills were covered. I'd planned to go back to school to finish my degree in business, but that never happened."

"Wow, I'm sorry to hear that."

"We tried really hard to make our marriage work. But when it became clear that we weren't made for each other, we divorced last year. My ex-wife stayed in El Paso and has custody of our fourteen-year old son, Shaun. Your children, Simon and Melanie, right? They remind me of him. I really miss my son." He looked at Tish. "How about you?"

"It's got to be hard to be separated like that from your child. How do you handle it?"

Tom looked away from her, took a deep breath, and noted that she kept the focus on him. "I guess you just accept that this is the way things have turned out and make the best of it that you can. You can't go through life being upset that everything didn't work according to your plan. So, I make every attempt to see him as often as I can and believe it's a better situation for him this way."

He watched, as she appeared to think about what he'd said; he detected a slight smile as they walked without speaking. Tom decided to move on with his question. "So, I assume you were married too?"

"Twelve years and I'm also divorced," she said as they approached the River Cruise tour. "If you like, we could take the river boat tour. It's a great way to see the whole River Walk and learn about its history."

"Maybe later. Right now I'm enjoying the walk. Let's stop someplace and have lunch. Is that okay with you?"

"Sure, whatever you'd like to do."

They crossed the river over a small stone pedestrian bridge and walked along the meandering, narrow sidewalk. "That's a statute of Saint Anthony over there in the foliage," she told him as she pointed toward some trees to their right. "The city was named after him."

On the opposite side of the river they saw a small, beautiful waterfall cascading over layers of ancient limestone. Both sides of the river were lined with an assortment of tropical plants and tall trees that seemed to almost surround them. The sound from the water rushing down the waterfall mixed in with the songs of mockingbirds and the buzz of the small motors used to operate the river boats helped create a unique atmosphere as people of all ages passed them going the opposite direction.

They turned right onto the main stretch of the River Walk and met a group of people wearing convention badges.

"Wow, it looks like this is the place to be today. It's going to be crowded at all the restaurants for a while. You want to walk some more before we stop to have lunch?" Tish asked as she pointed across the river. "That's Casa Rio, my favorite Mexican restaurant on the river. I'd like to go there when we're ready to eat."

Pleased to know she liked to eat what he liked, he smiled and mentally added another point to her scorecard. "Okay. That's where we'll go." A myriad of spices coming from the different restaurants made him ravenous. The smell of onion, garlic, cilantro, chili peppers, and grilled meats made it almost impossible for him to wait but he agreed.

They continued along the river, passing crowds of people all looking for a place to eat that could seat them right away. He followed Tish as she entered the Hyatt Regency Hotel where a small branch of the San Antonio River flowed through its lobby.

"Have you seen the Alamo yet?" she inquired.

"No, I haven't."

"Then follow me." She led him out the back door of the hotel to a walkway with an exquisite display of waterfalls and tropical plants. It ended with steps that took them up to the street level. They came out just across the street from the front of the Alamo.

"*Man*," Tom exclaimed with widened eyes. "I had no idea it was here in the middle of everything. I thought you'd find the Alamo out in a dusty prairie or something."

"Nope. It's right here in the heart of the city."

"I see some benches across the street." He pointed toward a grassy area shaded by a sycamore tree. "Let's grab that one before someone else gets it." He wanted to slow things down so they could talk.

Once they were seated facing the Alamo, Tom asked, "Okay, how did you end up in San Antonio?" He was determined to find out more about this gorgeous woman who had agreed to spend the afternoon with him.

"I moved here about three years ago following my husband and his great career. We met in Savannah where I'd moved after I finished my marketing degree at Howard University. We dated about six months, got married after he finished medical school. Melanie was born two years after we were married, then Simon came along."

"Where is Dr. Edwards now?"

"He's still in San Antonio." She shifted her position on the bench, sat back, and crossed her legs and her arms. "Except his name isn't Edwards. That's my maiden name. I chose not to keep his name when we divorced. Didn't see the point."

Her answer and body language told him it was time to change the subject. He wanted to ask about David, but decided against it in case she turned out to be David's woman. "So how do you know Dee and Aaron? Did you meet Dee in college?"

"No, actually I met her at a sorority meeting about a year ago here in San Antonio. She and I became best friends almost immediately. Soon after we met she told me about an opening at the advertising agency where she works and I've been working with her since then," Tish answered before turning the conversation back to him. "So how do you like San Antonio so far?"

"Oh, it's growing on me. Nothing like the East Coast, but I guess you know that, huh?"

"It's different, that's for sure. But that's why I like it. It's a good place to raise children and there's always something going on here. It's like the whole city's just one big excuse to have a party. It's also a good place for starting over and moving on."

She turned to him and gave him what looked like a forced smile. "What I'd really like to do is write books, travel, go back to school, and start a business of my own one day. I believe I'll get to do all those things, too." Her excitement grew with each word.

"What kind of books do you want to write?"

"Oh, I'm not really sure. I have this feeling that there's at least one really good story inside me that needs to be written. Sometimes I sense that much of this is familiar, like maybe I've been here before, you know, in another lifetime. As I get older, the feeling gets stronger. But when I sit down to write it, nothing comes out. So I guess that means whatever it is will have to wait."

As she spoke, she seemed to be more relaxed; it pleased him that she'd begun to open up. "I think it's great that you know exactly what you want to do. I haven't decided yet what I'm going to be when I grow up! You know, whether I'll make a long career out of the Army and retire or go back to school and do something completely different."

He paused and looked over to a group of pigeons that had gathered to eat the popcorn a young boy threw at them. "I'd really like to teach kids. In the meantime, I just signed up to mentor a couple of boys at King Middle School. We'll see how that goes."

Tish looked at him and smiled. "Let's go have lunch. I'm starved."

When he stood, he resisted the urge to reach for her hand to walk back with her as close to his side as possible. *Not yet, but one day I will.*

The couple returned to the River Walk the same way they'd left it. They crossed the river on the stone footbridge nearest the Casa Rio Restaurant and passed groups of convention goers who'd just finished eating.

"Table for two?" Miguel, the host asked Tom.

"Yes, thank you."

"I have one outside, right beside the river." He pointed to a small round table with two chairs covered by a large, bright yellow umbrella. "Will that be fine?"

"Perfect." Tom smiled at Tish and gestured for her to follow Miguel to their table. He pulled the chair out for Tish and then sat facing her.

"Wow, *this is* perfect," she said as she gazed out toward the river. "It's a beautiful, warm day; full of sunshine, and a nice breeze to keep it from getting too hot. Who could want more?"

"Well, as soon as I order my beef enchilada dinner and I eat it, I'll be complete in what I wanted." He rubbed his growling stomach. "I can say it's been a rather satisfying day, Tish. Thanks for sharing it with me."

"It's been my pleasure. The River Walk is one of my favorite places to be." She looked at the menu. "And I love the food here. I think I'll have the same thing you're having."

He smiled automatically and took a deep breath as he looked at her glowing face. *I'm with a beautiful woman, about to enjoy a wonderful meal in a picturesque setting.*

It was a perfect day that invited easy conversation for the remainder of his date with Tish on the San Antonio River Walk. When their meal concluded, he walked her to her car and they parted.

I wonder if she'll always be this easy to talk to? He scratched his head and watched her as she backed out from her parking space and drove away.

Six

My soul knew it first
what the mind could not perceive.
You are here for me.

Tish stopped at the Shoemaker's Inn on her way home from the River Walk. This place had a serious sale going on. The party season was coming and she needed to get her dress wardrobe together for the formal social events she anticipated being invited to by a number of the city's organizations. She looked forward to having fun and getting out and enjoying herself for a change.

No more sitting around watching TV as the holiday parties and events rolled by because her man worked long hospital hours or came home too tired to go anywhere.

After trying on several pairs, she found the perfect basic black evening shoes—stylish yet comfortable. However, Tish still had two major problems: evening dresses were non-existent in her closet, and she didn't have anyone to escort her.

She contemplated her situation as she drove home. *Next week I'll start shopping for gowns; that will take care of one problem. Maybe if I'm lucky, this afternoon will lead to a solution to the second problem. If not, the absence of a good man in my life won't stop me; I'll go solo.*

When she walked into her kitchen, the message light on the answering machine caught her eye.

"Okay, where are you? How was your date? I want all the details. Call me."

"All right, Dee, I'll get back to you in a minute." Tish chuckled, deleted the message, and went to the next, hoping it would be from Tom.

"Hey, Tish. David. I can be in San Antonio this weekend and wanted to know if you'd like to go out somewhere and do something. You have my work digits, right? Hope to hear from you."

"Fat chance. I'm losing the digits, even as we speak, Mr. Women-Don't-Listen." Tish erased that message with the flick of a manicured finger.

"Hi, Tish, this is Tom. I just wanted to let you know that I really enjoyed getting to know you today and appreciate you

taking the time to show me the very beautiful, yet small San Antonio River. I wanted to also give you my numbers in case you're interested in talking or getting together again. I'll leave that up to you. No pressure, but I'd really like to hear from you." He left his work, barracks, and cell numbers.

Oh, how sweet! There is a God and He's paying attention! Tish chuckled as she played the message again. *So I'm not the only one feeling good about our date! Maybe he has more potential than I originally thought.*

She had feared that she might have shared too much about herself. With everything she had going on she thought he might have decided to run for the hills. But she'd obviously been wrong.

She went into her bathroom, started the water in her whirlpool tub, and poured in a few drops of her most exotic bath oil—A Pharaoh's Favorite. She rarely used it because it was expensive and hard to find, but a little pampering while the children were away was exactly what she needed.

While the water filled the tub, she called Dee. "Hey, this is your girlfriend who has a smile on her face!" Tish said giggling as she sat on her bed. "What're you up to?"

"Oh, I'm not doing anything important. So I gather it went well with Tom? You like him, don't you? I can hear it in your voice. Give me the details!"

"Tom seems like a really nice guy." Tish went back into her bathroom to check on the water covered by a thick layer of bubbles. "He told me about himself and asked about me. He even listened to me go on once I got comfortable enough to open up about myself. By the time we sat down to have lunch I was really digging him. It's hard to explain. I didn't feel the need to be on the defensive or to hold back anything in order to protect myself or explain why I made the choices that I have. Hold on a sec. there's another call."

Tish switched to the call waiting and said, "Hello."

"Hi, Mom. What'cha doing?" Melanie asked.

"I'm on the phone talking to Auntie Dee, honey. What are you and your brother up to?"

"We're just hanging out with our new babysitter, Carmen. We're playing a video game while she's studying."

"Where's your father? And do I know Carmen?"

"Daddy left for a fancy dinner thing at the hospital. Mom, we went shopping with him today and he bought these shiny new black shoes, a suit and a bow tie!" She became as excited as a schoolgirl going on a first date. "He was soooo handsome when he got dressed. He modeled for us and everything! I wish you could've seen him, too."

"That sounds really exciting," Tish replied trying not to let the surprise show in her voice. She wondered why suddenly Dr. Marcus Brown had the time for and interest in formal dinners. "Now, who's Carmen?"

"She's a medical student and wants to be a pediatrician just like daddy. She's so cool. She's from Laredo and real pretty!" Melanie continued, "She even speaks English *and Spanish* and we're learning to understand some of her Spanish."

"Wow, so you're having a great weekend, aren't you?"

"Yes, ma'am. Daddy wants to know if we can come home at eight instead of six tomorrow night. He's gonna take us to a movie and it won't be over until seven-thirty. It's the only show he can go to because of some other stuff he's doing. Is that okay? *Please?*"

"Okay, but that means as soon as you get home, you have to take baths and go straight to bed. You have school on Monday. Did you complete your homework?"

"We're doing it right after this game is over."

"All right. I'll see you tomorrow night. Have fun. I love you."

"Love you, too! Thank you."

Tish switched over to Dee's call. "I don't know about that man I married, girl. How come he doesn't get it that Sunday night is a school night and children should go to movies during the day instead of in the evenings?"

"Maybe because he doesn't have to get them up, make sure they're dressed, fed, and at school on time. That's your problem, not his. Remember, he only does what's convenient for him. Why should this be any different?"

"You're right."

Tish put her wash cloth into her bath water and moved it around mixing the cold water she added to cool it down some before she got in. She didn't mention the babysitter to Dee, although she knew that a new pretty medical student in the house only meant that Carmen would soon be doing more for her ex-husband than watching his children.

"Now, back to Tom. You like him, right?"

"I do like him."

"And so, you're going to hook up again? Did you make a follow up date?"

Tish turned the water off and slipped out of her robe and slippers. Stepping into the tub, she smiled shyly. "He'd already called before I got home. He gave me all his phone numbers and left it up to me to make the next move but said he'd like to see me again. Guess that means he's interested. I'll call him, but not today."

"Okay, so you're going to do the make him wait, but not too long thing. That's cool." Dee replied sounding relieved that they were still talking. "I'm glad Aaron and I have been able to help out. A decent man in your life for a change is a good thing. Remember, take your time, and get to know him. He could turn out to be a true friend, if nothing more. That's my take on things, anyway."

"I agree," Tish said, splashing water on her legs with her wash cloth. "I feel like we're friends already and we just met. When we were talking over lunch, our eyes would meet in a certain way and his would draw me in. It felt kinda weird. Tom has a very kind face and familiar eyes. I can't figure it out. I'm sure I've never seen or met him before last week, but I feel like I've known him for a long time."

"Did you guys talk about that? Did he feel it, too?"

"I didn't mention it. How do you bring something like that up?" Tish asked, thoughtfully. "We don't know each other well enough to talk about those kinds of things. He may think I'm trying to be psychic or that I'm a psycho."

Dee laughed. "Girl, you tickle me. How can he think you're psycho? Huh?"

"I just don't want to scare Tom off about this feeling when I can't even figure it out. Maybe it'll come to me one day."

"I think this is just wonderful. Who knows, maybe you guys knew each other in another life." She chuckled. "There are people who believe in that stuff, you know. I don't, but I do find it intriguing."

"Yeah, who really knows? Maybe it's as simple as me wanting him to be the right guy for me, for the right reasons and right now. Maybe it's just me wishing that it'll all just magically work out so I don't have to live through the torture bad dating experiences bring."

Tish stared through the bathroom door at her neatly made bed that she'd become accustomed to sleeping in alone. "One thing I do know, I'm not going to just sit around and try to analyze it anymore, 'cause I'll just talk myself right out of seeing him again. Fantasy or not, real or not, if he's willing to spend time with me, I'm going for it because I feel good around him."

"So when are you going to see him again?"

"I have no idea. He had plans made already to do something tonight; he didn't say what. I didn't ask. Maybe he's seeing someone already. If he is, then good for him. If not, then I'll take my chances with him. I think he's worth the risk."

"Well, I hear you splashing around in that tub. Go ahead and turn those jets on and enjoy your bath. Talk with you later."

Seven

When you hold my hand
I am joined with you again.
Physically, as one.

Quiet. A wonderful quiet Sunday morning with no children in the house, no one to cook breakfast for, and no one to share the sports section with from the Sunday newspaper like she did when she was married.

Tish woke up with the urge to make love, and went straight to the gym to work off the sexual energy. She returned home two hours later and picked up the paper from the driveway on her way into the garage. She sat at her dinette table and checked to see what time the Redskins played the Cardinals in their first game of the season. Football was her second favorite sport. Basketball had always been her first love in the sports arena.

She showered and dressed; then turned up her stereo in the den. Listening to the Sunday morning worship service from St. Paul United Methodist Church helped her focus on what she knew were her priorities; her children, her faith, and learning to love herself better.

With a pot of Starbucks coffee brewing, she toasted some wheat bread and filled a bowl with fresh strawberries. She placed her breakfast on a tray, carried it out to the lower deck off of her kitchen, and sat on the swing in the sun to enjoy her meal.

She picked up the phone and dialed. “Hi, Tom, this is Tish. How ya’ doing?”

“Good, good. Just putting some things up on my walls in this small room trying to make it feel like home. I see you got my message.”

“Yes, I did. Thanks for leaving your numbers. I hope your evening was enjoyable.”

“It was. I had a date with one of the troops I met at a leadership training class. She’s an interesting lady; we’ve been out a couple times.”

Tish slowly lowered her coffee cup to her tray; blinked her eyes as she took a slow deep breath. *Damn, he is seeing someone else!*

"We'd talked about the movies that'd just come out and so I invited her to join me to see one last night. Like I told you yesterday, I'm getting out more. So, how'd you spend your evening?"

"I watched a movie, too, at home on my sofa with a bowl of popcorn." Her soft voice reflected the hurt she felt because he'd left her to be with another woman.

"Home alone, huh?" He sat on his bed. "So you aren't seeing anyone? How about David? I thought you guys might be kicking it."

"Well, for a very quick moment I thought we might be, too. But then he gave me the impression he might be remotely like my ex. Just an impression in that direction is all I need. I have no desire to explore a relationship with him."

As much as she hated to admit it at this point, she confessed, "And no, I'm not seeing anyone."

"Oooh," Tom said, his relief almost tangible. "Now that I have that straight, are you free today to spend some time with this newcomer to San Antonio?"

"Just as long as I'm home by eight. My children are with their dad and they'll be back by then." She didn't want to spend the rest of her day alone, especially if she had a better offer. "What do you have in mind?"

"Have you been to the zoo?"

"No, not yet. The kids have been there on school trips." She started gathering the sales sections of the newspaper she'd brought out to the deck with her.

"How about meeting me at the zoo?" Tom asked, as he stood and straightened the covers on the bed. "I haven't been to a zoo in ages and I hear that the one in San Antonio is great. Since it's the first time for both of us we might as well do this together, right?"

"Sounds good. Do you know how to get there?" She popped the last strawberry in her mouth.

"I have a map and it isn't very far from Fort Sam." He sounded eager to see her. "Why don't we meet in about an hour in front of the ticket booth? Does that give you enough time?"

"Yes, I can make that," Tish said, letting excitement creep into her voice as she stood up and stretched.

"Great. See you later."

She was surprised that Tom had moved things right along. *But what about Miss Thang last night?*

Tish shook her head. *I can't have any expectations about Tom and I certainly won't let my feelings for him go anywhere. He couldn't be ready for a serious relationship or he wouldn't have told me about his date last night.* She carried the tray back into the kitchen and rinsed out her dishes. She walked into the bathroom and brushed her hair, then checked her makeup.

But at least he's honest, she thought as she headed out.

She got to the zoo just as Tom arrived. "Shall we?" he asked, then walked up to the booth and bought the tickets. "So, what's your favorite animal in the zoo? Oh, let me guess, the elephant?"

"That's a lucky guess." Tish playfully pushed him with her arm. "Elephants are intelligent, beautiful, and the most graceful creatures on the planet despite their size. I have a large collection of elephant things at home. I've been collecting them since I pledged Delta."

"How many do you have?" He stopped to purchase a bag of popcorn from the first vendor he saw.

"I've never counted them. Maybe one hundred in all." She took a handful of popcorn and ate it one piece at a time as they continued to walk.

Tom smiled at her. "Maybe I'll get invited over one day and we can count them together. You think that's possible?"

"Yeah, I think that's possible." Tish smiled back. "What a smooth way to say, I'd like to come over sometime," she teased. "Do you collect anything?"

They walked past a flock of flamingos, their bright pink feathers shimmering in the sunlight.

"I inherited my dad's collection of bulldogs he'd started while in college. But the Army has me moving around so much that I try to keep my load as light as possible. So I left them at my mom's house until I get settled."

Tom stopped suddenly and stepped aside as a set of twin boys about eight years old, darted by them screaming about being the first one to see the monkeys. Their parents ran right behind them yelling for them to stop, but the boys were on a mission.

"I thought that I would buy a house someplace where I could retire, and then I would go get the bulldogs and add to the collection," he continued. "We got to El Paso and bought the house, but now I'm not there. I asked to be transferred to the post in San Antonio. My room at the barracks is no place for a collection of anything."

"I think we're getting closer to those monkeys…man do they smell bad!" Tish covered her nose as an acrid scent from the monkey house was whipped up by a strong breeze. "Do you think you'll retire here?"

"The jury is still out on that. I don't really like Texas that much; too many bad memories. I could end up anywhere at this point. I guess that'll be decided when it's time." He rubbed his chest and continued. "Right now I'm committed to Uncle Sam in San Antonio. So for the next three years this is where I'll be. It's close enough so I can get to El Paso to see my son frequently. I don't want to be too far from him when he's growing up."

"El Paso's a days' drive away, you know?" She lifted her eyebrows and looked at him with a smile.

"Yeah, I know. But at least we're in the same state and one flight away—nonstop on Southwest." He smiled. "Hey, it's better than being in the middle of a Gulf war or something…"

"It sounds like you're a good father; you care about spending time with your son. That's so important. I wish more fathers would do the same."

"I do the best I can with what I have." Tom looked at her again and admired her natural beauty. The warm breeze tumbled her hair making it flow softly around her neck and occasionally across her face.

She took another handful of popcorn. "Perhaps there's a chance that there'll be enough time to develop some really great memories in Texas before you have to leave it and move on—if you ever do."

"Yeah, who knows, maybe my destiny is right here. All it would take is the right woman at the right time." Tom answered, looking Tish directly in her eyes. Her glance back at him caused him to pause for a moment as he felt a lump begin to develop in his throat. Tom slowly reached for her hand and held it as they walked. "Look, the elephants are right over there."

He pointed toward the Animals of Africa exhibit where the heads of two giraffes bobbed above the crowd of people several hundred feet in front of them.

As they walked through the zoo, they talked about the animals and shared funny stories about childhood pets. Tom felt something he didn't understand and couldn't explain in words if asked to.

"Hey, here's the reptile house. Want to go see the big snakes from the Amazon?"

"Oh, absolutely not!" She pulled his arm to keep him from entering the exhibit. "I'm very afraid of snakes…have been my whole life. Seeing them in glass cages doesn't make it better."

Tish's cell phone rang and she checked the caller ID. "That's my ex. Excuse me for a second. I have to take this."

Marcus didn't wait for her to say anything or even greet her. As usual, it was an order. "I'm on the way to your house with the kids. Just wanted to make sure you're home."

"I'm not home. It's six-thirty. Melanie called last night and said you weren't bringing them home until eight," she told him, her irritation obvious in her voice.

"Plans changed. So how soon will you be there? The kids have school tomorrow, you know."

"I'm surprised you'd think about that," she snapped. "I'll be there in about thirty minutes." Tish closed the flip phone with a sharp snap. "Oh, that man!"

"Hey, don't let him spoil an otherwise perfect day, okay?" Tom squeezed her hand, stopped walking, and pulled her in front of him. "I really enjoyed my time with you and we got to see most of the zoo together." He smiled sweetly and gave her a soft hug. "Now I want to walk you to your car and see you safely on your way home to meet your children."

She squeezed him gently and replied softly, "Well, alright."

When they reached her car he opened the door and just as she stepped in front of him, Tom pressed his lips to the back of her hand. "I'll call you tomorrow, okay?"

He noticed her blush as she whispered, "Okay."

Eight

Tell me all your dreams
for they are all also mine.
They bind who we are.

The phone rang, jarring Tish out of a sound sleep.

"*Hel-lo.*" She checked the clock; the red numbers changed from six twenty-nine to six thirty, making her groan inwardly. *This had better be important!* She'd been forced out of a dream that had just gotten to the really good part.

"Good Monday morning. Did I wake you up?"

"Yes, you did, Tom," she whispered as she rubbed her eyes, and swallowed a mild retort. "And you yanked me from a very interesting dream."

She turned on her side, sinking deeper into the pile of oversized down pillows. "I think you were in it, too. How strange you would call—especially so *early* in the morning. Is everything okay?"

"Everything's fine. I really enjoyed yesterday. And since today is yesterday's tomorrow and I awoke with you on my mind, I thought I'd call like I said I would." He buttoned his shirt. "Now, what about that dream? Tell me about it before I go to work."

"There isn't much to tell,'' she said, sitting up, trying to shake off the sleep. "I stood by this large river dressed in this long, beautiful purple, green and red dress—an African design or something."

"Oh, so you dream in color. That's interesting."

"Lately my dreams have been in color," Tish answered as she tucked a pillow in her arms. "A man appeared, dressed in a white frock, and walked up to me." She closed her eyes as she recalled the details. "We faced each other and held hands. At first the man looked like you. Your features then melded and changed as if you'd become someone else."

"Oh, really?" Tom sighed.

"Yeah," she continued. "I looked down at our hands as we lifted them level with our shoulders. We opened our hands and he pressed his flat against mine. I looked into his face and it changed again. This time, his features were definitely all yours. You said something to me and I replied but I couldn't hear anything; I just saw our lips and mouths move."

"Was anyone else there? Which river? Surely not the big ditch?" He didn't give her a chance to answer. "Could it have been the James or Potomac?"

"It was just the two of us and I have no idea what river it was. The water's brilliant blue shimmer had a soft current that flowed away from the sand. The wind blew through the scattered palm trees at the river's edge."

"Well, it doesn't sound like one of our rivers. Is that all you remember?"

"We were just about to kiss when the phone rang. But other than that, yep, that's it." Curious about his reaction, Tish wanted to know more about his interest in dreams. "Do you remember your dreams?"

"Sometimes. I remember the *lusty ones*. You know the workings of my imagination about *things* that I sometimes wish could happen." He slipped on his belt.

"Do you mind sharing?" Tish asked with a throaty chuckle.

"Don't ask me to tell you about them," he said laughing. "I won't and you can't make me!"

"All right! You can keep your lusty secrets!" She giggled as she propped her elbow on a pillow and placed her chin into the palm of one hand. "But that still doesn't explain why you were thinking about me this morning. You didn't have one of those lusty dreams, did you?"

"No, or at least I don't remember a dream like that." He paused before going on. "You were on my mind this morning when I woke up; that happened for a reason. Maybe because you were dreaming about me. As they say, the mind works in mysterious ways."

"Indeed it does," she replied as she looked again at her clock. "Well, I'd better get my kids motivated and dressed for school. You have a wonderful day and thanks for calling," she said, shifting her legs to the side of the bed. "It's nice that you wanted me to know that you're thinking about me."

"You're welcome. I appreciate you sharing your dream with me. Who knows, maybe there's a message from your subconscious or something. Hopefully we'll figure it out one day."

Tom paused, and for a moment she could sense that he didn't want the call to end. "I'll call you later, okay?"

"Sure," Tish replied softly, as she put the pillow in its place and pulled the covers back.

"Until later," he said. He placed the phone on the nightstand and slowly grabbed his cap and keys.

"Wow, this is too much to believe," Tom mumbled as he headed out the door.

He had the same dream just three weeks earlier, *before* he ever met Tish and he remembered it the same way she'd described hers. The woman's face in his dream started as one person and then it became another. He didn't recognize either woman at that time. But now that he'd met Tish, one of them could have been her. As he'd listened to her tell him her dream, the word *"Teet"* had softly entered his mind, as if whispered in his ear.

What could it mean?

He'd call his mother as soon as he got in from work. Her sister, Louise, lived in New Orleans and she had friends who understood dreams, spirits, the psychic, and other such things.

Could Tish be one of those Creole women who knew how to work a mojo? Had she already been messing with my mind? The last thing I need is a woman who can put me under her control and lead me down some strange path.

He wouldn't allow any woman to have that kind of control his life, not ever.

Nine

Wait patiently to
confirm the love through kisses
poised upon these lips.

The answering machine light was blinking when Tish got home from work.

"This is David. I didn't hear back from you, so I went to Dallas for the weekend—hung out with the bruhs. The chapter in Austin is having a big party next weekend. Want to meet me there? Call me. Later."

"Nope, don't want to go." Tish hit the delete button and waited for the next message. She kicked off her shoes and pulled out a bowl of chili from the refrigerator to warm up for dinner as Dee's soft voice filled the room.

"Hey, girl. Sorry we didn't get a chance to have lunch and talk today as we'd planned. I have so much to do. These folks are working me like I'm a runaway slave or something. Anyway, call me tonight after you get the kids settled so we can catch up. Love you, sis."

Tish chuckled, knowing that feeling. Her boss also expected her to work way too many projects for one person. But the company paid her generously and she loved her profession.

I'll return Dee's call right after the dinner, dishes, homework, packing lunches for tomorrow; I finished paying bills, and the munchkins are in bed. Whew, just thinking about all that makes me tired; hope I have the energy left to call her back.

Tish looked at the answering machine, praying that the light would blink again. Nothing. She sighed disappointedly, took a deep breath, and exhaled. Tom hadn't left a message, but then he didn't say he'd call again today, just later. At least he'd started her day on a positive note.

She smiled and reminded herself that she shouldn't get her hopes up about the guy. *He's already too good to be true.* "Be careful, my heart," she whispered as she placed the chili in the microwave. "Don't fall too fast."

Tish flipped through the mail until she saw a letter from Marcus' attorney. *Damn, what does he want now?* She sat at the dinette table and opened it.

> "In light of your current ability to make a significant financial contribution to the support of your children, my client requests the opportunity to mediate an adjustment to the child support he agreed to pay at the time of your divorce."

Oh hell no! He's still mad that I found a way to afford to stay in this house and buy a new car—one I picked out all by myself. That's all this is about! She read the letter over again and slammed it down on the table.

"What's wrong, Mommy?" Simon walked toward her with a banana in one hand and a book in the other.

"Oh, baby, it's just some grown-up stuff mommy has to take care of that I'd rather not—that's all." She put the letter back into the envelope and held her arms out to him. "Come here and give me a hug. That's all I need right now."

"Okay, I can do that." He put his book and half-eaten banana on the table and gave her a tight hug. "Will you help me with my math homework? It's almost done, just need you to check my answers."

There were only a few times Tish missed having Marcus around—checking the kids' math was one of them; he was a math whiz. Since he was no longer a member of the family, checking homework fell to her and nothing numerical was at the top of her list of skills. She had to really apply herself to help her son the best she could. As a third-grader, Simon's homework hadn't gotten too difficult yet. But if she could have her way about it, she'd never look at another math problem.

Melanie joined them at the table with her homework. "Mom, if you'd like, I can help Simon with his math. We know you're numerically challenged, as dad says. I can handle third-grade math while you fix dinner."

"Okay," Tish replied, not sure whether to be upset with her daughter's comment or relieved at her freedom to now do what she was truly a lot better at—cooking.

"You know," Melanie hesitated as she seemed to contemplate her next thought. "If you and dad got back together before I go to high school, he could help me with my algebra and geometry every night. I wouldn't need a tutor. It'd be a lot cheaper to just feed dad and keep him around, I bet."

Stunned at her daughter's suggestion, Tish felt her face flush as her blood began to boil. In her defense, her first impulse was to ask her daughter, w*hat makes you think your father would start being around every night? He hardly spent any time at home. Between working late and chasing after every new pretty, young woman he met at the hospital...*

She held those thoughts at bay. She'd promised herself that she'd not speak negatively about their father to them and felt the need to whisper a short prayer before responding, *and lead me not into temptation....*

Tish took a deep breath. "Well, honey, that's just not going to happen," she said calmly. "Your dad and I will not be getting back together."

She stood and looked over at Melanie as she ran her fingers through the curls on top of Simon's head. "If you need a tutor for math, then we'll get you one. That's not going to be a problem. Thanks for helping Simon while I get the salad ready."

After completing her evening tasks, Tish slumped down in her bed; surrounded by sumptuous pillows that beckoned her to sleep. She resisted the urge to close her eyes and picked up the phone.

"Hello, Dee," she said, when the out-of-breath woman answered the phone. "So they're trying to break you from running away, huh?"

"What can I say but, *yes*!" Dee sighed. "I tell you…between the job and trying to keep things around this house covered, I just don't know, girl. They act like all I do in life is work for them."

Tish laughed. "I told you not to threaten to quit. They treat that stuff like you've already done it. And instead of being grateful you didn't, they work you even harder to get everything done just in case you do." She yawned and stretched. "You know we really should both quit this company and start our own advertising agency. Then we could just work each other to death."

"One day we'll do just that," Dee said, a hint of excitement lacing her soft voice. "But not until Aaron finishes his degree, and he's too close to make him quit and go back to work right now. I need one more really good income to keep things going around here so we won't all starve while establishing a new company. One day soon, it'll happen." She paused before asking playfully, "So, any new chapters in the Tom and Tish story?"

"You make it sound like a 'Dateline' update," she replied, pulling a pillow and holding it against her chest. "He called on Sunday and we met at the zoo. We had a good time. And he called me early this morning just to tell me I was on his mind."

"Early? What time was that?"

"Six-thirty. Isn't that sweet?"

"Isn't that sweet?" Dee taunted. "You mean you didn't cuss him out? You're not a morning person; I know 'cause I tried that once and waking you up isn't pretty. Do you even remember what you said to him? Is he still speaking to you? Oh, this could damage your future." She giggled.

"Oh stop the dramatics! I'm not that bad in the morning…*am I*?"

"Girl, you know how you are… and I ain't just making it up!"

"*Anyway…*yes I remember what we said. He woke me up from a dream and I told him about it because he was in it. It's kinda' weird. Why would he be in my dreams already? He hasn't even kissed me."

"Oh, he hasn't kissed you yet?" Dee said, with a little chuckle. "Soooooooo, expecting the kiss are we? That sounds good."

"It's been a very long time since I've had a real kiss. My ex didn't enjoy kissing. I guess 'cause he really didn't know how to." Her voice softened. "A really good kiss would just make my day. Well, a *reasonable* kiss would make my day, too." Her voice faded into almost a whisper. "Hell, at this point any kiss would be good."

"Gir-r-l-l-l, I just hope Tom has a clue what he's in for. You've been a deprived woman. How *do you* handle it?"

Tish sat up, bent her legs, and pulled her knees up to her chest. "I just try to keep things in perspective, I guess. I have two beautiful children who I love with all my heart. We live in a beautiful home that I can afford. I finally have the job I always wanted. I'm loved by family and have new friends who will do anything to help me out if things get tough."

She placed her chin on her knees, twirled her hair around her fingers and continued. "There are so many opportunities for me now that I didn't have just two or three years ago. I've been deprived of some things, but I have what really matters; most importantly I have my freedom. I can find love again and experience it the way it's supposed to be. I'll never let anyone take my ability to love away from me."

"You're a strong woman. Stay strong and wait for that kiss, girl! It's coming. I can *feel it*!"

Tish yawned again. "Look, I'll talk with you tomorrow. Got to get some rest."

"See you at work."

Tish hung up the phone, turned off her lamp, and slid under her covers with three calls not made: one to David to tell him to leave her the hell alone, one to Marcus to tell him to go to hell, and one to Tom to tell him how much she wished he was holding her as she fell asleep.

Ten

Now, what could this mean?
It's truly a mystery.
Help find the answer.

Tom came in from work, undressed, and stepped into the shower, allowing the steamy hot water to splash over his stiff shoulders and run down his strong back. He lathered the bar of Irish Spring soap in his thick navy blue wash cloth and slowly rubbed it across his skin. The day's built-up tensions were released and rinsed down the drain.

He stepped out of the shower and put on his favorite black robe, relishing the coolness of the silk against his naked body. He called and ordered the delivery of Chinese food he'd been thinking about all day.

While he waited, he turned on his stereo and listened to classic old school sounds, straightened the "Star of Texas" quilt his mother had made for him, and then sat on the bed.

As a rainstorm rumbled overhead and lightning flashed through his open curtains, his feelings of loneliness and restlessness grew. It would be a perfect evening to spend with a woman, someone whose company he could actually enjoy.

He rubbed his hands together, as Keith Sweat's mellow voice begged "Make it Last Forever." The song reminded him of how he missed being touched. It had been months since he'd been with a woman—an unexpected situation on this side of his divorce. Sizing up the two women in his life, Tish seemed to be the most unlikely candidate for a sexual encounter—at least not any time soon. She came across as a little guarded and had a lot going on in her personal life.

Sable, on the other hand, had possibilities. The more she was around him, the more he wanted to sleep with her. Her sexy appeal excited him when they sat in class together and talked about military leadership styles. The way she moved her body and cut her eyes at him got all his attention. She often touched his hand or his shoulder.

But what about this damn dream? Tom's thoughts went right back to Tish and the dream they shared. *How can that happen? How can two people have the very same dream?* He wouldn't know unless he asked his mother. He picked up the phone from the nightstand.

"Hello, Mama. How was your day?"

He imagined her dressed in the usual cotton snap-front housedress and slippers, her gray hair pulled away from her face and pinned in a French roll, with no makeup other than lip-gloss on her pleasant, toffee-brown face. Her silver, metal-framed, oval eyeglasses were probably halfway down her nose and he guessed that she'd have her evening cup of decaf with a thin slice of pound cake. She'd been cutting back on sugar and fats so she could lose that last ten pounds that would get her to her goal of one hundred fifty pounds by Christmas.

He'd told her how proud he was of her progress since her doctor told her she needed to eat healthier and trim down. She'd made some changes, but some old habits were hard to completely eliminate, like cake before bed.

"Hello, Tom. I'm fine and my day that was already good just got better. Haven't heard from you in a while. That's not like you." She sat at the kitchen table and poured another cup of coffee. "Is everything okay?"

"Everything's fine; just been busy trying to get settled in around here. I have more unpacking to do, and when it's only one person doing it with no help—it takes a while."

"I know, honey. Is there something else on your mind? I've been thinking about you all evening. I kinda' expected this phone call."

"You could always read me that way, couldn't you?" He took a deep breath before he continued. "I met this woman last weekend. We've seen each other four times, now. I called her early this morning—around six, because she was really on my mind and I wanted to talk to her before I went to work. My call woke her up from a dream."

Tom put his feet up on the bed and rested his back against the headboard. "Here's the kicker…I had the same dream about three weeks ago—to the last detail. She was in it and I hadn't even met her yet!"

"Oh, really?"

"Here's where I need help. I thought about those women in New Orleans, the ones that Aunt Louise calls friends; you know the ones who do mojo. How can I figure out if this woman is working some mojo on me? She has that same light skin, that nice hair, and looks just like those Creole women."

"I know something about the mojo and I'm certain it can't do that. This is something completely different. I don't know what it is, but it's different. Just because she may look a little Creole, doesn't mean she can work the mojo. Where are her people from?"

"From the East Coast, DC. I guess it kinda' freaked me out and I thought you or Aunt Louise might have an explanation." He scratched his head. "She doesn't know that I had the same dream and I'm not sure I should tell her."

"Well, honey, I don't have an explanation. But do you like her? I guess you do—calling her so early. You're just scared, that's all. Don't worry too much about it. She probably doesn't even have roots from Louisiana. It'll be all right. The dream means something and time will tell when it is time to know."

"Thanks, Mama." Tom sighed as he rolled over on his side and pulled a pillow under one of his arms. "You always know how to settle things for me when I go way off. I guess I'm a little scared, as you put it. She's a very beautiful woman and I do like her. I guess I wonder what she sees in me; I don't seem to be her type."

"And what type is that? What type is her type?"

"She's an attractive, professional, college-educated woman, divorced with two children and, according to her, she has a crazy ex-husband. I see her type of man to be handsome, with a degree, a professional career, someone who can give her what she's used to."

He paused, closed his eyes, and tried to create an image of the two of them together. Instead he saw himself watching her from a distance, just like the night he first saw her. "Not some guy like me who's the opposite of all that. I don't have anything to give anyone, not anymore."

"Now, don't you ever put yourself down like that again! You hear me! You're a beautiful person, inside and out. If she doesn't see that, then I feel sorry for her. And if she's so educated and has a professional career, why would she need you to give her anything anyway? She should have her own stuff." She took a deep breath.

Tom recognized that as a signal that she hadn't finished letting him have it.

"And stop and listen to what you've already said about the two of you. You just met her and have been with her several times since. If she didn't see something in you, she wouldn't have spent that kind of time with you."

She took a breath and continued, "She probably has all kinds of men waiting at her door including the kind you just described. But she chose to be with you. Stop and think about that. And she's dreaming about you too, and is willing to tell you. Just take your time and get to know this woman. She may be more special than you think."

"Yes, ma'am. I guess she can't be any worse than the women I've already had in my life. I don't want to play games or be played anymore. That's why I'm being so careful this time. I want to find the right woman who can make me happy, that's all. If she ain't right, I don't want her."

"I can tell you like her, so get to know her better and see if she's the one. I'm telling you, the dream means something, I just can't tell you what. But don't let it scare you. I believe it's a good thing."

"Yes, Mama. Will do. Talk to you later. Take care of yourself, now, okay?"

"Remember what I said. Good night, son."

Tom sat up on the bed. With elbows on his thighs, his face planted in the palms of his hands, he thought about what she said to him. "The dream means something. Time will tell when it's time to know," he repeated. *But how does any of that help me now?*

His cell phone jolted him out of his thoughts. "Hello?"

"Hey, it's Sable. Got a question for you."

"I'm listening." Surprised by the call, he stood almost at attention.

"I won't see you tomorrow in class 'cause I have a conference call with my unit back at the Pentagon in the morning and an appointment at the hospital in the afternoon. I wanted to know if you'd like to meet me at Tuesday Night Jazz downtown tomorrow night. I hear a really good band is playing and since it'll be my last night in San Antonio, I thought I'd spend it doing something fun. Interested?"

He kicked one of his slippers up in the air and caught it with one hand. "Sure, that sounds good. What time and where?"

"It's at a club called The Marx. I'll be at a birthday dinner with a group of lady friends first. Then I can meet you there around eight o'clock. Will that work?"

"Sure will. I know exactly where that is. There's someone at my door, probably my dinner. But hey, I'll see you tomorrow night."

"Looking forward to it," Sable replied almost in a whisper.

Eleven

Beware of the one
who may distract you from me.
I - am your soulmate.

The next day, eight p.m. couldn't come fast enough for Tom. When he walked into the crowded, smoke-filled club, he scanned the room looking for Sable. He found her seated at the bar.

She was facing the dance floor with her legs crossed. Her short, black form-fitting dress exposed a lot of brown legs and its low-cut top showed off her spectacular cleavage. Long bangs almost covered her eyes, and the rest of her hair had been pulled back in a ponytail that touched her shoulder.

"Damn, she looks good," Tom whispered as he walked toward her. He knew that if she had a mind to, Sable could very easily seduce him into doing just about anything.

"Hey." She lowered her frozen margarita and extended her hand toward him. "I saved you a seat, right here." She swiveled her chair toward the bar as he sat beside her. "So, how'd your day go?"

"Good, good." He smiled broadly as he got a whiff of her musk-like perfume. Something about the fragrance seemed familiar; he tried to recall who else wore it. He signaled the bartender and ordered a margarita on the rocks.

The band played Whitney Houston's *"I Want to Dance with Somebody,"* and the dance floor began to fill. "Wanna dance?" he asked.

She held out her hand and he led her to the dance floor. Her three-and-a-half-inch heels made her much taller than the five feet, three inches she stood in uniform. He watched her move; she had rhythm and could swerve that full butt with ease.

When the song ended, they returned to the bar but were unable to talk much over the loud music. The band took a break and a DJ took over with Jody Watley's "Looking for a New Love." They danced again.

The DJ immediately followed that one up with a slow jam. Tom pulled her into his arms and held her gently against his body. He closed his eyes and enjoyed the feel of a woman next to him as they danced to "Computer Love," an oldie by the group, Zapp and Roger.

Halfway through the dance, Sable teasingly whispered in his ear, "Why are you getting a hard on?"

Embarrassed that he hadn't even noticed, he told her, "Sorry…it's been a while since I've had any."

Sable pulled back and looked directly into his face. "I can fix that." Then she put her lips close to his ear again and whispered, "Come with me."

She took his hand, led him back to the bar, and picked up her small, black leather purse from the bar. She walked confidently into the parking lot still holding his hand.

"That's my rental over there." Sable pointed to a blue Malibu. "I'll pull up to the corner and wait until I see your car. Then, follow me back to the post. Okay?"

"Alright, I can do that." After he started the engine, he fumbled nervously with the radio searching for a smooth jazz station to calm the tension brought on by the sudden turn of events.

When they arrived at the post, she opened the door to her room, led him inside, and flipped the deadbolt.

"Sable, you don't have to do…" Tom started to beg off. His body urged him to go for it, but he wasn't used to this and it seemed much too quick and far too easy.

"Don't speak," she whispered, with a very seductive smile, placing a manicured finger on his lips. "It's okay. Just relax and let me do this." She gently kissed his cheek, then slowly walked to her CD player on the other side of the room. She swung her hips seductively for Tom's benefit.

He took a deep breath and tried to relax. *I guess I'll just let Sable have her way with me. Why not? We're consenting adults and there's no doubt I need her and apparently she needs me too.*

He noticed that the room smelled like her and he wondered if she'd used her musk perfume as an air freshener.

Selections from "The Best of Marvin Gaye" CD filled the room with soft velvety sounds. Before she turned to face Tom, she slid the palms of her hands up and down the sides of her hips as she moaned and slowly twisted her body. She pulled out a box of matches from her purse and lit several vanilla candles on her desk, dresser, and nightstand.

Then she turned to Tom and slowly opened the clip that held her ponytail letting her hair fall to her shoulders as she walked back to him. She flicked the light switch off, took his hand, and led him to the bed.

He closed his eyes as she slowly undressed him, teasing him with gentle kisses along his neck, chest, arms, thighs, and knees as she uncovered them. She gently pushed him onto her bed and as "Sexual Healing" played, she impersonated an exotic dancer intent on pleasing and seducing her male audience.

With the soft flicker of candlelight, she swayed her licentious body as she stripped for him, moving with the music, turning around, gyrating her hips, and tousling her hair. She peeled off her blouse and bra then lifted and caressed her firm breasts, bent her knees and dipped to the floor as she opened her legs so that he could see almost all of her.

Tom was having trouble controlling his urge to toss her on the bed and take her fast and hard. Huge goose bumps covered his body, followed by streams of hot sweat.

She gently pushed him down on the beige and brown Aztec-print comforter, and crawled on top of him. Her supple, bronze skin against his moist chocolate-brown body, full of anticipation, nearly sent him over the edge. His breathing became deeper and his heart pounded.

Her smell—that musk—intensified and made his head spin. He realized that he would lose control if he didn't act fast. He rolled Sable over on her back and kissed her cheek. "Be right back."

He went over to his slacks and retrieved a condom he'd thoughtfully dropped in a pocket—just in case. Once he had it in place he climbed on top of her, feeling her hard nipples and round, firm breasts pressed against his chest.

Tom kissed her lips, gently at first, then almost savagely as a surge of lust and longing passed through his body. He moaned as he touched her hair and caressed her body.

Sable lifted her hips, rotating to his rhythm of need. He entered her with one thrust, pulling her to him with each move of his hips, holding back to catch his breath each time as he edged her closer to a climax. He felt her abdomen tremble out of control; she held him tight, her arms taut and fingernails clinching his back.

He found the relief his body had long awaited. Tom shook and moaned so loud that he imagined every person in the quarters heard him.

Able to finally speak again, he whispered, “Damn, that was great.” He laid his head on her chest and said, “Thank you.”

“Welcome,” she responded, holding him in her arms and stoking his back. Before he’d expected to move again, she pushed him to roll over on his side. Then she turned over and went to sleep.

He’d always wanted a wild woman and Sable was as close to one he’d ever experienced. As he basked in the moment, he listened to Marvin’s smooth voice as he sang “Distant Lover.”

Tom thought of Tish. *Why am I thinking about her?*

After the great sex he just had with Sable, Tish had inched right back in his head, front and center. *This is crazy!* He couldn’t get her out of his mind. He tried hard to push the image of Tish’s face and the sound of her voice saying his name, out of his thoughts.

He looked over at the alarm clock on the nightstand. Time to leave. He slipped on his pants, shirt and socks, located his shoes, kissed Sable on the forehead, and said, “Thank you, again. You don’t know just how much I needed *all that.* You’re good. But then, I always knew you would be.”

He brushed the hair from her cheek. “Call me tomorrow before your flight back to D.C. will you?”

Sable moaned, smiled briefly, and whispered, “Sure.” She rolled over and pulled the covers tight under her chin.

Twelve

No one else can touch
or move the love that is yours.
It's kept inside me.

Thursday rolled in with more severe thunderstorms as the weather seemed to be fighting the seasonal change from summer to autumn. Tish hadn't heard from Tom since Monday. She hadn't had much time to talk with Dee all week either because clients had kept them scrambling at the office.

When she walked into her kitchen after work she automatically flipped on the answering machine.

"Tish, this is Dee. Aaron and I are going to an Omega party in Austin Saturday. Want to go? Aaron's going to ask Tom if he's free; maybe we can all drive up together."

She moved to the next message. *"Tish, David. Hey girl, I haven't heard back from you. What's up? Call me at work tomorrow. K?"*

No, this can't be happening. The guy she wanted to hear from had stopped calling and she didn't know what that meant. The guy she wished would lose her number was becoming a pest. She was flattered by his attention but not stupid. She really wanted to hear from Tom.

But what if he didn't call anymore? What if that woman is really in his life and he takes her to Austin on Saturday? What if he shows up with her instead of being with me?

Tish didn't know what to do. *Why does life have to be so complicated?*

She picked up the phone to call Tom and dialed all but the last number before she hung up. Instead, she spent the evening making dinner, helping the kids with their homework, doing a load of laundry and paying bills. By the time she had the kids' lunches made she didn't feel like calling anybody.

As she moved her purse on the kitchen counter her cell buzzed indicating someone had left a message. She'd forgotten that she'd switched it to vibrate during a meeting and had left it there all day.

"Hi. I hope you had a great day. I've been thinking about you and want to see you again when it's convenient. I know you're a very busy woman so call me back when you can."

"Ha!" she said with a big smile. "So he did call," she whispered. *All right, now.*

Tish skipped down the hallway and up the stairs to her bedroom. *Should I call him now or wait about four days? Well, it won't be tonight. I'm too tired and I might say something I'll regret. Maybe tomorrow.*

Thirteen

Thoughtful in all things
considering the motives—
desires of others.

Friday morning Tom sat at his desk, his radio tuned in to the oldies while he checked his e-mail. He returned a phone call to his commander, then checked his calendar to review his plans for the weekend.

Not much this weekend, unless we make it to that party in Austin.

Marvin's mellow, "Sexual Healing" played on the radio. *I wonder if I'll ever see Sable again.*

His phone rang. "Sergeant Manning."

"Hello, Sergeant Manning. This is Ms. Edwards. How have you been?"

"Quite well, ma'am, and you?"

"I've been doing just fine, Sir," Tish replied smartly. "I got your phone message late last evening. Thought I'd take a break this morning and return your call."

"It's good to hear from you." He picked up a pen, and started drawing circles on his notepad. "Are you are free for lunch? I'd like to take you to this really nice Italian restaurant on the River Walk."

"Let me check." She paused and checked her calendar. "So, where shall I meet you?"

"The Luciano Ristortante at noon. It's next to the Marriott. I have a table reserved on the patio," he said, tapping the pen on the desk.

"Great. I'll see you then."

Gee, what was that all about? Tish had been so proper with him and he just followed her game. He wondered if she might be upset because he hadn't called her every day.

But she wasn't the only woman in his life. *Got no time for that, not now.*

As he stood and headed for the door, his phone rang.

"Sergeant Manning."

"Hey, Tom, it's Sable. Got a question for you."

"Hey, there. What's up with you?"

"I just got a couple tickets for a Redskins' game weekend after next here in D.C." Her voice sounded more inviting. "Could I interest you in coming out here and going to the game with me? There's a Luther concert that night, too. I'm sure it'll be fun."

"Sounds good to me. Give me the date and the time the game starts. When I get back from lunch I'll see if I can catch a military hop your way. I'll call you back this evening. Will that work?"

"Sure."

Tom glanced at his watch knowing he was going to be late. "Have to run, Sable," he said as he headed for the door.

Tish arrived at Luciano's ten minutes before Tom.

"Sorry I'm late," he said as he slid into the seat across from her. "I had an unexpected call just as I was leaving the office. How's your day been?"

"Like most busy days go. Just a lot of work."

Tom sensed coolness in her voice. "Have you had a chance to look at the menu yet? I'm starving. What are you having?"

"The veal marsala with veggies," Tish responded. "It's really good here."

"Then I'll have what you are having," Tom said, hoping she wasn't upset with him for being late. "There's an Omega party in Austin on Saturday. Would you like to go?" He held his breath for her answer, then hedged his bet by adding, "Aaron and Dee are going."

"I'd like to go, but I'll have to get a babysitter," she responded hesitantly. "It's my weekend with the kids."

"Dee's already a step ahead of us. She said to tell you she has Cathy coming to watch Little Aaron and you can bring your kids over if you want. They can even spend the night so we don't have to worry about picking them up and bringing them home so late. I'll be happy to come by and get you guys and take you over there or meet you at their house."

He lifted his eyes and grinned at her. "Whatever you want. So what do you say?"

She smiled back. "I'll meet you over there. I have errands to do on Saturday, so I'll bring the kids with me after my last stop. It's not too far from where they live."

"I'm sure we'll have a great time. I've heard that they really know how to party in Austin," he added, as he looked squarely at her.

She turned from him and watched the waiter as he walked toward their table with two glasses of iced tea. "You know, Dee and Aaron have been lifesavers for me since I moved to San Antonio. They're the best friends I've ever had."

She paused until the waiter left. "I'm very happy that they introduced us." She leaned forward and looked directly into his eyes. "I hope you feel the same way."

He took a deep breath and straightened his uniform jacket. "Yes, Tish, I'm happy that we met, too. I've enjoyed our time together and hope to spend more of it with you."

"I'd like that," she replied in a soft sexy voice. "I'm actually excited about going to Austin. I've never gone there just to attend a party; it should be different."

"It'll be great." He reached for her hand she'd placed on the table in front of her. He lowered his hand on top of hers and squeezed gently. "You'll be with me and I'll make sure you have a wonderful time."

Just as the waiter served their lunch plates the sun broke through the clouds. Tish sat in the direct sunshine. He admired how the light made her complexion glow and her hair shimmer.

God, she's so beautiful.

Fourteen

The stars light the way
so that we may see a life
once ours together.

Tom convinced Tish that they should take his car to Austin and let Aaron and Dee drive theirs, just in case something happened to the children and someone had to return earlier than the others.

Interesting reason, she thought as she dressed and then smiled. *Apparently he wants to be alone with me; I can't argue with that.*

After they met up at their friends' house, Tom followed Aaron through the subdivision on the northeast side of the city. Once they got onto Interstate 35 heading north toward Austin, he slid a Teddy Pendergrass CD into his player.

As they passed the brightly lit, Retama Park Horseracing Track, he looked over at Tish. "You've been quiet this evening. Is something going on?"

"Oh, I'm sorry. I guess I've got some things running through my mind." She looked down as she played with her purse strap gently running her fingers across the stitches.

"You wanna' share or is it too personal?" he asked calmly.

Tish looked over at him and took a deep breath. "One of your frat brothers invited me to this party and I never got back with him. If he's there and sees me come in with you…well, I just thought I'd mention it in case he makes a scene."

"No problem…but thanks for the heads up. I'm sure it'll be okay." He looked over at her, placed his hand on hers, and squeezed it. "Is there anything else?"

"Yeah…there's something else," she replied hesitantly, glancing shyly at his face. "I've been thinking about how comfortable I feel when I'm with you. I've had some bad experiences with men and it's hard for me to let my guard down. The last thing I want is to be hurt again."

She paused and took a deep breath. "I'm not sure where this is going, but I hope you're feeling good about the time we've spent together, that's all."

"Tish, I thought you knew by now that I want to spend more time with you." He squeezed her hand again. "I want you to feel comfortable with me. Hurting you isn't part of my plan. Okay?"

"Thanks, but it doesn't have to be planned to happen." She looked down at her purse again as thoughts of former relationships and the pain associated with them raced through her mind. She had so much she wanted to say to him, but she didn't know what to share and what to keep to herself.

She took a deep breath and continued, "I just don't want to be played, you know…spending time with someone really nice, then start having feelings for him just to find out later that there isn't any room for me to be in his life."

"I don't want that to happen to me, either." Tom rubbed the back of her hand gently. "Let's just take this one step at a time and see where it goes. I'm willing to let our relationship develop naturally. I like you, Tish." He glanced over at her and locked his fingers in hers. "There's something very special about you and it's all good."

She felt a warm sensation flow through her body as she fought the impulse to reach over and kiss those luscious lips. "I agree. It's all good," she managed to whisper. "I like you, too, Tom, I really do."

"Now, that's settled. So tell me about how things are going on at work."

They talked about their jobs until they arrived at the party in Austin. Tom pulled into the crowded parking lot of Brown Suga's Night Club on the city's East Side and scanned for a parking space.

"Man, there's a lot of folk out tonight!" He pulled into one of three remaining spaces in the last row. "And I thought we were getting here early. I guess the parties in Austin start on time."

"It does appear that way." Tish unbuckled her seatbelt and waited for Tom to open her door.

"Thanks," she said as she stepped out of the car scanning the area as several couples walked through the parking lot toward the building. She spotted what looked like David's car backed in two cars down from Tom's. As they walked past the black Maxima, she spotted the "Que" symbol hanging from the rearview mirror. She took a deep breath.

As soon as they entered the nightclub, she saw a group of men talking near the doorway to the private party room where they were headed. The music played way too loud and the bass made the place vibrate. Mostly African- and Mexican-American couples were moving slowly through the door.

When she and Tom got in line, Tish looked over at the men again and she recognized one of them as David.

"You know, either this is a very popular place or everyone in town heard about this party and wanted to be here." Tom held her hand close to his side as they inched toward the party room.

David glared at her as soon as they entered. *Dang! I wish I had called him!* Tish thought as soon as she spotted him looking at her.

He strolled by them growling just loud enough for her to hear, "Trying to walk two dogs at one time, huh?"

"Not at all," Tish replied confidently. She took Tom's arm. "Let's dance," she whispered and led him to the dance floor as Luther Vandross' voice purred out the mellow sounds of "Always and Forever."

Tom looked over his shoulder at David and gave him a warning look. He took Tish into his arms, held her next to his body, and closed his eyes. "This is one of my favorite songs," he whispered in her ear.

"Mine, too." She took a deep breath as he held her firmly in his arm's, swaying smoothly to the slow tempo.

The DJ faded out that tune and turned up the volume of Al B. Sure's, "I'm Only Human." Tom didn't release his embrace; she didn't mind at all.

Pleasantly surprised at how secure and safe she felt with him, Tish imagined she'd found the place where she'd always belonged.

"You okay?" Tom asked, looking down at her with admiring eyes.

"I'm fine, thanks," she replied.

I'm melting...I'm melting...I'm melting down here. Oh, God, he smells good and he feels wonderful. If I could get a hard-on, I'd be in big trouble right about now.

"Yes, I'm fine," she repeated, closed her eyes, and gently ran her hands across his firm back.

Tom stayed close to her all evening, as if sending signals out that "she's mine, so hands off." She saw David glance over toward her as he worked the room with a beer in one hand, stopping to talk to and eventually dance with every woman without a man. She also took note of how Tom eyed David, which seemed to keep David in check. He didn't come near her.

"You must really like to party." She tried to speak directly into Tom's ear as they walked from the dance floor after working up a sweat from the fifteen-minute long back-to-back medley of Earth, Wind and Fire upbeat songs.

"I do." He leaned down to her ear so she could hear him through the loud music. "Besides, I like watching you dance. You're good." He pulled her chair out, waited until she sat at the table with Aaron and Dee. "I'm going to get a Coke. Want anything?"

"A Coke would be fine. Thanks."

Dee leaned over to her with a big grin. "Girl, I see how you're looking at that man. You *really* like him, don't you?"

She nodded.

"Well, we're about to head back to San Antonio," Dee said as she grabbed her sweater from the back of her chair. "You don't have to worry about coming for the kids tonight, you know." She lifted one eyebrow and then winked. "Enjoy him…I mean the rest of your evening."

Tish cut her eyes over at her friend and giggled. "You know, I think I'll do just that." She looked past Dee and saw Tom returning to the table with two Cokes. *Damn, this man is fine. And when he looks at me like that, he makes my knees weak.*

Tom smiled wide when the DJ played The Dells' "Stay in My Corner," as the last song. Without a word, he placed the drinks on the table, took Tish's hand, and led her to the dance floor.

She'd taken off her heels so when he pulled her into his arms, the top of her head met the bottom of his chin. She fit perfectly in his arms and against his chest. He held her close as they moved slowly to the romantic music. Her heart suddenly pounded in her chest and she held tight against his steady body.

Tom slowly caressed her back and she didn't want the song to stop or the evening to be over.

This feels so right.

On the way back to San Antonio, Tish sat very quietly thinking, *how can I stretch this evening out?*

As they approached Town Lake, she said, "Exit right here. I want to show you something."

Tom pulled around to the parking area beside the Town Lake Holiday Inn and parked the car. "Now what?"

She unbuckled her seatbelt. "I know it's rather late, but let's get out. I want to enjoy being near a real river. How about you?"

"That sounds good to me. I hadn't realized that I missed being so close to the James River until I met you. Water must be very important to you, huh, Tish? What are you, a Pisces?" Not waiting for an answer, he got out of the car, walked around, and opened the door for her.

"Actually, I am. Good guess. And what sign are you?"

"Taurus—very stubborn and headstrong when I want to be. Can you handle that?" Tom asked with a laugh as he closed the door and took her hand.

"I don't know. I never had to handle a Taurus before; could be a challenge," she answered as they walked toward the river.

"I see." He chuckled, released her hand, and put his arm around her shoulder pulling her closer to his body. They found a flat stone nuzzled in a patch of grass near the riverbank. He stepped behind her, holding her back against his chest, with his arms wrapped around her waist. She crossed her arms on top of his and enjoyed the warmth of his body.

Tish could feel his heart beating against her back; it matched hers. She relaxed silently taking in the moment. Standing by the river with the black sky sprinkled with a multitude of brilliant stars and having his arms around her felt more than comfortable; it felt renewing. She experienced an impression that somehow, somewhere, and at some other time they had done this very thing.

"Okay, that was the third mosquito bite," she said slapping her arm.

"Then I think it's time to head back to San Antonio." He gave her a tight hug then took her hand as they walked back to the car.

Fifteen

Material things
measure not the character
nor dilute the worth.

Tom didn't want to leave the river, but he didn't want Tish to be eaten alive by mosquitoes, either. *Why do I feel like I've done that before? I've never been here, and I've certainly not stood by a river with her before. What was that feeling all about?*

He opened her car door, "Entré vous, mon amie."

"Merci," she said and gave him the sweetest smile.

He cleared his throat and shook his head. *How can this woman take my breath away with just a look?*

He drove back to San Antonio replaying the evening over in his mind; happy that Tish had been his date and that he had the opportunity to let David know she was taken. He hoped David would be a good frat brother and leave her alone. *With him out of the way, I can take my time and really get to know her better.*

"Okay, now you're being quiet." She looked over at him. "So what's going on in your mind?"

"Oh…just thoughts about tonight and how glad I am that you came with me. I really enjoyed myself." He glanced over to her to see her reaction. "Did you have a good time?"

"Sure did. I love to dance, you love to dance, the music was perfect." Her voice became softer as she reached for his hand. "Thanks for inviting me. I wouldn't have gone if you hadn't asked."

"I'm very glad I asked and you said yes."

He replaced the CD with a Roberta Flack live concert CD. "Now, where do I exit to get you home? Remember, I haven't been to your house yet."

"That's true. The next exit—Loop 1604. Take it going west to Heubner Road. I live in the Grapevine Subdivision. But, what about my car? It's at Aaron's remember?"

"I'll come back in the morning and give you a ride. You can pick up your kids and car at the same time."

With Roberta's sultry rendition of "If Ever I See You Again" in the background, Tish sang along softly articulating every word. "That is such a beautiful song. I really love her music."

"So do I, and you can just keep singing, too. You have a sweet voice." He glanced at her and gave her a broad smile.

As he entered the gate to her subdivision he wondered how a single woman could afford to live in such an exclusive neighborhood.

"Wow, this is a very nice place." As he drove up the driveway, he thought, *Whoa, this woman is paying for this—alone?* He had always wanted to have an estate home like this for his family but never got the chance.

What does she see in me, when she could have any man she wanted? Nervousness crept into his previously composed demeanor as he glanced over at the very beautiful, successful, professional woman sitting in his humble, purple Neon.

"Come on in. It's very late; you should have some coffee before you head back to the Post. Don't want you to fall asleep at the wheel, do we?"

Tom turned off the car engine hoping she hadn't noticed that his hands were slightly trembling. "That'll be great."

He braced himself against the slight chill as he opened the door. "Something hot would be perfect."

"Great, hot is something I can do," she replied as he shut the door.

He opened the passenger door with a puzzled look. "I'm sorry, what did you just say?" He thought he'd heard what she said but checked anyway.

"Oh, I said I can make something hot for you, you know coffee, hot cocoa, tea…whatever you'd like." She grinned and gave him a gentle push as she got out of the car.

Tish escorted him into the house and turned on the TV in the family room. Soon BET's "Midnight Love" music video splashed onto the plasma screen. Tom sat on the soft, taupe leather sofa and waited as she went to the kitchen. She returned a few minutes later and sat beside him.

As Major Harris rendered the words to "Love Won't Let Me Wait," he reached over and pulled her toward him. Without a word, he gently pressed his lips against hers and felt her body relax.

Damn, she tastes good.

He released his kiss, moved back, and looked at her. She slowly opened her eyes, licked her lips, and moved back toward him with her inviting mouth set to let him in. Tom felt no resistance, no hesitance, just a welcome relief when she put one arm around his neck, and caressed his face with her hand.

They ignored the shrill sound of the coffeemaker's alarm as she sat quietly with his arm around her shoulder. He kissed her again and felt her hands caressing his body.

So kissing turns her on…that's a really good thing to know.

Sixteen

Be careful my heart-
Don't fall too hard and too fast
Think before you act.

Tish felt the earth shift as Tom's kisses became more passionate. Her hands, with a life of their own, roamed to places on his body she shouldn't explore yet. Her breasts ached to be caressed.

She pulled away realizing she needed the chance to decide before moving forward. She didn't want to have another first time with a man just because she got caught up in the moment.

Taking a deep breath to regain her composure, she said, "Let's go have some of that coffee." She took his hand, and led him to the kitchen.

"Would you like some of my lemon pound cake?" She took two mugs from the cabinet and then lifted the lid of the glass cake platter releasing the fresh lemony baked aroma into the room.

"How could I resist?" He sat at the dinette table and waited for her to join him.

She placed the filled coffee mugs and plates on the table, then sat beside him. *What am I doing? I want him so badly…Would it be wrong to invite him to stay with me the rest of the night?* She looked at her shaking hands.

"Tish, I don't want you to be uncomfortable around me." He held hands. "What's going on?"

"I…well, I'm a little nervous, I guess." She stared at the cake. "It's been a while since I've been alone with a man in my house—you know with kids and all. I don't get much private time these days."

"You deserve to have time for yourself, you know." He placed his fingers on her chin and moved her face toward his. Looking directly into her eyes, he continued, "I'll go as soon as we finish our coffee and cake. I'm not here to take advantage of you or this situation. So relax and let's enjoy the next few minutes of our evening together. Okay?"

A tear formed in the corner of her eye. *Who is this man who cares about how I feel and isn't trying to push the sex envelope? And where has he been all my life?*

"I can do that," she replied in a soft, yet reluctant voice. *But I really want to make love with you, right now.*

Seventeen

Make a simple wish
say that which your heart desires
have your dreams come true.

Tish awakened with bright sunshine beaming into her bedroom. A serious chill filled the air in her quiet house. Her emotions had been stirred and her physical need heightened. Not making love with Tom when she had a chance the night before had plagued her thoughts since he'd left. It was time to do something about it. She picked up the phone from her nightstand and dialed his number.

"Good morning," she said softly. "Did I wake you?"

"Hey, Tish," he replied, with a deep, sleepy voice. "Yes, you did. But I guess you owe me that one. So now we're even." He moaned as he stretched. "What's on your mind this early Sunday morning?"

"I didn't turn the heat up before going to bed last night. It's pretty chilly in here. I guess that woke me up. Then I had one of those empty rollovers that reminded me that I'm home alone."

"Empty rollovers?"

She turned to her side and pulled a pillow into her arm next to her chest. "You know, when you roll over in your bed expecting a warm body and you get a rude awaking because you come up empty. That's what I call an empty rollover."

"Oh, I see," he replied and cleared his throat. "I have those all the time." He yawned. "So what're you gonna do about it?"

"I guess I could go to the gym. That's what I usually do at times like this." She took a deep breath. "But I really don't want to do that today."

"No? So what do you want to do?"

"Well, I'd like…to be with you this morning." She paused and closed her eyes. "I feel really good when I'm with you. And when you kissed me last night, see I felt something very different going on inside, something I've never felt before."

"What are you saying, Tish?"

"Look, this is hard for me," she rolled on to her back and watched the ceiling fan slowly make its rotations. "But what I'm trying to say is…may I ask you to come back over here this morning? If you're feeling what I'm feeling, and I hope you are…well…I'd like for you to come over and pick up from where we left off before we had our coffee."

He rolled over in his bed, opened his eyes wide, and stared at the ceiling. "You mean the part where we were passionately kissing? Is that where you want to start this morning?"

"Exactly," she whispered. "That's exactly where I want to start. It's been a long time and I'm ready to make love again. I want it to be with you, Tom."

"Hey, I'd be honored and Tish, if you're serious I'll be there in forty-five minutes or less. Even if you aren't serious I'll be there anyway." He stood, dashed over to his dresser and opened a drawer, then pulled out clean underwear.

"See you in forty-five." She made a silent *yes!* with her mouth and a high-five gesture with one hand. She could hardly believe how easy that had been once she got the words out of her mouth. She heard him start his shower.

"As soon as I get dressed, I'll be right there."

"Great. See you then. Bye now."

Tish jumped out of the bed and threw her hands up in the air like she'd just scored a touchdown. Grabbing the white robe from the foot of the king-size bed, she covered her naked body as she walked toward the bathroom. She searched through the closet looking for the perfect thing to wear.

Nothing seemed right, so she rambled through her dresser looking for a seductive negligee. "*Right.* Like I have something provocative to wear." She stuffed everything back into the drawer and closed it.

"Shower. I'll just get that done while I think about what to wear."

She opened the glass door and stepped into the crème and beige marble shower at the back of the large bathroom and turned on the water. It looked more like a shower room, big enough for two people.

Then she flicked on the stereo that was on her vanity. Singing along with Natalie Cole to the words of "I Got Love on My Mind," Tish placed one arm across her chest and held the other up in the air as if she were holding a dance partner. She danced across the room to the linen closet and selected a large red, thick towel, hugged it in her arms and danced back toward the shower. She stood in place, swaying back and forth to the music still hugging the towel and singing her heart out until the song ended.

"Yes, indeed!" Enthusiastically she swung the towel and it landed on the white satin chair at her dressing vanity. As steam filled the bathroom, she removed her robe and stepped into the hot flowing water. "No cold shower today!"

When she finished, she wrapped the towel around her body and opened her new bottle of Red body lotion; it would soften, smooth, and perfume her whole body.

From now on, if he smells Red on anyone else, he'll think of me. She smiled as she lotioned her legs and arms.

Returning to the closet, she found a purple, green, and gold African print dress that she'd received as a gift from a college classmate for her last birthday. She'd worn it only a couple of times before around the house. She slid it over her head, brushed her hair, then her teeth.

Checking the wall clock in her bathroom, Tish saw that she still had time to spare before Tom would arrive. She looked at her image in the mirror.

"No makeup. It's time for him to see me without the Mary Kay magic." She found a lip moisturizer in the top drawer of her vanity and applied that.

Breakfast, I'll make some breakfast.

She suddenly began to feel anxious about having Tom come over especially since she'd pretty much told him she wanted sex.

I can't believe I just did that. She looked at her image again in the bathroom mirror and said, "You did it, now live with it."

Fifteen minutes later, Tish had biscuits in the oven, coffee brewing, bacon in the microwave, and eggs cracked in a bowl ready to be scrambled. Just as she walked into the pantry for a jar of honey, the doorbell rang.

Looking up at the kitchen ceiling, she put her hands together and whispered, "Lord, you know what I've been through. You know what I need. It's been so long since I've had it right. Please Lord, let him be good."

She took a deep breath and walked to the front door.

Eighteen

When I needed you
you came and took care of me.
My soul is thankful.

Tom had dressed casually in jeans, a gray Army T-shirt, and a navy blue golf jacket. He'd tucked three condoms in his pocket, hoping that one wouldn't be enough. As much as he wanted to make love to Tish and could hardly wait to get back to her, he suddenly felt anxious as he waited for her to open the front door.

What if I read her wrong? What if she really didn't mean what I thought she meant or had changed her mind before I got here? What then…what'll I do?

"Hi," she said in a soft voice as she opened the door. "Come on in."

"Thanks," he replied, as he looked into her smiling face that appeared flushed and innocent. He kissed her forehead. "Something smells awfully good in here. You've been cooking?"

"Yep. I had a few minutes so I did what I sometimes do when I don't know what else to do…cook."

"Wow, that's a great way to pass time, especially when I can benefit from your effort," he responded as he followed her to the huge kitchen. He noticed how the hardwood floors and mahogany stained cabinets seemed to have been recently cleaned and polished.

"I guess that means you're hungry?" She extended her hand to a bar chair. "Have a seat while I scramble these eggs. How do you like your eggs? You like eggs, right? I guess I should've asked you what you like, huh?"

"Hey, I'm not picky." He took off his jacket and placed it on the chair next to the one he sat in. "I can tell you I'll eat everything I'm smelling in here. So you just scramble them eggs any way you want and I'll eat 'em. It's really that simple."

Tish smiled at him before she turned to the stove.

As he watched he felt warm all over. *A woman who cooks. Period. How lucky is that? And she's beautiful…nice…smart…and successful… and she's cooking my breakfast…*

"I hadn't expected to find you working in the kitchen when I got here." He walked over to the coffeepot and poured two cups of coffee. "Not that I'm complaining or anything…trust me. Can I help you with something?"

"Thanks, but it's all done. Hand me the plates right there beside you and I'll get this food served up while it's still hot."

She piled the food onto the plates while Tom carried the coffee to the teakwood dinette table where gold place mats and silverware had already been set. She joined him and asked him to bless the food.

Halfway through the meal, Tish looked at him and asked, "I have to know, what is that cologne you're wearing? I absolutely love it."

"It's Paul Sebastian." He grinned, remembering what his father had once told him about wearing good cologne when he wanted to attract the attention of a woman with substance. He'd told him, "Not too much either, just enough to make a woman search for the origin of its placement."

"Okay, what's that look about?"

"I'm just glad you like it, that's all. It's one of my favorites." He placed his fork on the plate and finished his coffee. "And I noticed you're wearing Red, my favorite perfume. I find it quite seductive."

"Do you, now?"

"Yep. Thank you for breakfast. That was delicious." He stood, picked up his plate and coffee mug, and then headed toward the kitchen.

She followed him, placed their dishes into the stainless steel sink, and turned to face him. He backed against the counter and held out his arms. "Come here."

She walked right into his arms. He took a deep breath, closed his eyes, and held her tightly, caressing her back. "You're something else, you know that?"

"What do you mean?" she asked looking up at him with her head tilted.

"You're a beautiful, special woman and I can hardly believe I'm here with you, that's all." He leaned down, closed his eyes, and gently kissed her lips.

She took a deep breath and with her eyes still closed whispered, "I'm just me, being me. I've never been able to fake well so what you see is what you get."

Then she opened her eyes, looked directly into his, and continued, "So I hope you like what you see, 'cause this is it."

"I like what I see, so far...but I'm sure there's more of you yet to be discovered."

"Oh, most definitely." She reached up to kiss his lips.

Passion flooded over him and he pushed his tongue into her mouth and ran his hands through her hair as it hung loose down her back. He moved his hand up and caressed the back of her neck and along her hairline. She moaned and he felt her tremble slightly.

That must be her spot, or at least one of them.

She pushed back and said, "Let's go upstairs."

He followed her to her bedroom and closed the door. It had to be the largest master suite he'd ever seen. He scanned the room taking in the details that reinforced his thoughts—she appreciated very nice things and surrounded herself with them.

He studied the framed art hanging above her bed. "That's an interesting floral design," he said as he looked closer. He saw the words, *Lotus Flower*, below the profile of a softly painted water-color of a light-skinned, African-American woman's face, her eye closed. From the opposite corner of the piece her hand appeared holding a long, green stem that bent slightly allowing the single aqua blue flower to almost touch her nose.

"I've always been drawn to anything Egyptian and the lotus flower is a very special symbol in that culture. When I saw it on exhibit, I had to have it." She moved closer to him and took his hand. "It's an original and one of my favorite pieces of art."

Looking down into her eyes, again he felt a warm surge go through his body. "It suits you. Another original beauty, just like you." He leaned down and kissed her mouth.

She reached up and wrapped her arms around his neck, moving her body into his firm embrace. As he ran his hands across her back, Tish moaned and took deep breaths every time he came close to the back of her neck.

"I want to make love to you..." he whispered. "Let me take care of you."

"I want that, too."

Nineteen

Moment long waited
desired kindness, touch…
tender warmth of love.

Tish had made love with only two men in her life, her ex-husband and her college sweetheart. She had just decided to add one more lover to her short list and it made her think twice about it.

What if this is a mistake? I can never take it back, undo it or forget this moment…no matter what happens, this is going to be a memory. A good one or a not-so-good one.

Tom's hand gently caressed the back of her neck as he kissed her more passionately.

She could feel a melt down coming. *Damn! How does he know to do that? The whole time I was married, Marcus never found that spot and I'd forgotten all about it.*

As he continued to tear apart all her inhibitions about being intimate with him, she could hardly wait to feel his naked body against hers.

She pulled back from his kiss and took a deep breath. He loosened his embrace and silently looked down at her as she reached for the bottom of his T-shirt, lifted it up, and pulled it off. Her mouth fell open slightly and she blinked as she looked at his broad, muscular chest covered with a light sprinkling of dark, tightly curled hair. His stern body proudly displayed the six-pack that he'd kept safely hidden under his clothes. She kissed his nipples, then across his chest and slowly down his stomach.

Damn…This is going to be the best chocolate dessert I've ever had.

His breathing became deeper as he turned slightly and stepped toward the bed, bringing her with him. Stopping at the side of the bed, he reached down, took the hem of her dress, and pulled it over her head.

"Girl, you're so beautiful," he said as he sat down on the bed and looked at her body. "And so soft, so warm." He kissed her belly button and gently licked it. "Just tell me how to please you…" He continued to kiss her abdomen, then down her thighs and up to her stomach, as he gently but firmly squeezed her buttocks.

She trembled as she slowly moved her hands across his head and down his neck. He moaned and she tried to speak, but no words escaped her mouth.

Slowly he moved his hands to the front of her thighs and gently pushed her legs open wider. He touched her with his fingertips, gliding across the most private and protected part of her body, now wet and burning with desire. She closed her eyes and released a deep sigh.

If only he knew the depth of my need for him, how long it's been since I've been touched so tenderly. She began to shake uncontrollably as he gave her more pleasure.

"Come on baby, it's okay," he whispered as he stood and held her in his arms. "But we're not done yet. Lie down. I want to make passionate love to you."

She got on the bed and he reached into his pocket, pulled out the condoms; placing them on the nightstand. Then he pulled his pants and underwear off and climbed on top of her.

"You okay?" he asked as he wiped a tear from her cheek.

"I…I'm all right," her voice sweet and submissive. "It's just been a while, that's all."

She tried to smile as she looked into his gorgeous eyes, his face so close to hers that she felt his breath. "You've got me so excited, I don't know what to say."

"Then say nothing unless you don't want to go further." He stroked her face, carefully brushing the bangs from her forehead. "And if you do, I promise to be gentle. I won't hurt you."

She wrapped her arms around him, pulling him closer to her, and kissed his lips. Even if he wanted to, he couldn't hide that it had probably gotten past the point where saying "no" would be more than an evil thing. His arousal excited her even more. She wanted him buried deep inside her, not pushing against her thigh.

"You're gonna need one of those." Tish smiled, turned her head, and nodded toward the nightstand.

"Yes ma'am. Whatever you say."

He entered her slowly and gingerly as she felt the same tightness she'd experienced when she'd lost her virginity.

Had it been that long? Could time recreate such an illusion? She held him close as he continued to inch his way inside her, determined it seemed, to penetrate into her most scared place. "Oh, my goodness…" she whimpered.

"You okay?" He opened his eyes and looked at her.

"More than okay…" she could barely speak. "You feel so good…it's been so long…"

"Enjoy me, Tish," he whispered. "I'm here to please you."

He kissed her passionately and shifted his short, cautious motions to longer strokes that filled her up when he was deep inside. She heard him moan, then he whispered her name.

Gasping for air, she felt as if the room was spinning. He held her tighter as the first wave of bliss shimmered through her body.

"Hold on, now. We can do that again, if you want," he whispered.

"Please, please..," she whimpered, holding on to Tom as tight as she could.

Thirty minutes later, exhausted and satisfied, Tish rolled over on her side, taking his arm with her, wrapping it around her chest. With the front of his body against her back, his legs following the contour of her legs, they held on to each other. She smiled and took a deep breath realizing that she had never had better lovemaking.

Where has he been my whole life?

The phone rang; Tish let the answering machine get it. "Hey, girl, it's Dee. Just wanted you to know that we're all dressing for church and we'll be back to the house after we have lunch—about three o'clock. Call my cell and let me know if you need us to come get you. Remember, your car is at my house. Whatever you're doing…take your time and enjoy. You deserve the day off and you've got it. Use it wisely… smooches."

"Oh, that's great," Tom whispered. "Cause I'm not done with you. I just want you to know," he leaned in closer and kissed her neck, "that I enjoy making love to you, with you, and for you. And right after I take this nap, we are both having some more of that."

"Umm, yes sir," she whispered back, smiling with her eyes closed. "Whatever you say."

Twenty

With you I become -
I remember who I am;
it brings me great joy.

"Thanks for feeding the kids breakfast and taking them to church with you guys. I owe you one," Tish said, smiling at Dee as she led the children toward her car. "I'll call you later."

Dee, still wearing her navy blue designer suit and matching three-inch heels, walked up to Tish's car and stood by the open door. She raised one eyebrow. "Yeah, do call me as soon as you can talk. I can see we need an update, here…smiling like that," she replied as she handed the kids' overnight bag to Tish.

She shifted her braids that had fallen across her face. "I've got to get used to these things. They're always getting in my way. I don't know why I had this done. Short hair doesn't cause these problems."

"But they are soo cute, Auntie Dee," Melanie said. "They make you look like a teenager!"

"Gee, thanks, I think …" Dee chuckled. "I guess I never thought of it that way."

Tish looked over at Tom and Aaron standing by Tom's car talking and laughing. Tom looked back at her, nodded, and walked over to her.

"Hey, thanks for giving me a ride over to get my car, Tom."

"Not a problem, glad to do it. Call me when you get home." He hugged her lightly and kissed her cheek. Leaning into the car, he looked into the back seat and grinned at her children. "You guys have a good time at Auntie Dee's?"

"Yes, sir," Simon answered as Melanie nodded.

"That's good. Take care and I hope to see you again soon, okay?" Tom held his hand out and received a high-five from each of them.

He turned and gave Dee a brotherly hug. "Thank you for introducing me to your soror, here. She's a very special lady."

"*Well…* you are both quite welcome. It's nice to see such bright smiles today on both of your mugs! I'm so happy!" Dee replied. "Drive careful now."

Turning to Tish as she started her engine, Dee waved, saying, "Talk to you *soon*. Bye."

"Mom, when we get home can I call daddy to see if he'll come get us and go to Chuck E. Cheese today?" Melanie asked, sounding like her feelings had been hurt.

"Sure you can, honey," Tish answered, surprised by her daughter's request. She'd never asked to see her father on his off weekend before. "He may not be in town, you know. But you can call him and see. That's not a problem."

"Thanks, Mom." Her voice sounding more upbeat. "I just miss him, that's all."

"Oh, baby, that's understandable. You know it's okay with me if you see your daddy whenever you want." She reached in her purse and pulled out her cell phone. "Here, you don't have to wait 'till we get home. Use my cell and call him now."

Melanie found her father's phone number and hit the speed dial button. The call went straight to voicemail.

"Hi, Daddy. Call me when you get this message. Oh, it's Melanie." She pushed the end button. "He didn't answer. Maybe he'll call back. I'll keep the phone until he does, okay?"

"Sure, baby. Hold on to it until we get home. I'm sure he'll call you right back."

They drove home in silence.

Two minutes after they'd entered the house, the home phone rang.

"Girl, you know you got to tell me what happened last night," Dee said in response to Tish's "Hello."

"Damn, I just walked through the door. You anxious or what? Let me take my shoes off and turn on a movie for the kids. I'll be right back. Hold on."

After she got the kids settled in the game room, she hoped for the opportunity to have a conversation for more than five minutes without a serious crisis.

"Dee, I'm back." She took the phone out to her deck and sat in the sun. "Our evening was great! As you saw, he kept me busy on the dance floor and you know I like that. He made sure the brothers knew I was with him. I liked that, too. We stopped on the way back at Town Lake and walked along the river. He held me in his arms. That was so nice."

"Wow, sounds like you enjoyed yourself even after the party." Dee chuckled.

Tish pulled another chair in front of her and put her feet up. "The really cool thing is, Tom never tried to move too fast with me. Just enough to let me know he was interested, but also to let me know that he wasn't going to rush me. You know how some guys want to go straight to sex after the first date. So anyway, we finally got there, but not until he went home and I called him this morning. It was my idea."

"No! Not *Miss Victorian!*" she replied. "You suggested that he come over and have sex with you? I'm not believing this."

"Well, not quite like that, but yeah." She giggled. "I woke up thinking *I'm not going to the gym, today.* Girl, he is so good. Nothing like HBO or anything, just good, tender lovin'. We match each other—I felt like I'd found my missing puzzle piece."

She paused, thinking twice about her next thought, wondering if she should say it. "I don't know…but I think I could really fall for Tom in a big way. Is this just too good to be true or what?"

"Well, it could be that you were just horny, my sister! Ha-hah!! Hope you didn't hurt the brother!" Dee gave a hearty laugh. "He seemed to be smiling wide this morning, though. My, my. Got you some this morning. I'm scared of you!"

"Yeah, yeah." She stood, walked over to her potted red rose bush, and plucked off the dead leaves. "It was just a matter of time and the right man. I hope he is the right man. It'd be even better if Tom is feeling what I'm feeling. Cause if he is, he's gonna want to get with me again. But then, that might lead to other things—like commitment and proposal…" She stopped trimming the plant and looked down to the freshly cut lawn, her widened eyes gazing at the grass. "Oh, God, no. Not that—not for a long time!"

"See, here you go…scared you're going to get married already." Dee's scolding tone turned kinder. "Tish, remember, he recently came out of a divorce too. I'm sure his mind isn't on commitment with you or any other woman. So relax. Enjoy that man."

"I hear you. But I have this thing about sleeping around," she said thoughtfully. She sat back in the chair and admired the plants on the deck. "I don't do it and I don't want my man doing it with other women while he's doing it with me. So if he wants to have some repeats of this morning, we need to have a talk and come to an agreement. If he can't agree to my terms, I guess it's back to the gym for this ol' girl until I can't take it anymore. I had enough of that action when I was married. I had repeated yeast and bladder infections until I got wise and realized I was sleeping around every time I had sex with my husband, 'cause he had his women on the side."

"Child, you know, if my husband did that to me, I'd have to cut off his thing with a dull knife, no questions asked," Dee said. "And I think he knows it too."

She chuckled, then continued. "He heard me say that to somebody and every once and a while I see him in the kitchen sharpening the knives. I just laugh at him and keep on walking."

"Girl, you crazy. But you know I haven't had any problems since I left Marcus. What does that tell you?"

"It tells me you should always have your man wear a condom, 'cause you never know where he placed that thing last. Sometimes I think they believe their stuff has some kinda' natural super-reflecting shield and they can just walk away without wearing what they just dipped it in. It's a scary situation. But I agree with you. A monogamous relationship is still the best thing. It's healthier all around."

"Yeah, so I guess we'll have this conversation at some point. I hope we do, anyway. He's a keeper."

"You go girl." Dee opened the refrigerator and took out a package of pork chops. "Look, I gotta get dinner ready."

"Okay, talk to you later." Tish stood and stretched. "Tom asked me to call him when I got home. Bye."

"See you at work tomorrow."

Tish walked into the kitchen and dialed Tom's home number; she got his machine.

"Hey. Just calling to let you know that I got home safe and sound. The kids are watching a movie and I'm preparing dinner. If you'd like to come over and eat with us, I should have everything ready by six o'clock. Talk to you soon. Thanks again for a great evening…and wonderful morning."

She called his cell number and it went straight to voice mail. *Oh well, I did as he asked. Now, get to work.*

But in the back of her mind she wondered where he could be and what he might be doing.

Why would he ask me to call him if he couldn't answer the phone? Is he with another woman? Should I fear reliving that same pain all over again?

Twenty-One

Honesty brings truth
that sometimes injures the same
as not knowing all.

Tom picked up his messages as soon as he walked into his room.

"How you doin', Tom? I'm looking forward to seeing you this weekend. I've got plans for you... Mmm... mmm. Let me know what time your military hop will arrive and I'll be there to pick you up. Call me later. Bye."

He stopped the machine and thought for a minute. *Well, now. Miss Sable has plans for me...and I bet she does.*

The next message was from Tish. He sat on his bed and thought about how they'd spent the past evening and morning. As wonderful and loving as she had been, his desire for Sable hadn't faded.

Do I need to choose between them? He'd never had two such beautiful women wanting him—all of him—at the same time.

I enjoyed being with each woman and really don't want to stop seeing either. The right thing to do might be to let them know that I'm not ready for a commitment and that I intend to see other women. Then they can decide whether they want to be with me or not. That way I don't have to choose.

Tish's dinner invitation made him salivate, but it had gotten much too late for that, he feared. The thought of another one of her home-cooked meals made him want to go there anyway. He reached over to the nightstand and picked up the phone. Sitting with his back snuggled into the pillows stacked against the headboard, he dialed her number and hoped she'd ask him to come by.

"Hello, Tish. How's my Delta Queen this evening?"

"Hey, there. I'm doing good." She put the last of the leftovers in the refrigerator. "How about you?"

"Oh, I'm kinda tired, but otherwise, doing good, too. Sorry I missed your call earlier." He pulled his socks off and stretched his legs out on the bed. "I had some errands to run and forgot to turn on my cell. I can't believe I missed the invite for dinner. It's not often that I get a home-cooked meal. So you cook more than breakfast, huh?"

"Sure do. I've been cooking since I was about twelve years old. Some say I can really burn, too."

"Well, then, I'm real disappointed that I missed out."

"Maybe I'll have you over for dinner one night this weekend and you can see for yourself. It's the kids' weekend with their dad so I'll be free except for a sorority meeting on Saturday morning. Interested?"

"Interested? Yes. Available? No." Tom knew he needed to be honest. He'd take a chance and hope she would understand.

"Unfortunately, I made plans last week to see a friend in Washington, D.C. this coming weekend. She has tickets to a pro football game and concert on Saturday. So I'm kinda' committed to that plan. I won't be back until late Sunday evening. So this weekend is full for me. Sorry."

She didn't reply.

He took a deep breath and continued. "I hope that invitation is good for another time."

She said nothing.

"Tish, you still there?"

"Yes…sorry. I spaced out for a minute. I was thinking about what you just said."

Silence.

"And…what were you thinking?" Tom asked cautiously.

She sat at the bar and stared into space with one hand covering her mouth. "I, ummm, well," her voice almost a whisper, she continued, "I…I was just thinking that…it doesn't really matter." She took a deep breath. "Sure, I'll cook for you sometime. I hope you have a nice weekend. Sounds like you'll be kept pretty busy."

"Yes, Sable likes to stay on the go. I've never been to a pro football game so that'll be a real treat. I'm looking forward to it."

"Great," she said, sounding uneasy. "Look, I have to get to bed. I've a ton of work waiting for me in the morning, not to mention a presentation at eight o'clock for one of our major clients. Don't need bags under my eyes. I'll talk to you some other time."

"You rest well and I'll call you tomorrow evening. Will that be okay?"

"Sure," she responded with soft indifference.

Twenty-Two

Alone and despaired
untrusting again because
loving shouldn't hurt

Tish hung up, bent over in anguish, and let tears fall freely down her face. Slowly, she walked up the stairs to her bedroom, trying not to cry out and waken the children.

She walked into her room and went straight to the bed. Her stereo had been tuned in to KSJL and the DJ's selection of Donny Hathaway's "For All We Know," couldn't have been played at a worse time.

Mad that she'd given herself to a man who was involved with another woman, she punched the pillow. He didn't tell her—but she hadn't asked either. And now he hadn't even tried to hide it.

As much as we tell ourselves we want the truth, it still hurts.

Holding a pillow against her chest, she rolled over on her side as tears continued to fall. She couldn't help but think about what Tom had just told her and why.

If he's going all the way to Washington, D.C. for the weekend, surely he's sleeping with that woman, too. Pro football or not, he's sleeping with her. They're playing football all over the country and he could go anywhere else to see a game—hell, he could drive up to Dallas for that. But no, he's going to D.C. because that's where Sable is. So she must be more than just a friend.

"Then what does that make me?" she whispered as she sobbed out loud.

The pain became so intense, she could think of nothing else and the DJ didn't help as he played one sad love song after another. She discovered what songwriters meant about "drowning in my tears."

Eventually she cried herself into a dreamless sleep.

Twenty-Three

Listen to the dreams
remember what you forgot.
Your soul speaks to you.

Dee, sitting in her black leather executive chair behind the oversized cherry wood desk, looked up from reading the morning manager's report when Tish tapped on the half-closed door to her office. "Come in."

Tish walked in without saying a word and sat on the edge of the chair in front of Dee's desk clutching a folder against her chest.

"Damn girl, you look rough this morning. What's going on?"

"Good morning to you, too," Tish replied softly as she lifted her head and looked directly at her friend. "Do I really look that bad? Maybe I should just go back home. The Mary Kay magic didn't work, huh? Not even a little bit?" She looked down at her hands she'd flopped onto her lap.

"No, I can honestly say it didn't. What's wrong?" Dee stood and walked over to Tish's side. "You were so happy yesterday, so full of smiles." She placed a hand on her friend's shoulder. "What's up, my sister?"

"I don't have time to talk about it now," she responded, her head still lowered as she wiped a tear from her cheek." She slumped back in the chair. "Would you please take these notes and do my presentation? I don't think I should go in there looking like this." She placed the folder on the desk.

She took a deep breath and continued, "It's not anything I can't get over, trust me. I've been through worse."

Tish turned her head slightly and looked at the floor. Her voice dropped to almost a whisper. "It's just that it hurts the same no matter how often it happens. Just give me some time. I'll be fine—have to be."

"Well, all right. Show me what you have." Dee picked up the folder and opened it. "But I'm coming over so we can talk during my lunch break."

"That'll be fine." She stood, slowly took out the presentation notes from the folder, and spread them on the desk.

"Right now, let's go over what you have to do. We've only got fifteen minutes." She looked at Dee and forced a smile. "Thanks for doing this. I owe you…again."

When Tish got home she headed straight for the couch, turned on the TV, and surrounded herself with pillows as if building a fort around her.

Determined not to cry another tear, she closed her eyes and fell asleep. Her nap ended with the chime of Westminster Abby from her doorbell. As she sat up, the details of the dream she'd just had began to play back in her mind. She sauntered toward the door after the doorbell rang a second time.

"Hey, Dee. Come on in. I'd planned to make some chicken salad or something but I fell asleep watching a dumb soap opera and time got away. Sorry."

"No problem." She closed the door and followed Tish. "Call Pizza Hut and have them deliver a large Supreme. I'm paying and I'm hungry. So what's up with you today?" Dee sat on the sofa and crossed her legs.

"Hold that thought while I make the call," she said as she continued toward the kitchen, never looking back at Dee. "You can change the channel to something else. I'll bring out some drinks."

She placed the pizza order. As she filled the glasses with ice and poured the lemonade, details about her dream became clearer, more vivid, yet confusing at the same time.

"I hope lemonade is okay." She handed Dee a glass. "I'm out of Pepsi and I know that it goes better with pizza but I hadn't planned on pizza today."

Dee picked up the remote control and turned off the TV. "Now, *please* tell me what's going on with you. I can't believe the difference in you since yesterday. What happened?"

"Before I tell you what had me all messed up this morning, I have to tell you about this dream I had right before the doorbell woke me up." Tish leaned forward. "Remember the dream I told you I had when I was standing by a river with a man who became Tom? And we said something to each other but I couldn't hear anything?"

Dee nodded.

"I dreamed it again, except this time I heard what we said. It sounded like vows or something." She held her hands up, palms facing Dee.

"I told him to press his open hands against mine—and he did. I felt his life energy flowing from his body through our hands to me and mine back to him." She took a deep breath. "I told him, '*from this day forward we are one and our love will continue to grow.*' I don't remember everything we said to each other, but I do remember him saying, '*when I become Egypt's Pharaoh, you will become my queen.*' He also said, '*you will be near my side forever and ever.*' Now I know it was the Nile River we were standing beside."

Tish lowered her hands and crossed her arms in front of her. "That makes sense—the sand, the palms and how we were dressed. I felt so happy in the dream that when I looked into his face, tears of joy fell down my cheeks."

"Oh, Tish—that's so romantic." Dee's voice was soft and encouraging. "I wish I had dreams like that."

"You don't understand, girl. The dream was so real. I *felt it*. It was in color, too."

Tish unfolded her arms and lifted her legs onto the sofa, crossing them Indian style. "I heard the wind blow through the palms and felt it gently brush against my face. With his hands pressed against mine, I felt his energy. I woke up crying. This was not an ordinary dream." She looked down at her glass and her voice lowered almost to a whisper. "I don't know what it means, but I'm almost wishing I never had it. Especially after last night."

"What do you mean by that?" Dee asked with a curious look on her face. "It's just a dream."

"Somehow I don't think that's all it is." She paused, looked up, and gave Dee a half smile, and lowered her head. "Anyway, Tom is involved with another woman. He's going to D.C. this weekend to be with her. Dee, I had sex with that man *yesterday!* I didn't know he was involved with anyone. Now I know 'cause he told me. He even told me her name—*Sable*."

"Oh, Tish I'm so sorry—"

"And now...how am I supposed to feel about that? Huh? I know what I feel and it's not good. Not good at all."

A look of anger crossed her face as she shook her fist in the air. "What if he'd just slept with her before he came to me?

Men do that, you know…and I think that's just *gross*." Tish shivered at the thought.

"Remember, my sister. You don't want to get into a relationship with Tom or any other man. Those are your words."

She felt Dee shift into her counselor mode as she sat forward, eyes focused directly at her. "*So what* if he's seeing another woman? Isn't that what you want so he doesn't start looking at you for something you don't want—commitment? Did he use a condom? Hope so."

She nodded and sat silently listening to her friend going on and letting her have it.

"Have you had your talk about monogamy? Probably not; but remember you were the horny one; you needed him on Sunday morning."

Dee's voice reminded Tish of how her mother used to scold her. "You invited Tom over to take care of things. You told me he didn't try to rush you. So don't be mad at him. He did what most men would do. And you told me it was good. So what do you want now?"

A new tear fell down Tish's face. She knew Dee was right; she was always right, but it didn't make it feel any better.

"Honestly, I don't know what I want," she replied as she took a drink. She thought for a moment looking down at her fingertips. "Part of me wants a man like him to be in my life to enjoy things with, make me laugh, and have great sex with. Just one man—I only want one. But I want him to only want me, too. I know that could lead to other things, and that scares me."

"So what does that other part of you want, Soror?"

"The other part is asking could I share him with a woman in another state and be cool with that? That part wants to say yes, I could. That way I don't have to worry about him getting so attached to only me. And I realize from experience that even if you're married to a man, there's no guarantee that he's not going to sleep around. But knowing it and not just guessing about it doesn't make it easier; it still hurts." She shrugged her shoulders and looked over at Dee. "So I guess I'm right back to I don't know what I want."

"So why are you crying?" she asked in a very soft, caring voice.

"I don't know that either." More tears fell down her cheeks. "I started crying after we talked last night and I can't seem to stop. I guess I don't share well. Not my man, anyway. Hell, he isn't even my man and I'm crying. What's wrong with me?"

"I can't say. But why don't you make plans to get out of town this weekend and do something for yourself. You shouldn't sit around the house alone while the kids are gone. Don't you have a girlfriend in New Orleans you can visit? You can afford the trip. Right now you need one."

"I'll think about it. Thanks for listening and helping me put things in perspective." Tish wiped the tears from her face with the back of a trembling hand. "New Orleans sounds good. There's a brother there I'd like to see, anyway." She straightened out her legs and stretched. "Maybe he can help get my mind off Tom and I can have a great weekend."

"There you go! Be single, girl. You are, you know." Dee leaned back, crossed her legs, and waved her hand. "So, come out with the rest of it. What's this brother's name?"

"Maurice. I met him in Austin last summer and he invited me to come to New Orleans anytime I want." Her voice became stronger and the tears stopped falling. "He told me he'd make sure I'd have a good time. We talk on the phone every now and then. It's never been any more than that."

"So why didn't you tell me about him? Holding back?"

"No, not really. Just never thought much about it, that's all."

"Okay, so now I'm listening." Dee took off her heels and put her legs up on the sofa. "Tell me about him."

"He seems like a nice person with his head on straight. He's single, cute, smart, and I think he'd be fun." Tish pulled the ottoman closer. "He's completing his Ph.D. in psychology. Maybe I'll ask him what he thinks these dreams are all about."

"So you can have fun, be with a brother who has some brains and looks good, too." Dee chuckled. "He's already sounding like a much better deal than that dumb David, for sure! Not that we'd have you spend any more time on that loser."

"Oh, that's the truth." Tish laughed, and sipped on her drink. "I guess when you're a single woman, you have to take matters in your own hands and move forward when things don't work out and not waste any time doing it. Is that the lesson here?"

"I think that's true for any of us, married or single. But you must keep all your options open, my dear. So how are we going to get you and Maurice the hook-up this weekend?"

"He knows Tami Smith, the soror that hung out with us at the last regional conference. Remember her?"

"Yeah, the architect?"

"Yep. They've been friends for years. I'll call her and see if I can stay with her this weekend, that way I may be able to see him, too. So, if that works out, I'll go. I've talked myself into it. But right now I'm getting hungry. Where's that pizza man?"

Twenty-Four

You may run and hide
but the truth will soon find you.
Listen to your heart.

"Hey man, this Aaron. What's up?"

"Nothing much," Tom answered, surprised to hear from his friend. "Just getting ready to watch a movie on HBO. What's going on with you?"

"Same ol', same ol', you know..." Aaron cleared his throat. "Man, what's up with you and Tish?"

"Don't know what you mean."

"Something's going on 'cause Dee said Tish was upset about something...Dee won't even talk to me about it. She said I should ask you."

He took in a deep breath and let it out slowly. "Oh, man." He lowered his head into the palm of his hand. "I haven't talked to her since Sunday."

"Well, it's Thursday night now, brother. So whatever it is, I think you'd better try to talk about it, 'cause..." Aaron's voice faded out.

"That's the problem. I talked too much already. That's probably why she's upset. I was honest with Tish and told her about my plans to go out of town this weekend."

"So, what's wrong with that?"

"I told her that I'm going to see a friend and her name is Sable." Tom stood and paced the floor.

"Damn, man! *You crazy?*"

"I guess...." He felt terrible that he'd upset Tish. "But that plan was made before I knew Tish was really interested in me. I thought we were going to be hanging buddies, just friends. You know." He searched for the right words to explain himself. "And I thought I could tell her that and it'd be okay. I guess I was wrong."

"It sure looks that way."

"But I really like Tish and I don't want her to be upset with me about this." He scratched his head, hoping some bright idea that would fix things would surface. "I've got to see her before I leave tomorrow. She should know that I only meant to be honest with her, that's all. I didn't want to hurt her."

Aaron chuckled nervously. "Good luck with that, my brother. You know how women are."

"Yeah, I know what you mean, but I also know that I don't want to lose whatever chance I might have to get to know her better. There's something about Tish, man. I can't explain it, but it's all good."

"That sounds great, but you'd better get on it if you mean it."

"Right. I'll try to reach her one more time. Maybe she'll pick up the phone."

"Shout at you later. Good luck."

"Later."

If Aaron only knew just how much Tish has been on my mind.

Early that morning he'd dreamed that he entered a room where he saw her holding a baby wrapped in a golden cloth. She'd turned toward him, her face glowing. She handed him the child saying, *"It is your son, Teti. I have given you a son."* She wore a colorful dress with purple and green patterns throughout, reminding him of an ancient design he'd seen before. Her eyes were outlined in dark thick makeup. Tish looked like an Egyptian. *"Remember, our love is eternal,"* she said just as the alarm clock sounded, abruptly ending his sleep.

The dream had played over and over in his mind all day. *Who is Teti?* He asked himself again. *Why am I having dreams about Egyptians?*

The more time passed the stronger his desire to be with Tish had grown. Now that he knew that she was upset with him, he couldn't resist the desire to at least talk to her.

"Hi, Tish." Surprised to hear her and not the recorded message. "How've you been?"

"Oh, Tom," she replied flatly. "I'm doing fine, I guess. And you?"

"I'm alright." Taking a clue from her question that it might be alright to proceed, he asked, "I…um, I'd like to see you tonight; I'd like to talk."

"Oh?" she hesitated, pushing her chair away from the dinette table where she'd been reading the newspaper. "What's on your mind?"

"Nothing special," he said softy. "Just want to see you, that's all."

"O-kay..." She sounded unsure, but continued, "Would you like to come over about nine or is that too late?"

"No, not at all. I'll see you then."

"See you in a few…"

Twenty-Five

Find rest and comfort away from confusion in love's sanctuary.

Hmm, I wonder what that's all about? Tish hung up the phone and stared at the floor.

He's already told me he's spending his weekend with Miss Sable. What does he need to see me for? She'd made plans, too. Moving on. *New Orleans, here I come. Like Dee said, I'm single and I'm living like it, too!*

She could have told Tom no and made sure he knew that she didn't want to see him. But that wouldn't have been the truth. She didn't have to invite him over, but again, with the excitement she felt just hearing his voice, she couldn't bring herself to keep him at a distance, especially when he said he wanted to see her.

Maybe he's had a change in plans and won't be going to D.C. after all. That must be it.

But even if he wasn't going, Tish had no intentions of backing down from her plans to spend the weekend in New Orleans. Everything was set; her friends were expecting her and she'd bought her plane ticket.

At nine o'clock sharp the doorbell rang. Tish, wearing blue jeans and an oversized, cotton, Delta baseball shirt, answered the door in her bare feet.

"Hi," she said in a soft voice, looking him over. He wore blue jeans and a tight, long sleeve black cotton shirt that showed off his perfect chest. *Damn, he looks good.*

Without speaking he walked in and reached for her. Holding her in his arms, he softly ran his hands across her back. In his soft, sexy voice he whispered, "Hey there."

As he began stroking her hair and holding her closer to his body, she nuzzled into his chest and took a deep, long breath. *Oh... no...he's wearing Paul Sebastian again, too.*

He felt so good, so comforting next to her body. She liked the way he knew where she needed to be stroked and touched. They said nothing to each other for several minutes. They just stood there in her foyer holding each other; she began to fear they were about to say their last goodbye.

"Thanks for letting me come over. I've missed you," Tom finally said.

"I guess…would you like to sit in the family room and talk?"

"Sure, that's a good idea." He looked down at her with the sweetest smile and reached for her hand. Then he led her into the family room.

They sat on the sofa, silently looking at each other. Tish listened to Coco Lee's song, "Can We Talk About It," playing on the stereo. She realized that the song described how she felt and she looked away from him.

She picked up one of the burgundy throw pillows, placed it on her lap, and stared at it as she gently ran her fingers across the beige fringes. She frantically searched for the words, but there were so many things she could say; there were feelings that she wanted to talk about. Although foremost on her mind, she refused to ask about his weekend plans.

He asked to come over to talk, so I'll let him start.

Instead of talking, Tom leaned back into the corner of the sofa and stretched his arms out toward her. "Come here." She moved toward him and he held her next to his body. As he stroked her arm with his fingers, he softly kissed the back of her head. "I'm so relaxed with you."

They sat together on the sofa for more than an hour and listened to mellow tunes of various love songs—one right after the other—adding a romantic feel to the moments that passed without conversation.

"Tish, wake up," he said in her ear. As she raised her head, he continued, "I have to move out of this position and you should go to bed and cover up. It's getting rather cold in here."

"Wow, I really fell asleep, didn't I?" She sat up and rubbed her eyes. "Sorry, I didn't mean to do that…but I guess I'm tired, huh?"

"Well, you aren't by yourself. I got a good snooze in there, too." Tom stood and took her hands helping her to her feet. "Thanks for letting me come over and spend some time with you. You gave me just what I needed."

"I'm not quite sure what you needed, but you're welcome." She looked into those sexy eyes as he spread his luscious lips into a broad smile. She had to admit she agreed with him. "It's been a nice, quiet time with you, and very different for us. We've not ever been lost for words, before. I guess there're times when you really don't need to talk, just enjoy the moment for what it is."

"Yeah, that's just how I feel. Thanks for understanding. I'm gonna go now. I'll call you when my words come back." He stroked her face and moved the hair that had been misplaced in front of one eye. "You're so beautiful. You know that?"

Tom's quiet voice touched her as she watched him scan her face and then paused as their eyes met.

She couldn't reply. As she looked into his gaze, she realized that he was about to leave and hadn't said one thing about changing his weekend plans. She feared that she'd lose him to this other woman; that he'd fall in love with Sable and not come back and share any more special moments with her again. She felt connected to him in a very special way and wondered if he sensed the feeling too.

Tom took a deep breath, pulled her into his arms, and kissed her forehead. *Oh, how I wish I hadn't promised Sable that I'd come to D.C. this weekend. But I gave her my word and she's made plans. It just wouldn't be right for me not to go.* He stroked her hair. *I'm not ready to leave Tish, but I know I have to. This is crazy.*

Instead of sharing what he thought, he released her from his embrace and turned to walk toward the front door holding her hand.

Before he opened it to leave, he looked in her eyes. His mind played back the dream of them by the river.

He sensed he knew what he told her in the dream. *"A bond is pledged this eve, you will be near my side forever and ever."* He sighed as he hugged her tight one last time.

Who is this woman and what do these dreams mean?

"I gotta go," he whispered softly. "I'll be talking to you soon."

"You have a good weekend," she replied as she forced a smile. "Be safe."

"Will do." He kissed the back of her hand and opened the door. "You too."

Twenty-Six

Searching for answers
longing for confirmation.
Seek no more, I'm here.

The weekend found them in separate cities. Tish had been wined and dined in the Big Easy while Sable kept Tom occupied from the time his plane landed.

Tish dragged her tired body down the humid corridor and boarded the plane in New Orleans. She was stuffed to her eyebrows from Sunday brunch with Tami at Christian's Restaurant. She'd feasted on everything from spicy crawfish etouffee and perfect eggs benedict to rummy bread pudding and the best bananas foster she'd ever tasted. Before she buckled her seatbelt, she reached under her oversized T-shirt and unbuttoned her blue jeans, then unzipped them a little so she could breathe better.

The too-perky male Southwest flight attendant's cheerful humor made the otherwise routine announcements hard for Tish to ignore. She chuckled as she thought, *he must really love this job.* She wished for silence so she could get her nap on.

Closing her eyes and settling in her seat, Tish wondered why she'd had that last mimosa with her brunch. The effects of all that champagne had finally made a mad rush to her head leaving her eyes heavy and sleepy.

Those New Orleans folks sho' know how to party and keep people up all night, she thought as she adjusted the pillow against the window and wiggled again in her seat to find a comfortable position.

Happy that she'd followed Dee's advice and not stayed in San Antonio all weekend, she grinned as she closed her eyes. Going to New Orleans and making friends with such fun-loving people had been a good thing. She moaned as pleasant memories about how her weekend started and all the things she'd done began to replay in her mind.

Maurice and Tami had met her at the airport when she arrived on Friday night. They took her immediately to dinner at a crowded family-style seafood restaurant, where they were joined by six of their live wire friends.

They ordered what looked like way too much food and served themselves from dishes piled high with fried fish, shrimp, crabs, scallops, and side dishes. Everyone had been in such a good mood. They ate, drank, talked, and laughed for what seemed like half the night. Just when she thought the evening would end, the group left the restaurant and met in the French Quarter at their favorite jazz spot, The House of Blues. Before she knew it, four o'clock in the morning had arrived as she ate fresh beignets and drank strong chicory coffee at the Café Du Monde.

When the sun created the crack of dawn, Tami drove them to her house and parked in the driveway. Tish quickly undressed, washed her face, and brushed her teeth. She had planned to sleep at least until noon.

"Good morning, Soror," Tami called from the kitchen, waking Tish up from a deep sleep. The small guest bedroom, down the hallway near the kitchen, had been decorated in purple and crème, accented with African violets. The smell of frying bacon and brewing coffee filled her room with captivating aromas.

"It's eleven o'clock!" She walked to the bedroom door and pushed it open. Speaking in a softer tone, she continued. "Maurice called to see if you're up yet and ready to head out to see the city. Remember, last night you asked him to take you back downtown today. He's on his way over. So get up!"

"Ohhh, I did, didn't I?" Tish replied reluctantly, as she rolled over in the bed facing the door. "Dang, I didn't know he was going to start the day so early. Okay, okay. I'm getting up." She sat up as she rubbed her eyes. "I do want to see more of New Orleans, especially Jackson Square."

Tish adjusted the straps of her of white nightgown, placing them back on her shoulders. "Maurice is such a nice guy, isn't he, Tami?"

"Girlfriend, Maurice is a sweetie and a cutie,"Tami said as she entered the room wearing a blue terrycloth robe and black slippers. Pulling her shoulder-length, dark-brown curly hair back from her freckled face and securing it with a rubber band, she sat on the bed.

Even without makeup Tami was a gorgeous, thirty-year-old-woman with model-perfect skin and a size six body. "I'm glad you guys met. I believe he likes you, too. I saw how he looked at you last night. You had him hanging on your every word."

Tish hadn't paid much attention to what Tami had said until later that day when they were alone.

When Maurice arrived, she checked out his neat, professional, yet casual look. His dreamy, blue-hazel eyes framed by his dark, thick lashes and reddish-brown complexion seemed to pierce deep when he first glanced at her. He'd leaned over and planted a warm kiss on her cheek.

She enjoyed Tami's delicious breakfast of cheese grits dripping in butter, scrambled eggs, crispy bacon, homemade biscuits, fried apples, and the strongest coffee Tish had ever tasted. "How do you stay so small, eating like this?" she asked Tami as she pulled on her housecoat.

"Honey, I never eat this good unless company comes over." She laughed and smacked Tish's hand to get away from her hold on her housecoat. "Tomorrow it's back to a buttery, warm croissant and coffee for breakfast everyday—at least 'till someone else comes by!"

"Well, you ready to go?" Maurice asked after sipping the last of his coffee.

"Sure am." Tish stood and took their plates to the kitchen. "Thanks so much, Tami. I can't remember the last time someone cooked breakfast for me."

"Welcome," she said, taking the plates out of Tish's hands. "I got this. Now get outta' here, you two!"

She followed Maurice outside into the warm, breezy air to his clean, royal blue RX7, glimmering in the bright sunshine. They rode without talking as they headed downtown, enjoying the mellow sounds of a Wynton Marsalis CD.

He pulled into a public lot near the river. As soon as Tish stepped out of the car, the wind, much stronger than before, whipped her loose hair across her face. Brushing it from her eyes, she glanced over her shoulder and saw the Mississippi in all its majesty. She forgot all about touring Jackson Square or any other place New Orleans had to offer. She was captivated by the Mississippi—how it seemed to have a strange pull on her to come near it.

"Maurice, can we go over there and walk along the sidewalk?" she asked softly, pointing toward the river.

"Sure, doll, whatever you'd like to do," he replied giving her a wide smile. They were standing close together beside the car when he turned, looking at her eyeball to eyeball. His intense, light eyes made her blush as they stood in a suspended moment looking at each other.

He was about an inch taller than her. His broad shoulders and long arms made him appear larger than she'd remembered.

As they walked, she asked him to tell her about himself.

"Let's see. Last week I celebrated my thirty-fourth birthday. As you know, I'm not married, never got married, in fact."

"Any particular reason for not marrying?" She couldn't imagine how such a good-looking, smart, and well-put-together brother could remain single so long.

"A number. It's never been a priority." He put his hands in his pants' pockets. He looked over at Tish and paused a few seconds before continuing. "Besides that, I wanted to wait until I finished my education before settling down and it took me longer than I expected to return to college."

"So, have you completed your Ph.D. yet?" she asked as she led him to an unoccupied bench near the sidewalk facing the river.

"Not quite." He sat back and placed his arm behind her, resting it on the back of the bench. "This past spring I finished my coursework. Now I'm completing my dissertation, which I plan to defend in December."

"What do you plan to do after that?"

"A friend and I will be setting up a clinical psychology practice together here in New Orleans." He reached over and gently brushed the hair away from her face. "So tell me about a burning desire you've yet to accomplish."

Tish looked down at her lap and thought for a moment. "I've seriously considered writing a book when things in my life settle down some."

She cut her eyes up to his and smiled. "I really admire you for not letting go of your dream and sticking with it to get where you are today. You've got it all worked out. The rest is going to be a piece of cake."

Tish felt very comfortable with him. They talked about everything, it seemed, walked the length of the sidewalk along the Mississippi twice, then took the river paddleboat tour. By the time they got to Jackson Square the evening had darkened the streets and all the vendors had packed and left except for one tarot card reader.

"Well, here's something I've thought about doing…but never had the nerve." She nodded toward the woman seated at a table, shuffling cards. "I've been having some very different dreams lately. I wonder if she can tell me what's going on."

"You have nothing to lose but the tip you give her when she's done. You can either learn something useful or look at it as just another new experience." He encouraged her to sit down.

"Hello, I'm Madame LaSay." Her voice was deep, yet soft, almost whispery. Her very dark, intense eyes twinkled and widened when she looked up and found Tish seated at her table waiting to be her newest customer.

She looked to be about sixty-five years old. A long braid of dark brown and gray hair was pulled over one shoulder and hung down her chest. A silver scarf covered her head and was tied in the back of her neck. She wore bright red lipstick and dark eyeliner that matched her penciled-in thick eyebrows. Dark brown freckles accented her sun-baked, reddish-brown complexion.

She smiled broadly and took Tish's hand. "What's yo' name, honey?" Her deep southern accent added authentication to the whole New Orleans scene.

"Tish," she replied, timidly about the whole thing. "LaTisha."

Madame LaSay closed her eyes and nodded as she whispered, "Yes." She cleared her throat and continued, "What's yo' birth month?"

"March." She looked over at Maurice who stood nearby watching with his arms folded in front of him. He smiled and nodded his encouragement.

"Yes, of course." She opened her eyes and shuffled the tarot cards several times as she looked back and forth at Tish and Maurice, not saying a word to either of them. She stood and adjusted the long skirt of her African-print cotton dress, then returned to her chair, looking pleased, comfortable, and ready to begin.

"Miss LaTisha, let me see yo' hands," she said, as she carefully examined Tish's palms. Speaking softly she said, "My, you an ol' spirit."

She pointed to a spot on Tish's right palm. "See dis here? It's a pentagram. It means you been 'round for a ver' long time." She then placed one card on the table and smiled. "Having dreams of ol' times, yes?" She glanced up and looked Tish directly into her eyes and nodded. "No sense being frightened by it. You jus' remembering what has been befo'." Madame LaSay took a deep breath and picked up the cards then placed the deck back into a box.

Tish felt amazed and couldn't believe what she'd heard. She remained silent and waited to learn more from this very mysterious woman.

Madame LaSay sat back in her chair, placed her hands on her lap, and continued, "Dere people in yo' life to guide you to yo' destiny. Dey'll direct you to yo' one true love." She placed her hands, palms down, on the table. "Be patient, honey. You 'bout to be tested."

She reached across the table again for Tish's hands. "It's gon' take time fo' things work out in the matters of yo' heart, chil'. But dey gon' work out."

She looked at Maurice then back at Tish. "Dis man here, he's in yo' life for a very 'portant reason. He's been dere.., in yo' life befo'." She nodded, smiled, and slowly turned her head, looking Tish directly into her eyes. "Dat's why you feel good 'round him. You trust him. Dat's 'cause you always did. He ain't gon' hurt you nah, either."

Tish could hardly wait until she stopped talking. "Madame LaSay, I have so many questions. Can I—"

"Sorry, chil'." She raised one hand slowly to cut her off. "Dis here all I see for you nah. De rest you have to find. De answers are dere, but dey within yo'self."

Madame LaSay stood and pulled out the old, beat-up briefcase from under her card table. After putting it on the table, she quietly placed the items of her trade carefully in the case and closed it.

Tish put a twenty-dollar bill in her tip jar and thanked her. Walking slowing away from the table toward Maurice, she took a deep breath. "Gosh, I don't know what I should do about what she just told me."

"It'd probably be a good idea to write it down as soon as you can so you don't forget any of it." He reached for her hand

and pulled her close to his side as they walked toward the French Quarter. "Who knows, there may be some truth in what she's told you. You may want to refer to it sometime later."

"Yeah, I guess you're right." She remained silent as their walk took them to the corner of Chartres and Saint Philip's Streets where they joined numerous couples walking hand in hand, enjoying the coolness of the evening that the earlier breeze had blown in.

Maurice released her hand long enough to purchase a long-stem red rose from a street vender. Handing it to her, he'd kissed her check then told her, "I won't hurt you or disappoint you. Just like Madame LaSay said. I never have and I never will."

He stood in front of her and held both her hands. "I like you a lot, Tish. I wonder if it'd be possible for us to become more than friends."

She hadn't expected this move so soon. She had to think quickly. Her response must be honest but cautious. "You're a great guy and I've really enjoyed our time together. But we're still getting to know each other. How can you be so sure you want more from me than friendship?" She was lightheaded; this gorgeous, brilliant man had just asked for more than friendship and she stood there and questioned him about it.

"How can I be sure?" He tilted his head and paused. "I can't really answer that. I just know that since I met you in Austin you've been on my mind a lot." He took a deep breath, exhaled, then bit his bottom, luscious lip before continuing. "When you called to say you were coming here for the weekend, I felt my heart literally jump."

He hesitated again, smiled, and looked directly into her eyes. "You're someone very special, Tish, like no other woman I've ever met. I just want a chance to know you better."

A solo sax player on the opposite corner began playing "Secret Garden." Maurice held her chin as he gently kissed her lips. "Will you let me be more than your friend?" He kissed her again. "If not now, in time?" He kissed her softly as she took deep breaths. "I can wait, if I must." He kissed her again, this time a long passionate, tongue-involved kiss. "I think you're worth it. Whatever it takes."

Oh, damn…he's smooth. She felt her knees wobble, so she wrapped her arms around him to avoid falling. He held her against his firm chest as they stood on the corner by a gas streetlight listening to the smooth sax continuing to play that sexy song.

Tish didn't discourage his moves, but instead allowed herself to relish the moment with him. Although in her mind she kept replaying a line she'd heard somewhere before, *"A player only loves you when he's playing,"* his attention flattered her. It was a tender, sweet moment—one she'd never forget.

When they left the French Quarter, he drove her to his house. They sat on his black leather living room sofa and talked as they listened to his CDs. When "Secret Garden" played, Maurice pushed the repeat button on his remote control.

"I believe that's our song." He leaned over and kissed her on the cheek. Then he stood, her hand in his, and pulled her to her feet. Silently, they danced through the whole song.

He looked at her, "Girl, I don't know what you've done to me, but I like it." Then he sat back on the sofa and gestured for her to sit next to him.

As soon as she sat down, Maurice leaned back and pulled her on top of his chest and wrapped his arms tenderly around her. They fell asleep listening to the same song as it repeated through the night.

Warm, humid air had met them when they left his house and drove back to Tami's early that Sunday morning. The breeze had completely died down and made the outdoors feel like a huge sauna.

"I hope you come back to New Orleans again, soon." He'd told her as they pulled into Tami's driveway.

"I'd like that, too." She fumbled with her purse strap wondering what she'd say to her girlfriend about being out all night. "I've had a wonderful time and I appreciate you showing me around. New Orleans is a great place with great people. I'm very glad I came."

"Do you mind if I call?" He turned off the ignition and reached for her hand.

"Not at all; I'd like that."

"Great. Then I will. But right now, I need to get you back to Ms. Tami before she gets upset." He kissed the palm of her hand. "What time does your flight leave?"

"At two. We're going out for brunch before she takes me to the airport." She took a deep breath to calm the chills that had popped out all the way up her arm after that kiss.

"Peanuts?" The cheerful flight attendant had returned interrupting Tish's thoughts.

"No thank you," she answered flatly. She'd been in such deep thought about her weekend that she'd missed the takeoff. She pushed her seat back to relax and get her nap on.

I wonder how Tom's weekend went.

Twenty-Seven

This partner through life
brings loving joy to my soul.
None other can compare.

Tom sat quietly looking at the tall pine trees that lined the Northern Virginia highway as Sable drove to the airport. He took a deep breath and exhaled slowly; his weekend was almost over.

"Hey, thanks for a great time." He gave her a big smile. "I really enjoyed the game and Luther was off the hook!"

"It's been my pleasure."

"You can plan one hell-of-a weekend, I tell ya'. The dinner was great, too." He looked down at the short navy blue skirt that showed off her shapely bare legs. "Girl you sho' know how to spoil a man."

"I guess…" She gave him a quick glance before exiting for the airport. When she stopped for a traffic light, she looked directly at him. "What about the sex? I thought it was great but you didn't mention it. What's up with that?"

Tom hoped that subject wouldn't come up but it had and he couldn't ignore it. The sex had been good, in fact it was better than good, but it was just that: good sex.

How do I tell her what she wants to hear without giving her any ideas about the future? He focused on the dashboard. "It was great Sable; you're good at everything you do."

He couldn't tell her that each time they'd had sex someone else had been on his mind. As hard as he'd tried, nothing they did together kept Tish from popping up in his thoughts. When he kissed Sable, he thought about his first kiss with Tish. Sable dimmed some of the excitement for him because she was much more aggressive than Tish. He sensed she wanted more than a weekend with fun, food, and sex; that made him uncomfortable. Yes, they had some good times together but he didn't feel any real connection to her, not the way he did with Tish.

Yes, great sex is important, but I'm not that eager to lose my whole mind over any woman.

He remembered an earlier conversation when she said that she'd dreamed of having a husband and lots of kids. She was just months away from her twenty-ninth birthday and wanted to start that family before she got too old. *I think she wants those kids with me.*

"Well, here we are," she said as she pulled up to the terminal.

"You're a lot of fun to be with, Sable. Thanks for inviting me to come to D.C. and reminding me how the Army lives on this side of the world. If you get back my way sometime maybe we can get together again."

She gave him a half smile. "I'd like that; hey, take care of yourself. Call me when you land." She leaned over for a kiss. "Let's not let this to be the last time you come this way now…," she added as he slid out of the passenger side.

"Oh, definitely not. You haven't seen the last of Thomas Manning," he replied. He closed the door, then walked into the terminal.

Once he was settled on the plane he looked around. *Great. Looks like I'll have this whole row to myself.* He took a deep breath, stretched out his arms, and closed his eyes. He planned to sleep all the way back to San Antonio. His thoughts drifted back to how his weekend had begun.

He remembered how appealing Sable looked when she met him in the baggage pickup area inside the airport. She'd dressed in a long sleeve, purple dress that did everything to show off that shapely body. Her bare, curvaceous brown legs were shining as if they'd been polished. The matching purple high heels drew attention to her sexy calf muscles. Her hair was pulled up and away from her face; when he reached to hug her, he couldn't resist kissing her long, elegant neck first before their lips met.

Her fragrance reminded him of old school musk and heightened his arousal. He knew that as soon as he had her alone he would have all of her.

"I'm taking you straight to my apartment," she whispered as he opened the car door for her. As she got behind the wheel, her already short dress pulled up a few more inches revealing very inviting thighs.

She gave him a quick tour of her place, decorated throughout in a Japanese theme. The tour ended in her green tea colored bedroom with the sounds of water trickling over rocks and Japanese strings playing softly in the background.

She made it clear she was hot and wanted sex right away. She unbuttoned his denim shirt, kissing his exposed neck and chest. She stepped out of her heels and sat on the bed while she worked on his pants. She'd moaned softly when the pants fell to the floor and revealed his tight, black underpants bulging where it counted.

"Baby, I'd say you're ready for me, aren't you?" She cooed and unbashfully snuggled her face gently along his swell.

An hour later, they'd collapsed on the bed, naked, sweaty, and exhausted. He'd fallen to sleep for what seemed to be at least a couple hours before he felt her nose softly rubbing on the back of his neck.

"Tom, you hungry?" she whispered in his ear.

He felt her warm body lying against his back as she wrapped her arm across him, her hand gently stroking his chest.

"I cooked for you."

The smell of Italian spices and garlic bread made him realize how hungry he was.

He moaned and stretched his body. "You cook?" He didn't think of Sable as the type of woman who'd go through the trouble to cook for him or anybody else.

"Of course I do," she answered, sounding offended. "I slaved over that hot stove all day to prepare lasagna and fresh bread. I did it just for you."

"Well, now. That's real special and I appreciate it." He grinned to show his admiration, still not convinced that she cooked.

After he showered, they sat in the den and while they ate, they watched Tyler Perry's movie, "I Can Do Bad All by Myself." He helped with the dinner dishes and noticed there were no prep bowls or pots to be washed. "So, when did you cook that fantastic meal?"

"Today, while you were on your way here, oh curious one." She grinned, crossing her folded arms in front of her. "You really don't believe I made that dinner, do you?"

"I didn't say that." He thought about Tish's fabulous cooking. He shook his head to pull away from that thought and took Sable into his arms; she smelled like "new musk" all over again. He found it more than appealing; it was also sensually exciting.

"Tell me," he said as he licked her neck, "just what do you have on under that silky, black kimono?"

"Nothing," she whispered. Her fingers inched up his robe exposing his firm, naked behind. As her hands caressed his bottom, she lightly kissed his chest.

"Girl, you better be careful, nah…what'cha doing here in the kitchen." His breathing became deeper as his body heated up. He lifted her and sat her on the counter. "Let me see."

He slowly untied the front of her kimono to find her nipples standing at attention and her chest heaving up and down, matching his own ragged breaths.

"Oh, Tom, see what you do to me," she whispered, as she spread her legs inviting him to inch closer.

That move did it; he peeled the kimono off her arms and away from her body so he could feel, smell, and explore every inch of her. Being with a woman who didn't mind doing the kitchen counter thing sent his arousal to new highs. He'd heard of people doing it this way, but had never experienced it. He felt her advance her bottom to the edge of the counter top so he could enter her.

Damn, she knows what she's doing!

When he thought his legs might give out, he lifted her into his arms and carried her to the den, her legs wrapped around him. He'd lowered their hot, naked bodies to a white furry rug without breaking the connection.

That night Tom dreamed of lying on a purple rug by a river; he'd been with Tish. They'd made remarkable love as the wind blew hot sand against their bare bodies, soaked in the sweat their passion had created. "Our love is forever," he'd heard Tish whisper.

"Tom," Sable spoke softly as she awakened him from his dream early Saturday morning. Somehow, he'd made it to the bed during the night.

"Yeah, what's up?" he mumbled, as he looked around to be sure he was in Sable's bedroom and not with Tish on the riverbank.

"Let's get up and go out for pancakes." She sat on the bed and stretched. "I'm hungry. How 'bout you?"

"Oh, yeah." He rolled over on his back and saw that she'd already dressed and styled her hair. "Wow, how long have you been up?"

"Just long enough to shower and dress." She rubbed his leg, still under the covers.

"Where do you want to eat?"

"IHOP has the best pancakes." She stood and walked to the window, and looked out. "It's going to be a great day to drive up to Landover, Maryland for the game. So, let's get going!"

"All right, all right. I'm moving." He rolled out of the bed and ran into the bathroom, closing the door behind him.

"It must be nice to work at the Pentagon and be able to go to a Redskins' game whenever you want," he said as she maneuvered through heavy traffic, creeping toward the stadium.

"Well, yes and no. It's a least a nice thought. But I don't do this often…too much traffic and way too many people to come to a game on any regular basis." She slammed on the brakes as a car pulled into her lane without warning. "B - I ----!" she yelled. "I have no patience for fools!"

"Hey, just be patient. We have tickets and our seats will be there when we arrive." He tried to sound calm although he felt his heartbeat speed up. It looked to him like every man, woman, and child who lived anywhere close to Washington, D.C., had piled into their cars and were trying to get to the game at the same time.

"We're only going 'cause my commander has season tickets right on the fifty-yard line and he couldn't make this game. He got TDY orders this week somewhere in Arizona. It was my turn to get his tickets. So you lucked out that you could come this weekend. Any other weekend and we'd be watching the game on TV."

"It's an honor to be sharing this gift from the boss." He reached for her leg and ran his hand up her thigh. Her black miniskirt was almost invisible when she sat in the driver's seat. "Thank you for inviting me. I'm lucky I could come."

"And come you did!" She smiled and glanced over at him. "And you'll come again when I get you home."

"Girl…you scare me." He blushed, then wiped his face with his hand. "But I like it."

During the drive back to her apartment after the game, Tom was happy he'd made the trip. He couldn't believe he'd just watched the Redskins play the Cowboys from the best seat in the house.

As traffic slowly inched away from the stadium, she said, "When we get in, we need to clean up quickly and drive over to Crystal City for the Luther concert."

He'd dozed off and dreamed of seeing Sable as a younger woman, maybe even a teenager, dressed in a flowing white linen dress. She'd joined him inside a large tent where he unpacked a cotton sack filled with clothes. In the dream, Sable said, "I am for you, Teti." She looked Egyptian with dark eyeliner and thick, black shoulder-length braided hair. Reluctant to send her away, although he didn't want her, he allowed her to stay with him. The following morning, her parents, a Pharaoh and Queen, blessed their marriage.

"Tom?" Sable's soft voice brought him out of the dream. "Tom? Are you alright?"

"Yeah, right—I'm okay." He sat up straight realizing they were back at her place.

"You were mumbling and moaning in your sleep. Were you having a bad dream?"

"I guess you can call it that." He unbuckled his seatbelt. "But, hey, it's just a dream," he replied, wiping a trail of sweat from his brow.

Sunday morning had started pretty much the same. Marathon sex and IHOP pancakes. While they ate breakfast, a man stopped at their table and spoke to Sable.

"Oh, hi, what's going on?"

"Not much. It's good seeing you, though." He looked at Tom. "Oh, I'm sorry, man. I didn't mean to disturb your breakfast. Just speaking that's all." He tipped his head at Sable. "Check ya' later."

"Bye," she replied flatly.

Tom realized that he hadn't met any of her friends and this guy had been the first person they'd run into that knew her. He wondered if she had intentionally kept him all to herself or if she didn't want anyone to see them together. Even though the man had spoken to her in a very friendly manner, Tom thought that her response seemed strange.

"So, who's that?"

"Oh, he's nobody, believe me." She sipped her coffee. "How's your omelet?"

"Perfect."

I'm glad I didn't tell her about Tish, he thought. *Although she's been on my mind, Sable never knew it or felt it. Isn't that great? Soon I'll be on the plane and back to my life in Texas.*

Tom didn't know that before he woke up that morning he'd rolled over in his sleep and whispered "Tish" as he reached for and held a completely awakened Sable in his arms.

"Pretzels?" The flight attendant awakened Tom soon after the plane took off. "No thanks. I'd like a Coke, please."

He stared out the window and remembered the last evening he'd had with Tish. He missed having her close to him. He wanted to touch her, and to sleep with her in his arms.

Twenty-Eight

You cannot deny
the urge to come back to me.
It is destiny.

Tired from his long flight back to San Antonio, Tom placed his suitcase on the bed and turned on the stereo. Mellow sounds of the old school, S.O.S. Band's "Tell Me if You Still Care," filled the room.

Even though it was late he was tempted to call Tish. The red light on his answering machine blinked brightly when he reached to pick up the receiver.

He pushed the play button and listened, hoping she'd called. *"Hey, Tom. I hope you got in safely. Don't forget to call me."* Sable's voice paused. *"Thanks for coming. The weekend was great. Bye."*

He picked up the phone to call Tish, then placed it back down.

What if she asks me about my weekend and what I did? He stood still in deep thought, staring at the floor. *Of course I don't have to tell her any more than what I want her to know. But is that really fair to her?*

Tom slid his hands into the pockets of his jeans and slowly paced the floor thinking more about his dilemma. *That is, if she wants to have more than a friendship with me. But what if she doesn't? What do I want from her? That's the real question.*

He opened his suitcase and unpacked, placing his dirty cloths in the hamper and toiletries in the bathroom. He'd wait to see if she'd call him first.

Three days passed and with no word from Tish, and Tom couldn't resist his urge to talk to her. He dialed her work number hoping she'd be able to talk and at most, have the evening free so he could see her.

"Tish, hi." He smiled when he heard her voice answer his call. "How've you been?"

"Hey there. Oh, I'm fine. How about you?"

He heard her sigh.

"How'd your weekend go?" She sat back in the chair behind her desk and turned toward the window. She looked out to the tall cypress trees that framed her view.

"Oh, good, but I'm glad to be back into the routine of things. How did you end up spending your weekend?" he asked, taking the focus off his weekend story.

"Dee talked me into doing something fun. I flew out to New Orleans as soon as the kids' dad picked them up on Friday and spent the weekend with some friends. I hadn't been there before and had a really good time."

"Great. So you like to travel."

"Actually, I do," she replied, standing to see the activity down below on the river. "I plan to eventually visit every state and vacation in as many countries as I can. I've driven through Louisiana but never stopped long enough to say I'd been there. So now I can say, I've been there. How about you?"

"Yeah, I love to travel, especially by car."

This conversation had progressed easier than he'd thought it would. "I like being able to stop along the way and enjoy the scenery." He sat further back in the chair and pushed away from his desk. "Usually we're in such a hurry to get where we're going and then return home, that driving long distances doesn't work out for me much."

"Yeah, I hear you."

He took a deep breath. "Tish, I'd like to see you. Are you free tonight?"

"I will be for a little while, that is if the kids' dad picks them up like he's supposed to. They have a church activity tonight." She sounded very matter-of-fact. "He has a Wednesday visitation but I never know until the last minute if he's going to come through or not. Either way, I'll be home and they'll be waiting for him just in case he comes for them. One thing I never want my children to say is that I kept them from seeing their father."

"What time does he normally pick them up?"

"Six o'clock. I should know by five if he's coming or not. If he isn't, then I'll take them to church and stay until it's over. Why, what's on your mind?" She sat back at her desk, with one leg under her.

"I'd like to see you, that's all."

"If I'm free, I'll give you a call. Either way, the children will be asleep by nine."

"You're a busy woman. I bet you like having some free time on Wednesdays when they do go with their dad."

"Yeah, I guess you could say I have a pretty full life if you call spending Wednesday evenings in front of the TV with a bowl of popcorn for dinner having a full life."

"Well, in that case," he hoped an invitation to come over had been implied somewhere in her response, "may I come over at nine and spend some quiet time with you before you go to bed?"

He really didn't want to spend another evening in the barracks alone watching TV. "I'll even share your popcorn if you don't mind."

"Yeah, I guess so."

"Great. I'll let you get back to work; see you at nine."

Twenty-Nine

My love has found me
Here with the answers he seeks
Steady, unchanged love.

Tish hung up the phone and released a weary sigh. "Wow," she whispered, relieved that she hadn't lost him to Sable over the weekend.

Whatever they did, it appears that it wasn't enough to keep him from asking to see me again. For now, that's got to be good enough.

At nine o'clock, the doorbell rang as she placed the last dinner plate into the dishwasher. Tish sauntered down the hallway to the front door and let Tom in. He silently entered the foyer, took her by the hand, and pulled her slowly into his arms. He held her gently against his body and whispered, "Hi."

She wrapped her arms around his neck with her eyes closed. "Hey," she whispered back, hoping his actions meant he still wanted to be there for her. She stepped closer to him and held him tighter, allowing her body to fill the spot against his chest. She put her face right onto his neck. They continued to stand in place saying nothing, just holding each other.

"There's something about you, Tish," he said, speaking softly in her ear. "I don't know what it is, but being with you is so…I'm very relaxed. You make me feel so welcome, so…oh, I just…I can't explain it." He paused, then looked at her. "I think about you often."

"How about this weekend?" She leaned back and looked at him directly in his eyes. "Did you think about me then?"

"Yes, I did." He smiled gently. "And as soon as I got back in town the first thing I wanted to do was to see you."

"So what took you until Wednesday to call me?"

"I guess I'm not sure how you feel about me." His eyes drifted from hers to her lips. "I don't want to impose myself on you if you'd rather not have me around."

"So do you feel like you're imposing yourself on me now?" she persisted, determined to get him to talk to her about his feelings.

"No, I don't." He looked deeply into her eyes. "But I didn't know how you were going to respond to me until I got the courage to call. Now, I'm very glad I did."

He tightened his hug and kissed her forehead. "Thanks for allowing me to come over tonight. I needed to know that I could still be a part of your life."

Tish thought for a moment about what her comeback should be.

"I guess that's a good opening to have a discussion about just what that means…since, you know, what kind of relationship we can agree to have at this point. Is it going to be just friends, more than friends with occasional intimacy that doesn't exclude outside lovers? Or best friends who can have a monogamous sexual relationship for as long as we both agree that we can meet each others' needs? Which do you want?"

He pulled out from the embrace and held her hands. "Can we go in the kitchen and sit down with a cup of coffee and talk about this? I think it's important."

Tish looked back at him in almost disbelief. She finally had a man who wanted to talk about it. There would be no more guessing. Before she went to bed that night she might actually have a defined relationship. "We can do that."

"Cool." He leaned down and gave her a warm, passionate kiss that sent shivers down her back.

While the coffee brewed, she served him a slice of her sweet potato pie. They sat at her dining room table quietly at first. She wondered why he didn't start the conversation. He looked as though he had a lot on his mind. He didn't say a word as he broke off small pieces of pie, eating each one slowly as he stared down at his plate.

"I guess I'm a little confused." She broke the silence and went straight to the point. "When you told me about Sable and that you were going to spend your weekend with her, well, I thought that meant you had something going on with her. I don't want to come in between you and another woman. Nor do I want to be the other woman—you know the one you go to when you can't be with her because she's not here."

"I can understand why you're confused." He put his fork down, sat back in his chair, and rubbed his hands across his thighs. "I started talking to Sable before I met you and had a couple dates set up. One thing led to another and we planned my trip to D.C. before you invited me over that Sunday morning. I hadn't expected that we'd take our relationship up a notch like that, at least not that quickly. Not that I'm complaining or anything…it was wonderful, trust me."

He smiled and picked his fork up again and tapped on the crust of his pie. "But I didn't think it would be right to cancel the trip. I really wanted to go see her because she is a nice person and I enjoy her company."

Tom waited as she poured the coffee. "Anyway, I'm not sure I'm ready for a committed relationship right now. I think it's too soon after my divorce. But I want you in my life. What we have to decide is whether we're going to be just friends or do we want more."

"I can see your point," she responded, sipped her coffee as she realized that they were having the conversation she needed. "Well, here is where I am." She took a deep breath, pushing herself to be open, honest, and willing to take the risk to let him know how she really felt. "It's probably too soon for me to be in a committed relationship, too."

She nodded and glanced up to meet his eyes. "But, I'm afraid that my attraction to you will make me want more than just your friendship. I've been living by this standard or code of conduct, or whatever you want to call it. I've always been a one-man woman. The thought of having to sleep around to get my groove on with men who don't want to be exclusive, literally makes me sick to the stomach."

Tish paused. She knew she had to continue. Explaining herself to this man she wanted to be very close to was the right thing to do. "Besides, there is so much out there, stuff that'll kill you or ruin your life if you're not careful. I want to live a long time…meanwhile I plan to make healthy decisions."

"Yeah, you're so right about that." He sat forward in the chair, placed his arms on the table, and leaned toward her. His gentle smile and the look he gave her encouraged her to continue.

"So without a committed or exclusive relationship, what do I do about my sexual needs? Stay celibate and keep going to the gym?" Tish sat back in her chair and looked away from him, hoping he'd say something. He didn't. He seemed to be waiting until she finished.

She looked into her back yard where two fireflies fluttered together as if in a flight dance by the porch light. She silently watched them for a few seconds. “So tell me, am I to be your friend and wait until some mythical Prince Charming comes along and asks me to be his only sex partner?”

“I don’t think you have to do that,” he replied. “Honestly, I don’t like the idea of having multiple sex partners, either. I was a faithful husband the entire time I was married, even when she didn’t roll my way.”

He sat back in his chair, rubbed his palms together, and also looked out the window. “But I’m not married anymore. I just want some time to experience what that feels like and not have to answer to someone about where I’ve been, who I’ve been with, and what I’ve been doing. It doesn’t even have to be about sex.”

“Okay, so why are you here and why are we having this conversation?” she asked with a confused look on her face.

“Tish…I just know that you came into my life for a reason and now I have feelings for you that I can’t define.” He leaned forward and looked into her eyes. “I dream about you. When I’m not with you I think about you a lot. I can’t wait to be with you, to feel your touch, to look into your eyes like I’m doing right now. I long to hold you. This is all new to me. You move me like no other woman.”

He paused, shifted in his chair, and leaned closer toward her. “I can’t even believe I’m sitting here telling you this.”

“Wow, me neither,” She smiled softly, feeling very warm and special. “You know, I’ve been dreaming about you, too.”

“Yeah? Whatever this is…the dreams and all…I want to take some time to see what it’s all about. If we’re meant to be friends, then I’ll be the best friend you’ve ever had. I’ll do whatever I can to not hurt you or cause you to distrust me in any way. I’ll be honest with you and want you to be honest with me—about anything and everything. Is that asking for way too much?”

“That’s what friends are for, right?” She smiled. “So here’s some more honesty. When you came over that Sunday morning and made love to me…wow, you have no idea how wonderful you made me feel. I really wanted you and you gave me exactly what I needed. It seemed as if you’d known me all along.”

“I’m telling you, girl. You are so easy to be with.” He kissed the back of her hand. “And you surprised me when you let me know that you wanted me to come over and make love to you…and I'm very honored to have obliged, too."

She felt her body warm up and her face flush. Placing her hand on top of his she pushed herself to continue to open up and risk telling him how she really felt.

"My friend, you should know that I want you to stay in my life and I want you to be my lovemaking partner." Tish took a deep breath, and continued. "But for it to be right and comfortable for me, I need an agreement to be exclusive lovers. If it comes a time when you can't to do that anymore, just tell me and I'll understand. I'm not looking for a husband but I do have needs just like you. I'm simply asking to let me be the one for you and for you to be the one for me. If we can be there for each other and it works, then great. If it doesn't, just say so and then no harm done. Let's enjoy each other for whatever time we have, okay?"

He folded his arms in front of him and sat back in the chair. "Can you understand that I don't need to feel like I have to answer to anyone? I don't want to act like I'm married when I'm not?"

"I don't have a choice about that do I?" she responded. "I'm not asking you to marry me. I'm not asking you to act like my husband."

How do I get him to understand? Is this too much to ask? She thought for a moment then took a deep breath and continued.

"I only want you to care enough about me that you're willing to have me as your only lover for as long as that is a good thing for each of us. If someone else comes along that you want to be with, just tell me. I've been celibate for months before and it didn't kill me." She rolled her eyes up and made a smirky face. "I know I can go back and I'll survive. So either way, now or later, I know I can do without sex. I just don't want to. Not now. Not since I've been with you. Is that asking for way too much?"

"Girl, you're something else, you know that?" Tom said with a big smile. "In all seriousness, though, that's really what I want. I just needed to hear you speak your mind and to see if we were thinking the same thing."

He reached for her hand and squeezed it. "I enjoy being with you and our lovemaking was very special for me too. I can't wait to have you that way again. You tell me when and where and I will be there. You can count on it."

"Thanks for opening up and telling me how you feel. As long as we're honest with each other, we should have no problems." She looked lovingly into his eyes. "You can trust me. I won't hurt you."

"Thanks, Tish. I need to know that. And I'll do my best to not hurt you. My goal is to keep you happy and wearing that infectious smile." Tom stood up and pulled her into his arms. "Come here, girl."

He passionately kissed her and held her tightly as if clinging to every minute they had together.

"Thanks for letting me come over tonight. I'm glad we had this talk. I'd love to stay longer, but it's a school night and we have to get up early in the morning to start our day. I'll call you tomorrow morning and maybe we can meet for lunch. Is that okay?"

"That's fine. I hope we can have some alone time soon."

"Let's talk about that tomorrow."

Thirty

Touch me in your way
bring me back to you again.
Hold me in your eyes.

"Girl, I can't believe it'll be Thanksgiving next week." Tish gathered the briefcase and purse from her desk as Dee waited so they could leave work together. "I'm so glad you guys are coming over and sharing the holiday with us. It'll be great having a big dinner again with family friends."

"Yeah, too bad Tom won't be there," Dee said. "You two have been almost inseparable the last few weeks. I guess whatever you needed to work out you talked through. You've been so happy, too. What a difference a good man makes, huh?"

"No joke. Let's get outta' here and join the ladies at Thursday Night Jazz at Sunset Station. I need a good margarita."

"I'm with that. Ride with me and I'll bring you back for your car later. I want to hear what's been going on with you and Tom. I hardly see you anymore and we haven't had much time to talk."

"Well, he calls every day, sometimes two or three times," Tish said as she walked toward Dee's car. "The past three weekends he flew out to El Paso to take Shaun to his soccer games. He flew back early enough on Sundays to spend a few hours with me while Cathy had the kids at a movie or out for pizza."

"So you only see him on Sundays?" Dee unlocked the car and they dropped their briefcases in the trunk.

"No. During the week he'll come over for dinner with us, and once-in-a-while he helps the children with their math homework. He even went with me to one of Melanie's band concerts and joined us at her ballet recital."

"So how is Miss Melanie handling having a man around who's not her daddy?" she asked as she backed the car out of the parking space. "I've heard little girls aren't real cool about having their daddy replaced. And Melanie is one that'll tell you exactly what's on her mind."

"Oh, we've had our moments…" Tish smiled softly. "But when she watched him walk in during the ballet recital, her mouth fell open when he sat on the front row by himself. When he was the first to give them a standing ovation, well, let's just say that he's won her over."

She opened her compact and reapplied cranberry red lipstick that matched her suit. "Especially since her father was nowhere to be seen. She called him the night before each event and left him a message to remind him about the concert and the recital. And the dumb ass didn't show." Tish took a deep breath and shook her head. "What are men thinking, Dee? Marcus tells the kids how much he loves them and misses them, but when it's time to show up for important things, he just can't come through."

"We already know that if it's not about Dr. Marcus Brown directly, he's not interested." Dee waited for the light to turn green and continued. "But we can't worry about the decisions he makes, can we? The seeds he plants now will be the harvest he reaps later. The children see what's happening and they don't forget. I know I never did."

"What do you mean?"

She looked for a parking space by the historic, pink stucco San Antonio train station that had recently been converted into a nightclub. "Let's just say that I know too well about having a father who put himself before his children."

Dee took a deep breath and stared off toward the Alamodome. "Mine worked at the county courthouse as a bailiff. He had an affair with a young attorney right out of law school. When she won her first major lawsuit, he left mom and moved in with that heifer expecting she'd take care of them. He even quit his job. The child support stopped coming in for my two brothers and me."

She took a deep breath, then continued. "His woman got thirty percent of a ten million-dollar settlement and he lived quite well with her after mom divorced his trifling tail. Five years later, the woman kicked him out and she married a judge. Guess he wasn't good enough for her."

"Did he stop seeing you guys, too?" Tish could hardly believe Dee's story. She seemed so together all the time. There had never been any indication that she'd had anything but a great childhood.

"Girl, we never saw or heard from that idiot until he'd been left on the street with nothing more than the clothes she let him walk out with. Five years is a long time for a child to know that her father is in the same city and never hear from him. Then he shows up one day and wants to be *my friend*."

"So what did you do?" Tish asked.

"By then I was seventeen and used to him being out of my life. So, being a lot like your daughter and knowing I had nothing to lose, I looked at him with the sweetest smile I could fake and told him, 'You can kiss my friendly ass and stay out of my life.' Now, let's go in this place, have a strong drink, and enjoy our girlfriends. No more talk about men!"

Just as Tish stepped out of the car, Dee's cell rang.

"It's Aaron. Hey, baby. What's up?...Okay, I understand. I'll see if Tish and Tom can go. Talk with you later...love you, too. Bye."

"Aaron and I were invited to attend the Van Courtlands' Debutante Ball Saturday night. Something's come up and he can't go," she said. "How about you and Tom going? The invitation is at a soror's table and I'm sure she won't mind."

"Sure, I'd *love* to go, but isn't it a formal affair? I don't have a gown." Tish had shopped around, but hadn't found anything she liked.

"No problem, we'll find something for you. If you weren't so tall, you could wear one of mine," Dee said as they walked toward the nightclub. "Don't we know someone your size you can borrow a dress from?"

"Yeah, probably. Hey, remember Dionne? She used to work in our computer operations office. She's my size and has a fabulous wardrobe. I'll call her and see if she will help a sista' out."

"I bet that'll work. Meantime, call Tom and see if he wants to go. I need to call Soror Stacie Thomas and let her know that we're not coming and if you guys will replace us or not so she can have time to find someone else if she has to."

"Hey thanks, Dee. I haven't been to a deb ball since I was presented ages ago. This should be fun."

When they got to the door of the club, Tish said, "Go on in. I'll try to reach Tom right now. I'll be there in a minute."

Tish took the cell phone out of her purse and dialed his number. "Hey, sweetie. How ya' doing?"

"Better now. Funny, I'm sitting here in my office thinking about you. What's up?"

"I'm out with the girls for a drink. Dee just asked me to call you and see if you'd like to attend a debutante ball on Saturday night." She sat on the iron bench under a sycamore tree. "It's formal. She and Aaron have an invitation but can't go."

"Sure. I'll be in town this whole weekend and I want to spend it with you, anyway. Going to the ball will give me a reason to pull out that tuxedo I had made while I was stationed in Korea. I haven't had a chance to ever wear it. Let's go. I'm already looking forward to it."

"Great, I'll call you later with the details." Tish was thrilled. *Tom liked dressing up and going out! What a difference.* She hadn't been with a man who owned his own tuxedo before. *Wow!*

"This is your free weekend isn't it?" he asked.

"It's supposed to be. But as you know, Marcus has become less reliable about picking up the children when it's his weekend. I think they must've told him that I'm seeing someone and he's trying to mess things up for me." She couldn't hide her annoyance. "But I can get Cathy to come over and keep them for me Saturday night, I'm sure. I'll call her and get that set up just in case."

"If he comes for them, I want you to myself the entire weekend. Will that work?"

"Hmm, Sergeant Manning, what do you have in mind?"

"Not to worry. Just know I'll have it all worked out. You with me?"

"With you? Yes, Tom. I'm with you." She smiled, wondering what plans he may have in store for them.

"Good. Now get with your girls and enjoy yourself. We'll talk more about this weekend later. Take care."

"Okay, will do. Thanks, Tom."

"Thanks for what?"

"Just thanks, that's all. Bye."

When she joined Dee inside, she had the dress plan all figured out. "Hey Tish, Dionne lives on the next block down from me. Ask her to meet you at my place tomorrow with a few of her gowns and we can pick out your dress."

The following day Tish arrived at Dee's when Dionne drove up in her white Mercedes 450SL blowing her horn. She always made a dramatic entrance; today was no exception. She stepped out of her car, wearing designer jeans, a cashmere sweater, and navy blue heels, her long, auburn hair pulled back into a ponytail.

Tish helped Dionne pull out several evening gowns from her car and carry them into the house. "Girl, you sure have some nice evening wear! Where do you go to need so many dresses?"

"I only wear them once, unless I go to something out of town, then I might wear one or two of them more than one time."

Dionne entered the house and went straight to the guest bedroom. She hung three designer gowns on the doorway and removed the plastic bag from the cleaners. "Clothes are so cheap here in San Antonio compared to what I'd pay for them back east. So I just help myself to the bargains and look real good every time I go out."

"Wow, those gowns are fabulous!" Dee cupped her mouth with her hand as she examined the dresses. "I can't wait to see the ones Tish has. Hurry up, girl, let's hang those up too!"

Tish handed Dee the three gowns she'd carried into the house and pulled the plastic bag off. She had two black, one white, one red, one purple, and one royal blue evening gown to pick from. "You know red's my color, so I'll start with that one! It's just to die for!"

Tish slid into the cherry red sequined gown that fit her body like a mermaid suit. The slit in the back of the skirt went about three inches up past the back of her knees. The top had slender shoulder straps trimmed with onyx gemstones that matched the small brooch pinned in the slight v-neckline, revealing a teasing amount of her cleavage.

"My new black shoes will go perfect with this dress." She turned around, looking at herself in the mirror. "I have a black bag, too and the perfect bra—"

"And I have long black satin gloves you can wear," Dee added. "I've even got long black jeweled earrings that will be smashing!"

"Gosh, I haven't even tried on the other gowns…" Tish kept looking in the mirror not believing how stunning the gown looked on her.

Dionne put a hand on her shoulder. “I really don’t think it’s necessary. This one’s you, my dear. You look like a million dollars. It fits you a whole lot better than it did me! So I think you should wear it Saturday night.”

“Come over early and we’ll help you get all gussied up for the party,” Dee said.

Later that night Tish walked into her kitchen with her portable phone dialing Dee’s number and singing, “It’s Friday Night and I Just Got Paid,” while Tom looked for a movie for them to watch.

“Dee. Hey, girl.” She sat at her breakfast table and straightened the place mats. “Cathy can’t sit for me tomorrow night. She’s been booked for weeks by another couple who’s going to the debutante ball too.”

“No problem. I can. Just bring my babies over here.”

Tish tossed a bag of popcorn into the microwave. “Thanks, Dee. You’ve been such an angel. Don’t know what I’d do without you.”

“Hey, I’m doing no more than you’d do for me, right? So Marcus isn’t coming for them again this weekend, huh? That man should be shot.”

“No one’s heard from him either. It’s been about ten days. Simon left him three messages last night and one right after school today asking him if he was coming for them. No reply.”

“So life went on, anyway, I’m sure.”

“Tom and I took them to McDonald’s for dinner, then to a movie. We just finished a game of Boggle and sent them up to bed.” She took a liter of Pepsi out of the refrigerator and filled two glasses.

“So what’re you up to now?”

“Tom’s looking for a movie to watch.” She filled a bowl with the fresh, hot popcorn. “He’s coming over in the morning and having breakfast with us then we’ll go to Simon’s soccer game together.”

“Sounds like he’s gotten all settled in with you guys. Routine and all…watch it, now.” Dee chuckled. “Is this what you want?”

“He’s a wonderful man, Dee. He’s fun to be around and the kids like him, too. And remember, you told me to enjoy him; that’s just what I’m doing.”

"All right then, I'll see you at my house tomorrow afternoon. Tell Tom to pick you up here for the ball. The kids can spend the night with us."

Thirty-One

Our fantasy night
Better than the fairy tales
Found in children's books.

Tish enjoyed having Tom around and sharing the routine of her day with Simon and Melanie. During her son's soccer games Tom acted just like the rest of the dads, yelling and jumping up and down as their team ran with the ball. When Simon scored his team's winning goal, Tom met him at the sidelines and gave him a big high-five.

As she drove to Dee's house to get ready for the debutante ball, Tish thought about how stupid Marcus had been, missing the highlights of his children's life. *He must think he's punishing me by not spending time with them or he'd be there.*

Little did Marcus know that another man, a wonderful man, had filled the gap he'd created and no one, not even the children, seemed to mind.

I bet my own father wouldn't have been absent from my life, that is, if he'd had a choice about it. She glanced at her rear-view mirror smiling at her beautiful children sitting in the backseat. *If only I'd had a chance to grow up knowing what it was like to have a daddy around.*

When they pulled up to Dee's, Tish handed the overnight bag to Melanie. "Baby, go ahead and ring the doorbell so Auntie Dee will know we're here. Take this in for me, too."

"Okay, Mom." Melanie smiled. "Come on Simon, let's go find Little Aaron and play in his back yard!" The children ran toward the house as Dee opened the door to let them in.

Dionne and Dee were waiting for Tish and ushered her into the guest bedroom. "Now girl, get into that sexy gown; we got to work on your hair before Tom gets here," Dionne said.

"Yes ma'am," she replied as she slipped into the dress.

"See, all that working out at the gym has paid off!" Dee teased. "With a body like that in a dress like this one…honey, you'll be lucky if you make it to the ball after Tom picks you up. Better be glad the kids'll be here tonight!"

"Oh, I'm really happy about that, Dee. Momma needs a break! But now, my hair needs to be put up, don't you think?" She lifted her hair off her shoulders and turned around to look in the mirror. "I don't know how to style it so that it's glam like this dress."

"No problem. That's my department," Dionne said, reaching for a brush. "Dee, hand me some bobby pins. You can do her makeup when I finish with the hair."

Just as Dee painted Russian Red lipstick on Tish's lips, the doorbell rang. "That must be Tom," she said. "Right on time. Okay, girl, you can stand up and look in the mirror now and see what we've done with you."

Tish blushed when she saw how beautiful they'd made her look. Tears welled up in her eyes as she thought how lucky she was to have such good friends. "I feel like Cinderella," she whispered, wiping a tear from her eye. "Thank you guys so much for doing this. Dee, you sure it's fine for Simon and Melanie to stay here with you tonight?"

"Girl*, please*. We'll see you tomorrow after church. You go on now and have a great time," she said with a big smile. "You look marr-ve-lous!" She left the room to open the door for Tom.

Dionne gave her an encouraging hug. "Tish, you'll be the belle of the ball. Enjoy yourself. You deserve to have a great evening."

Tish walked slowly down the hallway and into the living room. "Hi, Tom."

"Damn, girl, you look fantastic! Wow…come over here." He hugged her and kissed her cheek. "I'm glad you're with me. You ready to go?"

"Thanks, you look great yourself." She stood back to admire him in his tux. She smiled guessing that the women at the ball would be green with envy when they see her with this handsome man.

"You're a smashing couple. Now, get out of here and have a wonderful evening," Dee said as she walked them to the door. "Tell Soror Thomas thanks for the invitation and understanding that we couldn't make it tonight. I'm sure she'll be very happy to see you two there."

Tom parked the car at the La Villita parking garage in downtown San Antonio and looked over at Tish. "Baby, you are so beautiful tonight." He smiled and took her hand. "You're always beautiful, but tonight you're more than radiant." He kissed the back of her hand.

"Thanks…you're very handsome, yourself, Thomas Manning." She blushed. "I'd better keep a very close eye on you all night or some woman may try to steal you right from under my nose."

"Not to worry. I'm all yours."

As they walked into the ballroom, Tish was astonished at the transformation. Hanging white roses, lilies, and baby's breath formed an arch over the doorway. Two over-sized, stuffed swans faced the door. Candlelight glimmered from each of the hundred or so tables covered with white tablecloths. White linens covered the chairs and were tied with big bows in the back; tall clear glass vases overflowing with white gladiolas, carnations, roses, and baby's breath decorated each table.

Graceful, elegant, life-sized, stuffed swans were positioned throughout the ballroom. The lights were dimmed as soft chamber music played in the background greeting the arriving guests. ROTC high school students sharply dressed in dark blue uniforms met the guests and escorted them to their tables.

"This has got to be the prettiest, most elegant affair I've ever attended," she whispered as Stacie walked up to them. "Soror Thomas, this is my friend, Tom Manning. Thank you for the invitation."

"It's my pleasure to have you two join us." She hugged Tish. "Nice meeting you, Tom," Stacie said as she extended her hand to him.

"Nice meeting you, also." Tom took her hand and softly squeezed it. "You look very elegant."

She pointed to his fraternity lapel pin and smiled widely. "Oh, so you're an Omega? You get a hug, too!" She embraced him then introduced he and Tish to the other guests at her table.

At eight o'clock sharp, the guests took their seats. The lights were slowly turned down and a spotlight illuminated the white flower-covered archway on the stage. The fifteen-member band, all members of the San Antonio Symphony, played the theme song from *Swan Lake.* The master of ceremony introduced the debutantes individually as each stepped into the spotlight. They wore full-skirted, white formal gowns, with long white gloves, and pearl necklaces.

The young ladies were met by their fathers who were dressed in black, full-tailed tuxedoes, white pleated shirts, and black bow ties. The father-daughter dance followed the presentation of the last deb. After they waltzed with their dates, the dance floor opened for the guests as the band played "The Harlem Shuffle."

"Let's go!" Tom took her hand and off they went, joining the other dancers who'd been waiting patiently.

As the evening progressed, Tish introduced Tom to her sorority sisters and people she'd met through her job. "You're so charming, " she whispered in his ear as they slow danced to "I've Got So Much To Give," a Barry White oldie.

"I'm very proud to be with you," he whispered, then leaned back, looked into her eyes, and smiled. She returned his smile and held his look until he pulled his eyes away and hugged her tight.

Tish relished the calming glow; she felt like she was dancing on a cloud in the arms of the man she should spend the rest of her life with.

"Thank you, God," she whispered and closed her eyes. *This is what it must have been like for Cinderella when she held her Prince Charming.*

Thirty-Two

With you I am safe.
My heartbeat is yours and my
spirit finds its home.

Tom grew closer to Tish as they attended a round of holiday parties between Thanksgiving and Christmas. By not pressuring him to do more than what came naturally, she left him feeling comfortable and safe with her. Knowing that she wasn't interested in rushing into marriage also helped.

They went to the Pal's Debutante Ball and the seasonal Greek letter organizations' parties together. The Delta's Poinsettia Ball had been the most elegant formal affair he'd ever been invited to. Tish wore a long white gown that had a sequin and pearl bodice and a full, almost sheer skirt. She'd curled her hair and it loosely flowed down her back. He almost lost his breath as she stepped into her living room because she looked so resplendent.

Then at the Omega's Christmas Gala, she wore the most impeccable purple and gold strapless evening gown with a full ballroom skirt that more than flattered her figure. The vision of her dressed up like an elegant queen remained in his mind. Not only was she always the prettiest, but also the most charming woman in the house.

Tom appreciated their sincere friendship and believed it had deepened. She'd agreed with his plans to spend Thanksgiving Day and Christmas in El Paso with his son; she'd completely supported him, even knowing that Katrina would be there. *How lucky can a man be?*

Tish had called while he was gone and told him how she, Simon, and Melanie had assembled six stick reindeer covered with clear lights, and positioned them in a cluster of cedar trees in the front yard. They'd decorated a ten-foot tall Christmas tree with lights and handmade ornaments that she and the children had made over the years. She told him that they managed to get it to stand straight in the foyer, just inside the front door.

During Tom's holidays in El Paso with Shaun, he and his ex-wife had actually gotten along. Katrina had considerably matured since their divorce. Dropping twenty pounds and dating a younger man probably added to her more positive attitude.

Two days after Christmas, Fort Sam Houston was quiet as Tom's taxi parked in front of his barracks. The only downside of his trip was the long wait at the El Paso Airport caused by severe storms that had blown in from the north and slowed down the crowd of holiday travelers.

He slowly lifted his black suitcase from the trunk. "Happy holidays," he told the driver, tipping him generously through the driver's window.

"Thanks, man," the young, Mexican-American answered before he drove off.

It was a warm sixty degrees; typical Christmas season, central Texas style. He chuckled quietly, recalling how he'd played touch football that morning with Shaun sporting shorts and a T-shirt in the seventy-five degrees of bright sunshine.

I see why they call Texas "God's country."

Tom dropped his luggage near the door and flipped the switch to the stereo, filling the room with the best sounds of the '70s. The first item on his agenda was to call Tish and ask her out for breakfast in the morning. As he looked at the phone he saw the message light blinking.

"Tom...hi. This's Sable. Why haven't you returned my phone calls? I really need to talk to you. It's important. Please call me back."

It'd been at least six weeks since Tom had spoken to her. She'd called his office the week before and left him two messages but he'd ignored them. The last time they'd talked, she complained about how sick she'd gotten with the flu, the cold weather, and how much she missed living in Texas.

I wonder what's so important now?

He flicked the erase button, then fell across his bed, and looked up at the ceiling.

I sure hope she's not thinking about coming here for New Year's Eve. I don't have time for that...not now.

He rolled over on his side and pulled a pillow into his arms. While Donny Hathaway's romantic ballad, "A Song for You," helped him relax, his thoughts went directly to Tish and how content he'd become with their relationship.

He looked forward to greeting the New Year with his arm around her at the upcoming Zulu's annual party. He cheerfully anticipated spending more time with her—his best friend and favorite companion.

The caller ID indicated that Sable had called his number twice in past three days. He sat up on the side of the bed and called to find out what she found so pressing. "Hey there. How ya' doing?" Tom asked with a congenial tone when she answered his call.

"Oh, I've been better. How about you?" she said indifferently. "I haven't heard from you in weeks. You must be pretty busy."

"I guess you can say that." He wanted to get to the point of her call. "Your message said you had something important to talk about. What's going on?"

"I'm driving right now…hold on a sec while I pull into this parking lot." She parked the car at a McDonald's. "Okay, now I can talk." She took another deep breath before continuing. "Well, I called to tell you that I'm pregnant." Her voice became faint. "And I believe it's your child."

"What?" The tenseness he felt resonated in his voice.

"I'm in my third month. My period kept coming and so I didn't know until now." She spoke faster as if terrified he'd hang up before she finished explaining. "When the morning sickness started I thought I had the flu. The doc says it happens like this sometimes. How was I supposed to know? I've never been pregnant before."

"Pregnant…? How can it be my child?" he asked, surprised and bewildered. "I used condoms, and you said you were on the pill. *Were you*?"

"Yes, I was on the pill," Sable snapped. "But remember that time you got me in the kitchen and didn't stop long enough to cover up? Just didn't get to it, 'cause we were so busy. I think that's when it must've happened." He heard her sign before she continued. "Besides, the pill doesn't guarantee a woman will never get pregnant. I'm carrying the proof."

"You *believe* it's my child…so that means that you aren't sure. You've had other sex partners then, right?" he asked, hoping for a way out.

"I did, but not at the same time I was sleeping with you. The timing makes me pretty sure you're the father."

"So what're you gonna' do?" Tom stood and paced the floor not knowing what else to ask at this point.

"I'm talking to you about it, that's what I'm doing," the timbre of her voice, now very resolute. "If you aren't interested because you don't care about me or think that it's not yours, then do what whatever you want to do about it! I'm having this baby because I want children."

A tear formed in her eye as she continued to explain her position. "I didn't plan this; it just happened. I'm telling you because I believe you should know. Whether you noticed or not, I really like you and want you to be a part of my life." The tear fell as another formed right behind it. "I had hoped you felt the same way."

"Sable, you're a really nice person and I do like you. But I've moved on and have a wonderful woman in my life right here in San Antonio." He continued to pace the floor. "Remember the last time we talked, I told you I wasn't interested in a long-distance relationship. But now this. I hadn't expected *this* phone call."

"Believe it 'cause it's true. As soon as the baby's born, I plan to leave the Army and move back to Houston to be near my family. Whenever it's convenient for you, you can arrange for a paternity test so you'll be satisfied that's it's your child. I know you'll want to do that."

"You're right about that—"

"The child *is yours* and if you want to have a parental relationship, I won't stop that." Her voice softened as she continued. "I'm sorry this happened. But, I don't expect anything from you that'll make you uncomfortable. I care much too much about you for that. I hope one day we can deal with it together, that's all."

"Oh, damn, Sable. You're no sorrier about this than I am. This was definitely not in the plan, trust me." He sat down, bowed his head, and glared at the floor. "Let me think about all this and I'll call you back later this evening."

"Sure. Think about it and talk to Tish about it too," she sneered before she hung up.

He threw the phone on the bed and jumped to his feet. "*Damn! Damn! Damn*!!" he shouted, as he waved his fists above his head and kicked the air.

How could this happen? Not again...not to me...not now. What did I do to deserve this? What if it's true and it's my baby? How can I tell Tish? How's she going to feel about this...about me?

He sat down again and then fell back, stretching out across the bed thinking about their conversation.

"Talk to Tish about it, too," Sable had just said that. How did she know her name?

Tom rolled over and located the phone on his bed. He picked it up to call Tish. As he stared at it, he realized he had to tell her about his conversation with Sable. He would ask her what she thought he should do. He trusted her as his best friend; they'd talked about everything. He'd opened up to her before and she seemed to accept him with all his shortcomings. But this problem presented something completely different and he had no idea how she'd take this news.

The phone rang. He checked the caller ID and saw Tish's number.

"Hey, Sweetie. How ya' doing?" His voice sounded a little shaky.

"Oh, I'm fine," she replied. "I'm putting some dishes away and you crossed my mind. Thought I'd give you a call and see if you were back. What's up?"

He sat up on the bed resting his back against the headboard. "Honestly…what's up ain't too good." He paused and scratched his head. "I just got off the phone with Sable."

With a softer tone, he continued. "I need to talk to you. Can you come over? I don't feel like driving right now."

"I had a feeling something was wrong," she replied as she folded the kitchen towel and hung it on the oven door to dry. "The children will be at their dad's until tomorrow. I'm on my way."

"Thanks, baby."

"No problem, see you in a few."

Thirty-Three

The truth should be told.
Share the pain, let it be ours
We are one, today.

Tish grabbed a wool jacket from the hall closet. A cold front was expected to blow into the area. By morning; San Antonio would feel like winter.

She was dressed for a day of comfort at home: black sweatpants, a red, short-sleeve Fiesta T-shirt and tennis shoes. Not taking the time to change her clothes, brush her hair, or put on makeup, she found her purse on the kitchen counter, took her keys from the side pocket, and headed for the garage.

As she drove toward the Army post, she tried to relax. She remembered how Tom had come to her rescue when she'd called him all stressed out after her day in court with Marcus acting the fool over his child support issue two days before Thanksgiving.

Thinking about it still made her blood boil. He actually showed up in court expecting a judge to cut his child support amount in half just because her salary had doubled since their divorce. Marcus had wasted her perfectly good vacation day and eight hundred dollars in attorney fees *and* would have ruined her holiday had the court not ruled in her favor. Tom had come over bearing a bouquet of red roses as soon as she called him. He took her to the Blue Moon Café for a quiet dinner and conversation. *That's what I call a good man.*

She ejected the Kenny G CD from her player and replaced it with Patti LaBelle, wanting something more uplifting. As she got closer to the post, she realized that she'd never been to Tom's place before and had no idea how to find it. She retrieved her cell phone from her purse and dialed his number.

"Hello…" Sadness resonated through his voice.

"Hey, baby. I'm less than five minutes away. I need directions once I get on post."

Tom sat up on the side of his bed and took a deep breath. "Come through the main gate at Harry Wurzbach Road then turn left at the first light. At the very next street, turn left again. Go down about a mile and you'll see the barracks on the right. I'm in the first building, room twenty-four."

"Thanks. See you in a few."

Tish turned up the volume on her CD player and the persuasive words of Patti's "Love is Just a Whisper Away," filled her car as she sang along, hoping deep inside that whatever had Tom in such a gloomy mood could be talked out and resolved.

She pulled up at the barracks and took a deep breath to calm herself as she stepped out of the car and walked up to his door.

"Hi, there," she said trying to sound cheerful. She walked in and gave him a hug.

"I'm glad you're here. I need to talk to you." He embraced her, holding her tightly against his chest.

"Sure, baby." She closed her eyes and caressed his back waiting for his next move.

He released his embrace and took her hand, leading her to a card table with two chairs in one corner of his room. She quickly scanned the simply furnished, modest room. It also had a double bed covered with a quilt and a nightstand with a black metal lamp and an alarm clock. A small screen television and a stereo component set filled one corner of the room.

No wonder he's never invited me over before.

She'd never seen him look so defeated. "Tom, what is it?" she asked as they sat close together at the table.

"It's about Sable. There was a message for me to call her when I got back." He shifted in the chair and leaned forward placing his elbows on the table, with his arms stretched out and hands cupped together.

"She said she's pregnant and that it's my baby.'" He looked down at the table, and paused as he bit his bottom lip. "She's about three months along. The timing makes it fit when I went out there to visit her." He glanced up and met her eyes. "I swear, Tish, she told me she was on the pill and I believed her. I used condoms ex-except once." He looked back at the table with a dull stare. "Maybe she lied."

"Oh, baby. I'm so sorry. She's just telling you this?" she asked, looking directly at him and stroking his arms. "What's up with that?"

He kept his eyes fixed on the table as he responded, "She said she didn't know until now." He took a deep breath and continued. "Well, she's been calling and leaving messages but I didn't return them. I decided to call her back tonight because of the way she sounded. I had no idea *this* would be what Sable wanted to tell me."

He turned and looked into her eyes. "Damn, Tish, how could this happen to me again? I don't want her; I want you in my life. What should I do?"

"I think you should make sure it's your baby before you do anything." The sharp stab she felt in her heart listening to him and seeing him this way almost made her cry.

Stay objective, sound understanding—just like I would with any of my other friends in this kind of situation.

"I say be supportive and concerned about her but make no promises until you know for sure you have an obligation. Then, if the test proves you're the father, you should do the right thing and be in the child's life." She tried to stay composed and not show how hurt she felt inside. "If you should do more than that, well…that'll come with decisions that you have to make."

"Are you upset with me?"

"Upset with you? No, Tom," she replied quietly. "I'm very sorry this happened, but everything happens for a reason. Every child is a blessing and never a mistake, including this one. If it's yours, I know you'll be a good father for it just like you are with Shaun." She took a deep breath, looked away from his eyes, and fixed her glance toward the door.

"If you decide you want to be with Sable and raise the child together, just let me know. I'll move out of the way. Don't worry about that. But take your time and don't panic. This isn't the worst thing that could ever happen."

She paused and looked into his eyes that were now teary. "More than anything else, know that I'm your friend, and I'll always be here for you. All you ever have to do is call me. You've been there for me through my stuff and I'll never forget that. You mean a lot to me, Tom."

"Girl, I'm so glad you're in my life." He stood and helped her to her feet. He pulled her into his arms and gave her a tight hug. Then he sat on the bed and pulled her onto his lap.

She wrapped her arms around his neck and silently stroked his face with her fingertips and looked into his dark, inviting eyes.

"I feel so good when I'm with you…" He kissed her forehead delicately. "It's like all the tension just left my body. Thank you."

"Welcome."

He closed his eyes as she placed moist kisses on his forehead, eyes, cheeks, and ears. Tom slowly caressed the back of her neck and she responded to his exhilarating touch with a passionate kiss. His hands roamed up her T-shirt, unfastened her bra and softly rubbed and squeezed her breasts.

Fully aroused, she pulled away from the kiss to catch her breath. She stared into his face and realized just how deep her feelings for him had become.

"I love you, Tom," she whispered.

"What?"

"Oh, my, did I just say that?" She quickly rephrased the statement that had just escaped from her mouth. "I care about you deeply, Tom. Make love to me. Please. That's what I wanted to say."

"But, I thought I heard you say—"

"Make love to me, please," she quickly finished his sentence. "I want you to make hot, passionate love to me right here, right now. More than I've ever wanted you before." She kissed his lips lightly. "I need you, baby."

"Nuff said, my queen," he whispered, then kissed her neck and reached for the hem of her T-shirt and lifted it over her head. He leaned over and placed her shirt over the back of the chair and then removed her bra, dropping it on top of the shirt. With her still sitting on his lap, he planted tender kisses on her neck, shoulders, and chest, working his way to her nipples, now firm and warm.

"Girl, I've missed you." His soft, sexy voice drifted to silence as he filled his mouth with her breast and sucked, breathing hard.

The piercing darts of sensation that awakened every nerve ending in her body became more intense as he again caressed the back of her neck with one hand and rubbed her upper thigh with the other. Tish threw her head back, moaning in pleasure, as she slowly raised her arms. He lifted her from his lap and carefully laid her on the bed, removed her shoes, and pulled off her pants.

As Robert Flack's sensual voice enchanted the room with "The First Time Ever I Saw Your Face," he stood by the bed gazing at her body while he removed his clothes.

She watched him as he uncovered his firm chocolate body, arousing her more than the first time she'd seen him naked. He reached for her sides and gently pulled on her panties, gradually sliding them down her hips, legs and then over her feet, dropping them to the floor.

"Baby, I need you," she whispered, barely able to speak.

"I'm here for you, sweetie," he whispered back. "I'm going to take care of you."

He opened the drawer of his nightstand and retrieved a condom.

She closed her eyes. *I could make love to this man all night... he just doesn't know...*

The next thing she felt were Tom's hands gently wrapped around her ankles, slowly moving them apart, then toward her body, causing her knees to bend up. She looked down and saw his head move between her thighs. One gentle kiss with his tongue, and the last words he spoke for what seemed to be half the night were, "Baby, you're so wet."

For the first time in her entire life, Tish learned what having fireworks go off from inside her body felt like. Tom's indulgence with the most sensitive area of her body created remarkable spasms along her thighs and lower torso as her whole body burned with desire and sighed with gratitude at the same time. Free to express whatever came out of her mouth, and with no shame or hesitation, she heard herself utter sounds and phrases that would have otherwise caused her pure embarrassment.

"Oh, shit!" she exclaimed, as a round of tremors seized her body. "Right there, *right there!...*don't stop…right there…o*h Shit!"*

Tom followed her reactions and kept touching each newly discovered spot bringing her heightened climax after climax until she yelled out something indistinct and hot tears fell down her face. "Hold me, Tom, please hold me," she whispered as she continued to tremble.

He moved from his position and lay beside her. Major Harris' familiar "Love Won't Let Me Wait" enhanced the moment as Tom held her in his arms, caressing her hair and face.

"Baby," she whimpered, "I want you in me, please, come in me…"

"Okay, sweetie. I just want to make sure you're all right." His voice soft and compassionate. "I'm not done yet…I've got so much to give you, Tish."

Still holding her in his arms, he slowly rolled her over onto her back. Looking lustfully down at her, he slipped the condom on in one quick fluid motion. He grinned at her and said, "If you're ready for Big Daddy, then open those legs wide and let me in."

She blushed at his mannish suggestion. "Big Daddy, come on home," she whispered, still breathing deeply from the pinnacle of excitement she'd already experienced.

Thirty-Four

Delighted to please
Joy in surreal ecstasy
Enchanted in bliss.

Tom had made love with Tish several times over the past few months. He'd enjoyed each and every intimate moment they'd shared. But this time he felt their lovemaking had reached a whole new level. As he gradually entered her, the silken warmth of her saturated welcome, enveloped him as if he'd slipped into a custom designed glove. Eyes closed, he moved in and out of her gingerly at first, savoring each second of the sexual high stirring up his whole body.

Her last words, *"come on home"* resounded softly in his mind. He moaned, as fragmented scenes of him making love to her flashed into his thoughts. In each snippet she'd looked like a different person, in different times, but the feeling remained constant.

Only Tish has ever made me feel this way.

Then an overwhelming sensation, more spiritual than physical, came over him. His head began to spin as his body felt as though it'd literally melted into hers. They became one being, sharing one heartbeat. Unable to open his eyes, he grabbed her hand to make sure she was still there.

"Oh, baby…," she whimpered, as the trembling of her body entered his and he experienced firsthand, the zenith of her emotional waves.

"Oh damn," he replied. "Girl, whatcha' doin' to me?" He gasped for air.

"It's okay," she whispered into his ear. "I got you."

He felt her hold him tighter.

Kenny G's tranquil sax played the sensual "Falling in the Moonlight" and the magic of the moment continued. Even though he embraced her firmly in his arms, he felt drawn from her. He closed his eyes and exhaled, not resisting the illusion.

Suddenly his body completely relaxed, and he experienced something he could never have imagined. His life energy left his body and hovered above them. Before he could speak he felt Tish's energy meet his and they danced on air together, resembling glowing fireflies without solid form. They moved in and out—their souls co-mingled in joyous reunion. This highly sensual experience, the most phenomenal interlude he'd ever encountered, had him almost speechless.

"Tom, do you feel what I'm feeling?" Tish whispered, not opening her eyes.

"I hope so." He felt a tear form in his eye, in awe of this experience they were sharing. "Why do I feel like I've left my body yet I'm still here?" His whispered response acknowledged the spiritual rendezvous as it unfolded.

"I have no idea." Her breaths were slow and deep. "This is the most unusual thing that's ever happened to me. It's beautiful..." She released a soft moan. "Let's be still and let it happen."

"Yes, let's enjoy this..."

Within moments, it ended. Tom rolled over on his side and held her in his arms, her back against his chest.

As they silently relaxed, a strange feeling came over him. The snippets of thoughts he had earlier included this experience in his distant past. He and Tish had made love on a purple blanket, beside a large river and again in a cotton field, in the hot summer sun. His thoughts suggested that this had not been the first time they'd shared an out of body experience together.

What the hell's going on here?

Thirty-Five

Know me now that our
spirits have danced, once again.
Like times, times before.

"Dee, we need to talk," Tish said as she hurried into her friend's office the next morning, still knocking on the half-closed door.

"Good morning, girl," she responded, as she looked up from stacks of files and papers spread across her desk. "What's got you so excited this morning?"

"I'm sorry. Good morning." Seeing the amount of work Dee had piled on her desk, Tish decided the talk could wait. "Let's have lunch. Meet you in the deli downstairs at eleven thirty?"

"No problem; what's up?" She pulled the braids from her face and pinned them back with a barrette. "Is everything all right? The children okay?"

"The children are fine. It's something else. Something happened and you're the only person I can talk to about this...but, not now. I see you're real busy…it can wait, I guess." Tish turned to walk out of Dee's office. "Lunch?"

"See you at eleven thirty."

Tish entered her office, closed the door, and flopped in the chair behind her desk. She moved clients' folders from one stack to another, peering in every other one searching for something interesting enough to get her mind off Tom and all that had happened the night before. Nothing caught or kept her attention. Questions she had no answers to persisted in her thoughts.

What if Sable's pregnant and it's Tom's baby? What if he goes to her? What if they get married? What happens then?

She sauntered over to the small, cherry wood, marble top table where her personal coffeepot had been neatly arranged in the center of a silver tray with a set of matching maroon and white mugs. Her administrative assistant, Michelle, had made a fresh pot. She poured a cup, then wandered back toward her desk.

Instead of sitting down, she stood behind her desk, leaned against the windowpane, and enjoyed the sunshine beaming into her office.

What do I do with these feelings for Tom that have grown deeper than I want to admit? She sipped her coffee, looking down at the city below her window, not really focusing on anything in particular. W*hat was that experience all about when we made love last night? Is that normal? Does that happen to other people?*

Tish couldn't wait until eleven thirty. She had to talk to Dee; she marched right back to her office, coffee mug in hand, and closed the door.

"Girl, I can't work." She didn't allow Dee to say anything. "Something happened last night and I need help understanding it."

"Okay, Tish." She dropped the paper she'd been reading. "What happened?"

"Tom and I made love last night. It was great—well it always is." She paused and sipped her coffee. "But something happened that I've never experienced before."

She sat forward and looked at Dee with a puzzled expression. "Have you ever made love and felt like you've left your body? That's the best way I can describe it. It's like I floated up and then danced with him in the air just above the bed."

"Yeah? Did he feel it too?"

"I think so…we didn't talk about it much." She sat back in the chair and glanced up at the ceiling searching for the right words to describe her experience. "It was wild. Kinda' scary now that I think about it, but actually I've never felt anything more exhilarating. Has that ever happened to you?"

"I wish I could say, I know what you mean, but I can't. At least not from personal experience." She sat forward in her chair, her elbows planted on her desk as she leaned toward Tish. "When my Jamaican grandmother gave me her version of the birds and the bees, she said if I'm truly blessed, one day I'd find my soul mate. I'd know him because when we'd make love, I would experience what she called "the spirit dance."

"*The spirit dance*?" Tish was astonished and she sat closer to the desk, eager to hear more.

"Yeah, that's what she called it. She described the spirit dance much the same way you just did. Grandma told me that at nineteen years old, a man named George came into her life and they fell deeply in love. He went off to fight in some war, but never came back. She said their spirit dance happened the night before he left the island. She made love to a number of different men during her life, she said, but none of them could take her to that special place that George did."

Dee sat back in her chair, looking at Tish with an unwavering stance. "Grandma believed that she and George were soul mates and were destined to meet and share that very special moment together."

"So, you're saying that your grandmother would tell me that Tom's my soul mate?" Tish asked with a perplexed look. "That's why this happened to us?"

"I think she might if she were still alive to talk about it. She also told me that even though he was the first man she'd ever made love with the feeling had been very familiar—like she'd experienced the spirit dance before and with him. Did you feel like that?"

"Yes! Oh damn!" Tish couldn't believe what Dee had just said. "I also felt this huge relief inside because I'd found someone I'd been looking for, for a long, long time. I didn't want the dance to stop."

"Well, congratulations, my sister. You've found someone who's very precious in your life." She stood and walked over to her friend, motioning her to stand up. "Give me a hug."

"Girl, you're serious, aren't you?" Tish stood and received the hug, still questioning the whole spirit dance theory.

"I am now." She sat in the chair beside Tish and leaned toward her. "Of course it hasn't happened for me yet, so I thought of it as just one of those juicy stories grandma made up."

She smiled widely and continued. "But you've made a believer out of me! See you didn't even know about it and it happened to you! And it doesn't sound like one of those things you can fake, either."

"How about you and Aaron? It hasn't happened?"

"No, and we've been at it for eleven years. I used to pray for the spirit dance, but it eludes me. Maybe Aaron isn't my soul mate, who knows?" Her voice drifted off as she added, "I love him to death, anyway."

"I know you do, girl." Tish's smile quickly faded. "There's something else." She paused and gazed down at her hands resting in her lap. "Remember Sable, the woman Tom went to see the weekend you talked me into going to New Orleans?"

Dee nodded.

"She may be having Tom's baby." She took a deep breath. "He called me last night and I went over to his place where we talked about it. I told him not to panic. I'd be there for him."

"Damn it!" Dee scoffed. "I knew that heffa' meant nothing but trouble." She went back to her chair behind the desk and picked up an ink pen. Tapping the pen on her notepad, she glanced cautiously toward her friend. "But Tish, you said you guys made love last night. After hearing his news, how do you do that?"

The pain that crushed her heart last night returned as tears filled her eyes. "Dee, there's more." She paused and took a slow breath. "Just before we made love, I told him that I loved him. I was thinking it and…girl, it just slipped right out of my mouth! It scared me as much as it scared him, I think."

"Well, that's because you've never have been able to do the poker face thing. Your expressions show all your feelings and when you know something that strong, you just say it. We need to work on that some more but in the meantime, have you fallen in love?"

"It appears so." She walked over to the window and stood with her back to Dee as tears fell down her cheeks. "But what am I going to do now? I can't tell him." Her voice began to tremble. "I really need to just back up some and let him decide what he needs to do about Sable. That's really the right thing to do, don't you agree?"

"I can't answer that for you." Her tone transformed into that counselor voice Tish had become accustomed to hearing. "You two shared the spirit dance. That means a whole lot more than Sable's having Tom's baby—if she is. Think about that before you make any decisions."

"I will." She wiped the tears from her face and turned to Dee. She sat on the edge of her chair and forced a smile before speaking again. "But one more thing before I go to work. How come no one ever told me about the spirit dance?"

"My grandmother said there are many lessons we've forgotten to remember." She walked over to Tish and placed her hand on her shoulder. "Because many of our African ancestors were born and raised in the Americas, they were taught ways of thinking that are not our own. Her people who lived on the islands were able to hold tight to ancient beliefs and customs and passed them on through generations."

She sat in the chair beside Tish and looked directly into her eyes. "What you've experienced is one of those ancient covenants of eternal love, my dear. It's very powerful and it's very real. You simply can't walk away from it."

"Oh, don't get me wrong, I don't plan to walk away from Tom." She sat back and crossed her legs. "I want him in my life, even if he ends up with Sable. I know that sounds strange, but it's true."

"And if he marries that woman, how do you handle these feelings you have for him, Tish? How do you have him in your life knowing this about him?"

"I'm not sure, but apart from our great sex and *spirits dancing*, I want him to always be my friend, at least that."

She looked down at her lap, pausing to think. "Because of the type of man he is, it wouldn't surprise me if he marries Sable. I have to prepare for that very possible outcome. And if I have to go through it with him, as his friend and confidant, I will. He means that much to me." She sighed and looked at Dee.

"Girl, I hear what you're saying but I don't see how it's going to be easy."

"I've learned that the right thing is hardly ever the easy thing to do." Tish leaned over with her elbows on her lap. "As a child I never knew my father because of decisions my mother made before I was born. I grew up feeling like I'd ruined her life."

She paused, drew in a breath, and exhaled slowly. "When I was in college I learned why she'd treated me with such indifference my whole life. I vowed I'd never be a part of anything that would damage a child the way I was."

"Oh, Tish…I'm so sorry." Dee leaned toward her friend and stroked her arm. "You've never said anything. What happened?"

"That's a long, sad story for another time." Tish brushed the hair from her face. "Right now I need to work through this situation with Tom. I want what's right for him and the baby, especially if it's his. That's all."

She looked at Dee with a forced smile. "This isn't about me or our spirits dancing. It isn't even about me falling in love with him. This is about a new little life that's about to come into the world who deserves a mother and a father. I don't plan to get in the way of that."

Dee crossed her legs and folded her arms across her chest. "This is going to be interesting."

Thirty-Six

With joy celebrate -
new years bring us back to this.
Our unending love.

Tom wondered how many people he knew in the dimly lit, crowded ballroom with loud, soulful music vibrating from a New Orleans brass band marking another New Year's Eve. Hundreds of multicolored balloons and laser beams darted past at least one thousand spirited, masked guests.

Couples packed the dance floor while others gathered around tables loaded with food. Wait staff dressed in black pants and crisp, gold shirts accented with purple, green, and red bow ties, served up plate after plate of enchiladas, black-eyed peas, fried chicken, smoked sausage, potato salad, red beans and rice, cornbread, and bread pudding.

"*Man,* the Zulus sho' know how to throw a party." Tom ordered his second Bud Light and a margarita at one of five cash bars stationed along the walls of the ballroom.

Aaron, wearing a bulldog party mask, brown turtleneck and slacks stood behind him in the line. "I've always heard about this party, but it's always been sold out. This year we lucked out, man; it's almost impossible to get four tickets from one of the Zulu members."

"I hear you, bruh and I can see why." Tom paid for his drinks, pushed up the sleeves of his purple, body-fitting, silk shirt that matched his slightly baggy wool blend slacks. He grabbed the Mardi Gras styled half mask covered with brilliant peacock feathers Tish had convinced him to wear because it matched hers. While he waited for Aaron to get his drinks, he repositioned his mask to cover his face. "I just don't get this *mask required* bit. Don't they know black folks don't do costumes?"

"Well, at least the costume part was optional. Hey, it's not so bad," Aaron said as he paid for his drink and turned to Tom. "But it's kinda' weird, too, 'cause you can't see who's under them masks. Like that woman standing at that table over there. The one with the Cleopatra mask and that long, white dress. I don't know, but I feel like she's been following us around. At least every time I look up, it seems like she's right there and watching us."

"Oh really? I hadn't noticed."

"Yeah?" Aaron began to walk away from the bar. "Maybe it's just me."

He picked up his drinks and followed Aaron back to their table. He made a mental note to be on the look out for Cleo, just in case Aaron was right.

As soon as they'd finished eating, the band took a break and the DJ played "The Electric Slide."

"Come on, da'lin…this one's for us! Just in time to start working all that food down!" Tom took Tish's hand and led her to the dance floor; other couples and individuals quickly joined the line dance.

Two minutes into the song, he made the next turn in the routine and out of nowhere, Cleo appeared dancing beside Tish, but she looked at him.

Then the group made the next turn. "Ooo, uuuh!" Tish yelled as she hit the floor. Everyone around her bumped into each other as the domino effect of one person stopping abruptly messed up the group's motion and they tried not to step on her.

"You okay?" Tom asked as he helped her to her feet. "What happened?" He placed his arm around her waist and slowly walked her back to the table.

"That *woman*! The one dressed like Cleopatra just *stopped*! When I turned around I bumped into her, tripped, and fell."

Tish pulled her hair back from her face and twisted it to keep it from falling forward. "She didn't even apologize."

Dee joined them at the table and removed her red velvet mask lined with white pearls. "I saw her throw her hands up in the air like it'd been your fault, then she walked off the dance floor in a huff. She went over there toward the food line."

"Well, I'd say she has a problem." Tish took a deep breath to regain her composure.

"Forget her. Are you all right?" Tom asked. "Can I get you anything?"

Tish sat at their table and took a sip of her margarita. "Yes. One more of these should do it."

"Be right back." As he headed for the bar he looked for Cleo but didn't see her anywhere.

An hour of the band playing jazz, then Earth, Wind and Fire favorites, they selected the best tunes of Barry White to bring in the New Year.

"Come here, girl." Tom reached for Tish's hand, leading her to the dance floor as the tall, thin, dark-skinned, baritone brother took the mic and in his best Barry-voice, serenaded the women with, "I've Found Someone."

They danced silently to the beautiful song. He felt flushed with satisfaction and desire. *If only she knew how much I adore her.*

"Five! Four! Three! Two! *Happy New Year*! Everyone shouted in unison as confetti and more balloons fell from the ceiling, noisemakers went off and the jubilant party-goers reached for their loved ones with hugs and passionate kisses.

He held her in his arms and looked lovingly into her eyes. "You know, you're the best thing that's ever happened to me." He kissed her nose.

"Oh yeah?" She blushed. "I can say the same thing about you. Yep, that's a fact!"

"Tish, no matter what this year brings, please promise that you'll allow me to be in your life." He kissed her forehead and took a deep breath, thinking about how everything could change if he was the father of Sable's baby. "I need you…I need to know that you'll always be my friend…no matter what."

"Well, Sergeant Manning, I'll always be right here for you." She smiled at him and then softly kissed his cheek "And I'll be your friend, no matter what."

His response was a fervent kiss that lasted until the band quit playing "Auld Lang Syne."

As he escorted Tish back to the table to get their complimentary champagne, he felt his cell phone vibrate. After assisting her with the chair, he pulled out his phone and checked the message that had been left at midnight.

"You didn't call me back...Oh, Happy New Year. Sable."

Thirty-Seven

Simple things in life-
Friendship, trust and thankfulness
Bind us together

"Aaron, brah...I just don't know." Tom kicked a rock in the parking lot of the HEB grocery store. He and Aaron had asked Dee to make her special potato salad and smothered chops for Sunday dinner and she'd sent them to the store with a list. "This thing with Sable…she's bugging, man."

"I hear you…but what cha' gon' do?" He handed the list to Tom and reached for a grocery cart. "Is it your baby?"

"Don't know." He hung his head and wished he could just turn back time and relive that defining moment that could've caused this whole mess. He followed Aaron into the store.

"When you gon' find out, man?"

"I don't know...not for sure anyway. She's already acting like I'm the daddy. Asked me to pay for her maternity uniforms. I sent her money last week, now she wants me to come to D.C. and go with her to pick out furniture, then to a baby shower and shit. Man, I don't want to do that stuff..."

"Well, you better than me. She wouldn't get a dime until I knew it was *my* baby." He looked at his friend and raised his eyebrows. "She's a tech sergeant just like you, right?"

"Yeah."

"So she makes the same money you do, but she ain't paying nobody child support like you do, right?"

"Nah, man, but you know how this thing goes, bruh..."

"Yeah, I do, but I'm just saying..." Aaron reached for the list. "So what we need to get?"

Tom read the aisle signage. "Turn right here and let's get some cold beer. I need a couple when we get back to the house."

"Right." They headed toward the cold case and Aaron reached for chips and dip. "We can catch a game while Dee cooks." He pulled two six-packs from the case and placed them in the cart. "So how you and Tish doin'?"

"I haven't seen her since the Martin Luther King Day March. She, the kids and I went together. I hooked up with the frat and they marched with her sorority sisters." Tom grabbed bags of corn nuts and pretzels from the snacks isle. “Man, there were so many people there I didn’t see them again until it was time to go and had to call her cell to locate them.”

“You know it’s the largest march in the country; big as the parade they have in Atlanta, they say.” Aaron tossed a bag of fried pork skins in the cart. “Who’d ever thought that San Antonio of all places would have such a big turnout?” He added some chocolate chip cookies and a pound cake to the cart as they passed the bakery.

“Aaron, we need pork chops, potatoes, onions and flour..,” he pointed to the meat department. “Let’s get the chops now.”

“So, the march was three weeks ago; you haven’t seen her since then?”

“I missed Simon’s birthday party the following Saturday, because I got called in to work that weekend.” He hung his head. “That wasn’t even my fault, man. Since then, when I’ve called and asked if I could come over, Tish is always busy doing something. I think she’s pulling away.”

“She’s probably shielding up. Dee asked her to bring the kids by today for dinner with us. She said she had plans to take them to the zoo.” He picked out a family pack of assorted chops and placed them in the cart. “So you might be right; she may be pulling away from all of us.” He placed a rack of baby back ribs on top of the chops. “Valentine’s Day is this Friday; so whatever you do, don’t mess that up. They take that day serious, you know.”

“I won’t even be here.” Tom felt defeated. “I got orders to report to the Pentagon on Wednesday and I’ll be there for a week. Can you believe that mess?”

“The *Pentagon? D.C.?* Ah, man, you kidding, right?” Aaron stopped shopping and looked at his friend and shook his head. “Does Sable know?”

“No, and I’m not telling her either until the last couple days I’m out there. Don’t want to spend my whole time with her.”

“But doesn’t *she work* at the Pentagon?”

“Yeah, but it’s a big-ass building, man. Probably never see her.”

“Shoot, with your luck lately, I wouldn’t count on it.” Aaron walked to the produce department and grabbed a bag of potatoes. “Have you told Tish about your TDY to D.C.? You know you got to explain why you won't be coming by on Valentine's Day."

"No, I'll call her tonight and tell her."

"Better do more than that. I think if I was you, I'd start sending flowers tomorrow. I'd have 'em coming every day of the week, too." He threw a sly smile at Tom. "Grab a bag of them apples and let's get out of here."

Thirty-Eight

The heart returns home
Comfort, love and nurture met-
Guidance sought, revealed.

Tom drove out of the rental car parking lot in Crystal City, Virginia and followed the traffic signs to Interstate 95 south. It was a perfect Saturday morning for February, east-coast style. The bright sunshine created a contrast to the brisk, thirty-two degrees and dusting of snow cover on the ground.

He and his planning team had completed developing phase one of a presentation they were scheduled to make at the Pentagon on Thursday the following week. Once they'd agreed to take the weekend off and start the last two phases of the project on Monday, he planned his surprise visit with his mother in Hampton, Virginia.

He turned on the radio, set the cruise control, and eased back into the driver's seat of the dark blue Ford Focus. The DJ introduced the next song, "for all the lovers out there."

As Tom listened to "Nothing Has Ever Felt Like This-" romantically performed by Rachelle Ferrell and Will Downing, he thought of Tish. He remembered her cool reaction to his phone call on Sunday evening when he'd told her that the Army was sending him to D.C for a week.

"Oh, really?" she'd asked. Her silence that followed left him feeling her thoughts might be directed toward Sable. Instead of saying what he'd expected, she deflected the subject by telling him about her children's report cards.

"Yeah, and I plan to drive down to see my mother over the weekend if time allows it..." he'd added to ensure her that this trip wasn't about Sable. So far, it hadn't been about her either. She didn't know he was in town.

Before he flew out of San Antonio on Wednesday, he'd picked up a Valentine's Day card and a dozen arranged long-stem, red roses and taken them by Tish's office. Tom smiled when he recalled her reaction when he entered her office with his gift. "These are for you..." he'd said, planting a tender kiss on her shocked lips.

"Oh, my. I didn't expect..." her response faded out and with a wide smile she ended with, "thank you, Tom." She accepted the roses and placed them on her desk. "They're so beautiful." With a curious look she added, "But I thought you were going to D.C. today."

"On my way to the airport right now. I couldn't leave without letting you know that your Valentine had remembered." He hugged her and kissed her cheek. "I gotta run. I'll call you…".

Tish had taken his hand and squeezed it. Her last words to him were spoken with a half-smile. "Happy Valentine's Day, Tom. Have a safe trip."

Tom pressed the dial button on the radio until he found a smooth jazz station. Two and a half hours later, he stopped at a florist in Hampton for a dozen roses and a card for his mother. He went straight to her red brick, split-level house. With his face hiding behind the flowers, he rang the doorbell.

"Who is it?" she asked behind the closed, locked door.

"Special delivery," he answered.

She carefully opened the door and peeked out. "Oh, dear..." she whispered.

Tom lowered the flowers so she could see his face and relax at having an unexpected visitor at the door.

"Hi, Mama! Happy Valentine's Day!"

"You rascal!" Her face glowed as she unlocked the storm door and let him in. "Why didn't you tell me you were coming?"

"Now that would've spoiled the surprise and I'd have missed seeing that priceless look on your face, too." He hugged and kissed her and placed the flowers on the dining room table. "What'cha got to eat?" He walked straight to the refrigerator.

"Not much since I didn't know you were coming." She stopped to smell her roses then joined him in the kitchen. "I can scramble eggs, make some grits, and toast a bagel for you. Will that do?"

"Sure will…that sounds good." He sat at the kitchen table and rested his arm on the back of the chair beside him and stared out the window.

"Baby, you okay?"

"I've been better." He took a deep breath. "Look, I need your advice on something…and before you let me have it about this, please hear me out."

"Yes, son. I'm listening."

"Well, see, there's this woman; her name is Sable." He looked at her and hesitated.

"Oh, that woman you told me about—the one in your dreams?"

"Ah…no, not that one; that's Tish." Tom shook his head. He knew this wasn't going to be easy. "It's like this. I went out to D.C. to see Sable last fall and…now she's pregnant and we think it's my baby."

He heard her gasp as she stopped beating the eggs. He waited to see if she would say anything. When she didn't he continued. "I'm working at the Pentagon this week and I plan to see her before I go back to Texas."

"So how do you feel about this woman—Sable?"

"I like her. She's single, beautiful, never been married, in the Army, and a lot of fun." He walked to the cabinet and got a coffee cup.

"And she doesn't have any children, right?" She added salt and pepper to the eggs and stirred slowly.

"No, not until this one's born." He lowered his head anticipating her next statement.

"So you like her. Is that all it takes these days to have a baby with someone, son?"

Tom knew she was trying to be kind. "No ma'am, it should take a whole lot more. This wasn't a planned event, trust me." He poured his coffee and returned to the table.

"If that's my grandbaby she's carrying, you'd better do the right thing. Accident or not, I don't want no child from this family clueless about all of his or her roots. Besides, I want to know my grandchild." She dropped the frying pan on the stove with attitude and snapped the on setting.

He stirred the sugar and cream in his drink. "I'm a bit concerned that if I don't bring Sable into my life in San Antonio, my chances of seeing the baby will be slim to none."

"So what advice do you want from me?"

"Mama, I need to know if I should marry Sable or not…that is if I'm the father. I care for her, I do. I mean I really care for her—"

"I think you know what I'm going to say about that, Tom." She drew in a deep breath. "That baby didn't decide on its own to come into this world. No, you made that decision sometime last fall when y'all were getting it on. Now, you're about to become a father and mother and y'all need to be together to raise this child because you share the responsibility from beginning to end." She paused.

"If you think you can live with Sable and y'all can make each other happy, then why not marry her? It's what's best for the baby. But make sure it's yours before you do anything. Don't let that woman trap you into a marriage that wouldn't have happened if you hadn't been careless."

"For sure. The baby's due in June."

"What about Tish? Did you stop seeing her?" his mother asked sharply as she dropped the sliced bagel in the toaster and pushed the lever down with snap of her wrist.

"Well no, not entirely. We still talk. She knows all about the baby." He wanted to tell his mother about how understanding and supportive Tish had been since the moment she knew about Sable being pregnant. Her calmness had amazed him. He wondered what she'd do if and when she learned that he had actually thought about marrying Sable.

"Honey, I can't tell you what to do. You a grown man and you've been down this road before. I want to advise you to follow your heart, but in this case I don't think that's what you need to hear. You'll figure it out on your own and you'll do the right thing, I know you will."

Thirty-Nine

I will find myself
When I again lose myself
Welcome my return to you.

Tom spent the night at his mother's house and went with her to morning church service. After they enjoyed a fresh seafood brunch at Phillip's Seafood Restaurant, he took her home.

"I got it," he said as he kissed her cheek and opened the car door. "I listened to the whole message this morning."

"Well, good Tom...God is good all the time. He brought you here 'cause He knew you needed that Word today." She hugged her son and stepped back from the car. "You drive safe now. Thanks for the flowers and surprise visit. I've enjoyed having you here."

As he drove back to Crystal City he listened to the DJ's featured gospel songs by Yolanda Adams. He set the cruise control and relaxed as the theme of the minister's sermon replayed in his mind.

"Any man can be a father," Reverend Washington announced. "But a *godly father* is also a daddy." The preacher paused and looked into the congregation then continued with, "So the question this morning—is what kinda' father are the men of Zion deciding to be?"

His mother had turned toward him and cut her eyes as if she'd caught him chewing gum in church as he did occasionally as a child. Then she sat a little straighter in the pew and placed her hands on her lap. As she listened to the message she nodded in agreement and said "Amen," each time the pastor made a salient point.

It was time to call Sable. He knew it would be wrong to be right there in D.C. and not at least try to see her before he returned to Texas. He picked up his cell phone and dialed her number.

"Hello," she answered.

"Hey girl, how you doing?"

"What's up, Tom? Oh, I'm having a better day. I'm over the morning sickness now, just getting used to my body getting bigger by the day." She sighed and sat at her kitchen table. "So where are you?"

"Funny you should ask. Actually I'm heading in your direction. I just spent some time with my mother in Hampton this weekend." He turned the radio off. "I'm working at the Pentagon next week. Go back to Fort Sam on Thursday evening."

"So where're you staying?"

"The Marriott in Crystal City."

"Umph, you could stay with me, you know?" She crossed her legs and fanned her face with the newspaper. "You don't have to stay at a hotel, Tom. You're always welcome to my place."

"Thank you ma'am, I do appreciate that. But the soldiers I'm working with are staying there too, so it's convenient when we need to stay up late and work on this project."

"I see...so are you going to come by before you leave?"

"How about when I get in town, I pick you up and take you to dinner?" He had no reason not to spend time with her...she was, after all probably carrying his child. "I should be there about six-thirty. Will that work?"

"Sure. I'll see you then."

Tom stopped by his room long enough to shower and change into dark slacks and a royal blue sweater. Refreshed and hungry, he parked his car at Sable's apartment exactly at the appointed time.

She opened the door as he walked up the sidewalk and watched him with an inviting smile, her face radiant. He noticed her pink sweater flared at the hem and covered down to her hips. The black, big-leg pants were accented with black low heels topped with pink bows. With her hair pulled back in a ponytail and hardly any makeup, she looked much younger than he'd remembered.

"Hey, Sable," he said and reached for her. "You are so beautiful..." He hugged her, then stepped back to survey her body. "Okay, so where's this baby? You don't look pregnant—is there anything in there?" He teased, lifting her sweater.

"Trust me, there's a baby in there." She smiled and placed her hand on top of his. "Come in and rest."

"I'm starved...let's go have dinner and I'll come in when we get back."

"Sounds good. Let me grab my coat. Where do you want to eat?"

"No matter, as long as it's seafood. I'm loving the fresh fish out here."

"Then it's The Flagship tonight. My favorite!" She smiled like a little girl and kissed his cheek. "It's so good seeing you, Tom. I'm glad you called."

After dinner, he followed her into her apartment with plans to catch the last quarter of the Spurs – Magic basketball game. Instead, she changed into that same kimono that got him into trouble the last time he visited her and once again, she had her way with him.

Three hours later, without knowing whether his team had won the game or not, he drove to his hotel. When he arrived, he drug to his tired body to his room and fell to sleep with a big, satisfied smile on his face.

Forty

A time to pretend
Celebration with dear friends
Enchanted moment.

Tish drove through historical Saint Paul Square just east of downtown San Antonio. Dee had invited her to her book club's annual 1970s theme party.

"You need to start getting out, my sister," Dee told her two weeks before as she dropped the invitation on her desk and walked out of her office.

Tish hadn't been too much interested in going anywhere lately. But this time she'd decided to take her friend up on this invitation – even though it meant she'd show up alone. The last time she'd spoken to Tom he said he needed to be out of town over the weekend and would miss the party.

As she entered the parking lot of the Delta House, she saw several couples walking briskly toward the two-story, white Victorian building, bracing against the strong gusts of the mid-March evening wind. She thought she'd arrived early, the invitation said six to nine o'clock. It was five forty-five and already the parking lot was just about full.

Strange, my people don't arrive before a party is supposed to start, not in these numbers anyway...There must be something else going on.

She flipped open the visor-mirror and adjusted her Afro wig and clipped on the large, oval shaped, peace sign earrings; then slid her feet into the platform shoes she'd removed so she could drive more safely. After she buttoned her paisley-print neru jacket she picked up the bag that had five decks of playing cards Dee had asked her to bring for bid whisk, she opened the car door to face the cold, bitter wind.

As Tish ran toward the house, careful not to trip over her bell-bottom jeans and those stilt-like shoes, it sounded as though the party was already in full swing. Stevie Wonder's "Isn't She Lovely" blasted through the doorway.

She entered the foyer and saw Aaron sporting a lime-green suit with a long polyester jacket and wide lapels, a yellow ruffled shirt and a matching yellow wide-brim hat. Dee stood beside him with a Tina Turner outfit, complete with wig, black leather mini skirt and high heels; and Tom, a dashing version of Bob Marley, with dreds, dashiki and beads.

Standing in front of the staircase with wide grins, they held a long, white sign with a bright red message, "HAPPY BIRTHDAY TISH!" A crowd of cheering people dressed in various interpretations of the late hippie era emerged from the back room while others came down the stairs holding red and white balloons.

Tish felt overwhelmed with surprise. "Oh, my God! You guys are just too much!"

The DJ switched the music to Stevie's "Happy Birthday" song and the guests joined in. As tears fell down her face, she gave Dee a big hug.

"No one's *ever* given me a surprise party before. When you said your book club was having this party tonight, I didn't have a clue. Thank you so much!"

"You're welcome. But thank Tom; this was his idea..." Dee glanced at him and winked. "I just facilitated the logistics and here we are."

Tish hugged Aaron. "Thanks, Super Fly. This is great...and you look wonderful."

"Yeah? I think I missed my calling." He tipped his hat and gave her a big kiss on the cheek. "Happy birthday."

She turned to Tom who had his arms extended toward her. She stepped into his embrace. "Thank you so much," she whispered and hugged him tight. "I thought you weren't going to be here this weekend. What happened?"

"I've missed too many important things with you lately and I wasn't about to miss celebrating your birthday, too." He squeezed her against his chest and kissed her forehead. "This evening's for you, Tish." He released his embrace as her friends and colleagues took their turns greeting her with hugs and well wishes.

Card tables and chairs were set up in the rooms downstairs for bid whisk and dominos while upstairs the DJ was stationed with a variety of 1970s music ready for the dancing to commence. Tish handed the bag of cards to Dionne, who'd found a big-hair wig and looked just like Diana Ross in her red sequined gown.

"Thanks for giving me an excuse to wear this dress again," she whispered as she hugged Tish. "Happy birthday, girl."

Couples teamed up with other couples and the games began. Beer and wine flowed and soul food was served from the kitchen.

"Hey, foxy mama..."

Tish glanced down the hallway and saw Tom looking at her holding two plates of food. He nodded then gestured for her to join him.

She followed him into a small room beside the kitchen that had a table set up with drinks, napkins and utensils for two. He deposited the plates on the table then pulled the chair out for her.

"This is nice..." she whispered as she sat, looking at her generous plate of food.

He closed the door and joined her at the table. "I want to make sure you eat in peace and that I have some quiet time with you before the night ends. I won't keep you from your guests too long."

"No, really, this is very nice." She felt flattered and very special. As long as the door stayed closed, she could pretend that they had entered their very own fantasy world - away from everything and everyone.

Forty-One

Hold on to your dreams-
Believe love lives on, because
Love trumps everything

"Girl, I can't believe you're not going to hang with us at 'The Taste of New Orleans' this weekend," Dee chided Tish after they placed their orders at Hoover's Cooking Cafe. The packed dining room had several groups hosting business luncheons.

Their voices were nearly drowned out by the piped-in jazz sounds of Kyle Turner. "Now that you're living in San Antonio, you have to plan to always be in town the third weekend in April and go to 'The Taste.' It's what we do here…and it's the best event of the year."

"I've heard so much about it, I'm sorry that I'll miss it." Tish squeezed lemon into her tea and stirred it. "The live jazz, the Creole and Cajun food, yes, I've been schooled on it. The southern cooking in here is sending enough luscious aromas from the kitchen right now to make me want to stay and eat my way through 'The Taste.' But this trip to New Orleans will give me the opportunity to work with the best marketing people around." She added a packet of sugar to her tea. "They've had the 'New Orleans Jazz Festival' account for years. Our team plans to learn everything we can from them to improve our promotion of 'Fiesta San Antonio' events on a national level."

"Too bad your flight doesn't get you back in time so you could at least come by on Sunday night." She folded her arms and tilted her head. "But Tish, you weren't on that team when we had our staff meeting last week. How'd you get on it and why?"

"Well, honestly, I didn't want to be here this weekend, so I pulled a favor." She slouched in her chair and took a deep breath. "Tom's leaving on Friday for D.C. Sable's been having complications with her pregnancy and is scheduled for an amniocentesis to check the baby's health. He's also going to have the paternity test done this time."

"This time? What do you mean? He's been to see her before?"

"Yeah," her response, slow and soft. "He's been to D.C. a couple times already this year."

"Why didn't you tell me?" Dee uncrossed her arms and picked up her napkin, snapped it and then laid it across her lap.

"Well…I didn't think it was that important at the time…" She grabbed the breadbasket and picked out a jalapeño cornbread muffin. "We haven't been spending as much time together as we used to. He seems caught up with the possibility that he might be the baby's daddy." She spread butter on her bread and sighed. "I guess we'll know for sure in a few more days."

"So, are you going to see Maurice when you're in New Orleans?"

"It's possible. I've e-mailed him to let him know that I'll be in town." She lifted her eyes and focused on Dee's face. "I guess I need to prepare to move on, just in case Sable wins, huh?"

"That woman won't win, my sister. Don't you let go and move on to nobody else unless and until you have to." She sat forward and placed her hand on Tish's wrist. "Girl, Tom loves you. I've seen it in his eyes."

"Maybe, but his attention is not on me, it's with her." Tish lowered her head and took a deep breath. "I haven't seen him since my birthday party. We've talked a couple times on the phone."

"What's going on, Sis?"

"Tom's concerned about Sable and her baby. He needs to take care of that for now, that's all." She lifted her head and smiled at her friend. "Meanwhile, life goes on, doesn't it?"

"Yes, Tish, indeed it does." She smiled back. "Let's enjoy lunch, now. No more talk about that situation for now."

Forty-Two

Time away, alone
Changes nothing, life goes on -
Seed planted survives.

Dee drove in heavy traffic through the downtown streets meandering toward the highway heading home from work for the day. "Hey, Tish, are you going to the May Day activities at the Delta House this Saturday?"

Tish stood on the balcony of her hotel room in the French Quarter and sipped cranberry juice with a straw, as a soft breeze blew through her hair. "No, I'll miss it. I'm still in New Orleans."

"New Orleans?" Dee responded. "You've been there two weeks? I thought you came back last Friday."

"No, last week was for work and I decided to take another one for me," she replied. She watched a couple at the corner across the street kissing under a tree. "I'll be back on Sunday when Marcus brings the children home. He's kept them for me - can you believe that?"

"No, ma'am...I can't."

"Well he did, and I've enjoyed my impromptu vacation."

"So what have you been up too?" Dee followed up. "Did you see Maurice?"

"We had dinner a couple times last week. This week he's been in Atlanta at an American Psychological Association conference. So I've been just hanging out mostly by myself and writing some." She didn't want to share all the truth with her friend. She'd spent most of her time in bed, feeling depressed. "So how was 'The Taste'?"

"It was the bomb! I'm sorry you missed it. But hey, there's always next year."

"No doubt..."

"So have you heard from Tom?"

"Well, yeah..." Tish had anticipated that question. "He went to see Sable like he said he was going to do."

"And?"

"We've talked a couple times since then." She sat in the white wicker chair and looked down at a group of people who walked the narrow street below her.

"Did she have that test done?"

"Yes, and they're having a healthy baby girl..." A tear formed in her eye. "The baby's his, Dee."

"Oh hell!" She exited the highway and parked her car in a Chevron gas station. "How'd he tell you?"

"Our first conversation had to do with how his trip went and how Sable was doing. She's been experiencing early labor symptoms and it's made her so uncomfortable that she's missed a lot of work lately. The doctor finally put her on house rest."

"So was your whole conversation all about Sable?"

"No, mostly though."

She paused and took a deep breath. Then she added what hurt more. "Dee, I told him that I'd missed our time together and had started going back to the gym again...you know, to work off my sexual energy like I did before. He didn't say anything, so I asked him if his distance from me was an indication that I just needed to continue going to the gym because he was taking care of his needs elsewhere."

"What did he say, Tish?"

"He said, 'If the gym is a good alternative for you and it's working, I think you should keep going. Maybe I ought to do the same thing.' Damn…" Another tear formed and fell down her cheek. "What kind of answer is that?"

"He's saying he can't be monogamous with you, Tish." Dee shook her head. "I think he's gon' back to old girl..."

"That's exactly what I thought he said, too, you know, without actually saying it." She wiped tears from her cheeks. "I've been dealing with that and the next thing he told me yesterday when we spoke again."

"Okay," Dee took a deep breath. "Let me have it."

"The baby's due in early July and right after she's born, Sable's scheduled to exit the military and move to San Antonio," she stopped and cleared her throat. "They're planning a late July wedding."

"What? You're kidding me, right?" She threw her hands up in the air. "So how are you taking this, Tish?"

"Oh, I've had my moments, trust me. I just can't believe this is all happening so fast. Last year ended on such a wonderful note. If it hadn't been for my way-cool birthday party, I'd say this year's the worse I've had in a very long time."

She blew her nose. "I'm not looking forward to what the rest of it is about to bring, either."

Forty-Three

Life's a miracle
arriving on cue and in
its own time and place.

"Hey Tom." Sable's voice sounded hushed. "I'm on the way to the hospital…water broke."

"What?" He stood behind his desk and dropped the ink pen on the tablet he'd been writing on. "But the baby's not due for another three weeks."

"Tell her that, would you?" She buckled her seat belt and locked the door of the taxicab. "I'm only five minutes from the hospital so I'll call you back as soon as they tell me something. Can you get a hop over here tonight?"

"A hop? Tonight?" He scratched his head and looked for his keys. "I'll see. I'll be there as soon as I can. Don't panic, okay? They'll take real good care of you at the hospital. They know how to help you have this baby."

"No kidding, Tom… that's what they do." Sable rolled her eyes and shook her head. "Gotta go now. See you when you get here."

Tom paced the floor in deep thought tossing the keys around his hand and rubbing his head with the other.

There's no way I can get to D.C. in time for the delivery. I guess I should try anyway. He checked his watch. *Two o'clock...it's still early. But I sure was looking forward to dinner tonight at Dee and Aaron's. There goes another chance to see Tish, too.*

He sat at the desk and stared at the phone.

Forty-Four

A new beginning
A family made of three
Vows said in July.

"Girl!" Tish exclaimed as she opened the car door and stepped out of Dee's car. "It's hot as hell out here!"

"Well, *it is* July in San Antonio, what do you expect?" Dee closed the door and threw her purse strap over her shoulder. She straightened the skirt of her yellow linen suit and took a deep breath. "Are you sure you still want to do this? We can get right back in that car and go have a great dinner someplace downtown, you know. We don't have to go in there."

"*You* don't. I gave Tom my word that I'd come to the wedding." Still standing beside the car, she turned and stared at the red brick building across the street from the parking lot. She'd attended St. Paul United Methodist Church several times before but this occasion would be different, very different. Today, the man who'd come into her life and stolen her heart would marry another woman. And she'd be there to witness the whole thing. She slid her hands across the bottom of her black and white paisley-print, sleeveless dress and brushed out the wrinkles. "Do I look nice?"

"Chil' you look as beautiful as always." She winked at her. "What? You worried about how you look?" She chuckled as the walked toward the church. "Girl, Ms. Sable's the one who needs to be worried. Don't let Tom see you walk into the church before he says 'I do.' He just might say, 'I don't!'"

"That's not going to happen, and you know it."

Dee lifted her eyebrows but didn't respond. As they approached the steep steps, a dozen other people walking from different directions joined them as they entered the church.

A very handsome male usher with mahogany skin and princely stature opened the door for them, flashing a killer smile that showed every one of his perfect, white teeth. The sharp navy blue Army dress uniform fit his well- developed body flawlessly. He extended his thick arm to Tish first, then the other one to Dee and escorted them down the aisle.

"Right here," Tish said as she stopped at the third row from the back. "This is fine, thank you." She quickly scanned the sanctuary and noticed that there were only about thirty people in the church…it looked almost empty.

Aaron had already arrived and had been ushered to a seat near the front on the second row.

The usher nodded. He looked intently at Tish and smiled again. "Ma'am," he whispered and walked back to his post at the door.

"Girl, that man's flirting with you!" Dee whispered with a wide grin.

"Oh, please, he was not! He's just doing his job and a fine job he's doing, too!" She giggled. "But damn, he looks good in that uniform, doesn't he?"

"Yes, and you can wipe the drool from your chin right now, missy."

"It's been a while, you know. I could use some attention from a good-looking hunk like him right about now." She tilted her head down as she played with the pearl button of her black satin purse lying in her lap.

"Tish, did you ever tell Tom how you feel about him? That you've fallen in love with him?" she asked in a hushed tone.

"No."

"I don't understand you. Did you at least talk to him about the spirit dance?"

"No." She looked away and took a deep breath. She didn't want to talk about this now; she didn't even want to think about it.

How could Dee be a friend and ask me these questions at this moment? Why didn't she bring it up yesterday when we had lunch if she wanted to know?

The pastor stepped into the church and walked to the pulpit, followed by Tom dressed in his dress military uniform. His best man and brother, Bryan, walked into the pulpit and stood beside him, simply dressed in a black suit, white shirt, and bow tie.

Seeing Tom dressed as someone else's groom hastened the beating of Tish's heart, and as tears filled her eyes, she consciously took deep breaths to maintain her composure.

The organist began playing the traditional "Bridal Chorus," and a young woman entered the sanctuary, wearing a sleeveless, peach chiffon dress with matching shoes and bouquet of dainty flowers.

"She must be Sable's sister. Tom said it would be a simple, small wedding," Tish whispered to Dee. "So she'll be next."

"No flower girl?"

"Nope."

Tish looked at the back door of the church and saw Sable standing in the doorway alone, dressed in a long off-white wedding gown with a full skirt, covered with pearls and rhinestones. The thick, layered veil brushed her shoulders, left bare by the strapless top of her gown.

"She doesn't look like a woman who just had a baby," Dee said very softly in Tish's ear. "How'd she get that body looking like that so quick?"

Sable walked unescorted down the aisle, passing them with a brilliant smile, her eyes fixed on Tom.

"Keep your eyes on the prize," Dee whispered.

"She's beautiful," Tish said under her breath as she returned to her seat in the pew.

"Where's her father?"

"He's in prison, Tom said," she whispered back. "Has been there most of her life."

"Oh, God. He's marrying a woman with criminal daddy issues?" She shook her head. "Not good."

"*Shhhish,*" a deacon of the church seated behind them admonished them with his finger at his lips.

They sat through the very short, simple ceremony without another word.

"I now pronounce you man and wife," the pastor stated flatly. "You may kiss the bride."

Tish wiped a tear from her cheek as Dee looked over at her. "Well, this does it for me. I don't think I'll ever bring myself to attend church here again." She wiped another tear and took a deep breath.

"Let's go." Dee nudged her friend and stood up.

Tish quietly stepped into the aisle with Dee following behind. They headed for the door before the bridal party left the altar. Once in the foyer, she turned to Dee. "I need a drink. Let's go for one of Blanca's stiff margaritas at Aldaco's in St. Paul Square."

"Sounds good to me."

Dee didn't say anything else until they were seated in the bar area of the nearly empty restaurant. After ordering their drinks, she broke the silence. "What's going through your mind, Tish? You look so sad."

"Yeah? Well, who said life could be fair?" She glanced toward the window and looked out at the pavilion being staged for an evening concert. "Cause this crap just ain't fair, Dee!"

"What part isn't fair?" She paused and dipped a corn chip into the hot salsa. "You supported Tom's decision to marry Sable, remember? You didn't tell him about your feelings for him, either. What else was the brother supposed to do?"

Tish continued to stare out the window and remained silent.

"Do you think you were completely fair when you didn't tell him that you've fallen in love with him?"

"It wouldn't have changed anything."

"How do you know?" Dee sounded surprised and annoyed. "He may feel the same way about you. Now we may never know; you just let him get away *and* he's married to another woman."

"Yea-ah, and she *just had* his baby girl, too. I didn't." Tish offered her best shot. "He's supposed to be married to her, don't you see. They're family. He and I are…we're best friends. That's all."

She ran her finger across the margarita glass. "I think I got the best of him, anyway, 'cause that'll never change. We'll still talk when something important happens, just watch."

"Girl, I hear you, but I'm not so convinced." Dee sipped her drink and looked puzzled. "You know him better than I do. But the real issue here is you're in love with him and he's married to another woman. How do you deal with that and still act like you're his best friend?"

"Hell, Dee, I don't know!" she retorted and took several gulps of her drink. "I've never done this before."

"Well," she placed her hand on Tish's arm, "I think you should give it some thought…that's all."

"I know." She folded her arms and leaned on the table wondering what the rest of her life would be like without Tom as a significant part of it. She really wasn't ready to let him go.

"When we were dating, we promised that no matter what happened, we'd always be friends. That's how we started and we should end that way, too. So as his friend, I have to be happy for his marriage to Sable, 'cause that's what he decided to do. I won't let her get in the way of our friendship."

"You sound so noble, my sister."

"Noble sounding or not, she'd better treat him right, that's all I'm saying."

"Well then. Tish has spoken." Dee lifted her margarita glass. "Let's toast to Tom and Sable's long and happy life together."

As Deborah Cox's sensual voice sang "One Wish" in the background, Tish slowly picked up her glass. She paused as she listened to the words of the song. As tears filled her eyes and fell down her cheeks uncontrollably, she placed the glass back on the table and whispered, "No, I'd rather not."

Forty-Five

As our lives go on
the memories remain strong.
Our bond growing more.

It's been almost a year since I met Tom. Tish rushed Simon and Melanie out the door and to the car parked in the garage. *So much has happened and I'm right back where I started before I met him. Single with children and going to the gym every other day to burn off that blasted sexual energy, 'cause I don't have a man. I miss him.* She opened the passenger door and dropped her purse, briefcase, and gym bag on the floor. *Regardless of his current situation, I need to talk to him. I'll call him as soon as I get to work today. I've waited long enough.*

"Mommy, are you coming to the PTA meeting tonight?" Simon asked as he climbed into his booster seat behind Tish. "I have to tell my teacher. She wants to know what parents are coming."

"Yes, baby, I'm coming," she replied as she buckled her seatbelt. "I wouldn't miss PTA, no way!"

Simon chuckled. "Oh, I have a book report that's due tomorrow."

"You've had plenty of time to read the book." She backed out as soon as the garage door completely opened.

"Yeah, I did…and I started the report, too. It's another one about volcanoes. Just need to finish it. That's all."

"That's great and you can do that right after school while you're at daycare. Miss Deborah can help you." She drove down the quiet streets of her neighborhood heading toward Le Petite Academy.

"Why'd you get us up so early, Mom?" Melanie rubbed her eyes and stretched her arms as if she'd just gotten out of the bed.

"Because I have a lot of work waiting for me and I can't stay late tonight." Tish peeped at her daughter through the rearview mirror. "I have to go in earlier so I can make the gym during lunch instead of after work today, that's all."

"Well, I'm sleeping all the way there," she whispered as she adjusted her position in her seat and leaned on the side of the car with her eyes shut tight.

Tish turned up the volume of the radio just in time for a lively commercial for the Omega's "Back- to-School Jam." With "Atomic Dog" playing in the background, the DJ embellished the details of the annual September event. "If you were there last year, you already know what a party it's going to be!"

Yes, I know...I was there. She drew a deep breath and slowly nodded in agreement.

"Mom, do you want to be a special speaker in my class next week? Each of us has to invite one person to come give a talk during our social science class." Melanie paused and released a big yawn. "I forgot to ask you before…but my day is Monday."

"Sure, sweetie, I'd love to." She turned the radio volume down. "What time would I need to be there?"

"Don't know for sure, but I'll find out and tell you this evening, okay?"

"Don't forget, 'cause I have to take time off from work, you know." Tish hid her annoyance that she daughter had waited until the last minute to ask her. "What do you want me to talk about?"

"I don't care." Melanie's voice faded off. "Just come." She grabbed her book bag as Tish drove into the parking lot.

"Have a good day. See you tonight," Tish said as her children got out and headed for the building. She pulled back into traffic and headed for her office hoping to get some work done before the routine of the day began.

Two and a half hours later Tish sat at her desk enjoying her second cup of coffee after the morning meeting that lasted an hour and a half. The exhausting staff review of the large volume of Christmas promotional work her company had picked up had consumed her energy. She sat back in her chair and stared at her children's pictures placed neatly on her desk.

I need a mental break. She'd closed the office door when she'd entered as a signal to Michelle that she wanted to be alone.

Tish placed her coffee cup on the desk and picked up the phone to dial Tom's number, then quickly returned it to the cradle, unsure if she should actually call him at work.

She reached for a small, black leather photo album in the bottom desk drawer. She scanned the pictures she'd taken in August when she took the children to the East Coast for their vacation.

It'd been the best thing she'd done for herself in a long time. She and the children had visited the Washington, D.C. sites, played all day at Busch Gardens in Williamsburg, and enjoyed cookouts in the homes of at least five different families she hadn't seen in years. The drive gave her time to think and reflect on her life, where she was, and the direction she should be headed. It also gave her physical distance from Tom and forced her to face the cold reality that he was a married man and unavailable.

She'd forgotten about the three photos placed in the back of the album taken when Maurice came for a quick weekend trip. While the children were visiting their father, they'd spent time on the River Walk, visited the Alamo, and attended a play at the Carver Community Center. Smiling as she viewed the photos taken of them together on the river, she remembered their conversations.

Maurice's new private practice as a clinical psychologist already had a promising start with clients referred by an established colleague. He'd started looking for a new house and had talked to her about resuming their relationship.

Tish softly brushed the surface of the photo with her fingertip.

Although she had no desire to move to New Orleans she'd told him that she'd consider it and get back with him. She hadn't thought much about it since. He hadn't brought it up either in the four phone calls after his visit.

Then there's David. She closed the album and placed it back in the drawer. After not hearing from him in months, out of the blue, David had called her yesterday at work. She leaned back in her chair and turned around to face the window. He seemed different, like he'd matured some. His tone sounded less hurt and the anger had not been as evident. He'd graduated from law school and taken the Texas Bar Exam.

"Will you at least talk to me, Tish?" he'd asked her. "I apologize for anything I said or did to upset you before."

She'd given him the okay to call her and start over again.

But the attention from these handsome, desirable men wasn't enough. She'd awakened that morning from a dream about Tom; her need to hear his voice again compelled her to turn back to her desk and dial his number.

"Sergeant Manning."

"Hi, Tom. This is Tish." She took a deep breath. "How you doing?"

"Hi there! I'm doing fine!" He sounded surprised and pleased. "How about you?"

"Oh, not bad." She felt her heart pounding. "Just sitting here thinking about you, that's all. I hope everything's going good."

"As well as can be expected, I guess. Can you hold for a second?"

"Sure."

He went over to the door and closed it.

"My daughter is growing up too fast for me though. Having such a little girl in my life is a real different experience. She's very special and definitely has her daddy's heart."

"I'm happy to hear that. She's very blessed to have you with her everyday. You should cherish all the moments you two have together. Before long she'll be grown and on her own." Tish paused. "So, is everything else going alright?"

"If you mean between Sable and me, well, it's civil. We're doing what we can to make it work." He picked up his pen and doodled circles on the notepad. "It's not easy, but we're at least trying. How about you? What's been going on with you, Tish?"

"Oh nothing much. Being mom, going to work, doing Delta committee work, and taking aerobics classes two—three times a week. I've joined a creative writing class in the evenings." She turned her chair around, facing the window. "You know, just normal stuff to keep myself busy and out of trouble."

"Now, what kind of trouble would you ever get in?" He chuckled. "You were the good one, if I remember right."

"Yeah, always the good one," she said softly. "Well, I just wanted to check in with you. Had to make sure you're being treated right," Tish replied, taking the focus off her feelings and how much she missed him. "Got to take care of my friend, you know."

"I'm so glad to hear from you." He paused, and cleared his throat. "I wanted to talk with you too, but wasn't sure if I should call. I know what we said about always being there for each other and being friends in spite of whatever else happens in our lives."

He dropped the pen, tore off the paper he'd drawn on and balled it up when he noticed he'd been writing her name over and over again. He resumed drawing circles on a clean sheet. "It's easy to say those things, but you never know how people really feel about it. Sometimes we say things that sound right and so you don't hurt someone's feelings."

"Yeah, I know what you mean." She stood and peeked out the window, remembering her first date with him, and their time on the River Walk.

"I'm serious about being there for you if and when you ever need me. I want you to know that I consider you my best friend. I can only hope you feel the same about me. No matter what."

"No matter what?" A bit surprised he was still using that condition; she waited for his answer.

"That's right, no matter what. I believe whatever we have between us is very special. It's more than friendship, the closeness, bonding, or whatever you want to call it…it's uniquely ours. And no matter what, I don't ever want to lose it or you. I don't know how else to say it, Tish."

"Then I guess that says it, huh?" She blushed, hearing that he felt that way about her.

"Yes, I guess it does." He paused and changed the subject. "You said you're taking a creative writing class. Which campus?"

"At St. Philip's College. I met a soror who teaches in the English department. She's published several books of poetry and written a couple of plays. She's a remarkable person to talk to, so I signed up for one of her classes."

Feeling more relaxed talking about something else, Tish sat back at her desk and took a sip of coffee. "I've always wanted be a writer; I've just not ever done anything about it 'til now. Plus, it's a good way to deal with pent-up feelings. Writing can be good, inexpensive therapy, you know."

"Sounds good. When does your class meet?"

"On Tuesday and Thursday from six to eight-thirty at night. Why?"

He smiled at her response. "*Interesting*. I'm taking a couple of classes at St. Philip's too." He rubbed his stomach. "The credits will transfer to Our Lady of the Lake University where I'll get my BA in business. At this rate, I'll probably be able to get that done in about two years. I just started last week. I guess your class just started too."

"Yes, it did. How about that?" She was pleased to learn he had taken this step toward completing his degree. "Maybe our paths will cross sometime in the parking lot or something."

"Oh, for sure…."

She wanted to talk longer but knew someone had to end the conversation. "Well, Tom, I need to get back to work. It's been good talking to you and catching up."

"I'm glad you called. Really, I am," he responded, tearing the sheet of paper from his notepad covered with circles, pyramids, and the word Tish. "Oh, by the way, are you going to the Omega's 'Back-to-School Jam' this Saturday?" He balled the paper up and threw it in the trash.

"No, not this year." She drew in a deep breath. "I'm going to a Harlem Globetrotters game with the kids and their dad. Imagine that?"

"So is he trying to make amends with you?" Tom penned question marks on the notepad.

"Not at all. One of the vendors at the hospital gave him four tickets. He isn't seeing anyone, I guess. So it was more like, 'I don't want to waste a good ticket, so do you want to go?' I said yes and he almost choked. He really didn't expect me to say that I'd go, I'm sure."

"Okay, just be careful."

"Oh, I will, trust me." Flattered by his concern, she added, "We're meeting him at the dome. So if he starts acting crazy, we can just leave. No sweat. Hey, a free ticket to see *the Trotters*? Why not?"

"Sure, I hear, ya'." He scratched his chin. "Well, I'll let you go. Hey, thanks for calling. It was really good hearing from you."

"Same here, Tom. You take care, now, you hear?" She needed to get off the phone before she couldn't hide the hurt she'd begun to feel inside. She'd missed talking to him more than she'd realized and hearing his voice sounded too much like an invitation to do something she'd regret in the morning.

Forty-Six

Silent moments touched
memories bitter and sweet
cold reality.

Tom hung up and stared at the phone, tapping the receiver with his fingertips. Tempted to call Tish back and tell her that he'd thought about her every day and that he'd never stopped waking up from dreams hoping to find her asleep beside him. He wondered what she'd say if she knew that every morning he'd fixed his own breakfast because Sable didn't cook. He remembered the great breakfast Tish had prepared for them before the first time they'd made love.

Would it be wrong to tell Tish these things? Whenever Sable had whispered "I love you" to him, he'd remember the only time Tish told him the same thing. Sable's words had never hit him like hearing it from Tish.

He leaned back in his chair and closed his eyes. *I had to make a decision...but did I choose right?*

As great as their lovemaking had been before marriage Sable never measured up after the ink dried on the license. She seemed to enjoy hot, passionate sex as a single woman but now that they were married Tom thought she was holding out on him.

He sat forward and begun to doodle again. This time he drew larger boxes with parallel lines down the middle, like prison bars. Sable had began to question him every time he'd been even a few minutes late coming home from work or when he went out to do anything that didn't involve her. She had to know where he'd been, whom he'd been with, and what he'd been doing.

He'd tried to find out why she was so insecure but got a limited response. She said she was doing what every newly married woman did. End of subject.

He crossed through the boxes on the paper, then stood, reached over, and switched on the radio sitting on the credenza beside his desk. He turned and looked out the window, listening to the DJ's excited rendition of the advertisement for the Omega's "Back-to-School Jam."

I'm not ready to give up. A good old school party is what we need.

They hadn't been dancing together since Sable became pregnant, nor had they attended a social function together as a couple. Now that he knew Tish wouldn't be attending the party he could be comfortable being there with Sable.

Tom stared out the window watching aimlessly as blackbirds pecked the ground, gathering in groups of two, then four, then ten.

The DJ selected "September" by Deborah Cox. The words reminded him that it was September a year ago that he'd met Tish. The more he listened to Deborah pour her heart into the song he realized that he missed Tish more than he wanted to admit and more than he had the right to miss a woman he wasn't married to.

He wiped away the tears that started to fill his eyes, returned to his desk, pulled out a pad of paper, and began to write: *Tish, I have loved you...*

In her downtown office, not too far from him, Tish stood quietly looking out her window, listening to the same song playing on the radio, with a warm stream of tears flowing down her face.

Forty-Seven

Yearning to see you
hurting as we are apart.
Please come back to me.

It was a crispy cool, late October evening with a light breeze ruffling the leaves on the campus lawn at St. Philip's College as Tom left his class and walked from the Sutton building to the Artemesia Bowden building. Daylight Savings Time had ended; he wasn't yet used to how early it got dark. He entered the Bowden building, went directly to the second floor and leaned against the wall opposite Room 222.

He had to see Tish. Talking to her on the phone had not been enough. He'd longed to have her beside him, if only for a moment, and to once more look into her eyes. He needed to feel alive again.

When the class ended, Tish walked out and without knowing it was walking straight to him. With books in one arm, she fumbled with her small black leather shoulder bag. She wore a dark purple and gold striped sweater, black jeans, and sneakers. Her soft, curly hair had been pulled back into a ponytail. She looked like a typical college student.

He smiled and stood still as she almost walked right into him. He extended his hand in her direction to keep her from tripping over him.

"Oh! Excuse me," she said then looked up to see who she'd nearly run into. "Hi, Tom! I'm surprised to see you here."

"Hello, my sister." He leaned toward her and almost planted a kiss on her cheek.

She cut her eyes toward him extending a mild warning that made him back off. "So, what brings you here?" She looked puzzled as he turned to walk with her down the stairs and out the door.

"It's rather dark outside, tonight," he replied evenly and thoughtfully. "I thought you wouldn't mind having an escort to your car. Is that all right with you, ma'am?"

"My, my, Sergeant Manning. You're a regular Sir Lancelot, huh?" She grinned and nudged him with her elbow. "I hadn't considered myself to be a damsel in distress, but I welcome the escort anyway. Thanks for thinking about me. How'd you find my class?"

"Easy. Looked on the website for a creative writing class that met at six p.m. on Tuesday and Thursday." He turned to look at her. "Actually, Tish I really wanted to see you. Well, and make sure you got to your car safely. This way I could do both."

"That's so sweet of you. Now, are you planning to do this every night until the class is over?" Her coy tone invited him to walk a little closer. "It's going to be dark for the rest of the semester and I might come to get used to this." She teased him just like before. "You shouldn't start something you can't finish, you know."

"That's a very good point. So since I've started this, I have to finish it. I want to anyway. Do you?"

"I have to admit this is a very pleasant gesture." She lowered her head as if in thought. "And it's great seeing you, Tom. Gosh, I haven't seen you since…well since your wedding." She looked up at him. "How are things going, anyway?"

"Just okay. I have this problem, though." He scratched his head wondering if he should talk about his wife's shenanigans. *Why not? Tish is my best friend.* "I think Sable believes I'm seeing someone." He hesitated as she looked at him with big eyes.

"Why do you think that?"

"Sometimes I feel like she's following me around. It all started when we went to the Omega party last month. She freaked when she saw me hugging the sistas like we do when we greet. Sable doesn't understand about the Delta-Que thing. When I tried to get her to see how all of us were greeting each other that way, not just me, she wasn't having it. She got upset with me because she thought I was disrespecting her. She even insisted that we leave the party early."

They stood by her car in the parking lot. "Man, what am I going to do about this? I hadn't expected that from her."

"You didn't marry a Delta, so why are you so confused?" Tish offered.

"Oh, thanks. That hurt." He took the key from her hand and unlocked the car door.

"No pain intended. Just pointing out the obvious, that's all." She motioned to him to open the door for her. "Would love to talk more, but you know, kids, homework, bedtime responsibilities. Thanks for the escort."

She put out her hand for her keys. "Let's do this again, sometime." She gave him a fake smile as she got in the car.

Tom closed the door and stood beside the car looking at her. *Yeah, I let my Delta Queen get away.*

Forty-Eight

Once moving forward
Allowing life to unfold
Jealousy follows.

As she drove out of the parking lot, Tish took a deep breath to calm the strong vibes running wild inside her chest. She glanced at the rear-view mirror and saw Tom with his hands in his pockets and his head lowered as he walked toward his car.

That may be the first and last time he does that. I didn't mean to hurt him. I just told the simple truth, that's all.

She noticed a black car behind her as she turned onto Martin Luther King Boulevard. The driver suddenly sped up so that their cars were beside each other at the stoplight.

She looked over and saw an attractive black female driver. The woman kept a firm, straight posture, never turning toward Tish, so she couldn't see her face. The light changed to green and the woman sped off. Tish noticed that the Camaro had a D.C. license plate and made a mental note of it just in case she came across her again in the future.

Tired from a long day at work and attending class right behind it, Tish dropped her books and purse on the counter top in the kitchen and spoke to Cathy as she headed toward the front door to leave.

"Thanks for babysitting for me, Cathy. How were the children tonight?"

She tossed her backpack across her shoulder and slid her car keys from jeans' pocket. "They were great. All their homework got done and they should be asleep by now."

"That's a big help. I know they enjoy it when you're their sitter." She reached to give Cathy a hug. "I really appreciate you being available for me so I can take this class. I need the break."

"No problem. Hey, the money I'm making is for prom this year." Cathy smiled and hugged Tish back affectionately. "This is the easiest cash I know. It sure beats flipping burgers."

"Well, great. We're helping each other." Tish opened the front door. "You drive home carefully, now. Tell your mom hello for me."

Tish closed the door after Cathy got in her car and started the engine. She walked back to the kitchen and checked the phone messages Cathy had left for her. She found one from Dee and one from Maurice.

She dialed Dee's number as she walked to the den. She sat on the leather sofa and plopped her legs on the cushions.

"Hello?" Dee sounded groggy.

"Hey, girl. You asleep already?"

"No, not really. Just sitting here trying to watch the news and dozed off. You just getting home?"

"Yeah," Tish replied, "just got here." She thought about telling Dee about Tom's unexpected appearance, but decided against it. "So, what's up?"

"Oh, I called to ask you if you want to share a table for the Poinsettia Ball. A little while ago Soror Taylor called and said she'd paid for a table but now she isn't going to be in town that night. She's looking for someone to host the table. Interested?"

Out of the blue, a sad feeling fell over Tish. Thinking about dressing up and going out to the all the balls and galas this year wouldn't be nearly as exciting as it had been last year.

"No, I'm not going to the Poinsettia Ball, the Alpha Toy Dance, the Omega Ball, Debutante Balls—none of those, not this year." She pulled a small sofa pillow from behind her and wrapped her arms around it holding it tightly against her chest. "So find another soror to do that with, please?"

"So what's up with you, Tish? Why such a mood?"

"Just not interested in going to those functions this year, that's all. Been there, done that." She took a deep breath and turned to her side on the sofa. "Have no man in my life this year and I'm not interested in going by myself, that's all."

"What about Maurice?" Her tone gave Tish the impression that Dee would not take no for an answer. "Didn't you tell me he pledged the graduate Omega chapter in New Orleans? Shoot, girl we both know he'd love to be surrounded by a ballroom full of Deltas. Ask him, I bet he'll come and be your date for the evening. And if not, there's always David."

"Yeah, sure. I'll think about it." Tish's soft response wasn't intended to convince her friend. "But I doubt it. Maybe next year."

"Ah, come on, Tish. At least go to the Poinsettia Ball and be with the sorors. I don't know enough people to invite to fill up the table so you should share it with me. Together, we can do it. And invite Maurice. You'll have a good time, I'm sure. Right now it doesn't sound like a good idea, but by then it will be, trust me, okay?"

"Well, all right. You do persist, don't you?"

"Yes, Tish. Especially when I know it'll be a good thing. I'll call Soror Taylor back and tell her we'll take her table. Thanks, sis. Now call Maurice, please?"

"See you at work tomorrow."

Forty-Nine

Nothing is the same
except my feelings for you.
How do I get through?

"I can't believe the semester is over already. It seemed to just fly by." Dressed in his military fatigues and thick jacket, Tom walked Tish from her class for the last time. "How do you think you did on your final exam tonight?"

As they left the building, Tish pulled the black cotton scarf closer to her neck as the cold north December wind blew through her not-thick-enough black and white tweet wool blend jacket and blue jeans. The weather had changed drastically in the two hours she'd been inside.

"I guess I did reasonably well. At least I don't need the grade to graduate." Although she'd declined his offer to go for coffee after class every week, she wished he'd offer again, because a good hot cup of anything would be perfect right now.

"Yeah, that's right. You already have a degree…lucky you." He pulled her close to him locking his arm in hers as they walked into the parking lot.

She was keenly aware of his marital status and she had kept her distance. She'd successfully resisted the urge to touch him—even for a simple hug or a brush against his shoulder. Now, she welcomed his gesture to protect her from the wind.

"I only wanted to become a better writer. I've been writing poetry and Professor Summers told me it's good stuff. I never expected that I'd write poetry of all things. I've started keeping a journal too. It helps me see things in new perspectives."

"Oh, so now you're a poet. That's great, Tish." He slowed the pace even though everyone else rushed to their cars to escape the cold wind. "Would you share one of your poems with me?"

"Maybe one of the short ones. Let's see, how about a haiku?"

"What's a haiku?"

"It's an ancient Japanese poem that is only three lines long and usually expresses one thought. The words in each line have to follow this pattern—only have five syllables in the first line, seven in the second line, and five in the third line. I've written several after we discussed them in class. The professor asked us to focus on a specific moment in time and write something that described it. Here's the first one I wrote.

When I needed you
you came and took care of me
and my soul thanks you."

"That's nice. So what moment in time were you writing about?" Tom slowed their pace even more as they approached her car, pulling her closer to his body.

"That Sunday morning when I needed you to take care of me so I wouldn't have to go to the gym." Her voice dropped to almost a whisper. "I think about that sometimes, especially when I wake up having an empty rollover and there is absolutely nothing I can do about it."

"What do you mean?" They stopped walking and stood beside her car. He pulled her from his side and held her by both her arms, facing him. "Aren't you seeing anyone, Tish? Surely you can be with any number of men in this city if you wanted to be…why aren't you dating someone?"

"I go out every once in a while but I don't want to sleep with just any man, Tom. If I could do that, I guess I'd never have an empty rollover."

She refused to look him in the eyes. "It's not just a warm body I need; I need a man who respects, understands, and wants me and only me to be in his life as much as I want him. Until that happens I'm on lockdown, you know, celibate—sweating at the gym and not in the bed."

"I see." He touched her chin and gently pushed it up forcing her eyes up to meet his. "So will you tell me another one of your poems?"

She knew it was a delay tactic to prolong their moment of departing as long as he could. She wanted to stay in that moment and talk to him all night, even if it meant standing in the blistering cold, she knew she couldn't and shouldn't.

"No, not tonight." She smiled softly as their eyes met. "I have to get to the house so Cathy can go home. It's a school night. Thanks for walking me to my car. It's been nice spending a few minutes with you after class. I guess I'll see you again when I run into you at some function. If not, have a blessed Christmas."

She handed him her car keys. After he unlocked the door, she dropped her backpack into one hand and prepared to enter the car. "Take care, Tom. Goodnight."

Before he opened the car door he pulled her into his arms. "Girl, how could I let you go and not get a quick hug?"

Feeling safe, warm, and welcome, she dropped her backpack to the ground and wrapped her arms around him expecting a nice friendly hug that Deltas and Omegas often exchanged.

However, he didn't release his embrace right away and feelings long filed away in her mind crept back into nerve endings as she felt an uneasy tremble moving through her muscles. The reality of the situation became clearer and more than she could endure. She remembered that he'd leave her momentarily and go home to Sable. Her body trembled stronger and he looked down at her as warm tears poured from her eyes.

"Please, Tom, please, let…me…go. I can't handle this." She pushed away from him. "I really can't do this. I have to go."

"Oh, baby, I'm so sorry." He released her and slowly opened the door. "I didn't mean to hurt you. I only wanted to hold you. I just wanted to hold you again, that's all."

"I've gotta go home, Tom."

He leaned into the opened door. "Thanks for our moments."

He waited until she drove off before he walked to his car two rows behind hers. He took a deep breath; and regretted he'd made her cry. He'd never wanted to hurt her.

Wow, I guess she still has strong feelings for me.

Just as he approached his car, a black Camaro pulled out of a parking space and sped past him.

Could that be Sable? Is she stalking me? No, it couldn't be...I haven't given her any reason to follow me around...have I?

Fifty

Avoiding the truth
does not stop reality.
Our love is still here.

"Hello?" Tish parked her car in the short-term parking lot at the San Antonio International Airport.

"Hey, doll, the eagle has landed," Maurice said smoothly with a hint of a southern accent. "We're pulling up at the gate. I'll see you in a few minutes."

"Great. I'm glad you're here. Did you have a good flight?" She turned off the ignition and unbuckled her seatbelt.

"A usual entertaining Southwest flight." The plane moved slowly, as the ground attendant guided it into the gate. "I can't wait to see you. Thanks for inviting me to San Antonio this weekend. I'd begun to think you'd given up on us."

"No, not at all. I've been going through some things…hey, I'm just happy you've been patient with me." She pulled the purse strap on her shoulder as she walked toward the terminal.

The chilly air had quite a breeze. It would be an enchanting night to dress up and go out two weeks before Christmas.

"So are you near the airport? Can I expect to see you outside at the curbside passenger pickup?"

"No, actually, you'll see me when you get to the baggage claim area. I'm parked and on my way inside."

"My girl!" he said proudly. "That's what I like about you, Tish. Somehow you know exactly what to say and do to make my day!"

"What?"

"I appreciate it when I'm greeted inside the terminal instead of being picked up curbside." He chuckled. "Inside is so much more welcoming and personal. It makes me feel like you really want me here and you're honestly happy to see me." He paused. "It takes more effort on your part, see?

"I hadn't thought of it that way, but it makes sense."

"Talk to you when I can see your gorgeous face," he said as he exited the plane.

"Sounds good."

"I'm almost there." His voice faded into a whisper.

Tish reached into her purse and pulled out the small mirror and quickly checked her hair and lipstick. She took a deep breath and reminded herself that she deserved to have a good time with Maurice and that's precisely what she planned to do.

David had called a few times since that first time when he wanted to try again, but had spent a total of thirty minutes on the phone with her. Something more pressing always seemed to be going on in his life. He'd never asked her to have lunch with him or out on a date.

Becoming a lawyer has apparently made him think he's better than I am. I wonder why he even bothered to call at all?

She'd been willing to let him redeem himself but he'd done nothing to earn her time or trust. Now that Maurice had eagerly accepted her invitation to come to San Antonio for the weekend and attend two formal galas as her escort, David was cold history.

She dropped the mirror back into her purse and turned toward the hallway. She saw Maurice standing at the corner, looking around for her with his garment bag slung over his shoulder. *Damn, he looks better every time I see him.*

His black jeans, white turtleneck, and black leather jacket fit as if they'd been custom-made for his body. He'd grown a nicely trimmed dark beard that outlined his chestnut brown face and made his eyes even more striking. He gave her a radiant smile as their eyes met and extended his arm as he walked toward her.

"My, my." Maurice pulled her into his arms for a tight hung. He kissed her forehead. "You're so beautiful, doll. I've missed you."

"Hi, Maurice, welcome back to San Antonio." She savored his embrace. His sensual cologne made her moan.

"Let's get this suitcase so we can be on our way."

"Yeah, we need to have a quick dinner and then get dressed for the Poinsettia Ball." She pulled from his arms and looked him into his eyes. "We have to be downtown by seven o'clock."

He took her hand as they walked toward the baggage claim area. "We have three hours." They stopped at the belt carrying the luggage from his flight and waited for his bag to appear. “Does that give us enough time to have dinner somewhere and get dressed?”

“Sure, I have dinner cooked and waiting at home for us.” She’d taken the day off and prepared his favorite Creole dishes. Marcus had picked the children up from school to start his week with them during their Christmas break. Having the house alone, she’d invited Maurice to stay with her for the weekend. “It’s only about twenty minutes from here.”

“I get a home-cooked dinner tonight?” He grinned as he reached for his suitcase and pulled it from the line. “I feel so special,” he added as he glanced over at Tish and winked.

“Well, you are special.” She liked him more and more and didn’t mind letting him know it. “You flew all the way from New Orleans to escort me the Poinsettia Ball and the Omega Christmas Gala this weekend. The least I could do is cook you a nice dinner.”

“It’s indeed my pleasure to be your escort, Ms. Edwards.” He placed one hand on his chest and looked her in the eye. “And I’m quite honored that you invited me, the most fortunate man, to be at your side for these most prestigious occasions,” he said with feigned formality.

“You’re just too cute.” She smiled and put her arm around his and they walked out of the airport and to the parking lot.

Twenty minutes later, she led Maurice into her home. Following dinner, she placed covered casseroles into the refrigerator. “I have lots of shrimp Creole, dirty rice, and gumbo left. So if you like leftovers, we can warm it up whenever you get hungry.”

He carefully lowered their dinner dishes into the sink and rinsed them off with hot water. “Are you sure you’re not from New Orleans? That was the best dinner I’ve had in a long time.” He cut his eyes over to her smacking his lips. “And yes, I’m gonna have more to eat later tonight, I’m sure.”

“No problem. Just leave those in the sink; we need to get ready.” She placed her hand on his arm and gently pulled him from the kitchen. “Grab your bags and follow me. She led him upstairs and into Simon’s room. “You can spread out and get dressed in here. The bathroom is clean and I’ve laid out towels and bath cloths for you in there.” She pointed to the private bathroom attached to her son’s room. “Let me know if you need anything. I’ll be at the end of the hallway.”

"Looks like you've got it all taken care of, my dear." He bowed slightly and kissed the back of her hand. "What time do you have scheduled for our departure?"

"We should leave no later than six fifteen."

"In that case, I'll be ready and waiting for you by six o'clock." He lifted one eyebrow.

"Oh sure...we'll see," she rolled her eyes at him enjoying his teasing. She left him and went to her room to get ready for an evening with a princely date.

Tish took a quick shower and then set her hair with her hot curlers while applying fresh makeup. She pulled her hair up off her neck and pinned the curls individually so that they'd fall in ringlets down her back. Next she went into the closet and removed the cranberry red satin evening dress with a full ballroom style skirt from the hanger, stepped into it, pulled the low-cut bodice into place, and adjusted the spaghetti shoulder straps. She zipped it up and then pulled the crinoline out of the shopping bag and stepped into it, filling the skirt of the dress to perfection.

She opened to her jewelry box and removed the Australian crystal and pearl necklace, the matching dangling earrings and bracelets and put them on. She slipped her feet into the flat black satin shoes that wouldn't make her taller than Maurice. Taking a few things from her everyday purse, she placed them into the black satin evening bag and completed her routine with a fresh coat of Russian Red lipstick and a spray of Red perfume.

At five after six Tish stepped out of her bedroom with a borrowed black mink jacket over her arm and saw Maurice standing outside Simon's bedroom, leaning against the doorway, hands in his pockets smiling broadly at her. A red bow tie and cummerbund accented his black tux and white pleated shirt. He looked sharp, all the way from his shiny black patent leather shoes to his rhinestone buttons and cufflinks. They hadn't planned to match; it just worked out that way.

They arrived at the LaVillia Assembly Hall in time for Tish to join nearly two hundred Delta women for their group picture. Members of the Omega fraternity served as hosts, escorting guests to their assigned tables. She saw four working the door when they'd entered.

Great, no sign of Tom. Maybe that means he's not going to be here tonight. She scanned the whole room just to make sure she'd not missed him. She smiled at Maurice as they walked arm in arm toward their table where Dee and Aaron stood waiting for them.

"Wow, you guys look like you just walked off an Ebony Fashion Fair runway." Dee's smile was as dazzling as the strapless, form-fitting red sequined gown against her ebony brown skin. She stretched her hands out to greet then. "Tish, the gorgeous southern belle, and Maurice, the perfect southern gentleman."

"Hi, guys," Tish said, blushing with joy. "Thanks. You are a smashing couple yourselves, you know!" She placed her hand on Maurice's chest. "I want you to meet Maurice Jones. He's here from New Orleans and he's your frat brother, Aaron."

"Nice to meet you, bruh." Aaron extended his hand for the traditional fraternity handshake.

"Good meeting you both." He shook Dee's hand. "Tish has told me so much about you, I feel like I know you already."

"Nice to finally meet you. We've heard about you, too. We're so glad you could join us tonight. I hope you enjoy the evening and your time in San Antonio."

"Oh, I'm sure it's going to be a wonderful time." He looked at Tish and gave her an endearing smile. "I'm surrounded by the most beautiful women in the state of Texas." He took her hand; his eyes fixed on hers. "How can I not enjoy this visit?"

"Oh, it's going to be a blast." Tish blushed slightly and turned to Aaron. "Hey, thanks for getting us the invite for the Omega Gala tomorrow night. That was a very special thing for you to do."

"Hey, just looking out…that's all." Aaron unbuttoned his tuxedo jacket that fit too snug around his stomach. He glanced over Tish's shoulder and bit his bottom lip. He spotted Tom, alone and walking toward them with a determined pace.

Dee saw him too. "Hey girl, let's go speak to Soror Thomas; she's at her table all by herself."

"Sure. Excuse us for a few?" She looked at Maurice and smiled.

"Hey, no problem. Go do your Delta thing. I'll be right here."

Tish and Dee walked away before Tish realized Tom was headed their way. He watched them walk away but continued until he reached Aaron with his hand extended.

Aaron spoke first. "Heeyyy, there Brother Manning." He received his handshake.

"What's up, man?"

"It's all good." He grinned nervously. "Hey look, I want you to meet Brother Maurice Jones from New Orleans. Brother Jones, this is Brother Thomas Manning."

"New Orleans? Hey, it's nice to meet you, bruh. Welcome to San Antonio. You couldn't have picked a better time and place to be, I tell you." He scanned the room then looked back at Maurice. "Nothing like partying with the Deltas at Christmas, man."

"No doubt." Maurice looked at Tish who chatted with a group of women unaware of his conversation with Tom. "They've done a great job decorating the place…all the poinsettias, the red and white everywhere. It's certainly their season to celebrate."

The lights dimmed and the band began playing "The Electric Slide" as the female lead singer said, "Let's get this party started!"

"Well, that's my cue to get back on the door. I have hosting duties tonight," Tom said. "So—you know Tish?"

"Yes, she's my date tonight."

"Great. She and I are good friends…would you mind if I asked her for one dance before the ball is over? I haven't seen her in a while."

"Sure, no problem." Maurice looked over and saw Tish waving for him to join her in the line dance. "Hey, man, it was nice meeting you. I'm being summoned to the dance floor. Check you later."

"Okay, bruh, later."

Fifty-One

Without you I'm not.
With you I can not be me.
How do I survive?

By ten-thirty, there were about three hundred couples on the crowded dance floor and in lines at the buffet and cash bars. Many guests strolled around from table to table greeting, laughing, and exchanging business cards. The band ended its first set with Sade's "The Sweetest Taboo," then left the stage for a much-needed break.

The DJ, a dark-skinned African-American man about fifty years old, took over. He flashed a gold tooth and introduced himself with a deep, smooth, sexy voice. "Hey, there now, this is Cool Ray. Please don't leave the dance floor. We're just gon' keep this party goin'."

As the first tune, "How Could I Let You Get Away," began to play he kept talking. "Now get ready for some of the best old school you haven't heard in a long time. We gon' let The Spinners set the stage and take us back, way back to the day…when music was real."

Tish had come to the end of the buffet line with a plate full of wings, roast beef, fruit salad, carrots, and crackers when the DJ made his announcement. She waited for Maurice who'd been in line behind her.

While they sat through several of the best songs of the 1970s, Tish wished they were still dancing. She couldn't believe she'd missed her jams, "Brick House" and "Flashlight."

She bobbed her head to the upbeat music while she ate. *At least we danced most of the night.*

Maurice wiped his fingers with the cloth napkin and leaned to her ear. "I'm going to get a drink. What would you like?"

"A white wine will be great. Thanks."

"Sure, be right back, doll."

Tish watched him as he headed to the cash bar on the other side of the ballroom. As soon as he disappeared into the crowd of people, she felt someone standing behind her. The DJ suddenly slowed the pace on the dance floor when he selected "A House is Not a Home."

Tom leaned over and whispered into her ear, as the piano cords, so familiar to her, made a chill roll down her back. "Wanna dance?"

Tish recognized his presence. She felt her heart skip from the sound of his voice. As Luther's seductive song suggested, she responded, "Yes." She stood, then turned around, trusting her initial instincts.

He had an almost pleading look on his face as he waited for her to step toward him. She took a deep breath and remembered what happened to her the last time she found herself in his arms. "I mean no. I can't Tom, not this song. Let's wait for something fast."

He took one of her hands and whispered in her ear, "Please?" He pulled her away from the table and into the aisle where they could talk.

"Don't you understand? I can't get that close to you. Not anymore." She felt a tear form in one eye. "Tom, I'm sorry."

"What have I done?" He cleared his throat and released her hand. "I see you're with an Omega tonight. He seems like a nice guy. I hope things work out for you."

"Maurice's…well, I like him a lot. We'll see how it goes." Tish answered as her mind said, *but he's not you! He could never be you.*

Tom reached for her hand again, kissed it on the backside. "Okay, then. It's been wonderful seeing you tonight, Tish. Enjoy the evening."

"Thanks…you too."

He walked away, his head tilted slightly to one side. She watched him saunter toward the door, his hands in his pants' pockets. He exited the ballroom without stopping to speak to anyone. She sat at the table, picked up her fork, and stared at her plate.

"Here's your wine," Maurice said as he placed the glass on the table and sat down. "You feeling all right?"

"Oh, fine. Thank you." She forced a smile and took a sip of her drink.

Although she felt like her heart would break, she consciously exhibited a cheery disposition until the ball ended.

Why shouldn't she? Maurice had turned out to be a great dancer and his social graces were wonderful. He looked at her with adoring eyes. When they slow danced with his arms wrapped firmly around her, she fantasized that she would run away with him that night and they'd live happily ever after.

When they left the party Tish handed Maurice her car keys and relaxed as he drove back to the house. She closed her eyes, smiling at the memories they'd created dancing most of the night. She'd delighted in introducing her handsome man to friends throughout the evening. Watching her girlfriends as they glanced at him with admiring looks, whispering to each other as he'd walk by, made her proud that he'd been her date.

"You asleep?" He drove to the gated entrance to her neighborhood. "I need the key code to get in."

"Oh, I'm sorry." She sat forward and stretched her back. "Just push the button on the black remote control on the visor. The gray one's for the garage door."

"Okay, got it." He looked over at her after he'd pushed the button and the gate opened. "Doll, did you have a good time tonight? You look pooped."

"My evening was wonderful, thank you." She placed her hand on top of his that gripped the stick shift. "I really appreciate you accepting my invitation for this weekend."

"You're welcome." He grinned slyly as he drove through the gate and toward her house. "But you know, I'm here not just so we can go to these formals together, Tish…" He pulled her hand toward him and laid it on his thigh. Then he put his hand on top of hers and stroked it softly. "I hope you know how much I care about you. I fell for you the first time I saw you."

She felt the strong tone of his leg muscles under her hand. Then the warmth and gentleness of his fingers continued to tease her physical senses and stir her emotions. *He has no idea what he's doing to me…it's been so long since I've been romanced…Hell, it's been months since I last made love.*

"Yeah?" she answered quietly.

"Yes, Tish. The thought of you has never left me." He clicked the garaged door opener as he drove into the driveway. "I'd hoped on many an occasion that a time such as this would come." He looked at her with a charming twinkle in his eyes. "I'm honored that you chose me to be with you this weekend and especially that you've invited me into your beautiful home. It's all been such a pleasant surprise."

"Well, this time your visit came when the children are with their father. It didn't make sense to have you stay in a hotel again when I've got all this room to myself." She felt very comfortable with him, even knowing that they would be staying in the house alone. She hadn't thought about the possibility that he'd want to sleep with her until that moment. *How naive of me...not to consider that...what do I do now?*

Before she could come up with an answer, Maurice had opened her door and held out his hand to help her step out of the SUV. "You are so stunning tonight, Tish. I bow to your elegance, even as you grace the garage with your brilliant beauty."

"My, my." She blushed at his compliments. "Thank you; you are so sweet and very handsome, dear sir." She took his hand and slid out of the seat and stood at the car door facing him.

He took her into his arms and pulled her close. "One more hug before we bid this formal evening adieu, my love." He winked, then kissed her nose. "I'm ready for something warm to drink and a serving of that bread pudding you told me about. I've never had it made with croissants before." He smacked his lips. "Sounds scrumptious! But let's get comfortable first. Enough with all these stuffy clothes!" He kissed her nose again and pulled her back slightly. "Let's see who can change into their PJs first! I bet I'll beat you. The last one downstairs in pajamas has to cook breakfast in the morning! Deal?"

"You're on!" He could let the little boy out and not always be so professional and grown up. She liked that. "But you gotta let me go."

"Oh, yeah." He laughed, kissed her forehead, and tilted his head. "Get ready. Get set." He took a deep breath and squeezed her tighter, then pulled his arms away from her. "Go!"

She took the lead as they entered the house and ran up the stairs, grateful that she'd worn the low slippers and not the usual toes-curling-with-pain evening shoes she'd worn on other occasions. Picking up the front of the long gown, she laughed as she ran down the hallway. She quickly kicked off the shoes, unzipped the dress, stepped out of it, then pushed the slip over her hips, down her legs and stepped out of it, leaving everything on the floor. She dashed into the bathroom and removed the jewelry and pantyhose. Then she stood in the middle of the room when it hit her. *Pajamas? I don't have pajamas.*

She walked into the closet and looked for something appropriate to wear. Her eyes locked in on the purple and gold African dress she'd worn when Tom came over and made love to her the first time. Slowly she stepped toward it, unfastened and removed her bra, then moved her panties down from her body and stepped out of them. Taking the dress off the hanger, she took a deep breath before she slid it over her head and pulled it down over her naked body. "It's just a dress," she whispered.

"Just so you know," she heard Maurice yelling from downstairs, "I'm in the kitchen making a note for you to use when you're cooking breakfast later."

"You win!" she yelled back, laughing. After stepping into her slippers, she left her bedroom and headed to the kitchen. "What's on the note?"

"Pancakes, sausage, scrambled eggs, and coffee." He chuckled. "I'm hanging it on the bedroom door so you'll know my breakfast selection. You know, just like in the hotels."

She entered the kitchen and saw him leaning over on the counter top. The black silk pajamas trimmed with purple tubing around the edge of the collar and arm cuffs made his body even more inviting. His bare feet even looked as if they'd been groomed. No apparent ash, excessive hair, corns, or bunions. In fact, they were the most beautiful feet she'd ever seen on a man. She took a deep breath and refocused when she realized that her attention had taken a strange path.

"Oh, so it's like that, huh?" She smiled at the appreciative look he gave her as he turned around when she entered the kitchen. *Yes, it's just a dress, but it's working again.* "Next you'll want room service, too."

"Doesn't that come with this reservation? Or do I get breakfast in bed…being that this is better than staying in any hotel I know." He stood straight and extended his arms out to her. "Come here, doll. I love that dress. Not pajamas, but it's so nice on you."

She walked into his arms. He stroked her back and kissed her cheek. Her eyes closed, she held him tight and exhaled slowly. *Relax…this is really going to be more than okay.*

"Tish," he whispered in her ear.

"Yes?"

"Do you think," he paused. "How do you feel about…" he paused again and pulled her back and looked into her eyes. "Tish, I really like you a lot and I've wanted you to be my special lady for a long time. I need to know if your heart is available to me. I've felt as though there's been someone else all along."

He kissed her nose softly and continued. "But as I stand alone with you in your kitchen, pajamas and all, it's because you asked me to come here this weekend. I've gladly done so and have enjoyed my time with you. But I want more and you need to know that."

Feeling the caught-by-surprise dilemma, Tish lifted her eyebrows and breathed deeply, quickly gathering her thoughts. *Just be honest with him.*

"Wow, Maurice, I'm very flattered." The tone of her voice was soft and her words carefully selected. "I could always tell that you wanted more with me and appreciate that you've never been pushy about it. Your patience and understanding have attracted me to you the most."

"That's good to know."

"And, I guess I should tell you what's going on with me." She pushed away from him. "There *had been* someone else in my life, someone I fell in love with. He's no longer available to me because he got married a few months ago. I've come to terms with that, but there're times when something unexpected happens that creates some doubt about whether I've actually gotten over my feelings for him."

She smiled at his expression of concern. "I'm trying really hard to move on. Emotionally…well, it's still a struggle."

"Oh, Tish, I understand how that can be." He pulled her closer and hugged her lovingly. "If there's anything I can do to make this easier for you, just know that I'm here for you. And you can talk to me about it…about anything, ya' hear?"

"That's so sweet of you, thanks," she whispered in his ear, enjoying the comfort of his embrace and the sincere sound of his caring words. "So, do you still want that bread pudding and coffee?"

"No, actually I don't, not now." He replied softly. "What I'd rather do at this moment is take you upstairs and lie in bed with you in my arms for the rest of the night. That's all I want to do."

She knew it would come up and what a cool way to do it. She hadn't decided that she wanted to have sex with him yet, but the idea of sleeping with a caring, gentle, man who also happened to be gorgeous and digging her…it was appealing at the very least.

"You're quiet, Tish. Are you considering it or wondering how to tell me no, you're not having it?"

"Actually, I'm thinking about how nice it would be to have you sleep with me tonight…I know I need to be held and touched. It would be very comforting and reassuring." She pulled from his embrace and looked at him. His generous smile told her that she'd just made him a happy man.

"I want to hold and touch you, doll. Very much." He gently kissed her lips. "And I have strong self-control, too. So if that's all you want, I'll be the perfect gentleman and not go any further than you feel comfortable with, okay?"

"How can I refuse that?" She dropped her arms from his back. Then she took him by one hand and led him out of the kitchen, turning the lights off as they headed toward the stairs.

Tish remembered what Madame LaSay had said. *"He will not hurt you; he will not let you down."* The thought of waking up to a full rollover for a change brought a smile to her face as they entered her bedroom.

Fifty-Two

They say moving on
is not ever that easy.
When you love someone.

Tish dialed Dee's number with her cell phone after she dropped Maurice off at North Star Mall to pick up some last-minute Christmas gifts while she made her hair appointment.

"Hello?" Dee sounded tired.

"Hey girl. What you up to?"

"Nothing much. I'm resting on the sofa watching a movie." She yawned. "Excuse me. You sound so chipper. What have you guys been up to?"

"Oh, we got up early, cooked a huge breakfast together."

Tish maneuvered the SUV through the heavy traffic onto Loop 410, heading toward the northeast side of town. "Girl, for it to be Saturday, there sure are a lot of people out here. You wouldn't believe it!"

"Well, it gets like that during the holiday season, Tish."

"Yeah, I guess you're right." She turned the radio station on 101.9 FM to listen to the nonstop Christmas music. "Maurice's shopping while I get my hair braided for the Omega Ball tonight. I have this long, beautiful dress from Ghana that's beaded all over it's batik print in purple, turquoise, gold, and cream colors. Purple's the dominant color."

"So, you're going to completely change your look tonight." Dee chuckled. "And you're going to fall into that ball, breaking the heart of every Omega who's not with you, too. I can see Maurice now, his chest all poked out with pride."

"You so crazy." She beamed with pleasure, because she knew Dee was right. "Just keeping it fresh, that's all."

"You two sure look good together, my sista'. You seemed to be having a good time last night. So how did everything go after you got home?"

"Good, good." She didn't feel the need to go into details about the rest of her night with Maurice, especially since she'd allowed him to sleep with her but didn't yield to his passionate gestures to do more. She had no desire to explain any of it, not now. "So, I'll see you guys tonight. Get your rest, girl, you know how the brothers like to party."

"You know I know." Dee stretched and rolled over to her side. "I'm staying right here until I have to warm up dinner for Little Aaron. He's at a movie with his dad right now."

"Sounds good. Well, I'm here." Tish drove into the parking lot of the beauty salon and parked the car. "I can't wait to see what they do with my hair. Talk to you later tonight."

"Okay, girl. See you at the ball. Bye."

The rest of the day sped by as Tish and Maurice did their own things until they headed back to her place to get ready for the evening.

She stepped out of her bedroom wearing her evening dress, flat gold sandals, and her long braided hair with purple and gold beads dangling from at least three dozen ends. She looked down the hallway and saw Maurice waiting for her dressed in his tuxedo, accented with a purple bow tie and vest.

"Wow, Tish. You're a Nubian queen. That's a fabulous look." His wide grin reminded her of what Dee had said earlier "Don't you wander too far from me tonight, either. The bruhs are gonna be all over you...just wait and see if they don't try it."

"Thanks, Maurice." She blushed at his sincere compliment. "I'm glad I'm with you. I'm sure you'll keep them at bay."

"Oh, no doubt!" He laughed and extended his arm to escort her down the stairs. "You're *my queen* tonight...and I'll let all of them know it, too."

At the Marriott Rivercenter Hotel, Maurice handed the keys to the valet, met Tish on the other side of the SUV, pulled her arm into his, and escorted her into the lobby.

"Man, this is a very beautiful hotel. The Christmas decorations are awesome." He looked around as they walked toward the escalator.

A twenty-foot Christmas tree dominated the center of the lobby decorated with children's toys, angels, red, green, gold and silver glass balls, and thousands of tiny twinkling clear lights. Tables had piles of toys, bows, and holly carefully arranged on snowflake-embroidered linen covers. The check-in desk was trimmed with bright red ribbons and bows; large poinsettia plants graced each end.

"It's my favorite hotel in the city."

The Omega Christmas Gala was in the second-floor ballroom. As they entered, they met Tom and Sable waiting to be escorted to their table by one of the Delta hostesses.

"Hi, Tom." Tish spoke first, extending her hand. "It's good seeing you."

His surprised reaction to her handshake gesture made her grin. "Hello, Tish," he said softly.

"Tom, I believe you met Maurice last night?"

"Yes, how you doing, Maurice? This is my wife, Sable. Sable, I'd like to introduce Tish and Maurice," Tom replied, obviously uncomfortable.

"*Tish*? Oh, hi," Sable responded with one eyebrow lifted and her head slightly tilted to one side. She extended her hand to Maurice. "Good to meet you, Maurice." She quickly turned to Tom, put her arm around him, and pulled him away toward their table. "You guys have a good evening," she called as they walked away.

"Thank you, you too." Tish felt like she'd been politely slapped with the handshake that hadn't happened.

"Why didn't she shake your hand?" Maurice asked with a puzzled look. "Does she have something against you?"

"I have no idea. I've never met the woman before tonight." She suddenly felt sorry for Tom. He didn't deserve such a rude, selfish, and possessive woman. *What could have attracted him to her?*

"Let's not let that spoil our evening, doll. You look fabulous; we're partying with the bruhs and the band sounds hot tonight! Let's find our table and enjoy ourselves."

"Absolutely!" She smiled broadly at her handsome, intelligent, loving escort and followed him in the opposite direction that Tish had dragged Tom.

Fifty-Three

Darkness shadows love
Beguiled by swift confusion
Enraptured voices to sing.

"What's up with you, Sable?" Tom asked as soon as they were out of hearing range from anyone.

"So that's Tish, huh?" She spoke without looking at him. "Those yella' girls kill me, trying to look black wearing braids and African garb. Why don't they just be themselves? Half white is what she is. Why can't she and Alicia Keys get that?"

He couldn't believe what his wife had just said about Tish. He felt heat steaming from his collar. "What the hell are you talking about? You don't know anything about her." He stopped walking; Sable's arm still locked in his. He looked at her as his irritation grew. "And how can you have the nerve to say that about her? Look at you—you don't wear braids *or* your hair natural. You just spent ninety dollars and four hours doing whatever it took to have your hair cut and styled to look like Princess Diana's. So what is it that you don't get?" His evening had already been ruined over some stupid mess.

She glared back at him. "Why you defending her? Is she *the Tish* you've been wanting to wake up to? Calling her name out in your sleep, walking her to her car. You still trying to take care of her, or what? Don't think I don't know."

Don't know what?

"Okay, okay, we have history. She's my friend, but I'm married to you. You know this isn't the time or place to have this discussion. Let's please find our table and quietly sit down. Then let's try even harder to have a good time this evening. I'm not going through this with you again, Sable. If you're going to make my night miserable, we can leave now and you won't ever have to worry about going to another one of these functions with me. Are we staying or are we leaving?"

"Staying. I won't say another word about it tonight, Tom. We can talk later. Besides, the band sounds really good."

Oh shit, this woman is crazy.

He shook his head as they walked to their table. He pulled the chair out for her. She smiled graciously at the other guests as she sat down.

"I'm going to get a drink, you want anything?"

"A glass of white wine will be fine," she responded, giving him a charming smile.

"K, be right back."

Tom walked briskly out of the ballroom, past the bar, exited the building, and stood alone on the River Walk. He took a deep breath to calm down. A brisk fifty degrees and the beauty of the seasonal lights twinkling from the tall cypress trees that lined the river created a much-needed, peaceful refuge. A mariachi band playing Christmas music in the distance made the moment even more serene as several couples walked by him holding hands.

He walked to the railing, placed his hands on it, and leaned facing the river.

Oh, damn, my instincts were right. Sable's been following me. I've got to do something about this situation, but not tonight. I refuse to allow her to spoil my evening. Not again.

He took a deep breath, remembering the times he and Tish had spent on the River Walk. He missed her so much. Seeing her with Maurice again looking so beautiful, being so charming and graceful made him wonder how his life had ended up the way it had—without her at his side.

It is…what it is. He spun around on his heels and returned to the ballroom.

Fifty-Four

Just for a moment
With a simple, loving look
Renewed pain and tears.

Tish made it through the buffet line and back to their table before she saw Dee and Aaron; he walked toward her ginning from ear to ear.

"Hey, Tish," Aaron said holding his hands out to her to stand up. "Dee told me you were promoted on the job to division manager! Congratulations, my sister! I'm so proud of you." He gave her a big hug.

"Oh, yeah, thanks." She'd forgotten all about her good news. "That just happened on Friday. They're not playing around either; I start in the new position first thing Monday morning."

"And I understand it comes with a substantial increase in salary."

"Yes, otherwise it wouldn't be worth the substantial increase in stress and hours!"

"I'm sure you can handle all that." He released his embrace and took her hands. "You're a very talented, special lady, Tish. They did a good thing for the company and for you. Don't let 'em forget it either!"

"Thanks for your vote of confidence, Aaron."

"No problem. You guys having a good time tonight?" He leaned over to Maurice and extended a handshake. "Man, I like that purple bow tie and vest set. That's tight."

"Thank you." Maurice stood and straightened his tuxedo jacket and touched the bow tie.

Dee gave Tish a hug. "My sister, you look as gorgeous as I thought you'd be. Queen Nerfertiti, herself, up in here."

"Oh, you're so sweet." She blushed as she hugged her friend. "That's the most regal purple velvet gown I've ever seen, Dee. Where'd you find it?"

"My hubby drove me to Austin to this fabulous evening wear store in West Lake." She smiled with pride telling her story. "He wanted me have a solid purple dress for tonight. That's the place to go, girl. They have the most beautiful gowns."

"I'll keep that in mind for next year."

"Sounds good," Aaron said, rubbing his stomach. "We're off to get out some of the delicious-smelling food before it's all gone."

"Cool, see you in a few." Tish returned to her seat as they walked away holding hands.

The band played Kenny G's "Falling in the Moonlight" and her thoughts went to Tom and the night their spirits had danced to that song. She scanned the room as couples met on the dance floor, embraced, and moved slowly to the tranquil music. She hadn't seen him since they entered the ballroom; for that she felt grateful.

For the next thirty minutes, she and Maurice talked with the other couples at their table and to each other. Then they'd danced to almost every song before they took a break to rest.

"We've come to the last hour and a half of the evening, folks," the lead singer announced as the bass player strung a solo piece. "We're going to take a break right after this next song."

He extended his arm out to a young, attractive woman who walked on the stage from behind the band. "This is one of San Antonio's newest and best local talents, Maria Munoz."

She approached the microphone wearing a little black dress and pearl necklace and earrings. Smiling shyly, she waved at the guests and then took the microphone. "I'm sure you've heard this Deborah Cox song on the radio lately; it's one of my favorites," she said with a soft, sexy voice. "Don's going to help me out and I hope you enjoy."

As the musicians began playing, it became obvious that it would be a slow tune. Maurice smiled as he reached for Tish's hand. "Your break is over…let's dance."

Without a word, she followed him to the dance floor, then stepped into his embrace and closed her eyes. As they moved slowly to the band's rendition of "We Can't Be Friends," the lyrics hit Tish's emotions so hard she felt as though daggers were being pushed into her heart. Tears formed in her eyes and as she carefully opened them, Tom stood directly in her view, looking as sad as she'd ever seen him.

With more unexpected emotions than she could handle, she pulled from Maurice's embrace. "Please, excuse me for a moment?"

"Sure. Everything alright?"

"Um-mm, be right back." She walked off the dance floor and then ran into the ladies' room once she got into the hallway. Before she could get into a stall and be alone, the tears fell.

Midori, one of her sorority sisters, dried her hands at the sink and saw Tish crying.

"Oh, my," she said. She took Tish by her arm and led her to the sofa. She sat with her quietly, handing her tissues from her purse.

"Don't ask," Tish said with a trembling, soft voice. "I can't talk about it. Please, just sit here with me for a minute. I'll be all right."

Fifty-Five

Trying to move on
is more than a small notion.
You are inside me.

"Are you sure you're okay?" Maurice asked Tish for the third time after she returned to their table. He placed his arm on the back of her chair. Taking her hand he looked into her eyes and whispered, "We can go whenever you're ready."

His kind understanding lifted her spirits and made her face beam. "Yeah, I'd like to go home now, if you really don't mind."

"Anything, anything at all for you, doll. Just keep smiling, that's all."

They gathered their things, said goodnight to the couples at their table, and left the crowded ballroom. As they rode down the escalator to the hotel lobby, Tish saw Tom and Sable slowly walking toward the door. With hands shoved deep into his pockets and his head lowered, he sauntered seemingly unaware of his wife beside him.

Sable glanced over her shoulder and met Tish's stare. She glared back and then rolled her eyes as she stepped closer to her husband and put her arm through his.

Girl, I'm not trying to get your man! Tish shook her head and took Maurice's hand as she stepped off the escalator. He placed his arm firmly around her waist as they continued toward the exit. *Please let them be gone when we get to the door.*

"Why don't you wait inside while the valet gets the car?" Maurice helped her with the gold wool wrap, then kissed her cheek. "I'll be right back."

"Thanks, I like that idea." She watched him walk away and as the hotel door opened, she saw Tom and Sable waiting patiently outside for their car. She turned away from the door and took a deep breath enjoying the beauty of the decorated lobby, once again. *This will be over in minutes.*

"Tish, you haven't spoken one word since we left the dance," Maurice said as he drove into her subdivision. "Will you please tell me what's been on your mind?"

"Oh, I've been thinking about how wonderful the weekend's been having you here. I'm so glad you were able to come and attend the galas with me." She glanced at him and smiled.

"And thank you for inviting me." He grinned. "I feel so special."

"You're an exceptional man, Maurice. And I'm the lucky one to be with you."

"I can't wait to get you home and snuggle up since this is my last night with you." His sly smile and lift of his eyebrow hinted that he planned more than a snuggle.

As he reached to open his door once they were in her garage, Tish took a deep breath and placed her hand on his arm.

"Maurice," she said softly. "Wait a minute before we go into the house. There's something I need to say."

"Sure, doll. What is it?"

"I want you to know just how much I really appreciate you coming all the way to San Antonio and spending the weekend with me. I've had a wonderful time with you." She paused. "You mean a lot to me but somehow I feel like taking our friendship to another level would be a mistake. I'm not sure why I feel that way, I just do. It's not that I'm not attracted to you, because I am, Lord knows, I really am."

"Are you saying that you don't want to make love with me, Tish?" He took her hand and held it gently. "Is that what you're trying to tell me without hurting my feelings?" He politely kissed her knuckles.

"Well, yes, that's kinda what I wanted to say." She blushed at his straightforwardness.

"Baby, no worries. I wouldn't want to do anything that you're not completely comfortable with. While I can't think of anything I'd rather do than make passionate love to you until dawn, if you're not feeling it, that's cool." He continued kissing her hand. "Will you let me sleep with you tonight? I loved holding you in my arms last night. I slept really well. Didn't you?"

"Yes, I did." She had to admit it felt good to sleep with a man, one who cared for her as Maurice seemed to. But the fear of falling in love again created that damn wall again because he could steal her heart if she'd let him. *Such a sweet man, so handsome, so perfect.* "And yes, of course, we can sleep together tonight. I…I just don't—"

"I know, you're not ready to make love, not yet." He finished her sentence. "Somehow I get the impression that you're dealing with a broken heart that's not willing to open up and let me in." He brushed the hair from her face. "Is that it, Tish?"

"Yes, I guess you could say that." She looked down at her hands resting on her lap. "But I know that I'll be letting go and moving on soon…have to. It's just that right now, I'm still hurting and until that's healed I'm on lockdown emotionally. Sorry."

She looked up and met his sad eyes. "It has nothing to do with you, really. I'm very happy that you're in my life. You're making this easier for me, even though it may not appear that way."

"My dear," he took a deep breath and continued, "whenever and wherever you need me, you can count on me to be there for you." Maurice took her hands and squeezed them. "You are a very, very special person. I believe that I came into your life for a reason and that I'll always be in your life. So, like it or not, you're stuck with me."

She smiled at his kind face. "I like it." Tish leaned over and kissed his warm, firm lips. "Can we go in, now?"

"Sure, my lady." He grinned and opened the door. "I'll be there directly to escort you into the house."

Fifty-Six

Truth hurts more sometimes
Than not knowing all the facts
Learn to live in peace.

Tom fought his emotions too, as he drove his wife's car in silence hoping Sable wouldn't talk. She'd already done enough damage to his evening; he couldn't think of anything he'd welcome from her lips for the rest of the night.

It started when they left the house to come to the gala when she refused to ride in his car. "Why take the Neon when we have a Camaro?" she'd sneered at him talking down about his car. "It's black and it's elegant…."

His car had been quite acceptable any other day, but all of a sudden, it wasn't classy enough for her. He'd bit his lip and asked her for the keys.

Tish drives a Lexus and she never put my Neon down or acted in any way uncomfortable when I picked her up to go anywhere…what a difference.

Relief washed over him as he pulled into the parking space of their apartment complex. He was more than tired; he was totally spent. Before he could get around the car, Sable had the door open and was struggling to slide out of her seat with the tight-fitting silver sequined gown and spiked high heels.

"Would you please wait and let me help you?"

"I don't need your help. I've been getting in and out of cars by myself long before you came into my life," she snapped.

"I'm sure you have..." Tom watched as she pulled herself out and closed the door. They walked in silence from the lot to their second-floor apartment.

He paid Rhonda, the teenager who lived next door, for babysitting and watched her until she entered her apartment safely. Sable barely spoke to her before she left.

Tom walked back in as Sable tossed a pillow and his grandmother's quilt on the black leather sofa. She flashed him a look of pure hatred.

"You don't have to worry about ever inviting me to go to another one of those Omega affairs. I'm not interested. In fact, I'm not the one."

"What are you talking about?" Her moods had been flopping all over the place that evening; it looked like she was ready for a fight.

"I'm tired of running into your women friends when we go out together. They seem to have no respect for the fact that you're a married man." Her voice was calm and deliberate. "And you don't appear to mind it at all."

"If I knew what you're talking about, I'd explain."

"No need." She pointed to the sofa. "I slept alone long before I met you." She turned, stomped into the bedroom, and closed the door with authority.

"Whatever, Sable." He removed his tuxedo jacket and loosened his tie.

I don't want to sleep with you tonight anyway. He stretched out on the sofa, the pillow in his arms, as memories from the evening played back in his mind. *How did I ever get myself into this mess? I'll talk to Sable first thing in the morning. I can't forget the way she treated Tish. We need to settle this if we're going to live together. And I won't be sleeping on the damn sofa again, either.*

Tom woke up early Sunday before his wife and daughter stirred. He washed up quietly in the guest bathroom and grabbed some jeans and socks from the laundry basket. While the coffee brewed he started blueberry pancakes and bacon.

"Smells good in here," Sable said as she walked into the kitchen. She sat at the kitchen table and pulled a coffee mug toward her. "Is it ready yet?"

"Just about." He flipped the bacon and turned the burner off. "Is Sheila up?"

"No, she's still asleep. Which is a good thing. We need to talk."

"Yes, we do," Tom agreed as he poured her coffee. He drained the bacon, then put a stack of pancakes on the table.

"So, tell me about Tish."

His first instinct was to tell her that Tish was really none of her business but he knew she wouldn't let it go. He also knew it was a waste of time trying to explain all of it to her.

"We had a short, romantic relationship that ended not long after you called me and told me you were pregnant." He sat at the table across from her and looked at his coffee mug. "We stopped seeing each other because I wanted my daughter to have my name and her daddy in her life. I did what I believed was right."

"So you broke up with her to marry me because of Sheila?" She sounded genuinely surprised.

"What more can I tell you? Tish was in my life and now you're my wife."

"Do you love me?"

"Sure, I love you Sable."

"But did you ever fall in love with me?"

"No, I don't think I ever have…" Tom didn't finish his sentence as he stared at the floor.

"Are you in love with Tish?"

"You know, sometimes it's best not to ask questions that you really don't want answered. That would be one of those questions. I suggest we not talk about this anymore."

He walked out of the kitchen not waiting for a reply.

Fifty-Seven

I dreamed you'd come back.
And then each day, time goes by
Alone, I remain.

Tish opened her journal and wrote:

March 15: Today, I celebrate my thirty-sixth birthday. Happy Birthday to me. Oh what joy…I can't even keep up with my journal between the kids' after-school activities and the new demands of my job.

Marcus does as little for the children that he can get by with. Lately he's only seeing them sometimes on his weekends.

I just need to settle down and review where I am and where I need to be going…especially with my love life.

Divorced from the man who appeared to be the Prince Charming of all times and turned out to be all but that. Romanced by the finest and most compassionate man around and I can't let him into my heart because I'm hopelessly in love with a married man. How dumb is that? Feel like I'm tied to him by some unknown force that keeps us running into each other…well, used to, anyway. Haven't seen him since the Omega Gala. Haven't heard his voice either.

I miss him so much. Wish he would call. Last night I dreamed of him again. It was so romantic. We made love outside at the bank of a large river under the cover of tall pine trees with stars and the moon shinning so brilliantly. Our spirits danced again as the gentle breeze perfumed with honeysuckle cooled our bodies burning with passion. It felt so real; but when I woke up, I had another empty roll over that brought me back to the cold cruel world. I wonder why Tom ever entered my life since he wasn't the one to stay?

She closed the book and dropped it into the top drawer of the nightstand. As she reached to turn off the lamp by her bed, the phone rang.

"Hello?"

"Hey there, doll." Maurice's soft voice seemed even more deep and sexy. "Happy Birthday."

"Wow, thanks." She beamed with excitement that he'd remembered. "You're so thoughtful. I'm sitting here on my bed thinking about you, too. How special is that?"

"I think that it's wonderful that you're thinking about me anywhere near your bed!" He laughed. "But of course there's nothing I can do about that from here but talk to you."

"At least we can talk." Tish knew she'd make passionate love with Maurice if he'd appear in the flesh at that very moment. He sounded better to her than ever before.

Oh, God, that's just my horniness talking.

"I must admit that I remembered this evening and a day too late to have flowers delivered on time. Look for them to arrive at work tomorrow." He paused briefly. "I've missed you, Tish. I'd hoped that you'd come out this way to see me by now."

"You are the sweetest man." She sighed and pulled the bed pillow into her arms. "Thank you for the flowers, you're so thoughtful."

"And I'm inviting you to come to New Orleans for the Jazz Festival as my guest. You can stay right here, in my new house. It's almost furnished. There's plenty of room for the two of us."

"Oh, that's right. It's about that time of the year again." She blushed at the thought of going back to New Orleans and spending time alone with Maurice in his home.

"The best time to come is the first weekend in May. Just say you'll come and I'll purchase your tickets. I want to see you so much."

"That's so nice of you. I'd love that, but I need to check my calendar in the morning and see if I have any commitments that weekend. And of course I need to make arrangements for the children in case their father doesn't show for them."

"Great. Please let me know how things work out. I'll get your tickets as soon as I hear back from you."

She wasn't comfortable about him buying her ticket in case she changed her mind at the last minute. "Thanks, Maurice, but you don't have to do that. I have a flight credit for a trip I didn't take at Christmas and I need to use it soon."

"I hear you. But do come. We'll have fun."

"I'll plan on it. Thanks for the invite."

"I know it's late, so get some sleep and we'll talk later this week, okay doll?"

"Definitely."

Tish fell asleep and dreamed she and Tom were walking along the Mississippi River holding hands. They silently walked into a field and as the sun set, they made love in the middle of mature cotton plants.

Fifty-Eight

Thoughts are mute, lifeless
Through breath expelled into life...
Words spoken are born.

The day after Tish's birthday, Tom arrived at his Fort Sam office an hour before anyone else arrived. He'd been awake since four o'clock after a restless night. He'd dreamed of seeing Tish crying and covering her face with a red veil as he silently walked past her and into Sable's arms. He remembered hearing Tish whispering, "Why have you done this to me again?" He woke up in a sweat and couldn't go back to sleep.

He reached for a spiral notebook he kept locked in the middle desk drawer. He wrote a note describing the dream as he'd done on a number of other occasions. There were at least ten entries about dreams of Tish.

I wonder what this one means? What did I ever do to her before?

Then he remembered the night of the Omega Gala; he'd seen and felt her pain when the band played "*We can't be friends... 'cause I'm still in love with you.*" He'd never seen her look so sad; it hurt him deeply.

Not picking up the phone to call her on her birthday had been the hardest thing he'd ever talked himself into doing. He tried to convince himself that time and space would help them let go and move on; that wasn't going to happen if he kept popping up in her life.

As Tom walked toward the door to start the coffee in the office break room, his phone rang. *Who's calling me at six-thirty*?

"Good morning, Sergeant Manning."

"Oh, so you went to work?" Sable's sleepy voice sounded irritated.

"Where did you think I'd be?" He sat back at his desk, picked up his pen and started doodling on a note pad.

"How would I know? You didn't bother speaking to me when you got up or when you left." She rolled over in the bed and pushed his pillow to the floor.

"When I get up Monday through Friday, I come to work, Sable. Nothing's changed about that. You were asleep, it was very early, and I didn't want to wake you just because I couldn't sleep. I was trying to be thoughtful."

"Know what?"

"What?"

"I think you went to work early so you could call Tish."

"I haven't called her and don't plan to either."

"Right. You're still in love with her and you're not going to be happy until you're with her. That's what I really think."

"So…what're you saying?"

"I just said it," she replied flatly. "Mull that over and have a nice day."

Fifty-Nine

An April shower
rains tears for the love I miss
through the bright sunshine

Tish served up another bowl of some of the best gumbo in San Antonio for a hungry customer at Miz Monique's booth, The Krazy Kajun, during the "A Taste of New Orleans" celebration. Thousands of people of all ages and nationalities walked by, savoring the delicious tidbits from two-dozen food vendors specializing in Creole and Cajun cuisine. As the brass band straight from New Orleans played "O Parka Ray," hundreds of people danced behind them following their lead around the park in the early evening sun, bouncing brightly colored umbrellas and waving handkerchiefs in the air.

When the last of the "Second Line" participants passed her, Tish glanced up. Her eyes focused on the booth directly across the walkway where the Omegas were handing out pamphlets about the Red Cross Blood Drive they sponsored. She realized that she'd almost made it through her three-hour commitment in the booth without running into Tom.

Now with only thirty minutes left before she could leave quietly and get lost in the crowd, she saw him check in with his brothers, and then he turned and looked directly at her.

Her heart pounded as she dropped her eyes and adjusted her apron after seeing him walk toward her. His purple shorts and gold T-shirt with the Greek letters of his fraternity in royal purple boldly displayed across his firm chest made him look very appealing, all the way down his muscular legs to his brown leather sandals.

"Hi, Tish. Long time no see. How you been?"

"Oh, just fine, Tom, how about you?" She looked up and saw him smiling.

"Doing okay. I like your haircut. What do they call that, a pageboy?"

"Thanks. I guess you could call it a long pageboy cut. It's easier to take care of when it's shorter." She pulled her hair back and fastened a hair clip making a ponytail. "And I can still get it out of my way when I want to."

He gave her a boyish grin. "Would you like to donate some blood for a good cause?"

"No, I don't think so." She struggled to keep her cheeks from blushing. "It's good seeing you."

"Yes, I do know what you mean." He let his eyes move from the top of her head down as far as he could see. "That apron looks good on you. But all work and no fun isn't what Fiesta is all about, you know. When does your shift end? I'd like to talk."

"At six o'clock. Then I plan to go down to the end of this aisle and get some of that fried fish and a roasted corn. I'm ready to pig out." She licked her lips. "See you at six if you'd care to join me."

"Count on it." He winked at her then turned and walked back to the Omega booth.

A new wave of people arrived in Tish's booth. She worked nonstop filling bowl after bowl of gumbo and rice until six o'clock came with the mellow sounds of Richard Garcia's jazzy saxophone charming her from center stage.

She looked up and saw Tom walking back to her booth with a fried fish in one hand and two roasted ears of corn in the other.

"I think I have enough food here to share, that way you don't have to wait in line; it's gotten pretty long for the fish," he said flashing her a broad smile.

"You're so thoughtful." She couldn't help but grin. "Thanks, Tom." She removed the apron and handed it to her replacement.

They walked to the back of the park and sat on a large limestone boulder where they could hear the live jazz performed from the stage and not be caught up in the crowd.

"So you're doing okay, huh Tish? That's great." He glanced over at her. "You still seeing Maurice? That's his name, right?"

"Yes, that's his name and no, I haven't seen him since December," Tish replied, softly. "We talk once in a while," she answered before biting into her corn.

"Oh, I thought Maurice was "in there" so to speak. You looked so gorgeous at the balls I thought you were trying to hook a brother." He grimaced. "Ooo, that didn't come out right…not that you aren't gorgeous all the time." He took in a mouthful of fish and bread.

"Thanks, but I wasn't trying to hook *a brother*. I just wanted to look nice."

"Well, you sure had me looking. But you've always had my eyes." He wiped his mouth. "Tish, I've really missed talking to you."

"I know that feeling. So how are things with you and Sable?"

"Not great. She told me I talk in my sleep; apparently I say your name. She's still mad at me about that. Something I have no control over—imagine that?"

"Really? Imagine that," she replied, giggling as she elbowed him lightly in the side.

"You think that's funny, huh?"

"Yeah, a little. I'm just picturing it in my mind, that's all," Tish answered still laughing.

"I guess I miss having you in my life more than I want to admit. Do you think we'll ever have a second chance, Tish?" he asked somberly as he looked directly into her eyes.

"Wow, I didn't expect that question. I guess that's something time will have to tell. Right now you have your life with Sable and your daughter. That has nothing to do with me. I'm sorry that somehow I'm in your subconscious and it's spilling out at night messing up your relationship with your wife. But again, I can't do anything about that, now can I?"

"No, I guess you can't," Tom answered softly.

They sat quietly as they listened to the music and ate their food. When there were no crumbs left, he stood and took the food containers to the trashcan.

When he returned she got ready to leave. "It's been nice chatting with you. You look great." She smiled at his gorgeous and inviting eyes. "Thanks for dinner. Take care of yourself and maybe I'll see you again at the Zulu's Juneteenth picnic."

"Can I walk you to your car? You know, it's getting dark out there," he replied with a shy grin.

"It's not dark at all." She placed her hand gently on his arm. "I'll be okay. Goodnight, Tom."

He watched her walk away and cautiously started to follow her, slowing when she did. He stopped as she picked up a to-go bag from the Naw'lings Creole Kitchen booth and then went across the walkway to the Alpha's booth and paid for one of their famous sweet potato pies.

Before she walked out the gate, she looked back to where she'd left Tom. She scanned the area until she saw him. He looked directly at her from the middle of the walkway, with his hands in his pockets. She took a deep breath and waved before she turned and continued to walk toward the parking lot.

It took every fiber in her body to keep her from turning around and going right back to him.

Sixty

In your arms I melt
As you move into my heart.
Will you stay this time?

"Next weekend is the Juneteenth picnic in Comanche Park. Are you going?" Dee asked Tish as they stepped off the elevator into the lobby of their office building and headed toward the exit.

"I plan to." She pulled the purse strap onto her shoulder and opened the door allowing the arid, nearly one hundred-degree temperature slap her in the face.

"You know, they missed teaching us in American history that slavery didn't end in Texas until two years after the Emancipation Proclamation. June nineteenth should be the day we observe the abolishment of slavery all over the United States because that's when everyone finally became free."

"I agree." Dee removed her baby blue jacket, revealing a cream, sleeveless cotton shell that matched the linen skirt and dressy sandals. "We call it the Texas emancipation day and celebrate it with family barbecues, church events, and community gatherings. Every year the celebrations get bigger—even some concerts. I heard they celebrate Juneteenth in Detroit, now."

Tish removed her sunshades from the red leather designer purse and put them on. "I think that's wonderful. Maybe it'll become a national holiday sometime during our life. Who knows?"

"Well, if that's ever going to happen, we'd better start the lobbying process now!" Dee sighed and pointed toward the Rio Rio Cantina. "Feel like Mexican today?"

"Girl, I can do Mexican any day."

"Good. Looks like we got here before the crowd, too," Dee said as they walked into the restaurant and were seated inside where the air conditioned room felt more inviting than the patio by the river.

"Did I tell you that I saw Tom at 'The Taste?'"

"No, you didn't. You haven't said one word about him in months. I thought you'd just stopped talking to him altogether."

"Yeah, that had been the case until we sorta' ran into each other. We talked for a few minutes before I left."

"So what did he have to say? Anything worth repeating?"

Tish bit her bottom lip before responding. "He asked me if I thought we'd ever get a second chance."

"And did you remind him that he's a married man?"

"Of course I did." Her voice was soft and distant.

"So what, pray tell, made him ask that question?"

"Dee, he's been dreaming about me and apparently calling out my name in his sleep…which is upsetting Sable."

"Oh, I bet she's pissed!"

Dee's eager laugh surprised Tish. "I see you think it's funny, too." She smiled as she remembered how she'd giggled when Tom told her about it.

"But Dee, here's the thing. I've never stopped dreaming about Tom either. Last night's dream was rather disturbing." She folded her arms, placed them on the table, and leaned forward. "I dreamed I was dying. Tom sat on the bed beside me and held me in his arms, in tears. He kept repeating, 'You can't leave me, not now.' I looked at him and his face changed to look like an ancient Egyptian, you know with the dark eyeliner and shaved head."

"Okay, here we go again with the Egyptian dreams. Girl, I think you're watching way to much TV."

"I watch very little TV. You know I don't have time for that." She sat back reluctant to continue sharing the details of her dream.

"I'm sorry. I shouldn't have said that." Dee reached for Tish's hand and squeezed it briefly. "So how do you know you were dying?"

"Because I died. But before I did, I told him, 'I will come back to you. Find me and let's start this love story over again."

Dee straightened up, put her elbow on the table, and cupped her chin in the palm of her hand. "Did he get a chance to say something back before you died?"

"Yes, he said, 'I just want to hold you again. Please let me find you and hold you again.'"

"How would he find you in another life? I don't get it."

"This is all new to me, too you know." Tish paused and looked out the window as a riverboat pass the restaurant. "In my dream, I told him we'd know each other by our hands, our eyes, and how we touch each other."

"What about your hands?"

"Girl, I don't know. That's all that was said about the hands." She picked up the menu and hoped to change the subject. "I think we should order so we can eat and get back to work."

"You're going to call him today, aren't you?" Dee asked.

"I believe so." She placed the menu on the table and tapped it with the tips of her fingers. "I can't stop thinking about Tom. So I guess it's time for us to talk. Don't know why; just know I'm feeling that way."

"Then I say, go with your feelings, my dear." Dee said. "Girlfriend, you know I got cha' back, right?"

"Yes, Dee. I do know that. Now let's eat so we can get back to the office. I've got an appointment right after lunch."

Before her meeting, Tish closed the office door and just as she reached for the phone, it rang.

"LaTisha Edwards."

"Tish, this is Mom." Her tone seemed calm with a touch of sadness Tish hadn't heard before. "How are you?"

"Hi, Mom. I'm doing okay. How about you?" She reached for a pen to take notes. Her mother rarely called unless something important had happened.

"Honey, I'm fine. I've got some very sad news, though." Her mother was never much for chitchat.

"What is it, Mom?" She began to feel a somewhat uncomfortable. She could hear the wind blowing in the background, which meant her mother had called from her cell phone. Tish imagined she was somewhere sitting under an umbrella either by a pool or the beach, sipping her favorite vodka and orange juice.

"It's your father. He passed in his sleep last night." Tish heard her take a deep breath. "I got a call from his wife this afternoon. The funeral service will be this Saturday in Washington, D.C."

"Oh, no-o-o-o," she replied almost in a whisper.

"Of course I don't plan to be there. I guess she wanted to make sure you know about it. So I have passed it on to you."

"Do you know what happened?"

"He had a stroke," Mrs. Edwards replied flatly.

"Is that all you know? Is that all you can tell me?"

"Well, Tish, one good stroke and it's all over." Her tone resonated even and direct. "What more do you want me to say?"

"Mom, I guess that's all you can say." She wished her mother would show some emotion just once. "I'll try to get out there as soon as possible. You sure you don't want to go to the funeral? I'll come by and get you. We can go together if that would make you feel more comfortable."

"No, baby. He was your daddy," she said, then took a breath. "We'd only had a very brief affair. I really don't have a place with his family and it would make his wife feel uncomfortable if I showed up there, I'm sure. So I'll save everyone some additional grief and stay right here. You do what you need to do and don't worry about me. I'll be just fine."

"Okay, Mom. I understand. Thanks for calling me. I love you."

"I love you too, Tish."

She placed the phone down gently and took a deep breath.

This can't be happening. I just got to know my father fifteen years ago and all I get is fifteen years. This just isn't fair. She shook her head as tears filled her closed eyes and ran down her face.

Someone knocked on the door. "Come in," she said just above a whisper, blotting her cheeks dry with a tissue.

Tom walked in dressed in his full military uniform and closed the door behind him. "Hi," he said, smiling at the shocked look on her face.

"Hi," she responded, surprised at his unannounced visit. She stared with her mouth open as she realized that she'd not seen him in full greens since his wedding.

Damn, this man is wearing that uniform.

She stood and instinctively walked toward him. He met her and gently pulled her into his arms and gave her a hug. Her strength to be objective began to melt away as she took a deep breath and stepped back.

"I've been missing you, girl. How's my Delta Queen?" He looked at her face as she wiped away the tears. "Are you crying?"

"Yes, you caught me at a really bad moment." She walked back to her chair behind the desk. "My mother just called to tell me that my father died in his sleep last night. His funeral is on Saturday in D.C."

"I'm so sorry, Tish. You are going, right?" He sat in the chair facing her desk.

"Yes, of course. I haven't had a chance to look at flights, make arrangements for the kids or even ask for a couple of days off or anything, yet." She sat back in her chair and crossed her legs. "I'd just put the phone down from talking with her when you knocked."

Tom placed one hand on his chin and shook his head. "Once again I'm amazed at how we seem to be connected. I woke up thinking that I couldn't leave town today without seeing you and letting you know I'd be gone for two weeks. I wanted to see you and tell you in person. It seemed so important at the time and I couldn't figure out why. Now I know."

"Okay, so tell me. What's going on?"

"I'm leaving today for Washington, D.C. I have a project to work on at the Pentagon. I'll be there over the weekend; if you need me to help you through this, please call. You have my cell number. I'll be staying at the Crystal City Marriott on Jefferson Davis Highway. I'd like some time to talk, anyway."

He shifted in the chair and straightened his tie. "There are some things I want to say to you that I should've said long before now. Tish, I've missed you so much. You have no idea."

She looked at him for a couple seconds before responding. "Just before my mother called, I'd reached for the phone to call you. I really need to talk to you, too. I wanted to hear your voice and to know you were okay." She paused and smiled at him. "I had a dream this morning that I wanted to share with you."

"You still having dreams, too?"

"Yes, and I wanted to tell you about it." She leaned forward placing her elbows on the desk. "But then, I got this awful call and when my life takes a dreaded turn, just like magic you appear when I need my best friend the most."

He stood and walked around the desk, took her hands, and pulled her to her feet. Tom kissed the backs of her hands and then wrapped his arms around her, pulling her close.

She breathed in deeply and closed her eyes. "There's something very special about us, Tom. And no matter what, I love you for it. Yes, I said it. I love you. I've always loved you. Thank you for being in my life."

"Tish…I…I…know. And I'm so blessed to have you in my life, too." He pulled back and looked at her with a shy grin. "I've got to get to the airport. Please call me when you get to D.C."

"I will. Have a safe trip and thank you for coming by."

He kissed her forehead before releasing his embrace. "I'm really sorry about your father. I want you to tell me all about him this weekend, okay? And I want to know about that dream, too."

"Sure, but there isn't much I can tell you about my father, so that won't take too long." She gazed into his eyes, wishing he didn't have to leave. "Be careful out there and take care of you for me, okay?"

Tom walked toward the door. "Always." He opened the door and winked at her. "Talk to you soon. Be strong."

Sixty-One

Consider our fate,
remember our pledge of love
for eternity.

Tish sat quietly as Dee drove past the mature palm trees and lush tropical landscapes into the San Antonio International Airport passenger drop-off area. "Cheer up, my friend. It's going to be okay."

"I know Dee. It's just that no matter what we know about life and death, nothing ever really prepares us for losing a parent." She stared straight ahead wishing this had been a bad dream and she'd wake up any minute. "My daddy was a really nice man. I wish I'd been raised by him so I could've known him all my life."

"So how long did you know your father?"

"I met him while I was in college. Look, it's a really long story. Maybe I'll tell you all about it one day. Right now, I've got to be a big girl and deal with this."

"And I know you will, girl. Remember, you are a strong woman."

"Thanks for the ride to the airport in your brand new Escalade. Man, that account with HEB really paid off, huh?" Tish forced a smile as she looked up at the sunroof and slowly stroked the soft taupe leather seat. "Who'd guess that an account with a grocery company would equal Cadillac money?"

"You know? And all my credit card debt is gone now, too. That's the only way I'd ever try to afford something as luxurious as this car." She ran her hands around the steering wheel. "I just love it!"

"It suits you and you deserve it. I'm happy that you treated yourself and that I get to ride with you in such style. You just go, girl! I'm so proud!"

"Well, it's time to *go girl*, yourself." Dee chuckled. "We don't want you to miss that plane. Don't worry about the kids. Aaron will pick them up from school today and we've got the whole weekend planned with nothing but fun things to do. Especially Saturday when we have Aaron's graduation family barbecue celebration. I'm so sorry you'll miss it."

"Oh, I'm sure it'll be off the hook and the kids will have a great weekend. I'm so glad he finished his degree and you're taking the weekend to party. I wish I could be there, too." She unbuckled the seatbelt. "You guys are such wonderful friends, Dee. I don't know what I'd do without you in my life." A new tear formed in the corner of her eye.

"Please don't start the crying thing again. You've got to get on that plane and I've got to get to work." Dee turned off the engine and also unbuckled her seatbelt.

"Okay, I'll be fine. I'll call you from the hotel and let you know when I'm all checked in. I'm staying at the Marriott in Crystal City, Virginia." Tish gathered her purse and computer bag, and met Dee at the trunk, removed her suitcase, and placed it on the sidewalk. "Oh, did I tell you that Tom will be in D.C. this weekend, too? He's picking me up from the airport."

"No, you didn't mention it." Dee arched her eyebrows. "Interesting."

"It's merely a coincidence, Dee. Nothing more." She gave her friend a hug and picked up the suitcase. "I'll call you later. Thanks, again."

"Have a safe trip, Tish. Talk to you later today!"

Tish checked her bag with the Continental Airline curbside porter and proceeded to the security screening. The line was unusually short and she completed the process in less than five minutes. Just as she finished, her cell phone rang.

"Hello?" Her voice lifted with a surprised tone when she realized the number on the caller ID belonged to Maurice. She continued to walk toward the gate.

"Hey, doll. How are you this lovely day?"

"Oh, I'm doing good. How about you?"

"Never better." He cleared his voice. "Look, there's something I need to ask you. Got a minute?"

"Sure." She sat at a closed gate with no passengers sitting or standing around.

"See, it's like this. One of the ladies I dated in grad school has invited me to go with her on a cruise in a couple months. She's an expert bridge player and will be giving lessons onboard. She can take a guest with her for free." He paused and took a deep breath. "She's not dating anyone seriously right now and we've always gotten along, well…and …I've never been on a cruise and—"

"Maurice, what's the question?"

"I'm kinda' going on, huh?" He chuckled, nervously. "Okay, here's the question, well maybe two. Is there any future for you and me? I want to know if I say no to her, will I be holding out for you and find that you're not there for me? There, I said it."

"Wow, I can't say for sure right now." Taken aback with his news she dropped her purse to the floor and sat back in the chair.

"You know how I feel about you, Tish. I've been waiting for you to feel something special for me, too. But it seems that you've been avoiding me lately." He paused. "You're the woman I want. But how long do I wait?"

"I can't answer that for you either. But I think that this sounds like a wonderful opportunity to go on a cruise with someone you obviously like." She sighed as she remembered looking into his gorgeous eyes and falling asleep on his chest. She'd always felt comfortable with him and could imagine that he'd be a great travel companion.

"So are you saying that you don't have a problem with me going and being with her?"

"How can I have a problem with it, Maurice? We aren't committed to each other." Tish realized that this moment would bring an end to them taking their relationship to another level. Unsure she wanted to let him go completely, she added, "But if it doesn't go as well as you'd like, call me when you get back, okay?"

"Yeah, Tish, I'll do that."

The gate announcement chimed in loud and clear.

"Where are you? At the airport?"

"Yes. I'm on my way to D.C. for the weekend." She picked up her purse and stood. "My father passed and his funeral is tomorrow." She slowly walked toward her gate.

"Oh, doll. I'm so sorry. I wish you'd told me that before I went on about this cruise thing. That could've waited."

"Hey, no problem. You had it on your mind and needed to say what you said. I understand."

"I'll let you go. If you need anything, anything at all, let me know, will you?"

"Sure, Maurice. I will. Thanks." She arrived at her gate just as the attendant called for her seating group. "Look, I gotta go. Thanks for calling and have a marvelous time on the cruise."

"Will do. You take care of yourself and travel safe now, ya' hear?"

"Okay. Check you later."

She felt more forlorn than ever as she turned off her cell phone. She handed her boarding pass to the gate attendant and wiped a tear from her cheek before boarding.

She found her seat and settled her head against the window; she was asleep before the plane took off.

"Welcome to the Reagan National Airport." The flight attendant's abrupt announcement awakened Tish from a deep sleep. "The local time is 12:50 p.m. and it's a sunny 82 degrees."

She stretched and opened the window shade as the sixty-passenger jet rolled down the runway slowing its approach toward the gate. As she peered out at the bustling activity of airplanes of all sizes moving to and from gates, people driving trucks and luggage trans moving in all directions going about their work, she took a deep breath and whispered a brief prayer.

"Lord, thank you for the ability to make this trip and for our safe arrival. Please be with me when I meet my brother, stepmother, and others at this family gathering tomorrow. Give me strength as I come face to face with the harsh memories of my past. Give me wisdom, patience, and grace as I search for the proper words. Thank you for seeing to it that Tom would be here. Thank you for not allowing me to go through this alone. Amen."

Tish gathered her purse and computer bag and followed the other passengers out of the plane. At the first ladies' room she spotted, she dashed in and freshened up before meeting Tom. Her anticipation heightened in the moments it took for her to enter the public area and search for signage that would direct her to baggage pickup.

She stopped suddenly when Tom appeared wearing his green Army uniform minus the tie and jacket.

With a broad smile and opened arms, he walked toward her. "Hey, there." He gave her a strong hug.

"Hey, Tom," she whispered, allowing her whole body to press against him, absorbing his energy she needed so badly. "Thanks for meeting me."

"My pleasure." He released her, placed his arm around her shoulder, and pulled her close to his side. He pointed to the right. "Baggage claim is this way."

As they walked Tish felt safe and welcome. She smiled at his silent glance at her realizing just how much she adored his greeting and how much she wanted to be close to him.

"I really appreciate you being here, Tom. This is a very difficult trip for me."

"I'm glad I'm here too." He kissed her forehead. "You hungry? I am. Let's go have some lunch." He grabbed her suitcase from the luggage belt.

"Sounds good. You know they only feed you peanuts on these flights and I slept through that serving." She felt him take her hand as they walked out of the airport. "So if you have time to eat with me, then that'll be great."

"I've made time to have a quick lunch with you, Tish." He smiled and squeezed her hand. "After we eat, I'll take you to the hotel. You can check in and get some rest. I'll be back after work, around five-thirty. If you want, we can get together and talk over dinner unless you have plans to be with the family."

"I'll call Mrs. Shaw, my father's widow, and see what I should do this evening, if anything, with the family. I may just go to the funeral tomorrow." Softly, she finished speaking her thoughts. "It'll probably be the best thing for all of us if that's all I do."

"Why do you say that?"

"It's a long story. I'll tell you about it when we have time and you're not in a rush to get back to work."

"Okay, sounds good." He pointed to a red Mustang rental car. "There's our weekend ride, my dear."

Tom drove through busy traffic exiting the airport. "The hotel is only five minutes from here. There's a sandwich shop on the corner across the street from the Marriott. The food's pretty good."

"That'll do just fine."

He parked in the hotel parking lot and they crossed the street and entered Fin & Filet Café. They ate fried fish sandwiches, onion rings, and coleslaw.

"That had to be the fastest fast food in the country," Tish teased Tom as they entered the hotel. "The flounder must have just been pulled out of the oil when we walked in the door. It was so good."

"We're right on the Atlantic Ocean pretty much. The fish here is fresh every day." Tom stopped and pointed to a lounge chair in the hotel lobby. "I'm going to park myself here while you check in. Then I have to hurry back to work."

"Okay, I'll be right back." At the registration counter she found out her room wasn't ready. Frustrated, she rejoined Tom. "I can't believe I can't check in. I told them when I made the reservation that I had an early arrival. Now they're saying my room won't be ready until about four."

"That's not a problem, Tish. You can relax in my room until yours is ready."

"You sure that's okay?"

"Why not? It's my room. I have to go to work anyway. By the time I get back, you'll be moved into your room, right?"

"Sure, and I can set up my laptop and finish a marketing plan or something," she said as they walked toward the elevator.

"Or you can rest. You've had a long day and you have an emotional, potentially stressful day ahead," he replied as the entered the elevator.

"Yeah, you're probably right," she answered as they walked into his room.

He placed her suitcase on one of the beds and turned to her. "Get some sleep. I'll put the *Do not Disturb* sign on the door." He kissed her forehead and left.

Tish completely undressed. Instead of moving the suitcase from the bed that hadn't been disturbed, she sat on the still unmade bed. Tom had slept in this one and she wanted to be next to his sheets.

Slowly, she slid into the bed and pulled the covers over her naked body; his scent was all around her. She thought about all that she'd been through with him, and she realized how much she'd missed him. Losing him to Sable made her cry. She wanted Tom back; she wanted him all to herself.

She rolled over on her side, hugged his pillow, and fell asleep. She dreamed of watching Tom and she as they made passionate love on a royal purple rug alongside a huge river. She saw the stars twinkle and glitter from one side of the horizon all the way to the other with brightness she'd never seen before.

Suddenly, she heard them moan with joy and she saw their "spirit dance." Tears flowed down her cheek making a wide wet spot on the pillow against her face. She felt the urge to be a part of what was transpiring, not just an observer. She whispered to Tom, *"I will love you for eternity. I will come back for you. Please find me and let's continue our life story together forever."*

Just as Tom began to respond to her in the dream, the hotel door opened. "I'm sorry if I woke you," he whispered as he walked slowly toward the bed. "I didn't expect you to be here."

"I guess I was more worn out than I thought." She wiped the tears from her face. "I'd planned to take a short nap and then move into my room by now."

"Not a problem, but you look as surprised as Goldilocks when the bears found her sleeping in Big Bear's bed. There's no Mama Bear here, though," he said as he sat next to her. "Hey, have you been crying? Are you okay?"

"Yeah, I'm all right."

He gazed at her for a moment and then said quietly, "I want you Tish. I really want you."

"Do I have to remind you that you're a married man?" Her heart began to race. "And you're not married to me. It wouldn't be right and you know it."

She kept the covers pulled up to her chin. "I'm so sorry to still be here and to put you in this compromising situation. Believe me, I hadn't intended for this to happen. Let me just get dressed and I'll get out of here."

"Okay, Tish, but first can you tell me that you don't want me? Can you tell me that when you were crying in your sleep, you weren't dreaming about us?"

He reached for her hand and kissed her knuckles. "Can you honestly tell me that you aren't in love with me? If you can tell me all this, I'll let you get dressed right now and I won't even look."

Her heart pounded and she felt her body heat up. She hadn't expected any of this, especially not now. She took a deep breath and tried to calm her wild emotions. "I can't tell you that I don't want you. I can tell you that I can't have you because you're not available to me. I can't tell you that I'm not in love with you, because I am and I have been for a long time."

She paused, hesitating before putting all her feelings out in the open in fear that he'd leave her hanging again. "I'm not sure how you feel about me because you haven't told me. And yes, I was crying in my sleep because I was dreaming about watching us make love under the stars by a river. I cried because it was just a dream; I wanted for it to be real. It was beautiful."

"Interesting. Last night I had a similar dream. We were making love outside on a beautiful purple rug on the bank of a river. I'd climbed a cypress tree and watched us as we left our bodies and floated on air right in front of me." He leaned over and kissed her lips. "And yes, it was a beautiful thing to see."

"The stars and moon were so bright—"

"Yes, we were alone and the night air was still. I heard you say, *'Please find me and continue loving me forever,'* or something like that."

"Oh, Tom! That's exactly what I dreamed. How could you know that?" She sat up in the bed holding the sheet against her body. "I'd just gotten to that part when you opened the door. I didn't hear what you said back to me."

"Well, in my dream I replied, *'I will look for you until I find you. Help me know who you are. My love for you has no end. You will be near my side forever and ever.'*"

He moved the hair from her face and smoothed it back against her shoulder. He touched her chin. "Damn, Tish, what is this? I need to know what this is all about."

"I don't know, but I sure would like to know how two people can have the same dreams."

"I can't help you with that." He reached for her hand and squeezed it gently. "But I can tell you that I love you. I can't get you out of my mind no matter what I do. I believe that my marriage was right as far as my daughter goes, but not what my heart wants." He kissed her hand. "I love you, Tish. Sometimes it feels like I loved you even before we met. I know that sounds weird, but how weird is it that we're having the same dreams?"

"I say it's pretty damn weird, Tom. I've had so many dreams about you that I've been writing them down. Once I dreamed that I had your son and I handed him to you wrapped in a golden blanket. I guess that dream was out of frustration knowing that Sable, not me, gave you a child."

"I had that one too. In the dream you called me Teti. You said, '*It's your son, Teti. I have given you a son.*' You looked like an Egyptian. I wrote that dream down too. Maybe we can compare notes one day. We've got to find out what this all means."

They sat quietly. She felt safe and cherished as Tom looked lovingly into her eyes and stroked the back of her hands with his thumbs. In that moment she decided that she could not let him go, not ever again. She took a deep breath and lifted her arms allowing the sheet to fall revealing her bare breasts.

"Be it right or wrong, Tom, you're my man and you've been my man all along."

"I believe that's the God's honest truth, Tish."

"All I ever needed to do was open up to you and let you all the way into me." She lifted one hand a stroked his face. "I'm no longer afraid of what might come of our relationship."

"It seems we have no choice; whatever is happening is something neither of us can control." He leaned toward her and lightly kissed her lips. "I adore you and want you in my life every day, Tish."

"I want that, too," she whispered.

"Look, it's almost six p.m." He had a pleading look in his eyes as he caressed her neck. "Are you going to keep your room reservation…or stay with me?"

"Come here." As tears fell down her checks she pulled Tom into her arms. "I want you back, Tom. I need you."

"I need you, too." He gently held her against his chest and ran his fingers through the soft, curly hair and stroked her back. "You," he whispered in her ear, "are more than welcome to stay right here, you know…"

She took a deep slow breath. "Hand me the phone."

Sixty-Two

I open myself
and pour out all my old pain,
protect me with love.

Tom held Tish's hand as they entered the Marriott's CC Bistro Restaurant for a late dinner. He asked the hostess for a table for two, then admired the dark red walls and very contemporary décor of the dining room. He hoped they'd be as impressed with the food as he was by the romantic setting with flickering candles and freshly cut flowers on every table.

The hostess, a blonde woman in her mid forties, adjusted her black necktie, and unbuttoned the top of the white long-sleeved shirt in anticipation of her shift ending. She picked up two menus from the neat stack on the table behind her. With a half-smile she led them to a window table.

Tom pulled the chair out for Tish and as she slid into her seat, he inhaled the fresh scent of her body. He closed his eyes briefly as a quick memory of the shower they'd just shared together crossed his mind. He leaned down and kissed the top of her head. The fragrance of her hair reminded him of honeysuckle, freshly rinsed from a summer rain.

"This is lovely," Tish said to the hostess. "Thank you."

"No problem, ma'am. Your waitress is Sheryl and she'll be with you in a moment. Enjoy your dinner." She placed the menus on the table and walked back to her post at the door.

Tom peeked over the top of the menu. "I'm starving, Ms. Edwards. You really made me work up an appetite."

"Mr. Manning, it has been more than nine hours since we had lunch, you know." She smiled gently and nodded her head. "I could eat a big steak about right now, and not even feel guilty about it."

"In that case, order one and anything else you'd like. I don't want you to be hungry—ever." He lowered the menu and took a deep breath, fighting the urge to tell her that he never wanted to leave her side again.

He felt a chill crawl down his back when she looked up from reading the dinner selections and met his eyes. He remembered how wonderful she'd felt when their naked bodies met in a familiar love lock in his bed.

"I will. And a baked potato with everything and some broccoli." She placed the menu on the table and sat back in her chair. "That ought to bring my energy back, you think?"

"I sure hope it does 'cause, well, that was the best lovemaking I've had in a very long time, Tish." He reached for her hand. "Baby, I hope you're okay with what just happened. It seemed so natural."

"Yes, it did." She placed her hand in his and as they rested on the table, she gently stroked the back of his wrist with her thumb. She dropped her eyes and turned her head to one side. "But, Tom, you're the one who's married. How do you go back to Sable after what just happened?"

"Maybe I won't."

"What?"

"Good evening," Sheryl suddenly appeared with pen and an order pad. "May I take your order?"

"Yes, you may," Tom told the young, attractive Asian woman, dressed just like the hostess. He gave her a broad smile and she returned a grin that revealed braces on her almost perfectly straight teeth.

"But first, let me do this." Tom slid the wedding band off his finger and dropped it in his shirt pocket. "And let me amend what I just said. I meant to say I don't."

Sheryl blinked as she jerked her head toward Tish. She stepped back as though expecting a fight. "Oooo, my," she whispered.

Tish giggled at the young woman's reaction. "It's not what you think. This is a good thing, trust me."

"If you say so. I wish I could stay for the rest of this conversation, but I need to get your order in before the kitchen closes."

"Great. We'll both have the eight-ounce ribeye, medium well, baked potato with everything and steamed broccoli. For dessert, my date will have the chocolate cake, I'll have the peach cobbler, both with vanilla ice cream."

"And to drink?"

"Iced tea and water with lemon."

"Thank you, sir. I'll get this right out for you and your date." She smiled and winked at Tish before she walked away.

Tom leaned toward Tish and placed his folded arms on the table. "I don't want to talk about Sable tonight, okay? Right now I'm with you and only you. You've got enough to think about with the funeral and getting with your family tomorrow. Besides, you promised to tell me about your father, remember?"

"Oh, I see you didn't forget." She rolled her eyes and bit her lips. He saw her look somewhat perplexed before she spoke again. He waited hoping she'd trust him enough to share whatever seemed to be difficult for her to start.

"I've told very few people about how I met my father. Dee doesn't even know." She leaned forward, placed her elbows on the table, and planted her chin on top her cupped hands. "It's a pretty painful chapter in my life, one I hoped that I'd never have to face again. But then, who really prepares for the death of a parent?"

"I'm not sure how anyone does that, Tish. I don't know that you can.'"

"What I'm going to share with you is something that no one in Texas knows about. I'm going to tell you because I believe you'll never hurt me by passing it on." She took a deep breath and continued. "So just know, you're very special."

"Hmmm, this sounds interesting already."

Sheryl placed their drinks on the table and walked away.

"We can say it's certainly *different*. But, let's see, where do I start?"

Tom squeezed the lemon in her tea. "How about the beginning?"

"Okay, but if I start there it gets to be a long story."

"Baby, we've got all night." He opened a sweetener and poured it in her tea and stirred. "I'm not leaving you until you give me all the details. I want to know the whole story."

"All right, here goes." She took a drink of her tea and slowly placed the glass back on its coaster. "My mother's husband, James Edwards, died when she was about four months pregnant with me. I grew up with my brother, mother, and no father in the household because she never remarried. Although I'd been told James was my father, I often wondered how that could be. I look so much different than pictures of him or my brother Carl."

"What do you mean you look different?"

"Their complexion is much darker than mine. Most of my family has dark skin, including my mother, so my color doesn't come from her. My hair is nothing like theirs, even my mother's, and I'm so much taller. I used to think my mother adopted me, especially because she always treated my brother better than me. I grew up feeling like I'd been a really bad mistake she'd made."

"That's a hell of a beginning, huh?" He moved his chair closer to her.

"It gets worse." She paused and placed her hands, palms down on the table. "My mother was very strict with me the whole time I was growing up. She wouldn't let me date until my senior year in high school and made such a fuss about the guys I wanted to go out with that I didn't even have a real boyfriend until I went to college. She'd tell me that I shouldn't have sex until I got married cause the boys only wanted to get between my legs, then spread rumors and ruin my reputation."

She took a sip of tea and held on to the glass. "I listened to her and kept pretty much to myself until I met this really nice, great looking guy at Morgan State. He told me that when he first saw me he was amazed at how I reminded him of his little sister. Charles and I dated from the day we met my freshman year until spring break of our sophomore year. He was my very first love. Everyone on campus knew us as a couple and my best friends always told me we were a perfect match."

She looked at the glass of tea. "I pledged Delta my sophomore year in the fall and he pledged Omega that spring. We were both number seventeen on our lines. Isn't that odd?"

"Sounds special to me," Tom said softly. "So did you marry him? Is he your ex-husband?"

"No, that would've made this a happy story, but marrying him wasn't possible. We talked about getting married after we graduated. But then Charles took me home to meet his family in Washington, D.C., during spring break."

"Sounds like the brother was serious about you; he took you home to meet mom." Tom paused while Sheryl placed a basket of hot dinner rolls and butter on the table. "That's a good sign."

"I thought so too." She waited for Sheryl to leave. "But I met his father first and during the introduction, he looked at me kinda' strange and asked me to repeat my name. Then he asked where I grew up. His name was Albert Shaw and like Charles, he was a tall, light-skinned man with a beautiful smile. He'd been a guard on the basketball team at Morgan State just like Charles. He even played pro ball with the New York Nets a couple years until he injured his back."

"Wow, that's exciting." Tom sat back as Sheryl reappeared and refilled their tea glasses. "So did dad act like he was pleased with his son's girlfriend?"

"Your dinner will be out soon," Sheryl said before Tish could answer. "Can I get you anything else?"

"No thanks," Tom replied.

Tish sat back in her chair and watched Sheryl walk away from the table. "He seemed to be more concerned about who I was and where I'd come from. So I couldn't read *pleased* in anything he said or did at that point."

"Okay, I want to know what you mean by that."

"I'm getting to it." She took a slow deep breath. "Then he asked me, 'Who's your mother?' I answered, 'Loretta Edwards.' Just then Mrs. Shaw, Charles' mother, walked into the room. Charles' dad introduced us, and she just stared me down as if she already knew me. Then they both looked at Charles, then back at me, looking extremely stunned."

"Don't tell me he's your twin." Tom felt uneasy with the way the story was headed; he could see how difficult it was for her.

"Close. He's my half-brother." She took a long drink of tea. She removed a dinner roll from the basket and broke it in half with trembling hands. "That's why I look so much like his little sister. She's my half-sister! What he missed was how much I look like *our father!*"

"Oh *shit!* Tish, what'd they do?" He pushed the basket and glasses from the middle of the table and reached for her hand. "Who told you the truth? How did they handle that? How did you?"

"Oh, it wasn't easy and it got ugly." She wiped a tear from her eye. "My father asked me for mom's phone number. He went into his study, closed the door, and called her. When he came out he had all of us sit down in the family room. He explained that he'd had a brief affair with my mother one summer here in D.C., when she came to visit Aunt Alice, one of her sisters. They were introduced at a political party and he'd been very attracted to her. He didn't know my mother was married and didn't find out until he tried to reach her by asking Alice for her information. She'd told him to let it go because Mom was a very happily married woman."

"If she was so happy, why'd she have an affair?" he asked.

"That's a great question. I'll get to that." She paused as the waitress placed their steak dinners on the table.

"Thank you," he said to Sheryl. He reached for Tish's other hand and blessed the food. "Do you want to finish this story now or wait until after we eat?"

"No, I'm on a roll, so let me get to the end." She opened her potato and filled it with butter. "Besides, I'm starving. I can finish this up quickly so we can eat."

"Okay, I'm listening," he replied as he stuffed his mouth with a chunk of steak.

"Mr. Shaw went on to tell me that he never knew mom became pregnant with his child. She *never* told him about me. He said that when he talked to her on the phone that she told him that she'd become so ashamed about how everything had happened between them, she didn't want to talk to him again. She created a lot of pain through her indiscretion. She'd kept this a secret all this time."

"And you look at people like you and think their lives are drama free—"

"Yeah, well…it gets worse," she softly replied as she wiped her lips with the napkin. "I cut spring break short and went home to confront my mother. I found out that the reason mom had an affair was because her husband had been taking a strong high blood pressure medication after having a serious heart attack in his thirties. He'd become impotent."

"Impotent in his thirties? Damn. That's gotta be rough."

"Apparently it was…for both of them." Tish sat back in her chair, dropped the folk on the plate, and stared at her steak. "My mother was horny. Plain and simple, horny." She lifted her pain-filled eyes after a brief pause. "She later told me that she'd been 'without any relief' for two years when she met my father. One thing had led to another and before she knew it, they were in bed 'doing it.' Mom wasn't on the pill because she hadn't been worried about getting pregnant."

"Too bad she didn't know about going to the gym, huh?" Tom asked, trying to lighten the mood. "Maybe she could've worked things out there."

"Okay, smartie." She grinned. "Anyway, when she realized she was pregnant, she couldn't do anything about it. She actually told me she'd thought about aborting me, but it wasn't legal. That really made me mad. When her husband found out that mom was pregnant, he knew it couldn't be his child. He became so enraged he suffered another heart attack and died."

"*Damn*, Tish. Hearing that must've really hurt you."

"You have no idea. It really changed my relationship with my mother. I was so mad at her for not telling me the truth." She picked up her fork and stabbed her potato in frustration. "All my life I thought my dad was that man in the picture on the piano because she told me he was. Even when I doubted it, I still believed her. Then I go to college and fall in love with *my brother!* We planned to get married. Damn, I get mad every time I think about it. What if I had gotten pregnant?" She dropped the folk and picked up her water.

Tom couldn't think of anything to say to her; nothing seemed appropriate. He continued to work on his steak as he silently waited for her to continue.

"Of course we broke up and I was heartbroken. I wanted to marry the only man I had slept with. But that would never happen. Finding out that I was the reason that my mother's husband died was almost too much." Tears ran down Tish's face.

He stood and moved his chair around to the other side of the small table until it was beside her. He sat down and wrapped his arm around her shoulder.

"Baby, don't cry," he whispered. "I'm so sorry all this happened, but you had nothing to do with any of it." He took her napkin and wiped her cheeks. "I'm so glad you told me, though. Knowing this helps me understand who you are and why certain things are so important to you. I remember you telling me that no child is a mistake and you won't do anything to keep your children from seeing their father."

Tom took her hand and slowly kissed her knuckles. "I see why you were so supportive when I told you about Sable being pregnant. I know now where your strength and beliefs come from. I'm so proud of you. You're such a strong woman."

"Thanks, I need to hear that right now. This is a very difficult trip for me and I'm glad you're here."

"So, what happened after that?"

"I didn't return to Morgan State after spring break. Charles had a full basketball scholarship and stayed to graduate. I'm sure everyone wanted to know what happened to us when I dropped out of school."

"Did you get to know your father and his family at all?" He handed Tish a glass of water. "Did you return to college later?"

"I stayed so angry with my mother that I refused to have anything to do with her after I learned the truth; not so much because of what she did but more because she had lied about it to me all those years. I packed my bags and left. I refused to go home, return her calls, or take any money from her to finish college. My father ended up being there for me; he treated me like the long-lost daughter he never had and worse, never knew he had. We became as close as possible in the little time we had."

"So where did you live?"

"I moved in with Aunt Alice and finished my degree at Howard University." She took a long drink of water before continuing. "Charles' mother eventually warmed up to me and allowed me to come around their house so I could get to know my family."

"What do you mean? Why wouldn't she like you right away? What had you done?"

"Oh, I forgot to tell you that she and my father were engaged to be married when he messed around with mom. They moved up the wedding date when she found out that she was pregnant. Charles is only a month older than I am."

"Gosh, this is too much for TV." He shook his head. "That man was busy."

"Indeed, he was. They'd occasionally invite me over for dinner and a couple of family gatherings but I avoided being there when I knew Charles would be home. I haven't seen him in years."

"So at least you got to know your father. That's a good thing, right?"

"Yeah." She smiled and held her head up. "In spite of all that drama, he was a wonderful man. He always had my back when I needed anything. He even gave me away when I got married. That was so special."

Tish took a deep breath and lowered her head again. "The messed up part is that so many people were hurt just because my mom couldn't control herself."

"Oh, now don't be so hard on mom" he responded. "Remember, she's human too and she didn't make you by herself. I'm not saying what she did was right, but it must've been difficult for her to go through this and keep that secret for so long."

"Perhaps. But it's still hard for me to forgive her sometimes. Well, forget it is more like it. I forgave her. But, now I have to face my other family tomorrow, including Charles. After all this time, it's still going to be hard."

"You want me to go with you?" Tom asked. "I will."

"Yeah, right. I can just see me with you tomorrow…the man I'm in love with who happens to be another woman's husband, escorting me to my father's funeral…who happened to impregnate my mother while she was married to another man. Oh, Tom, am I just repeating what my mother did? Am I no better than she?"

Tish shook her head slowly as her voice softened. She stared at the window as a tear fell from her eye. "I've tried so hard to be the best woman I could be. I've never slept around or tried to take a man away from another woman. Maybe I should find another hotel room." She turned and looked at him with a confused look on her face. "What am I doing? Why am I here with you right now?"

"Tish, baby, please clam down," he replied as he reached for her hand. "You're a wonderful person. You're not your mother, not even close. Our story is not your mother and father's story. They met, 'did it' but didn't have a relationship or friendship. What you've learned about them has made you a better person and you know what?"

He kissed her forehead. "I love you for the person you are. They didn't have love, we do. They needed to meet so you could find your way back to me, and you did. Now I know I can't let you go."

He squeezed her hand, slid off his chair onto his knees and told her, "If you'll have me, Tish, I plan to be with you for the rest of our lives. Just give me some time to get my life together when I get back to San Antonio. You'll see. I'll be knocking on your door asking you to run away with me. But for right now, I want to go with you tomorrow. Please…I'll be right by your side if that's what you want."

"I need you with me, Tom. Thanks."

"No, Tish, thank you," he said, as he stood, he pulled her into his arms, and kissed her passionately as the waitress and hostess looked on and smiled.

Sixty-Three

Dawn renders a life
bringing new birth to old love
before the sun sets.

Tish made it through the funeral the next day with Tom constantly by her side. She introduced him to her stepmother and other family members as a dear friend from San Antonio who happened to be in D.C. at the time. She was grateful for the coincidence, especially when she came face to face with her brother at her father's home after the service.

"Hello, Charles," she said. She hugged him and kissed his cheek. "It's really nice seeing you— it's been quite a while…"

"Sure has…" he responded and gave her a shy smile.

"This is my friend, Tom. Tom, this is my brother, Charles."

"Nice to meet you. Sorry about your father, man."

"Thanks. Good meeting you, too." He shook Tom's hand. "You guys both live in San Antonio?"

"Yeah, I'm there with the Army. It's where Tish and I met," Tom replied. "Have you ever been there?" He took a plate from the serving table set up in the dining room and picked out a golden brown, fried chicken breast. "It's a great place to take a vacation, especially if you have children."

"No, and no children…so I'd need a different reason to come to San Antonio…" He looked at Tish and grinned. "So I hear you have children?"

"Yes, a girl and a boy."

"And what about Marcus? He didn't come with you?" Charles tilted his head and peered at her curiously.

"He and I aren't married anymore." She stepped to the table, grabbed a plate and handed it to her brother. "Hey, aren't you hungry, too?"

She took another one and picked up the long fork and stabbed a chicken leg. "This food sure smells good. I'm starving…"

"You guys enjoy the spread. I'll get my appetite back soon." He returned the plate to the table then placed his hand on Tom's shoulder. "Take good care of her, man. She's a good woman and deserves nothing but the best… and I believe she's well overdo for all her blessings."

"I agree, and will do what I can to make sure her blessings are never blocked again." Tom reached for Charles' hand. "I'm glad we got a chance to meet and hope to see you again under different circumstances."

"For sure…" He shook his hand and turned to Tish. "You take care and kiss my niece and nephew for me. I'll have to come to Texas sometime soon so I can meet them."

"That'll be wonderful. Anytime…now, hear?" She hugged him goodbye and he walked away.

"Baby, I tell you… I don't know how anyone couldn't see that you and Charles were related. You could be his twin. I can't imagine how your father felt when he saw the two of you together that first time. And when I viewed your father's body—man, it's amazing how much a daughter can look like her father."

"Yes, that's what everyone says…" She lowered her head as her voice faded out.

"Tish," Tom reached for her hand as he drove her to the airport later that day. "I wish you'd stay. Couldn't you reschedule the flight and leave tomorrow?"

"I wish I could, but I need to get home to the children." She took his hand and gently kissed his knuckles. "They know that this is a sad trip and they are worried about me in their own way. I'm sure Dee and Aaron are taking good care of them, but it's a mom thing."

"I can't blame you for returning home to your family." He stopped at a traffic light and looked at her. "You know, I'm happy that this weekend happened—not the losing your father part—but that we were able to be alone and talk. After all this time, we've connected on whole different level. Thank you so much for sharing your very private life story with me and allowing me to be with you this morning at your father's funeral."

"I really appreciate having you with me, Tom. It made such a difference." She smiled and squeezed his hand.

He drove in silence for several minutes while Tish thought about the morning's events. She'd awakened as the first light of morning peered through the slightly opened curtain of Tom's room. She smiled, remembering that he'd held her in his arms all night. Not once had he attempted to turn her willingness to join him in his bed for a repeated sexual interlude. The morning brought her renewed sensations of love, belonging, joy, and security.

She'd left the bed, careful not to awaken him. She stepped quietly to the window, pulled the curtain out just enough to slide between it and the glass. The orange glow of the sunrise was soft and warm. As she enjoyed the dawning of a new day, it felt like spiritual arms enveloped her with love and assurance that everything would be okay. She'd closed her eyes when she realized that she'd experienced this before, that there'd been something very familiar about the moment. She just couldn't remember when or where it'd happened.

"You okay?" Tom glanced over at her as he turned into the airport property.

"Yes, I'm okay." She realized that their time together would end in minutes. "You don't know how difficult this could've been for me if I had to do it alone."

"Well, I have an idea…" He slowed down and pulled the car over to the outside lane, allowing the airport traffic to pass. "I think the hardest part of the day happened when you introduced me to Charles. I noticed how uncomfortable you became when you told him about your children and divorce."

"Yeah, he's never married, has no children. He didn't get the pro ball contract. I just hope that what happened between us didn't damage his ability to go after what he wants in life."

"Tish, don't go there. He's a grown, intelligent, and good-looking man. His executive banking position doesn't hurt anything either. Trust me, he can get whatever he wants. He's doing alright for himself."

"I'm sure you're right. That was the first time Charles and I had an unemotional, rational conversation in a very long time."

She took a deep breath and turned to the man she loved. "Tom, thank you for being at my side and holding my hand every time I needed some silent support. The little things like that make a difference in how we handle difficult situations."

"It's my pleasure to be here for you. And if you let me Tish, I'll always be right here for you. No matter what," he replied as he parked the car at the passenger drop-off.

"No matter what?" She looked at him expecting an explanation.

"No matter what," he repeated. "I have some things I need to take care of when I return to San Antonio next Friday." He released the seatbelt and turned toward her. "For now, just know that I love you more than I've ever loved another woman and I want you with me for the rest of my life. Not only now and then when fate brings us together."

He leaned to her and gently kissed her lips. "Tish, please wait for me."

"I don't plan on going anywhere."

Sixty-Four

Now walking away
becomes the only option.
He walks toward his life.

Friday hadn't arrived fast enough for Tom. As he deplaned in San Antonio, he was relieved that he'd taken steps to get his life back on track. He'd made a mental map of everything he needed to do and say as soon as he landed on Texas soil.

Before he left Washington, he'd searched the Internet, found a one-bedroom apartment near the post, and completed a three-month lease. He'd also contacted an attorney to handle his divorce.

Jonathan had reassured him that Texas family law hadn't changed since his divorce from Katrina. It was still possible to end the marriage on the sixty-first day after filing the petition if Sable didn't contest anything. Tom quickened his pace and whispered, "Thank God." He raised his head and looked forward with renewed determination.

As he turned the corridor and walked toward the baggage claim carousel, Tom sensed an old reality—he'd have to wait for Sable. Since their marriage, she'd made little effort to arrive on time for anything important to him. He'd asked her to get a babysitter for Sheila so they could have dinner together before going home.

He grabbed his suitcase from the conveyor and walked purposely toward the exit. He stepped outside and gasped as the blistering heat of the late June San Antonio day blasted his body. He scanned the slow moving SUVs in the passenger pickup lane. People rushed past him and toward their loved ones as he sauntered the length of the sidewalk and back. When he didn't spot Sable's car anywhere, he sat on a shaded, vacant concrete bench and waited patiently for ten minutes before pulling out his cell phone and calling her.

"Hello?" She sounded short and impatient.

"Sable, are you on your way to the airport?"

"Yes, as a matter of fact, I'm exiting onto Airport Boulevard. I'll be there in a few minutes." She turned the radio off. "Do you have your luggage yet?"

"Yes, I've been waiting outside for you." He stood and slowly paced the sidewalk.

"Oh, I'm sorry." Her tone softened. "I didn't expect your flight to be on time. They never are."

"Well, this one and the last five flights I've taken arrived on time; you were the one that didn't."

Never again...never again. He shook his head and rubbed the back of his neck to ease the tension. "Do you have any idea how hot it is out here?"

"Sure, the car thermometer says it's ninety-eight degrees. That's cooler than yesterday. You know we hit one hundred already!"

"That's nice, Sable." He took a deep breath and rolled his eyes. "Did you get a sitter for Sheila?"

"She's at the post daycare. We have until seven to pick her up." She drove into the passenger pick up lane. "I'm here."

He stood and looked for her car. He saw the black Camaro approach and reached for his suitcase. He opened the trunk and slowly lowered his bag as a memory of meeting Tish in the Washington airport crossed his mind. *What a difference...*

"Hello, Sable," he said as he sat down.

"Hi, baby." She smiled sweetly. "How was your trip? Did you get a lot of work done at the Pentagon?"

"Yes, I can say a lot got accomplished on this trip." He took a deep breath. "There're some things we need to talk about. I'd like to get some Mexican food where it's not too noisy."

"Sounds good to me." She tapped her fingers on the steering wheel before glancing over at him. "Well?"

"Well, what?"

"Where do you want to go? I need to know which direction to drive."

Tom rubbed his palms against his thighs as he pulled his mind from rehearsing one more time how he'd tell her he wanted a divorce. "It really doesn't matter to me. Let's go to your favorite place tonight."

"Then let's go to Aldaco's in Sunset Station. It's early enough that we'll beat the dinner crowd."

"Good choice. I've missed real Mexican food. And I don't eat it anywhere but San Antonio."

"You've said that before," she answered sounding bored as she navigated the near rush hour traffic that headed south on U.S. Highway 281. She turned the volume up on the stereo that played a Prince CD.

Tom took that a signal that she'd rather hear the music and sing along than talk to him. He relaxed against the headrest and closed his eyes. *Fine. Just fine.*

Twenty minutes later, he pointed to a vacant table near the back of the restaurant. It was next to a window that allowed them to have some privacy and a view of the plaza outside.

He watched the palm trees swaying in the tropical like breeze as mockingbirds perched on branches of live oak trees in the cobblestone-paved plaza. The ambiance of the Mexican restaurant with its brightly painted tiles and framed art, the festive Mariachi music playing in the background, and the ethnic aroma of chili peppers and cilantro created a wonderful illusion of being south of the Texas border.

A waiter approached their table with a basket of corn chips and small bowl of hot salsa. "Bienvenido. My name is Jose. I'll take your orders when you are ready." He looked at them with a polite smile and waited.

"Sable, do you know what you want?" Tom asked.

"I'll have my usual, the divorced enchiladas. You know the plate that has the beef enchilada separated by rice from the chicken one. I think that's so clever." She handed the menu to Jose without reviewing it.

Tom closed his menu and looked at Jose. "I'll have the beef enchiladas and iced tea. Sable do you want anything to drink?"

"Water is fine—no ice."

"Gracias, I'll be right back with your drinks."

Tom watched Jose walk away and turned his attention to the chips and salsa; he hadn't eaten since breakfast before he checked out of the hotel in D.C.

"You said we needed to talk about something. What's on your mind, Tom?"

"Something very important, but not an easy thing to say." He bit the chip and glanced up and met her eyes, which reflected concern.

"What? You've got orders to Afghanistan and you're leaving tomorrow?"

"No, I wish it was that simple." He dipped another chip. "Actually, I have a question. What's the most important thing to you about our marriage?"

"Sheila, of course. Isn't she why we got married in the first place?"

"Exactly." He could hardly believe she actually said it. "So do you think if you hadn't gotten pregnant with our daughter, that we'd be married at all and having dinner together right now?"

"I seriously doubt it." She dipped a chip and looked at him curiously. "Where're you going with this, Tom? Because Sheila did happen, she's your daughter and we're married. There's no what if about it."

"I know. I just wanted to know where you stand." He sat back as Jose placed their drinks on the table.

"Your turn," Sable said. "What do you think is most important in our marriage?"

"Sheila's best interest has driven every decision I've made about my life lately, including marrying you because you gave birth to my child."

"So are you saying that if Sheila hadn't happened, you wouldn't have married me?"

"There's no doubt in my mind that we wouldn't have had a relationship beyond my first trip to D.C. to see you. If you hadn't gotten pregnant, we wouldn't be having dinner together tonight."

"I bet," she replied sarcastically. "You've been in love with another woman the whole time I've known you, haven't you? Don't lie, tell the truth." She cupped her hands together and rested her chin on her fingers.

"Yes, I have been. I thought I could get over having to shift my life and realign my priorities when I learned you were pregnant. I believed I had to do the right thing for the right reason to improve the situation. Trust me, I wanted this to work, between you and me. But it just isn't—not for me."

He squeezed the lemon in his tea and continued, "Sable, I've been down this road once already. I married Katrina because she was pregnant with Shaun. We lived together for years and we weren't in love. It's a miserable existence. You convince yourselves that it's in the best interest of the child to have both parents in the same household. And in most cases that's true because the parents love each other."

"Are you saying you don't even love me, Tom?" She slouched back in the car and pouted.

"I do, but not enough. Not in the way I'd need to if I were to honestly say that you're the one I want as a life partner. No, Sable, I can honestly say you're not her."

"I'm not her, huh?" She smirked and threw a chip on the table. "Would *her name* be Tish?"

"It doesn't really matter what her name is. It isn't you." He kept the tone of his voice steady and just loud enough for her to hear. The last thing he wanted was a public scene.

He looked toward the front of the restaurant and saw Jose bringing their dinners on a large round tray. "Here comes our food."

The way Sable stared at him with her arms folded tight across her chest reminded him of a spoiled teenager whose father had just grounded her and taken back the keys to her first car.

"Could you box this to go?" she asked Jose as soon as her plate hit the table. "I've lost my appetite."

"Of course, ma'am." Jose had a puzzled look as he picked up the plate and turned to Tom with his hand extended toward him.

"Oh, no, man. I'm hungry. My plate stays right here. Thanks." Tom silently blessed the food and began eating as Jose walked off with Sable's dinner.

"Tom!" She slapped the table with her hand. "How can you sit there and eat that food while we're having this conversation?"

"I'm hungry, that's how. I haven't eaten since about six this morning. I've been traveling all day. If you're not hungry, don't eat. I am, so I will. It's really that simple."

"You men are all alike, selfish bastards! You sit here and tell me you're in love with another woman, telling me—*your wife*. Just look at you eating them damn beans and rice like it's nothing."

"Sable, calm down and lower your voice. No one in here needs to know what our conversation is about." He wiped his mouth and drank some tea. "I'm trying very hard to have a civilized conversation with you about this. You asked me to be honest and that's exactly what I want to do. But if you can't handle the truth, perhaps I need to explain less and just do what I need to do without talking about it."

"Do what?" She laughed nervously. "You gonna divorce me?"

"I want to know if we can reach an agreement about going our separate ways in a manner that preserves our ability to raise our daughter as level-minded, caring adults. That's what I want, Sable. More than anything else."

"If you think I'm going to let you and some heffa' take my daughter away from me…like hell I will!" She took the napkin from her lap and slammed it on the table.

"No one said anything about taking Sheila from you. Where'd you get that idea? She's still a baby and you've been a good mother. This conversation is not about that. Haven't you heard anything I've said?"

"So you just want to walk away from us and let me deal with all her needs by myself? I ought to walk outta' here and leave your ass right now. You and your Mexican dinner."

"You're free to do whatever you want, Sable. I know how to catch a cab home."

"Don't toy with me, Tom. I'm the mother of your child. Remember that," she said with a voice and look of pure hatred.

"Trust me, I'm reminded daily; nothing will ever change that." He placed the fork on his plate as Jose returned with her to-go dinner. "Thank you. Could I have the check, please?"

"Si. I will be right back with it. More tea?"

"No thank you, Jose. This'll be fine."

"Okay, Sable, here it is. I want a divorce. If you want full custody of Sheila, no problem, you've got it. If you don't, that's not a problem either. I'd be happy to take her full time. What I don't know, I'll figure out. All you have to do is tell me what you want. It's that simple."

"What's simple about that Tom? I haven't worked since she was born. I left the Army and moved the hell out here to be with you. I don't have a job, no income, and no daycare. What am I supposed to do next?"

"I suppose a resume is the next thing you do. With your degree in computer technology, the Army experience working in

IT, and managing the installation of that new personnel software, there's a job out there with your name on it. Go find it."

"Sheila's birthday is coming up. She's just a baby and you want me to go back to work already?" She shook her head. "What kind of father are you anyway?"

"One who wants what's best for his daughter. Both our mothers worked right after we were born, didn't they? We turned out all right. Most mothers these days work while raising children. What's the big deal? Fathers do it all the time."

"Oh yeah? If you really want what's best for your daughter, we wouldn't be here talking about divorce, now would we?" She gave him a disgusted look and rolled her eyes at Jose when he dropped the check on the table and cleared Tom's dinner plate.

"I'm not divorcing my daughter, Sable. I'm divorcing you. My decision is in Sheila's best interest. I have to start taking better care of me. I don't see how I can make this marriage into something more than what it is. And that's just not enough. I refuse to settle any longer."

"Your decision? So this isn't a discussion about whether we should get a divorce or not. You've decided already?" Her voice softened as she looked at him with a puzzled expression.

"Yes, I have. As a matter of fact I'll be moving my stuff out of the apartment in the morning. I don't want any of the things we've purchased since we got married. Most of what we bought was for Sheila anyway. I'll be taking what I already had."

"You're moving out? So soon? To where?" She held her hand up in front of her face. "Wait, don't tell me; you're moving in with this woman?"

"No, I'm moving into an apartment and will be living by myself, Sable. Our divorce will take about sixty days. Until then we're still married. I wouldn't move in with another woman while I'm still married. Give me some credit. *Damn*."

"Sixty days and it's done? Really. So who's paying for all this?" She sat back as her shoulders slumped in defeat.

"I have it covered. Jonathan Andrews will file the petition for us on Monday or Tuesday if we can sit down sometime this weekend and work out the terms of the divorce settlement. I've set up an appointment with him Monday morning. I've jotted down some things that you and I need to discuss. It'll be easy. We don't have much to agree on, just who'll be Sheila's custodial parent, who pays child support and how much, and then a few other details."

"You make it sound so mechanical, so… procedural. What about marriage counseling? What about kissing and making up? Why does it have to be so fast? So final?"

"Because it's not negotiable, Sable. The simple truth is I don't want to be married to you any longer. And I don't want a lengthy, complicated divorce that costs a hell of a lot of money for the very same outcome, just thousands of dollars and months or years later. Let's just do it now, plain and simple. I want to move on with my life."

"So, it's like that, huh?" She hung her head as a single tear fell down her cheek.

"Yes, that's exactly the way it is." He stood and picked up the check from the table. "Now, let's go home. I want to spend some time with my daughter before she goes to bed."

Sixty-Five

Anger follows loss
triggering the pain forward
shaded truth unfolds.

"Hey, girl." Dee's soft, yet excited voice sounded like music to Tish's ears. "I haven't heard from you in three weeks. What's going on with you?"

"Yeah, I know." She sat on the bed that beckoned her to crawl back in and sleep more of the day away. "I've been working really hard lately. I'm so tired when I get home that all I want to do is sleep. The kids are with their dad this weekend. Dee, I slept until noon today."

Tish slowly lowered her back on the bed and curled up around two fluffy pillows. "I think I'll take a nap until it's time for dinner."

"What? Sounds like you're depressed. Get dressed. I'm coming over there."

"Oh, I'm okay, Dee. You don't have to do that."

"I know I don't *have to do* anything but die, but that's for way later. Right now I'm on my way to your house."

"Well, all right…." Tish knew it was useless to argue with Dee when she'd made her mind up about something. "Have it your way. I'll be right here."

"Good. Get up, take a shower, and get dressed. We're going for a ride."

"What? I thought you were just gonna come over. Where we going?" Tish sat up and crossed her legs, pulling the oversized, black and silver Spurs T-shirt down over her knees.

"Austin." Dee entered her car with the cell phone in one hand. "Look, I'll tell you more when I get there. Throw on some jeans. We're going shopping."

"Okay. See you in a few." Tish hung the phone up and stared into her bathroom. It took all her energy just to get up and walk to the bathroom door. *I'm hungry. I didn't eat dinner, no breakfast either. That's all, I just need to eat. I'm not depressed... just hungry.*

She showered and dressed in jeans and a white sorority T-shirt. After brushing her hair and teeth, she slid her feet into her slippers and sauntered to the kitchen.

Banana, that's all I need. Some pure potassium. That'll get my energy back. She took the last piece of fruit from the bowl on the counter and peeled it as she sat at the kitchen bar. After she took one bite, the doorbell rang.

Tish walked to the front door, banana in one hand as she wondered how Dee could have arrived so quickly. She hadn't even rung her from the gate.

She opened the door and to her surprise, it wasn't Dee after all. The woman who stood alone on her porch had one hand planted firmly on her hip.

"Sable?" Perplexed with the unexpected visit, Tish opened the door, but didn't invite her in.

"Look," Sable lowered her hand from her hip and relaxed her stance, "I came over to personally apologize for how I treated you the other day when we ran into each other at lunch." She took a deep breath, licked her lips, and continued. "David, my lawyer, and I were going over the terms of my divorce settlement and it was a really bad moment for me when you walked into the restaurant."

"Apparently." Tish looked beyond her to see if anyone had come with Sable and was still in the car. "How'd you know where I live?"

"Don't you know you can go to findanyone.com and literally find anybody? All you need is a name and city. I plugged your address into my new GPS system and here I am. The gate was already open, so I just drove in." Sable looked into the open doorway and lifted her eyebrows. "You got a really nice house. This is a good neighborhood, too." She nodded as she continued to survey the premises.

"Yes, we like it here." Tish felt as though she'd been checked over.

"*We*?" Sable's tone lifted in heightened interest.

"Yes, my children and I." *Now, where's Dee?*

"Oh, I see. But what about that man you were with when we met—let's see, wasn't it the Omega Ball?" She tapped her forehead. "Maurice? Isn't that his name?"

"Yes, he was my date that evening. You have a good memory."

"So he doesn't live here with you?" She peeked over Tish's shoulder trying to get a better look inside.

"No, he doesn't." She felt more uncomfortable with the line of questioning.

"Well, it sure looks like a mighty big mortgage for a single woman, that's all I'm saying."

"Sable, thank you for coming by to apologize for the other day. You really didn't have to drive all the way out here. I'm expecting company and…" before she finished her sentence, Dee drove up and parked her car in front of the house. "There's my girlfriend right now."

"Look Tish, before I go, let me just say this one thing…" She planted her hand back on her hip. "I know my husband's in love with you. Now I can really see why. I don't blame him for wanting you. You're a pretty damn good package, my dear. But you will *never* get my daughter, you hear? She's mine. She'll always be mine."

Sable tilted her head and lowered her voice. "And I hope you have all the money you need to pay for this ranch of yours. By the time David and I get done with Tom he won't have a dime to help you pay your light bill."

Tish looked over Sable's shoulder at Dee as she approached the house. "I can assure you my relationship with Tom has nothing to do with your daughter or my light bill. So if you don't mind I have things I need to do and—"

"Hi, I'm Dee. You're…?" She asked as she stopped on the porch and threw Tish a frown.

"Sable, Sable Manning." She ignored Dee and kept her eyes glued to Tish. "And I can assure you that I know better. But you do what you need to do and I'll wish you well. Tom's not the man you think he is."

She turned and walked toward her car as she continued to talk. "So you can have him. By the time this thing's over, I'll have David. So, thank you for messing things up for me and Tom. David brings so much more to the table than Tom ever could. Have a good life."

Dee pointed toward Sable and looked squarely at Tish. "Is that Tom's *wife*?" She stepped into the doorway and gently pushed Tish into the house. "What's going on around here?"

"Just come in, close, and *lock the door*…please." The banana still in her hand, Tish turned and walked toward the family room. "I'm still trying to believe this—"

"Are you going to eat that thing or just carry it around?" Dee smiled at Tish as she sat on the sofa.

"Oh, I forgot I had it. I was hungry before that heffa' showed up." She laid the fruit on a napkin and left it on the table. "I don't know where to start, Dee. So much has happened lately."

"Let's start with three weeks ago. Ever since you came back from D.C., your father's funeral, you've been missing, girl. I come by your office and your door's closed or you're not there. You haven't returned my calls. What's happened?"

"Tom came by the office the week after I got back and told me he'd filed for divorce and moved out. He told me to give him about sixty days and his marriage would be over if everything goes without any problems."

"Problems? Does he think that woman won't give him problems?" Dee sat beside her friend and took her shoes off. "Tish, she's trouble coming and going."

"Oh, you don't have to tell me. He suggested that we not see each other or talk until he's divorced just in case she's having him followed or his phone tapped. He thinks she'll hold anything she can find against him in court."

"So that's why you're depressed. You're missing Tom. I can understand that, but what was Miss Thang doing over at your house? What was that all about?"

"Last week I went over to the eastside to get some Chadwick's fried chicken and instead of doing the drive-thru, I went inside to place my order to go." She lifted her legs and folded them under her. "Big mistake. Sable and David, yes the same David that tried to date me, were there. He's her lawyer; can you believe that? Anyway, as soon as I walked through the door she recognized me and stood up with this angry, pissed-off look. She shouted, 'You bitch!' David took her arm and tried to make her sit back down. Everyone looked at me as she ranted on, 'You family destroyer! I hate you!'"

"Oh, my God! What'd you do?"

"I turned right around and walked out the door. Girl, you know I don't know how to fight and I wasn't about to get my butt kicked over a man by some insane woman." She lowered her head. "I called Tom when I got back in my car. He didn't pick up any of my calls to his cell or his new place. He still hasn't called me back."

"Damn, Tish. That hurts. Now she shows up at the house. What did she want?"

"She claimed that she wanted to apologize for how she'd treated me and gave some lame excuse about having a bad day. I think she just wanted me to know that she could find me if and when she wanted to, to intimidate me. Girl, she was checking my stuff out, too. Then, you heard her, right? 'You can have Tom, I got David….' Like this is some game and we just traded tokens or something."

Dee looked at Tish with a friendly smile. "That woman's got issues and if she winds up with David, they deserve each other," she said, then walked over and turned on the stereo.

"Amen to that." Tish stretched on the sofa. "I bet David advised her to apologize to me to make sure that whole hollering scene at Chadwick's goes away. You know I'm not trying to get involved in their divorce. I don't plan on showing up in court testifying for or against anybody either."

"Yeah, but they don't know that." She sat back on the sofa and crossed her legs. "Look, give me Tom's cell number. I'm going to call that Negro myself and tell him he needs to talk to you. He can't be running scared from that witch. Not talking to you isn't going to make Sable act better. She's already crazy."

"You know that's right." Tish stood, picked up her banana, and walked toward the kitchen. "You can call him later. Right now I need to eat something. I just realized how hungry I am."

"Let's get a burger or something. Then we'll head to Austin. I need to get a couple pieces of art for Aaron's office from Mitchie's Gallery." Dee followed her to the kitchen. "He's got this new state job that pays mo' money than he's ever made."

"Sounds good. I need to get away."

Sixty-Six

Remember the night
I fell so in love with you.
It was in late September…

Tish loaded the dishwasher with breakfast dishes. Melanie wiped the counter clean, and Simon lifted the trash bag from the stainless steal trashcan and carried it to the garage.

"Mom, I loved the blueberry pancakes," Melanie said softly. "I hope I can cook like you one day."

"Next weekend I'll wait until you wake up to make them again and you can do it." Tish smiled at the thought of having her child by her side cooking their meals together. "I'll show you how it's done. That's the best way to become a cook. You have to just do it."

"Okay, that'll be fun." Melanie sat at the bar and looked at her mother. "Are we going shopping today? My friends are going to the Labor Day sales at the mall."

"No, I hadn't planned on it. It's just nice to have the day off to relax."

"Can I go with Celestina and her mom?" Melanie looked at Tish with soulful eyes. "They're going to North Star Mall and I'd just like to go and look. I don't need anything."

"I guess so. I'll call Colleen and see when they're planning to leave." Tish smiled at her daughter and brushed her cheek with the back of her fingertips. *My child is growing up…shopping already at the mall…who'd have thought.*

"Okay. I'll go take a bath and get dressed. Thanks, Mom!" She skipped from the kitchen and down the hallway.

Just as Tish closed the dishwasher and turned it on, the phone rang.

"Hello?"

"Hey, Tish. What's up?" Dee's voice sounded upbeat.

"Not much here, how about with you?"

"Oh, just enjoying a Monday morning for a change. Girl, ain't nothing like a three-day weekend." She pulled her housecoat closed and flopped on her sofa. She picked up the remote control and turned the TV off.

"I know that's right." Tish sat at the kitchen bar and poured a cup of coffee. "So how was the Omega's party on Saturday? Many people there?"

"The same ol', same ol'. You didn't miss much," she replied as lifted her legs and rested them on the sofa. "But I have to say, I'm glad you decided not to come this year."

"What was so special about this year's event? Why are you glad I decided to stay away? Did you see Tom there?"

"No, he didn't come either." Dee drew a deep breath. "Tish, Sable was there with David."

"Really? So I guess he's doing more than giving her legal counsel."

"Girl, she was sporting a huge rock on her left hand. You'd think her arm was paralyzed in place, all stuck out for everyone to see her finger."

"A diamond? They're engaged?" Tish stood up in surprise.

"They probably wanted everyone to think it's the real deal, but I'm sure it was just a zirconium. It was way too big to be a diamond." Dee paused before continuing. "Look, Tish. They were just flaunting, that's all and he should know better. No class attracts no class."

"We certainly can say that. But damn, Dee, she must be putting out some hellified hoochie-coochie. How can a brother be so stupid? Dating his still-married client who doesn't know better than to be braggadocio about their alleged engagement." She shook her head, sat down, and took a drink of coffee.

Dee chuckled as if someone had tickled her. "Just wait until she finds out that he tried to date you first. She'll probably go ballistic!"

"I just don't want to be around when that happens. She's scary enough already."

Just as Tish put her coffee cup down, the doorbell rang. "I wonder who that could be. I'm not expecting anyone this morning."

"Girl, the last time that happened, your unexpected visitor was that crazy Sable. Take the phone with you and be careful."

Tish walked toward the front door and saw someone holding red flowers through the thick cut-glass design of the windowpane. It was a florist deliveryman.

"Hello. Are you Latisha Edwards?" he asked.

With a huge smile, she replied, "Yes, I am."

"Then these are for you." He handed her the flowers and tipped his hat. "Have a wonderful day, ma'am." He turned and walked back to the truck.

"What's going on-n-n?" Dee's voice suddenly went up an octave.

"Girl, there must be two dozen red roses in this vase!" Tish walked back to the kitchen smelling each bud. "Oh, they smell sooo good. And they're so beautiful."

"Okay, tell me, who sent them!"

"There's an envelope attached. Looks like a card. Hold on, let me open it up and see what it says." Tish placed the phone on the counter as she opened the envelope and silently read the handwritten note.

> It's the sixth of September, the exact date two years ago when we first met. I remember how I couldn't keep my eyes off you and how my heart jumped inside when I touched your hand. My life will not be perfect without you in it and I want to live the rest of it like I finally got it right. Please wait for me. I'll come to you correct, and will have a very, very important question to ask you. It won't be long now….
>
> I love you, Tom

She sat at on the barstool with one hand over her mouth, as she stared at the note. "*Oh shit…*" she whispered.

"Tish!" Dee's loud voice brought her attention back to their conversation.

She picked the phone up and took a deep breath as tears formed. "Well…the flowers are from Tom." Tish wiped her eyes.

"So what does the note say?"

She read the note to Dee.

"Oh, damn, Tish, he's going to ask you to marry him, I *bet* that's what he's going to do!"

"You think?" She slowly folded the note and laid it on the table. "Maybe, maybe not. Let's not jump to conclusions. He's not even divorced yet. It could be anything."

"Right. Anything." Dee giggled. "Girl, you tripping. The man loves you. You love him, too. Nuff said. I'm hanging up this phone to have a strong cup of coffee. This call has made my day!"

"K. I'll talk to you later. Thanks for calling."

"My pleasure. Go do something fun today. Later!"

"Bye, Dee." She read the note again and then again.

Sixty-Seven

A new adventure
Our beginning starts again
Love everlasting...

"Hey, baby. Please call me as soon as you can. Thanks."

The only message on her office phone left Tish perplexed. She tilted her head and looked directly at Dee who'd made herself comfortable in the chair facing her desk.

"That was Tom. He must've called while we were at lunch." Tish sat in her chair and swiveled it toward the phone.

"Okay, so call him back." Dee folded her arms across her chest and crossed her legs. "Aaron told me last night that Tom's divorce would be final today. Maybe he called from the courthouse. It is the sixty-first day..."

"The sixty-first day? What's that?"

"Since he filed for the divorce. He expects it to be final today, according to what he told Aaron."

"So why hasn't he called me before now?" She pulled her chair closer to the desk. "And today, I'm his baby? What's up with that?"

"Tish, now don't go there." She picked up the phone and handed it to her friend. "Call him. See what he wants."

She dialed Tom's phone number and waited.

"Sergeant Manning."

"Hey, Tom." Tish paused and exhaled slowly. "I just got your message. Is everything all right?"

"Yes, all is well in the River City." He pushed the heavy wooden door as he left the red sandstone county courthouse. The bright San Antonio sunshine almost blinded him as it reflected against the faded gray sidewalk. "How are you, Tish?" While he waited for the traffic to clear, he looked back at the Romanesque building that had been standing in that spot for more than one hundred years.

"I'm doing great. So what's going on with you?" Tish nervously played with the phone cord.

"Well, baby, I just want you to know that my life is much better now. The judge signed my divorce papers just a few minutes ago and I'm a free man again." He cleared his throat and continued. "I'm eager to resume our relationship and do it right this time."

"You are?" She felt her cheeks blush. "So soon? The ink's hardly dry on the divorce decree, Tom." She glanced over at Dee who sat grinning from ear to ear.

"I don't want to waste any more time, Tish. We don't get it back, you know. It just keeps moving forward," he said as he crossed the street and walked toward the four-story parking garage.

"Yeah, that's true." She sat back in her chair and twisted one long curl between her fingers.

"Baby, remember when I asked you to wait for me?"

"Yes, and I've done just that." She paused, tempted to admonish him for not calling her the past few weeks. Instead she made a confession. "I've also been going to the gym a lot and it's getting old—"

"Say no more. Are the children with you or their dad this weekend?" He waited for her answer before entering the parking garage.

"He's picking them up from school today. They're going to Corpus Christi until Sunday evening."

"Can I come get you and have you all to myself until they come back?"

"I suppose so…what do you have in mind?"

"Let's get away."

Tish could hear the excitement in Tom's voice.

"I want to take you to New Orleans. We can be close to a real river…we can walk down the streets holding hands. I want to be able to kiss you in public, sit and listen to live jazz, and enjoy my time with you in total peace. How about it? You with me?"

"That sounds really nice. But…" Tish looked at Dee, searching for support. She wanted to put Tom on hold and talk to Dee before answering. Instead, she took a deep breath and looked away from her. "I'm with you, Tom. When shall we leave?"

"Right after work. I'll come by the house when you get home. I'll check the Internet and find a late flight out tonight and book it for us. My attorney told me about a great last-minute deal at the Marriott on Canal Street for the weekend."

"You're really serious about this?" She stared at Dee, wide-eyed; her mouth open, and one hand fanning her face.

"I've never been more serious. I want to spend my whole weekend with you—but not here. So throw some things in a bag and I'll see you real soon. Tish, I love you."

His words struck her with a gentle shock. She hadn't heard him say the "L word" since her father died. *I guess he really meant that and everything else he'd said.*

Her face flushed. She smiled and told him, "I love you too." She picked up a folder and fanned harder.

"Thank you, baby. Now I'm gonna' let you go. I'll see you about five-thirty, okay?"

"Yes, see you then." She sat forward and placed her elbows on the desk. "Tom?"

"Yes?"

"Thank you."

"For what?"

"Just thank you."

"Welcome, then. See you later."

The rest of the afternoon dragged in slow motion as Tish waited until she could make a dash for home and throw some things in a bag. She was ready and waiting when Tom arrived at five-thirty right on the dot.

On the flight to New Orleans they discussed finding a jazz club in the French Quarter and having dinner right after they checked into the hotel. Didn't happen.

"Wake up, Tish. It's nine-thirty in the morning." Tom slowly sat up and propped his elbow against the oversized pillow. He gently stroked her hair and whispered close to her ear. "Wouldn't you like to go have some breakfast since we missed dinner last night?"

Tish felt his warm, naked body next to hers. She opened her eyes and saw Tom looking at her with the sweetest smile. His enchanting expression made her feel happy and content.

"Hey…" her whisper was almost inaudible. She stretched and looked about the room to establish where and why she was in the bed with him. Memories of their evening flooded over her as she shook off the sleepiness.

He lowered his head toward hers and kissed her lips. "You are so sexy." He gently touched her nose with his. "And you've made me the happiest man in all of New Orleans this morning."

"And the hungriest, too, I bet." Tish felt her stomach growl as she wrapped one arm around his body. "Thank you for making such passionate love to me last night. I've missed you so much."

"Baby, that goes both ways. You have no idea how long I've wanted to have you back into my life just like this." He pulled her tight against his hot, firm chest. "When you took your shower last night and stepped out of the bathroom with just that towel on, I couldn't help but take you into my arms and love you the best way I know how."

"Well, Sergeant Manning I tell you, that was the best sexual marathon I've ever had. Four hours?"

"What? You think it's over?" Tom grinned and tickled her stomach. "Baby, we just got started."

"We do need to eat, though." She managed to get the words out between giggling.

"Of course. I don't want you to think that I brought you all the way out here to starve you to death." He stopped tickling her.

"How about room service? Let's eat in, okay? I'm not quite ready to get dressed."

Tom touched her face with his fingers. "Sure, baby. We can do that." He kissed her lips. "You're so yummy though. I could have you for breakfast, you know." He ran his hand down her stomach. "But I also want to keep your energy up. I'm not done with you, yet."

"Mmm, that sounds very good." She felt her body heat increase from his sensuous tender touch. "Call and place the order. That'll give us about thirty minutes to take care of some of that for you."

Tish couldn't get up and walk anyway, even if the room was on fire. Not after last night.

Sixty-Eight

Come, journey with me
Fate beckons our destiny-
Our past lives revealed.

"New Orleans is so nice in the fall." Tish reached for Tom's hand as they walked down North Peters Street toward the French Market. "It's not nearly as humid and muggy this time of year."

"Yeah, you're right about that." He pulled her hand up and kissed her fingers. "But it wouldn't matter if it felt like a sauna out here. I'm with you and that's all that matters."

They silently strolled past tourist shops as Cajun music blared through open doors and by seafood restaurants with people lined up waiting to be seated for dinner. The evening sun cast long shadows from the historic buildings along the sidewalk. A smooth breeze had made it pleasant to be outside.

"Tom, there's this woman in Jackson Square I met the last time I was here. I want to look for. Her name is Madame LaSay."

"I know her. She's one of Aunt Louise's friends. How do you know Madame LaSay?"

"Oh, here we go again." She shook her head and continued. "She read the tarot cards for me and told me some things that didn't make a lot of sense, but I found them to be very interesting. If she's in her spot, let's ask her to do a reading and see what she says now, okay?"

"Sounds good. Maybe she can tell us something about these dreams we've been having, too."

Madame LaSay sat at her seasoned card table looking out through the crowds of people who wondered around checking out the artists and vendors. As Tom and Tish walked closer she stood and waved them to come to her smiling and nodding as they followed her instruction.

A long, cranberry red, silk scarf covered her head and was tied behind her neck. Her carefully braided hair hung down her back. She stepped forward to greet them and pressed the simple, beige linen dress with her hands. Her face brightened with a charming smile when Tom opened his arms to embrace her.

"Madame LaSay, how are you?" he asked as he gave her a strong hug.

"Is dat you, Tom?" She returned his hug, peering at Tish who stood beside him. "Boy, I haven't seen you in years. Where you been? And who dat pretty woman witch you?"

She released Tom and looked at Tish. "Wait, I know…I seen you befo', haven't I, chil'?"

"Yes, ma'am. We met here last year." Surprised that she would remember meeting her, Tish had a strange feeling in her stomach.

"Yes, last year. I remember." She took Tish's hand. "I see you done found yo' way, nah. I don't needs to read the cards dis time, neither." She pulled Tish closer and examined her face. "I see it in yo' eyes, nah."

Madame LaSay took a deep breath and sat in her chair. She pointed to the empty chairs at her table. "You know, don't you?" she asked Tish.

She slowly sat beside Tom, bewildered by her question. "I know what, Madame LaSay?"

"Umph. What's yo' name, honey?"

"LaTisha, or just Tish."

"Mm-mmm. Tom, let me see yo' hands, yo's too." Madame LaSay silently examined the palms of their hands, gently nodding her head. She closed her eyes and softly chanted a song as she held their hands in hers.

After about a minute had passed, she opened her eyes and looked directly at Tish. "Miss LaTisha, you know dat dis here man is yo' soul mate, don't you? You been told about the spirit dance and you ain't told 'em, have you?"

"Well…no, ma'am I, I, haven't…just, no not yet." *How could she know that?*

"How come, Miss LaTisha?"

She felt like Madame LaSay's eyes pierced her soul. "It…it just never seemed to be the right time, I guess." She tried to tear away from Madame LaSay's glare but couldn't. "I'd just forgotten about it."

"Dis here's a ver' important thing, you know?" Her face remained serious. She looked at Tom and gave him a slight smile. "You in love with someone you've loved for thousands of years. But how would you know? By the spirit dance, dat's how."

"What's the spirit dance?" He looked from one woman to the other. "Is this some kinda' woman thing and I wouldn't understand?"

Tish opened her mouth to explain, but Madame LaSay spoke first. "You know what it is…you know mo' than you'll admit. The spirit dance, now dat's the real proof." She looked down and nodded. "Now look at yo' hands. The same lifelines, and see? What cha know? Yo' hands have all the same pa-terns."

"Oh, my God!" Tish was amazed. "They're duplicates of each other!"

He didn't speak at first but continued to examine their hands more closely. "Wow. How can that happen?"

"It's not easy and it rarely comes to our attention, cha." She released their hands and sat back in her chair. "Now, tell me about yo' dreams? You dream the same, no?" She waited for an answer, but they were still looking at their hands.

"I know, yes. Dat too is the same." She continued, "You're remembering yo' lives befo'. Yo' souls let you know this way sometimes, dat yo' past is connected with this one." She grinned at them and crossed her arms in front of her. "Tom, you can stop looking. She's right here." She pointed at Tish and paused. "And Miss LaTisha, yo' king's eyes and his heart are open for you. He's ready, nah." She nodded at Tom.

"But how could you know so much about us? How'd you know the answers to questions we haven't even asked yet?" he asked.

"Cha, I been reading yo' eyes since you were just a lit'l boy. I saw Miss LaTisha in yo' past and in yo' future long before you ever kissed a girl. Yes, and I know 'bout dat, too." Her tender smile was brief and as she looked more intensely at him her mood changed. "What's mo' important here is you've experienced the spirit dance with Miss LaTisha. It's mo' than a great gift; it's sacred and it's ancient."

"But what does it mean?" he asked softly and deliberately.

"Dis is why you're here today, Tom. You want meaning to what's been happening to you because you don't understand it." She extended her hands and placed them on the table, palms up. "Cha," she whispered, "I can tell all that I know 'bout dis and you'll just walk away and not believe. You think of me as an old woman who works magic. Well, I didn't have anything to do wit' what is done. *Dis* is not magic."

"No, no, that's not it, Madame LaSay. Really." Tom scratched his head and sat forward. "It's just so amazing that you've said things we've experienced without us telling you anything, that's all. It's just damn amazing." He repeated and looked at Tish. "Isn't that right?"

"Well, yeah. Please, tell us more. I'm so intrigued by all this."

She stood. "No, I'm finished here." She looked at Tish. "Dat young man who was with you befo'. He'll help you understand in a way better than I."

She picked up her suitcase and placed it on the table. She opened it and placed her cards inside. "He's part of yo' ancient story. His role is to guide you. Go nah. It's time to find him."

"But, Madame LaSay, we haven't even asked you a question. Can't we talk some more with you?" Tish pleaded and reached out one hand toward her.

"No, there's no mo' for me to say."

Tom stood with his head hung in defeat. He reached in his pocket and pulled out a twenty-dollar bill. As he attempted to place it in her tip jar, Madame LaSay placed her hand over it and stopped him.

"You never asked me a question, remember? I told you only what was placed on my heart. Dat was not work. You cannot pay me for telling you dat which I have always known." She untied the red scarf that covered her head. "I've waited for you to come by so dat I could finally tell you."

She removed her scarf and handed it to Tish. "Take dis. It's my gift to you. As a symbol from yo' past; it may help you to remember."

"Thank you so much." Tish stood and took the scarf and held it in the palm of her hands. She looked at it and wondered how this piece of cloth could help her understand her quandary.

Tom hugged Madame LaSay. "Thank you. It's been good seeing you." He took Tish's hand. "We'll go now and see what we can piece together."

"Bye, now. Take care of one another. Love every moment you have." She placed her hand over her mouth and turned away from them.

They silently walked from Jackson Square and toward the Mississippi River.

"Tish, I need to sit down and talk about what just happened." He pointed to a vacant bench near the bank of the river. "And will you please tell me what the spirit dance is all about?"

"Remember when we made love after you found out that Sable was pregnant?" She sat beside Tom and turned toward him.

"Yeah, you were over at my place on post."

"Do you remember how you felt right after we climaxed? Maybe it was just me, but I felt like I'd had a true spiritual experience. It was as if our life energies had lifted from our bodies and danced on the air just above us."

"Oh, yeah…I remember that. We didn't talk about it, but that's exactly how I felt, too." He rubbed his hands together. "But how'd Madame LaSay know about it?"

"I don't have a clue. But not only that, she seemed to know that someone had explained it to me and that I hadn't told you. Now, that's just wild."

"Nothing about this seems normal, Tish." He lowered his head and ran his hands across his forehead, unsure how she'd take what he was about to say. "I'm not into this mojo stuff. I've known about it all my life and heard stories about how it can mess with people's minds."

"It seems there's more to it than mojo. And it's not just people like Madame LaSay who know about it, either." She reached toward him and placed her hands on top his. "Tom, I'm convinced that we've lived in times before this and we've been lovers more than once."

"You are, huh?" He stoked her hands and looked into her eyes. He drew his lips inside his mouth momentarily, and then said, "Then tell me, Tish, what else do you know."

"The experience was so powerful to me that I had to tell Dee about it. I don't usually talk to anybody else about my love life, but this was so different than anything else that'd ever happened to me."

She paused and waited to see if he'd say anything, but he didn't, so she continued. "Dee told me that it was the spirit dance that we'd experienced. Yes, she called it the very same thing."

"How does Dee know about this?" he asked. "I've never heard of such a thing."

"Well, me neither until she explained it to me. She told me that her Jamaican grandmother had experienced the spirit dance and told her about it when Dee was learning about sex."

"So what does it mean?"

"It means that we're soulmates, Tom. It's an ancient, spiritual ritual of sorts that only happens between two people who are destined to be together."

"So that's what Madame LaSay meant when she said I could stop looking 'cause you're right here?"

"I believe so."

"Okay, so who's this other man that you're suppose to talk to?"

"Remember last year when I came to New Orleans? I was with Maurice when I met Madame LaSay. I suppose she's referring to him."

"So what's he got to do with all this?"

"I can't even imagine. You guys met at the balls in San Antonio. He's never asked about you, so he knows nothing about our relationship."

"Well, she was very direct about him being a part of our past." He stood and paced a few steps.

"I agree that it seems strange that she would tell us to go find him. I wonder how he can help," Tish said as she stared toward the river.

Tom sat back on the bench. "Does he read cards and crystal balls?"

She chuckled. "No, he's a clinical psychologist. I doubt he uses those tools in his practice. He just doesn't seem to be the type."

"Do you have his number? You guys are still friends, right?" He seemed anxious to get to the bottom of this.

"Yes, I have it. You want to do this, Tom? Are you sure?"

"You know, Madame LaSay made a believer out of me." He rubbed his hands together. "If there's more we can find out about this and if Maurice can help, let's do what she said. I want to know."

Sixty-Nine

What more can be said
to make it clearer for us.
Believe in our hearts.

Tish and Tom sat close to each other on a plush loveseat and patiently waited for Maurice to meet them at the hotel piano bar. Located down the busy hallway from the hotel's lobby, the cozy room had piped-in traditional jazz music that created a soothing atmosphere with mellow saxophone melodies. Two nearly bald and a couple of gray-haired African American gentlemen entered, dressed in neatly pressed dark slacks and white shirts. They sat at their positions on the stage and picked up their instruments. On cue, the quartet of jazz musicians began playing Louis Armstrong popular tunes with the same passion one would expect from Louis' very own band members.

Through the first two numbers, the couple sat silently and sipped wine and snacked on cheese and fresh fruit.

"So, Maurice said he's coming, right?" Tom fidgeted in his chair and scanned the doorway to see if his frat brother had entered the room.

"He'll be here. Let's give him a few more minutes." She crossed her legs and sat back in her chair.

He began to doubt anything would come of this meeting with Maurice. *What could he possibly tell us that we don't already know? Why would Madame LaSay send us on this aimless assignment?*

Tish stood and waved her hand, motioning someone to walk toward them. "He's here," she whispered.

"It's too noisy to talk in here, now. Let's meet him and go out to the lobby."

"Great idea," she responded and picked up her purse from the table. They walked toward Maurice and she greeted him with a hug.

"Hey, there. Thanks so much for coming over." She extended her hand toward Tom. "Maurice, you remember Tom?"

"Right, yes. What's up man?" He eagerly took Tom's handshake.

"Good seeing you again, bruh," he said and wondered if their impromptu meeting felt as bizarre to Maurice as it did to him. "I appreciate you taking the time to come talk to us, too."

"Well, Tish said you guys needed to discuss something important and it couldn't wait because you're leaving for San Antonio tomorrow." He pushed his hands into the pockets of his navy blue casual slacks and shrugged his shoulders. "However I can help…"

She pointed to a quiet spot in the hotel lobby where they could talk in close proximity. "Let's go sit down over there. We need to explain what just happened to us."

"Maurice, remember when I came to New Orleans last year and we met Madame LaSay in Jackson Square?" She sat forward in her chair and made direct contact with his eyes.

"Yes, I remember her." He folded his arms across his chest and sat back.

"Tom and I just saw her again today. She said some things to us that left us with more questions but she wouldn't even listen."

"Like she did you last year, huh?" He smirked and rubbed his chin.

"Yeah, just like she did before. But the difference is she told us that we needed to talk to you. She said you'd know how to explain things—like why our hands match, and about our dreams….so we'd understand and believe." Tish glanced at Tom then turned toward Maurice. "What do you suppose she meant by that?"

"I'm not absolutely sure what she had in mind…actually I only have a theory." He hesitated before he continued. "See, nothing's going to prove any of this…it'll sound more like a hunch than fact."

"Okay, man, *what* are you talking about?" Tom's patience with all this had begun to fade.

"All right, here's the deal…and all that I know about any of this. You can take it with a grain of salt—it doesn't matter to me." Maurice sat forward and spoke in a very serious tone when he continued. "One of my classmates is practicing past life hypnosis and apparently with a lot of success. He uses it primarily with his patients who live with constant, chronic pain."

"I heard about that on an Oprah show one night last week." Tish looked at Tom and gave him a nod.

"Yes, it's becoming a more recognized form of psychotherapy for some forms of disorders." He took a deep breath and continued. "I was very interested in it and asked him to process me through a past life hypnosis just for the heck of it. I was curious to see if it'd work on me."

"And what does this have to do with Madame LaSay? Was she there to witness your trance?" Tom's composure had shriveled more with this explanation.

"No, that's not the connection. I know this sounds incredible, but Madame LaSay is a true psychic, a gifted woman who can actually read people and see things we can't even imagine." He looked at Tish and continued. "Remember when she told us that I'd been in your life before and that I'd never hurt you?"

"Yes…"

"Well, during my past life hypnosis you appeared as a Queen of Egypt and I was the Pharaoh's best friend and also his head of state. My role was to protect him, his national affairs and his secrets. His name was Teti and your name was Nadjet-M-Pet, but your nickname was Teet."

"Oooo, my goodness..." Tish whispered. "How'd you know that?"

"Know what? I'm just telling you what I learned while I was in the trance, that's all." Maurice looked at Tom. "What?" He lifted his shoulders and waited for Tom to speak.

"Ah…man, just keep talking." Tom couldn't believe any of this. Surely Tish had told him about their dreams.

"Tish, you were one of Teti's biggest secrets. You were the only one of his queens that he ever truly loved. You bore his heir, his first son. But your life ended tragically and my job was to ensure that your position in death would guarantee your ability to find each other again in the afterlife."

"How'd you get all that from a hypnotic trance, huh?" Tom couldn't believe any of this. It was so unscientific, so preposterous.

How'd any intelligent Black man with any scruples get caught up in such mumbo jumbo?

"Bruh, you guys asked me to meet you. Remember?" He turned from Tom and looked directly at Tish. "Look, I didn't come to you with this information because I wasn't sure how'd you take it. Now, I'm only reporting to you what I've experienced. If this is scary or you think I'm just making it up, I can stop talking about it and we can leave it at that."

"No, no, please, Maurice." She shook her head and leaned toward him extending her hands in his direction. "It's just that you've said some things that I've already dreamed and I think Tom has too." She glanced at him and nodded gently.

Maurice turned to him, also. "Tom, you're Teti. You were Teet's husband in a life lived more than four thousand years ago."

Tom didn't respond, so he continued. "If you don't believe me, I'll call Dr. Lee Chung right now and ask him if he'll meet us in his office tomorrow morning. You can do the past life regression yourselves. See if I'm lying."

"Why we need to see him? Weren't you trained in this stuff when you got your Ph.D. like him?" Tom felt like calling this man's bluff.

"No, actually this isn't something we're taught in our Ph.D. program. He studied past life hypnosis independently after reading about its successful uses by a psychologist somewhere in Florida," he answered matter-of-factly.

"Madame LaSay told us we'd been having dreams of our lives before," Tish chimed in. "What's so strange, Maurice, is that we've had the same dreams. She wouldn't let us ask her about it though. What do you think?"

"I've learned that dreams can be more than dreams," he replied. "Sometimes they're memories that are replayed in our sleep state. Some are so old that we think that they're simply imaginary stories because they couldn't possibly be real."

He cupped his hands around his cheeks and paused before making his next statement. "Think about it… if you two are dreaming the same thing, how could it not be a shared memory?"

"So, how did Madame LaSay know you'd had a past life hypnosis? This looks like a set-up to me…" Tom shook his head, still in disbelief.

"I have no idea how she'd know about it. I haven't seen her or talked to her since it was done." He sat back in his chair and crossed his legs. "See, she's not like us. She has her very own way of knowing things without someone ever telling her."

Tish tilted her head and frowned. "But Maurice, she told us to have you explain this stuff because she said you could help us understand and believe. Why would she do that?"

"Again, I don't know. She perceives information different than us and we don't even know how to study it," he answered. "Maybe when we first met she sensed something or saw our past and our future. Perhaps she thought if I suggested the past life regression approach to you that you'd find it a more plausible answer to your questions. You know, some people just don't trust cards and crystal balls."

Tom rolled his eyes. "Okay, this all sounds like something straight-up from a reality TV show."

"Yes, it does seem extraordinary. But I'm so intrigued by it." Tish turned to Maurice. "Please call your friend, Dr. Chung. I want to do the past life hypnosis before we leave tomorrow. We have a four o'clock flight, so if he can meet us in the morning, I'd love to go through the regression."

"Sure, I'll call him and see if I can set it up. He's a good guy. He'll probably do it."

"How about you, Tom?" she asked. "You said you wanted to know."

"Yeah, I did say that." He stood and scratched the back of his neck. "But I don't know about all this though...it's going a bit far for me."

Seventy

Stepping back in time
Reliving moments once lost
not just memories.

"Tish," Dr. Chung's comforting voice suddenly seemed so much closer to her as he spoke. "I'm going to count to ten." He waited a couple seconds then continued. "Unless you have something else you want say, I'll start the count and when I get to ten, I need you to open your eyes."

"Yesss," she whispered. She understood, but felt compelled to delay ending the experience reliving her past that seemed so familiar.

"Wait." She felt her body go limp. Warm tears fell down her cheeks and she whispered, "I will be back. Find me and we can be together again. Remember, life is eternal and so is love."

The embrace she'd felt wasn't there anymore but she heard the man as he spoke very softly, "Please stay with me. I have no life without you…."

She then watched him from above the doorway of the room as he sat on her bed holding her body and rocked back and forth, crying with agony.

Tish felt her legs fold up and she curled into a fetal position on the psychologist's coach and cried through her own anguish. "Come back and find me again," she whimpered. "Life is eternal and so is love."

"Tish," Dr. Chung's soft voice again broke into her fantasy-like experience. "Are you okay?" He stopped writing on the notepad and looked patiently at her.

"This is Teet, why do you call me Tish?" She surprised herself hearing the question.

Tom sat back in his chair and crossed his legs. He picked up a magazine and opened it, then softly laid it back on the end table. Then he leaned forward and waited for the next round of questions.

"Okay, Teet." Dr. Chung went along with her clarification of to whom he was speaking. "I'd like to know if you're okay and if you're in a safe place right now."

"My soul has left my body," she replied. "It is sad. He thinks that I am still with him." Tears continued to fall from her closed eyes. "I am safe. It is dark here, now. I can not see my love anymore."

"Where are you?" Dr. Chung asked.

"Nowhere. This is the nowhere place." She answered with a very matter-of-fact tone in her voice. "I have to stay here until it is time to come back."

"When will you come back?"

"Not before it is the right time. He must be there, too," she replied. "We will come back again and again. We must continue our life together. Our love is too strong. It will never die."

"Who is your love, Teet?" Dr. Chung asked.

"He is the Pharaoh Teti, the father of our son, Pepi I, who will rule Egypt when it is his time."

"Teet, how will you be certain that you've found your love when you come back?"

"When we first meet, we will feel what we know. The river, like the Nile, will draw us near. Our hands will look the same, more than with any other hands. We will have the spirit dance."

She paused, wondering if she'd just said that from her current experience. But then she added, "There will be a man in our lives who will bring us together. He is Mereruka, Teti's vizier. He will come back with us and assure our meeting."

Tom picked up his notepad and added the name to the list of others and then drew a line under it. He'd recorded places and events she'd talked about while in the trance. Then he wrote in bold letters, THE SPIRIT DANCE.

"Okay, now I need to speak to Tish."

They'd been at this for more than two hours and she felt that Dr. Chung needed to bring this to a close, especially since it was Sunday and his day off.

"Yes…." she forced her mouth open to reply. "I never left."

"Good." He smiled and placed his notepad and pen on the table beside his black leather chair. "Now, I'm going to start counting. When I get to ten, I need you to open your eyes and be aware that you are in my office in New Orleans. Ready?"

"Yes."

He counted to ten and she opened her eyes. The first person she saw was Tom, as he stood beside her biting his bottom lip and trying to smile.

"Hey, baby." Pleased to see her man, she sat up slowly and reached for him. He leaned down and pulled her to her feet and gave her a strong hug.

"Welcome back, my queen," he said as he rubbed her back and stroked her hair. "You've had quite a trip, huh?"

"Yeah, I suppose I did." She sat on the sofa and pulled him to sit beside her. "Dr. Chung, I'm confused. I thought when you're hypnotized that it would be like you're sleeping and talking from your subconscious state. I was aware of everything you said – all your questions. I didn't lose awareness or control over what I said, either."

She scratched her head. "I don't think I did it right."

"No, Ms. Edwards, you did it perfectly correct." He touched her hand gently and looked directly into her eyes. "You were a Pharaoh's queen and you mothered his heir. Your love was the most profound of all time."

"How can you be so sure?"

"Because you told us in quite some detail." He sat back and relaxed with his arms crossed on his chest. The plain brown T-shirt matched his cotton trousers and the leather loafers he wore without socks. He was a small man, in his early forties. He removed the gold, wire-rim glasses and pointed them at her when he continued to explore for an explanation. "Have you ever heard the names Teet or Teti before?"

"No…well, yes, but only in dreams," Tish replied. "Maurice mentioned them, too."

"I see. How about Mereruka, or Pepi I?"

"No, never those names before." She looked at Tom. "How about you, have you heard those names before?"

"Nope, not me." He shook his head and glanced back at Dr. Chung and waited for him to say something more.

"Okay, let's see what we can find if we Google the names." He stood and walked to his desk. He sat in front of his computer and began to type away.

Tish was very curious about what had occurred and the possibility that she might find out that she'd lived in ancient times in Egypt and had been a queen. *How many women I know can say that?*

After a few minutes, Dr. Chung looked up from his computer and smiled. "It looks like I'm in the presence of royalty. It's all here. Pharaoh Teti lived during Egypt's sixth dynasty and his son, Pepi I, became the next Pharaoh after his death. Mereruka was Teti's vizier. If you hadn't looked it up or no one had ever told you these things, how would you know unless you'd been there?"

"Oh, my God!" Tish stood up. "Does it really *say* that?"

"My dear, yes, it does. I'll forward the sites I've found to both your e-mail accounts and you can read the history yourselves when you return home."

"Damn…" Tom said, just under his breath. "I guess I'm a real believer now. Google don't lie."

"Well, there's more than just what Google tells us, Tom. You mentioned dreams. Have you told each other about the dreams you've been having?"

"Not all of them. But we've each been keeping journals where we write them down. I guess it's time now to pull them out and see what we have, huh?" Tish sat beside Tom again and looked at him hoping to see agreement in her plan.

"The dreams and this session explain a lot, even why we're so drawn to rivers. This is truly amazing stuff." He glanced at Tish and continued. "I'm more certain than ever that we're supposed to be together."

"That's exactly right, Tom," Dr. Chung responded. "Hold on to this woman, she's very special. And you're very lucky to have found her."

"That I do know," he replied, with a big smile, tenderly touching her face. "And hold on to her is exactly what I intend to do." He looked at Dr. Chung. "Thanks again for coming in to meet us on your day off. We really appreciate your help."

"No problem. Maurice and I work together on interesting cases like this. We don't have much control over life you know. You just have to be ready to do your thing when life beckons you to listen." He stood and extended his hand to Tom. "I'm happy that I'm the one who helped you discover your past life experiences. So, thank you. I'm honored."

Tish opened the door to leave. “I wish we could stay longer in New Orleans so we could talk more with you about his. But we’ve got to hurry to the airport now and catch our flight back to San Antonio.”

“Sure, travel safely.”

Tom held her hand as he drove them to the airport in silence. He glanced at her and smiled at the beautiful woman who’d returned into his life.

I’ve found my queen.

Seventy-One

Quiet solitude
Moments to reflect and think
Souls revealed in verse.

"Let's take some time to think about what happened in New Orleans, okay?" Tom asked Tish as he opened the car door for her after taking her home from the airport.

"I'd say we have a lot to consider, huh?" She touched his face and smiled softly.

Concerned that he may be frightened by what they'd learned about their past and the manner in which the news came about, she'd honored his effort to avoid taking about it on the flight back to San Antonio. "I'll call you later tonight after I pick the kids up from Dee's house. You take care."

She watched him drive away and then walked into the house and sat at the desk in her quaint oval-shaped office. She stared at the built-in walnut bookcase positioned directly across the room and felt the urge to write something.

She found the quiet solitude helped spark a creative moment. Instinctively, she picked up a pen and began to write a poem. She named it, "Our Hands" and copied it into her journal after she completed the last draft.

When God created me, he must have known
that one day I would need an extra pair of hands.
So when he created you, he duplicated my hands
making them more masculine
so that they would suit you.
But they were still so much like mine that
when I finally found you and held your hand
it felt almost like I was holding my own.
So, now when I'm alone and I miss you,
I cup my hands together and close my eyes and
pretend that you are here
and it is your hand that I am holding.
This may seem silly and maybe even odd,
but it is true.

I believe it is a way for me to know when I have found
the one God created just for me.
And when given time to be still, mature and reflect
on all that we have learned about each other
I have come to understand that no matter what happens,
you will always be the one for me, because when I long
for you, I lie in bed and remember how you pressed your
open hands against mine as we made incredible love
and the energy of our souls passed through our
duplicated hands reminding us that we are a
perfect match, a perfect fit, and perfect soulmates.

Seventy-Two

Often it takes time
to get things right and in place,
I am ready now.

The week that followed had been unremarkable. When Tish told Dee about their weekend in New Orleans she'd listened intently to every detail. She encouraged Tish to stay hopeful that Tom would come around and accept the news the regressive session with Dr. Chung had revealed as a reliable source. She'd even admitted that Tish's story was convincing enough to make her a believer in such things.

On Friday morning, Tish sat at her desk reading the manager's morning report when the phone rang. "Hello?"

"Tish, how are you?" Tom's soft voice was a welcomed sound to her ears.

"Great, how about you?"

"Good, good. Hey, are you free tonight? I'd like to take Aaron and Dee out for dinner to celebrate his graduation since we missed his family party. I'm thinking Luciano on the River Walk."

"Sure, I can do that. That's a great idea." She hadn't seen him since he took her home from the airport and had only briefly spoken to him a couple times since. He hadn't said one word to her about New Orleans or about their future. Having dinner with their friends would be a good way to end the week.

"Terrific. I'll pick you up at seven." He took a deep breath.

"Okay, see you then. Bye."

Tish arranged for Cathy to come over and stay with the children. She selected a casual denim pants suit and flat, brown leather sandals. When Tom arrived she scanned his handsome body decked out in a sharp black, double-breasted suit with a lavender shirt and dark purple necktie they had picked out together in New Orleans.

"My, my you look nice. I feel so underdressed," she said as he entered her foyer. "Give me a minute to change into something less casual."

"Okay, I'll wait," he replied smiling broadly. He walked into the family room and watched Simon and Melanie play a video game. "Hey guys. What's up?"

Tish went to her bedroom, puzzled because she had no idea this would be that kind of evening. She searched her closet and selected a new cranberry red, silk pantsuit she'd saved for the perfect occasion. She removed the silver loop earrings and replaced them with the pearl studs Tom gave her in New Orleans. She had a necklace that matched, so she put it on as well. After she changed into black patent leather sandals with a slight heel, she reviewed her new look in the mirror. *Okay, this is better.*

"I'm ready," she announced, as she stood in the doorway of the family room.

"You look wonderful." He hugged her and landed a quick kiss on her forehead. "Let's go."

Tom parked his car in the garage at the Marriott River Center Hotel. They took the elevator up to the lobby and walked through it and then down the stairs to the River Walk. As they turned right they saw Aaron and Dee seated beside each other at a four-top table just outside the Luciano Risterante with the best view of the river.

"Hi, guys!" Surprised to see Aaron also dressed in a suit and tie, she greeted her friends with hugs and kisses. "Wow, this is my first time having dinner out here at night. It sure is beautiful, isn't it."

Tom helped her into her chair. He hugged Dee and gave Aaron the handshake.

"Yes, it's a beautiful night," Dee replied. "Gosh, that's a pretty suit. Where'd you find it?"

"My favorite store, Stein Mart. Where else? A Delta can never have too much red in her wardrobe."

"I know that's right. I wish I'd found that one before you did. I love it."

Tom picked up the wine menu. "This is a very special night. So let's order some wine to start the celebration. What's your pleasure?"

"Aaron and I prefer Riesling; we like it sweet," Dee replied.

"That sounds good to me, too," Tish nodded.

"Then that's what it'll be." Tom ordered the wine and sat back to relax. "Dinner's on me, guys. So order whatever you want. Let's enjoy the evening and our friendships."

The couples reviewed the dinner menu and placed their orders. Luis, the waiter, arrived with the wine, opened and poured everyone a glass.

Tom proposed a toast. "Aaron, we're so proud of you and your accomplishments. You persevered until you reached your goal. Congratulations on your graduation from college and landing that great job." He tipped his glass toward his friend.

"Here, here," Dee and Tish chimed in.

Luis took their orders and while they waited for their dinner, the couples talked about current events and enjoyed the music from the Central American band that played on the other side of the lagoon. At eight o'clock, they ended their performance and left the River Walk.

After everyone finished eating, Luis cleared the table. Tom leaned toward Tish and took her hand. "Guys, not so long ago, you introduced me to this wonderful woman. Dee, you even suggested where we'd go for our first date, right here on the River Walk. I think it's fitting that the four of us end up here tonight."

He paused. "I want to thank you for bringing us together. I *really* love this woman."

"Ooo, I can tell…" Dee grinned and lifted her eyebrows. She waited until Luis served their coffee. "We're so glad that you're back together, too. From the beginning I felt like you were supposed to be with each other. I don't know how I knew, I just did."

"Yeah, man…" Aaron said, as he rubbed his chin. "You two show look good together."

"Well, this is how I want it to be, from now on." Tom reached into his jacket pocket and pulled out a black box, the size of a deck of cards. It fell to the floor. He leaned down to retrieve it from under the table.

Tish scooted her chair a little to give him more room and saw Aaron nod at someone behind her. Before she could turn to see who was there, she heard a violin playing, "When I Fall in Love."

The musician walked from inside the restaurant, dressed in a tuxedo and bow tie and stood by their table. She looked at

Dee, surprised by the sudden serenade, and whispered, "What's going…."

Tom retrieved the box and from the corner of her eye she saw him beside her, on one knee. He placed the closed box on the table in front of her then looked directly into her eyes.

"Tish, it's taken me almost two years to really understand why you're in my life. In that time I've come to know what real love is all about. I've experienced how wonderful and pure it feels when you're with the right person." He took her hand. "I've fallen in love with you all over again. And just like the song says, my love for you is forever."

He picked up the box. "I don't have much to offer when it comes to material things. But I have everything to give you when it comes to my love, time, help, friendship and companionship. If you will have me, Tish, I want you to be my wife, best friend, and only lover. You're already my soulmate, we devoted ourselves to each other long ago." He opened the box and two fireflies flew out blinking their lights as they glided upward and toward the river.

"Wow, that's just beautiful, Tom." Tish whispered as she watched their glowing lights fade into the sky. She returned her focus to Tom as he removed a ring.

With tears in his eyes he reached for her hand. "In this small chapter of our eternal lives, Tish, will you marry me?"

She looked resolutely into his eyes as her tears fell. "Yes, Tom. I will marry you."

"Thank you," he whispered and slid the gold ring, with a ruby surrounded by four small diamonds, on her finger. He stood; pulled her into his arms and gave her a passionate kiss.

Bianca, the owner of the restaurant took pictures and the entire wait staff applauded along with Aaron and Dee. The serenade concluded and the musician shook their hands in congratulations and returned to the restaurant.

"You guys had this all planned, didn't you?" Tish wiped the tears from her face and looked at her ring. "Oh, it's so beautiful… thank you, Tom." She showed it to Dee.

"The ruby is your favorite color," he explained. "And red is the color of love. When you look at it, I want you to remember how much I love you."

He held her hand and looked at the ring as he continued. "The four diamonds represent our children that we'll raise together. Our perfect family; two girls, two boys, you and me. We are truly blessed, Tish. Thank you for not giving up on me."

"Okay, so when will the wedding be?" Dee pulled out the calendar from her purse. "I'm ready to set the date and get the planning started. There's no better time than the present!"

"Dang, girl. We just got engaged!" Tish laughed at her friend's eagerness to get them hitched. "I'm not sure I want a big wedding..."

"Hey, who said it had to be big?" Dee lowered her enthusiasm and thought for a moment. "How about a red and white December wedding? It's the perfect month for a Delta wedding..."

"No. Did that already and it was big and beautiful." She looked at Tom for support. "December is out. Red and white—not doing that again either."

"How about purple?" He grinned and laid his hand on his chest. "You know *I love* purple."

Aaron smirked. "Man, you also know that it's never about what the groom likes when it comes to the wedding thing... why do you think this one will be any different?"

"Oh, that's how you see it, huh?" Tish looked at Aaron in disbelief. She then turned to Tom and crossed her arms and rested them on the table. "Here's your chance to call it. When, where, what colors and how big. Tell us how you'd like the wedding to be and that's what it'll be, Tom. I mean it."

"Ah, see, man...there you go." He looked at Tish and Dee. "I didn't say that. That was Aaron."

"I know, but he's probably right. I bet you didn't have much to say about your first two weddings. This one will be your last, you know..." Tish poked his arm.

"You're right about that. Not ever again, not in this lifetime, anyway." He laughed and took her hand. "If you really want to know what I think, I'd like to have a small wedding this October at the Fort Sam Chapel. I want Aaron to be my best man, I see Dee as your maid of honor. Rather than having a bunch of other people, let's have Shaun, Melanie and Simon as our attendants."

He kissed her fingers and looked lovingly into her eyes. "It's not just us getting married, you know. We're bringing our families together as one."

"October?" Tish asked. "Don't you think that's kinda' soon?"

"I'd marry you today if I could, but my attorney said I have to wait at least thirty days. That's just in case Sable files an appeal." He took a deep breath. "It ain't happening, though. I don't see her doing that."

Aaron cleared his throat. "Right and I want to hear you say you want the color purple, man." He sat back with a smart grin and waited for Tom's reaction.

"You don't have to say it, Tom. I want to have a purple, gold and green wedding. Somehow I see those colors together." She couldn't believe what she'd just said, she didn't even like green.

"You're kidding right?" Dee retorted. "You want me to wear those colors?"

"No, maybe one or the other…it'll be up to you."

"Well, it'll be purple," she replied and signaled Luis for more coffee.

"Enough about the details, already. We can have a planning lunch or something as soon as we find out when in October the chapel will be available." Tish held her hand out and looked at the ring. "It's just beautiful…"

"I'm glad you like it," Tom replied. "Oh, by the way, October twenty-second." He sipped his coffee and blinked his eyes at Tish.

"What?" She tilted her head and thought for a second. "You've already checked on the chapel?"

"Yeah, and booked it, too. You know…just *in case* you said yes." He rolled his eyes and flashed a twisted smile. "It's always easier to cancel than to wait too late and then can't get in at all. That's all I'm saying."

"Man, you on it." Aaron laughed. "And that's all I'm saying!"

Seventy-Three

Talking things over
Free, seasoned advice given
Support the process.

"So, Tish, tomorrow's the big day...are you ready for this?" Dee asked as she stacked the dirty dishes on her dining room table. Aaron and Tom stood and headed for the family room.

"I'm ready," she replied with a wide grin. Tish handed Dee her dinner plate. "Who'd have thought I'd be saying I'm ready to get married again with all I've been through? I never expected this would ever happen."

Tom's mother lowered her coffee cup and tilted her head as she gave Tish a nod. "You should never say what you'll never do, 'cause you just don't know what the Lord has in His plan."

"That's right," Tish's mother chimed in. "And by the way, have you taken care of, you know, did you get an appointment with your doctor so you could get back on the pill? You don't want to have an accident on your honeymoon, you know. That's how so many babies get made. It's best to plan ahead." She picked up the last fried catfish nugget and bit it in half, then turned toward her daughter.

Tish glanced at Dee and watched her roll her eyes up to the ceiling and press her lips together as if trying to control laughter. She turned and stared openly at her mother and blinked her eyes. "I've seen my doctor and nothing has changed since Simon was born. He said I don't need the pill because the chances of my getting pregnant again are slim to none."

"Well…anyone for dessert?" Dee spoke up quickly wiping her fingers with a napkin. "I have Blue Bell ice cream and pecan pie."

"I'll have a scoop of ice cream, honey," Mrs. Manning replied. "And another cup of this delicious coffee, please."

"One more glass of wine and I'll be done for the night. Tish, hand me that bottle." Mrs. Edwards reached for the wine then filled her glass. "How about your wills...have you updated them?"

Dee shook her head, picked up the dinner dishes, and went into the kitchen.

"No, Mom. We're not even married yet."

"You've at least talked about it, right?"

"Yes, we have…"

"And what about the children, what are they going to call him?" She gulped the wine down and stared at Tish, waiting for an answer.

"Mom, why all the questions?" She felt as though her mother was interrogating her for no reason. "Can you just be happy for me? We'll work all that out as a family. It'll be fine."

"I'm just concerned, that's all, dear. You can't blame me for trying to help you think about the things that could create havoc in your marriage." She poured more wine in her glass. "So is Tom moving into your house or are you going to buy a new one together?"

"Mom…" Tish took a deep breath and paused before answering. "We've decided to stay in the house so the children won't have to move and disrupt their lives. There's no reason to do all that."

Mrs. Manning cleared her throat and gestured a wave. "Honey, I think that's the best thing you could do. Children need stability."

"Sure they do." Mrs. Edwards nodded then turned to her daughter for one last shot. "So when are we going in for the night? I had a long flight to get here today and I'm tired."

"We can go anytime you and Mrs. Manning are ready. I have your bedrooms ready for you at the house," Tish replied. "The children will stay here with Dee tonight. Tom's going to pick them up in the morning and take them with him to the airport to meet his son, Shaun. Then they'll go over to the Chapel and walk through the wedding together."

"So you didn't have a rehearsal today?" Mrs. Edwards asked.

"No, I was told to write my vows and pick out a song for the wedding. All I have to do tomorrow is walk down the aisle, say my part and kiss my groom." She smiled and glanced at her ring. "My friends have worked out the details with Tom and I'm not sweating any of it."

Dee returned to the dining room and placed the ice cream on the table. Mrs. Manning picked up her spoon and said, "As soon as I finish this, I'll be ready to leave, too. We have an exciting day ahead of us."

"Yes, we do!" Dee stood behind Tish and hugged her shoulders. "My girl is getting married and we're going to be right there to love and support her. We've planned a small and very simple wedding. But it'll be one to be remembered – just wait and see."

"Indeed," Mrs. Manning said with a big smile.

"So when are you leaving for the honeymoon?" Tish's mother had one more question.

"On Wednesday. First thing Monday morning, Tom's taking the kids and I to Fort Sam to get our military dependant ID cards made. He wants to get that out of the way as soon as possible—to get us in the system."

Tish sat forward and placed her elbows on the table. "On Tuesday we meet our attorneys to revise our wills. Then to day care and the children's school for Tom to meet their teachers and administrators and to get him added to the children's emergency contact info."

"You guys are so organized. I'm impressed." Mrs. Edwards stood and stretched. "That wine's made me sleepy."

"So where are you going on Wednesday?" Mrs. Manning asked.

"To San Francisco, just until Sunday."

"That's nice. San Francisco is a beautiful city," she replied and took her last sip of coffee. "I'm ready, now. It's gotten late and we all need to get some rest tonight."

Seventy-Four

Best friends get married...
Breath takes on a new meaning
eternity saved.

"So, Tom, do you have your wedding vows memorized?" Aaron glanced over to his friend after he drove past the security gate at Fort Sam Houston.

"No, not really..." he replied, looking down at his typed notes that captured the essence of what he'd planned to say to Tish when it was his turn to speak from his heart. "I think I'll just end up saying whatever I feel at the moment. Trying to remember what I've written and revised about a dozen times now seems kinda' ridiculous."

"Yeah, I hear ya', man." He scratched his head. "Whatever happened to just repeating what the preacher asks you and then saying I do?"

"I can't say. But now that Tish has become a poet and all, I think she wants this to be more personal and creative than the standard vows." He folded the paper and carefully placed it in the jacket pocket of his dark blue formal military uniform. "Just in case I freeze and lose my words, I can pull it out and use this." He tapped the pocket with his hand.

"Sounds good." Aaron nodded and turned into the chapel parking lot and stopped beside the only car there. "Looks like Chaplain Scott's here already."

"Great, so we can get inside and meet with him before anyone else arrives," Tom said. He opened the door and stepped out into what had to be the most glorious late-October day San Antonio had ever had. Even with the full sunshine of the early evening hour, the temperature was a mild seventy degrees as a pleasant breeze kept the almost no-humid air in a constant stir.

Aaron got out of the car and reached for his tuxedo jacket hanging in the backseat. "Man, if I hadn't put on a couple pounds after leaving the Army, I'd be wearing my uniform, too. You sho' do look sharp in yours."

"Hey, thanks." Tom adjusted the jacket and straightened his bow tie. "I'm still in, so I have no choice..."

They walked side-by-side up the limestone steps toward the building. "So, Tom, you ready to do this again?"

"Yeah, bruh, more ready than I've ever been. This time it's the right thing to do because my heart is in it."

"All right, then. That's the right answer...so let's do it." He opened the door and they stepped inside and headed toward the chaplain's office.

An hour later, Chaplain Scott, a red-haired Irish-American, about fifty years old, escorted Tom and Aaron from his office into the sanctuary. They stood facing family and friends who'd come to witness their wedding ceremony.

As the organist played Stevie Wonder's "Ribbon in the Sky," Tom beamed when he scanned the faces in the sanctuary. On the front row closest to him sat his brother, Bryan and his mother smiling proudly at him. Behind them, to his surprise, were Madame LaSay, Maurice and probably the new woman in his life, Liz. He hadn't met her yet, but Tish had told him about her.

He looked toward the back of the church and saw Katrina walk in with her new husband, Derrick. She smiled shyly at him and flashed a quick wave before they sat near the rear of the church.

Tom turned his attention to the other side of the aisle. Mrs. Edwards sat smiling in her gold silk suit, her ankles crossed and hands cupped together. Beside her was a young man who looked a lot like her. Tom decided that the man must be Tish's brother Carl, who was expected to fly into town that morning from Sacramento.

He looked behind them and caught a nod and wide grin from Jonathan, his attorney sitting and holding hands with Tish's friend, Dionne. About a dozen Deltas and Omegas, along with a few people from Tish's office, looked back at him and waited patiently for the wedding to begin.

Midori sat near the pianist, ready to sing the solo selected for her by Tish. Michael, one of Tom's fraternity brothers, with a voice like Luther Vandross, sat beside her waiting for his turn to sing the solo Tom had selected for the wedding.

The middle aisle had been decorated with pots of blooming purple and yellow chrysanthemums and bows at the end of each pew. The organist finished the song and nodded to the audio staff to start the recorded music Tom had selected for Tish's entry.

As “You Were Meant for Me” by Donny Hathaway began to play, Shaun entered and walked down the center aisle toward his father. Dee followed Shaun, wearing the same purple gown she’d purchased for the Omega gala. She stood on the other side of the chaplain and faced the congregation. Then, Melanie and Simon walked slowly down the aisle together, followed by Tish just a few steps behind them. She wore a simple long, white, sleeveless gown with a high waist trimmed with jeweled stones of purple, red, and emerald green. The red scarf Madame LaSay had given her was draped loosely over head and around her neck. She carried a single, white water lily.

She arrived at the altar just as the song completed. Tom looked at her and nodded with pleasure. Tish’s face was beaming, she looked so happy.

The chaplain began the ceremony with the traditional readings from the Bible and said a prayer to bless the couple.

Then he addressed the guests, “The couple will now say the wedding vows they prepared in their own words.”

Tom turned toward Tish and as he looked into her loving eyes, he couldn’t remember one word of what he’d prepared to say. He blushed, then said the first thing that came to his mind, “Press your open hand against mine,” he lifted his right hand and waited until she raised her left hand and placed it against his. He took her other hand and held it by his side.

“Today we are one and our love will continue to grow.” He paused, hoping he’d remember the rest of what he’d written.

Tish took this as her cue to start with her vows and begun to recite them.

“The measured heartbeat accelerates the flow of life through my being; excited hands tremble in anticipation of touching your face. Our eyes lock in search of the inner spirits we share; I surrender my love, my life, and forever into your safekeeping, witnessing everything that I am covered with your sincere protection. Our journeys, long-destined, merge as one with common purpose—encountering the ultimate love free of boundaries, conditions, or limitations. Neither time nor space can define or capture its perpetuity. Gratefully, and with much contentment, you have joined me again; now, you reach for me as breath takes on a whole new meaning. My whole existence is yours for an eternity.”

Tom almost lost his breath. "Damn, Tish, that was beautiful," he whispered. He cleared his throat and took a deep breath. With a stronger voice, he began his vows.

"Well, I'm no poet, but I want to express to you how I feel in my own way. Since the beginning of time man has needed to share his journey in life with the woman God created just for him. Often, we grope in darkness, just passing time until the veil that blinds us is lifted when she finally walks into our life. The challenge we often face is to recognize the significance of that moment and to never turn away from the gift her life brings to ours." He lifted her hand and kissed her knuckles.

"Tish, when we first met, I could tell you were a very, very special woman. Little did I know then that we'd share this incredible love and extraordinary journey. All that we've experienced, even through the ages, has prepared us for this sacred occasion. Today, I marry my best friend. I promise to always love, honor, cherish and protect you. All that I am, and all that I will become, I share with you by my side, forever and ever. Thank you for loving and trusting me enough to become my wife. I can honestly say I've found my rib."

Midori stood and stepped next to the pianist as he started playing the opening chords to the Heather Headley song, "If It Wasn't for Your Love." As she sang her solo, Tish and Tom continued to face each other holding hands as tears fell down her face. He took the scarf off her head and held it in his hand. He kissed her cheek. "You're so beautiful," he whispered. "Thank you for such a beautiful song."

"Welcome," she replied, barely above a whisper.

When the song concluded, Chaplain Scott placed his hands gently on the couples' shoulders and directed them to turn toward him. "I now pronounce you man and wife," he smiled and nodded. "You may *now* kiss your bride."

It was the moment Tom had waited for. He pulled her into his arms and planted a kiss that made his mother blush and cover her face. Michael stood and with the pianist accompanying him, he sang, "You for Me" by Johnny Gill.

When the kiss concluded, Tom stepped to Melanie and placed a gold necklace around her neck with a heart-shaped charm that had engraved, "My Princess" on one side and "Love, Tom" on the other. He then turned to Simon and placed a gold ID bracelet on his wrist that was engraved "Man of God" on the top and inside "Love, Tom."

Tish placed an ID bracelet on Shaun's wrist engraved like Simon's, but with "Love, Tish" on the inside. Then they took two red roses from Dee and approached their mothers and with kisses, handed one to each.

The couple turned and looked at the congregation. Tom raised his hand and with a broad smile said, "Thank you!" They walked down the aisle and out the door as Michael finished his solo.

Seventy-Five

A brand new chapter
Our book of life continues
Joy with adventure.

"So, Tish, how's San Francisco?" Dee asked the Friday following Tish's wedding. She sat at her desk and closed a folder then placed it in the file drawer.

"Ah, it's beau-ti-ful," she replied, sitting across the table from Tom sharing a sundae at the Ghirardelli Ice Cream and Chocolate Shop. She pushed the speaker button on her cell phone. "Tom's here and we're stuffing our face with the best chocolate on chocolate, with chocolate in the world." She licked her lips. "So you know I'm happy…"

"Hey, Dee," Tom said looking at Tish. "Your girl's grinning like a nine-year-old over here."

"I bet both of you have more than enough to smile about. So have you taken in any of the sites yet?"

Tish placed her spoon in the dish and wiped her mouth. "Yeah, yesterday we drove down the crookedest street and then rode the cable car to Chinatown. We started to go out to Alcatraz, but it didn't seem like the thing to do on a honeymoon. Today we drove over the Golden Gate Bridge and had breakfast in Sausalito."

"And now we're having lunch at Ghirardelli's!" Tom chimed in.

"Sounds *healthy...*" Dee giggled. "I'm just checking in to let you know all's well here in San Antonio. The children are enjoying having their grandmothers around. We took them to the River Walk last night and tomorrow we're all going to a show at the Carver."

"Great, sounds like you guys are having fun, too." Tish picked up her spoon and took another bite. "Mmm, this ice cream is sooo good. Well, hug the kiddos for me and let our moms know we're doing fine. We'll see you guys on Sunday afternoon!"

"And, Dee," Tom scrapped the last spoonful of the sundae and offered it to Tish. "Thanks again for helping with the kids and hosting our mothers. You and Aaron are real friends. We owe you…"

"Not a problem," Dee smiled and pulled her purse out of the desk drawer. "You'd do the same for us." She removed her keys. "I'm taking the rest of the day off and heading home. Enjoy your trip and travel home safely."

"Okay, will do," Tish replied. "Take care. Love you girl! Bye." She dropped her cell phone in purse and turned to Tom with a pensive expression. He could tell she was about to tell him something intriguing. "Know what we should do?"

He smiled at her and leaned closer. "No, what?"

"When the children have their Christmas break, we should all go to Hawaii for vacation."

"Hawaii?" He hadn't expected that answer.

"Yeah, I inherited a timeshare ownership from my father," Tish explained, sounding more excited. "The company has resorts all over and I'm entitled to a three-bedroom property. Even when it's not my week, I can rent one for not a lot of money. I've been eager to use it. See, we'd have a bedroom, the boys could stay in one room together and Melanie in the other." She tapped her chin. "And we can always get another room for Dee, Aaron, and Little Aaron."

"But why Hawaii?" Tom was still on the place, not the logistics.

"Because we haven't been there before," she nodded. "Just like we chose to come to San Francisco because it was one place we both wanted to visit and hadn't yet. Besides, Simon is really into volcanoes now. Don't you want to go to Hawaii one day?"

"Sure, but isn't that going to be expensive? Especially for five of us?"

She nodded. "It'd be a bit more than what we'd spend on Christmas presents for all the kids, but the trip could be our gifts to each other. No shopping involved." With a thoughtful grin she continued. "The more I think about it the more I like the idea. Dee and I get Christmas bonuses every year from the company. It would cover the airfare. So what do you think?"

"I think it sounds like a great idea. I like it." He rubbed her back and looked lovingly into her eyes. "Tish, you're the best thing that's ever happened to me."

"Oh yeah?" she replied as she lifted of one eyebrow. "Is that 'cause I shared my chocolate ice cream with you?"

"Yeah, that and because you're sharing your whole life with me, too." He kissed her lips. "I like that you love to travel and explore new adventures. I can see it's going to be an exciting journey with you. And I treasure every moment of everyday."

"That's how I like to roll…no more dull moments." She stood and wrapped her arms around his neck. "Tom, I love you. Thank you for a wonderful honeymoon in this beautiful city. I'll never forget this."

He stood and pulled her into his arms. "Baby, I'm here to be with you always and to keep you safe and happy. Whatever you want you got it, okay?"

"Thanks, sweetie," she whispered.

Tom gave her a passionate kiss in the middle of the busy restaurant. Then they left and walked down North Point Street holding hands and enjoying the warmth of the bright California sun.

Seventy-Six

Wish upon a star
that in paradise sparks the
miracle of life.

A distant thunderstorm rumbled above the dark horizon. Soft flashes of lightning broke into the constant ebony sky and reflected like a mirror against the ocean waves.

Tom sat next to Tish in warm sand, sharing their wet towels on the once crowded Waikiki Beach. He could hardly believe he'd spent the past two days on the big island of Hawaii with his new family, exploring volcanoes, rain forests, and black sand beaches. Now he and the love of his life were together in complete solitude enjoying the end of their first day on Oahu Island, watching a storm as it slowly approached land.

"It's so beautiful here," he whispered into her ear. "So peaceful." He grabbed his t-shirt that matched his navy blue and white, tropical print swim trunks and put it on.

The wind shifted and the temperature dropped as the storm moved closer. Tish, wearing only her swimsuit and white linen cover-up, shifted her position, leaning back against his chest. He wrapped his arms around her and held her tight.

"Thanks for helping make this vacation work, baby." She kissed his arm. "I'm the most blessed woman in the world."

"You deserve the good that life has to offer, Tish. It's my job to make sure that you have nothing but all the love and happiness you can stand from now on." He kissed the back of her neck.

"Mmm, my husband is sending chills down my arms, just so you know…" she wiggled and added, "I could really get used to this."

"That sounds so good to hear you say… 'my husband.' I just wish I could've found you years ago. I've never been so much in love before. This is how life is supposed to be, Tish."

"I agree. But now that we're together, let's make the most of every moment we have, okay?"

"Deal. As Patti says, 'the best is yet to come.'"

"We'd better go inside before that storm gets any closer," Tish replied. "I'd like to live to see the best that's coming." She chuckled.

"I hear ya'. This Marriott Resort hotel is awesome. I bet the kids are having a blast at the pool with Dee and Aaron."

"Yeah, and I'm ready for a spa treatment, maybe a nice massage."

"Baby, I'll give you a massage right after I bathe you—I can give you that Manning Touch. They don't have that on the menu in the spa, you know…" He stood up and grinned looking down at her.

"Oh really? So what's the Manning Touch?" she asked as he helped her to her feet.

"It starts with a hot bath with sensual oils. You'll relax as I wash all your tension away." He took her hand as they walked toward the hotel. "Then you'll lay naked on your stomach while I start working on your toes, then your feet. I'll massage each leg and slowly move up your back to your arms and neck. Then I'll roll you over and start all over again."

"So how will it differ from the spa massage?"

"Well, for one, you'll be naked the whole time…and also, you might get your toes and feet kissed and loved on. I bet they don't do that at the spa…"

"No, I've never paid money to have my feet *kissed and loved on* before…but it sounds interesting. I can hardly wait for this new experience."

She placed her arm around his waist and pulled him closer to as they walked from the beach. "I'm so happy, Tom. This is the life I've always wanted. Thank you."

"I'm with you on that. So, thank you for letting me be right here so we can do this together. I've never had a better Christmas."

"Is there anything I could give you to make this an even more special gift?" she asked.

"You know Tish, I wish you and I could have a child together. That would be the greatest gift." He looked down at her as she slowed the pace of her steps.

"Oh. I did tell you that my doctor advised that I'll probably never be able to have another child, didn't I?"

"Yes, we talked about it." He stopped walking and held her in his arms. "Baby, it's okay. If we don't ever get pregnant we have four beautiful children to raise and I'm happy. But, if we did…then that would be absolutely the ultimate blessing, you agree?"

"Yes, Tom. It would not only be a blessing it would be a miracle."

"Miracles do happen…you just have to believe. So let's go get that bath and massage going so I can get you all relaxed. Then, let's make that baby." He grinned and squeezed her tighter. "I love you so much."

Tish looked up at the sky. "Look, the clouds have moved out and there's one star. Let's each make a wish."

"I wish for a healthy, beautiful child that has your smile, personality, and optimism in life," Tom responded.

"I wish our love will survive all the changes life will bring for the rest of eternity." She looked at him with a shy smile. "I also wish we could have a healthy baby. I just don't…"

"Hey, let's just leave it at that." He cut her off. "If it's meant to be, it'll happen."

He took her hand and began walking again. "For now, let's not sweat it, let's go make love and enjoy our spirits dancing. I can't wait."

"Me either."

Seventy-Seven

Love lasts forever
Vows pledged, lives lived as thankful
Valentine sweethearts.

"So Tish, are you and Tom still seriously trying to get pregnant?" Dee picked up her menu and glanced at the lunch specials at the crowded Tommy Moore's Café on the eastside of downtown San Antonio almost in the shadow of the Alamodome complex.

"Yeah, but so far nothing's happened." Tish grinned at her friend. "But we're sho' enjoying the process!" She giggled and pointed to her selection on the menu when the waitress approached their table. "I want the pork chops, greens, and mac n' cheese, please."

"Yes ma'am," Yvonne, a middle-aged African American woman replied, wearing black slacks and a long-sleeve white shirt. She looked at Dee and waited.

"I'll have the catfish, green beans, and mashed potatoes, please." Dee looked up at the waitress and smiled, "and some more cornbread, too. Tish ate it all already…"

"Yes ma'am, I'll bring some right out." She picked up the menus from the table and walked toward the kitchen.

"Sorry, I guess I was really hungry, huh?" Tish wiped her lips and drank some tea.

"Well, yeah, that's why I asked about the pregnancy. I thought you were eating for two already, the way you went after that cornbread."

"It was hot when it hit the table and I love my bread hot, so once I got into it…you see what happened."

"So, what are you guys doing for Valentine's Day next week? Aaron and I are going to see "Phantom of the Opera" at the Majestic on Friday night. Can you keep Little Aaron for us?"

Tish nodded. "Sure. We'll be home with the children. We'll hang out, order pizzas and watch a movie at home. He can spend the night, too if you want. Marcus is supposed to come for the kids on Saturday and take them to the matinee ice show."

"Thanks, that'll be perfect. Maybe we'll try to get pregnant, too." Dee laughed out loud. "Girl, can you see me with a new baby? Please…"

"What? Of course I can."

"I'm only kidding, so don't even go there."

"Dee?"

"Yes?"

"Do you think it's silly of me to want to have another baby? I mean, I'm nearly forty years old…and…well, should I do this?"

Tish paused. "I mean, shoot, it may not even happen, but what if I do get pregnant?"

"I think it's a wonderful thing that you and Tom want a child together and you're trying. If it's supposed to happen, it will and nothing can stop it. So relax and let go of any doubts you have." Dee waited as Yvonne put two huge portions of hot cornbread on her very own bread plate. "Thank you, so much."

"Ma'am," the waitress turned to Tish. "Would you like more cornbread?"

"No, I'd better not. I won't have room for my meal. But thanks."

Yvonne walked back to the kitchen and Tish watched Dee spread butter all over her cornbread. "Girl, you sure you can eat all that?"

"I guess we 'bout to find out, huh?" She grinned and blocked her plate with her hand. "Don't even think about coming over here with your fork, either…"

"Getting back to V. Day… Tom and I are going to the Links' Western Dance on Saturday night. After church we'll go to the downtown Marriott and have brunch. I think it's going to be too cold to walk the River Walk, especially since we'll have Sheila with us. But if not, we may do that for a bit until it's time for Melanie and Simon to come home."

"Sounds like a great way to spend time with your sweetheart. You guys seem so happy. Are you really?"

"Yes, really. I've never been happier, Dee. I honestly feel like my life is perfect. I wouldn't change anything. Tom is so loving, so attentive and supporting. I had no idea that being married could be this wonderful…it never was before."

"You never shared your life with your soulmate before, either. It makes all the difference in the world." She sipped her iced tea and sat back in her chair as Yvonne placed their lunch plates on the table.

"Will there be anything else?"

"Yes, Yvonne, would you bring us some hot sauce, please?" Dee replied. "Gotta' have it for this catfish."

"Sure, be right back and I'll bring more tea, too."

"Thanks." Tish took the last sip of her drink and placed her glass on the table.

"So sounds like you've had Sheila every weekend lately. What's up with that?" She looked puzzled. "Not that it's a problem for you guys, just I'm surprised that Sable would let her spend so much time with you."

"Oh, I didn't tell you…Tom said she's pregnant and having terrible morning sickness. During the week she puts Sheila in daycare and works part time at home as a database administrator for some military contractor." Tish paused as Yvonne filled her tea glass. "Apparently David isn't around anymore and she needs help on the weekend."

"Pregnant? With David?" She smirked. "She thought he'd be the daddy type? I could've told her that'd be a losing bet if she'd asked."

"Yeah, that's her dilemma. We're just happy to have Sheila when we can. She's a doll and the kids adore her. They think it's really cool to have a little sister."

"You know that if you need a break, Miss Sheila can come stay at my place anytime. I love having little girls around, too."

"Dee, thanks for always being there for me especially with the children." She wiped her mouth with her napkin. "You've also helped me understand and accept so much about Tom and I. I wouldn't have gotten any of it if left to my own devises."

"I'm glad to share with you what I know." She took a mouthful of potatoes and nodded. "This food is sooo good."

The following Sunday, Tom and Tish filled their plates with the chef's best dishes at the Sunday brunch and followed the hostess through the busy restaurant to their table. Once they were seated, Tom reached for her hand and offered a prayer.

"Dear Lord, we are grateful for this beautiful day and this wonderful meal we are about to eat. Bless the food and the hands that prepared it. May it nourish our bodies, strengthen our minds, and replenish our spirits with renewed energy and purpose. Thank you for my lovely wife and our beautiful children. Keep us close, protect us from harm, and envelop us with your love, forever. Amen."

"Amen," Tish said. "You know how to say a lot with a few words. That was a nice prayer, thanks."

"Hey, I'm a very grateful man and I know from where my blessings flow. I believe you wouldn't be here now without His hand guiding all that happened." He looked at his wife and smiled broadly. "I thank God everyday for sending us to that party so we could meet."

"Yeah, that's right," she replied. "Did you know that I wasn't going at first? I had this idea that a back-to-school party was for youngsters, not grown folks in their thirties. But Dee insisted and since I didn't have anything else going on, I gave in and went."

"I'm glad you did…I fear what would've happened if we never met…ooo, let's not even go there." Tom shook his head briefly, then filled his mouth with sausage and eggs.

"Okay, deal. Let's think forward." She smiled at her handsome husband. "I have another idea to share with you…" she said softly, lifting one eyebrow.

He looked up from his plate and waited for her to continue.

"Each of the children has done fantastic work in school making all A's and B's on their report cards. No discipline problems, just praises from their teachers." She put her elbow on the table and rested her chin in the palm of her hand. "Shaun's science project is going to be presented in the school's science fair, Melanie has progressed superbly with ballet and Simon's volcano research project was judged the best for his grade level."

"Somehow I feel another trip coming up…" he said, then drank some coffee.

"Exactly!" She was pleased that he anticipated her next thought so well. "I think it's important to reward great work and behavior from our children. Plus, spring break is coming up and we've never been to Orlando. I'd like to go and I know they wouldn't object too much." She paused, looking at his surprised expression. "What you think?"

"Orlando—as in Florida?"

"Yep. Where all the theme parks are and tons of other things to do." She felt more excited. She'd done her homework and priced everything out already, too, just in case he'd ask.

"We can stay at a timeshare again?"

"I've already checked and one is available the dates we need. I've done our income taxes and we should get at least half of what we need to cover the cost back in the refund. The rest can come from my savings account."

"You sure you want to spend that much money on another vacation so soon?"

"Yes, I'm sure. That's exactly why I saved it, for our vacation time. It's important to take time out to enjoy life and each other, Tom. The children will be grown before we know it. You can't get this time back."

"True, true." He scratched his head. "You know we'll probably have Sheila too. Did you factor her in?"

"Of course. Shaun, Sheila, Simon and Melanie." She smiled sweetly, feeling she was getting through to him. "All six of us. It'll be so much fun."

"Okay, if that's what you want to do. I'm with you." He kissed her hand. "You and the children are my life—the reason I live. If you're happy, I'm delighted." He kissed her fingers. "So I look forward to spending a week in Orlando with my family playing with Mickey and them. I know if you plan the trip, it will be wonderful. Let's do it."

Seventy-Eight

Best made plans revised
Yet the journey continues
Destiny unfolds.

Tish drove away from Sable's apartment breathing deeply to calm her nerves. With Sheila safely strapped in her car seat, she sighed in relief that they were finally on their way to the airport.

She glanced at the clock and saw that they had just enough time to park the car, check in, and hopefully make it through security without missing their flight to Orlando.

She picked up her cell phone and dialed Tom's number.

"Hello," he answered, standing by the hot tub at the resort watching the children playing in the water.

"Hey, baby, we're on our way to the airport."

"Good, good. You okay? You sound flustered."

"That's putting it mildly." Tish released another big sigh and continued. "When I went to Sable's to get Sheila she was not happy. I guess she expected to see you. When I explained that you and the kids had left already for Orlando on Friday, she flipped. 'He didn't tell me he was going *to Orlando*!' she huffed. I calmly told her we'd already purchased our tickets when she called last week saying she wanted Sheila to be at her baby shower last night."

"Right, right. We did this for her."

"You wouldn't have known it from her reaction. She kept looking at the car, I guess to see if you were in it. I explained that I'd changed Sheila's and my tickets to leave this morning but we couldn't afford to change everybody's."

"You've picked Sheila up before so what's her beef today all about?" He scratched his head.

"Who knows? She was in a ticked-off mood; that's all I know. Maybe she's mad 'cause she's not going to see Mickey, too." Tish turned down the radio and sat back in the seat to relax her body while she drove.

"Well, it's a public place and she can come down here just like anyone else, you know? Anytime she pleases." He sat in a deck chair and sipped his root beer.

"*We* know that. She's a trip, Tom. She didn't even thank me for coming for Sheila, taking her with us to Orlando or making changes to our flight." Tish rubbed her forehead. "She's given me a real headache."

"Baby, don't let her get to you."

"Oh, I don't plan to. I'm on my way to Orlando to play with my family. That's all that's important right now."

"Sure is. And thank you from me for changing your flight, picking Sheila up and bringing her with you." Tom smiled and leaned forward in his chair. "I adore you, but you know that, right? I can't wait to see you."

"Good. I need your hands all over my neck and back. There's stress that needs your attention, mister." She felt her stomach suddenly feel sick. "Oooo, now my stomach is upset a little bit. Hope I'm not coming down with something."

"It's just the drama of your encounter with Sable settling in, I'm sure. Look, just get here. I'll take care of all that when you're in my arms again."

Tish turned into the airport parking lot. "All right, sweetie. We're on our way. What's the weather looking like in Florida?"

"It's warm and the sun is shining bright right now, but they're talking about thunderstorms this evening. Hopefully y'all be in before any of that happens."

"We'll do our best!" She parked her car. "Tom, I love you. Kiss the kids for me and tell them I'll see them in just a little while."

"I love you too, my wife. Travel safe and get to me soon."

Five hours later, Tom drove toward the Orlando airport and scanned the angry sky, as dark, thick thunderclouds blew in and swiftly transformed the sunny afternoon into a dark, scary looking night. This was not how Tom had expected his family would start their spring break vacation when he and Tish booked their flights four weeks before.

He parked the rented SUV as a loud clasp of thunder echoed through the garage. "I bet no planes'll be landing here for a while," he whispered as he walked toward the tunnel that led him into the terminal.

Sure glad Aaron and Dee came along so the kids didn't have to come out here with me. Tom checked his cell phone to see if he'd missed any messages. He found none.

Crowds of people waited inside the airport for their loved ones to land; some upset that the ticket agents were helpless in offering any encouraging words. The thunderstorm had traveled from Houston, closing airports and delaying travelers along the way. Tom checked the status for arriving flights and saw that Tish and Sheila's was scheduled to land in forty-five minutes. *We'll just see*...he thought as he walked toward the coffee shop to wait it out.

An hour passed and Tom went to the passenger arrival hallway and glimpsed his wife holding Sheila in her arms as she walked toward him. The pulse of his heartbeat quickened when their eyes met and she smiled at him. Relieved that they had finally arrived safe and sound, he opened his arms and welcomed them with a warm hug.

"How are my ladies?" he asked, then kissed his daughter's soft, brown cheeks and brushed his hand across her hair, braided and clipped with six pink and green ribbons that matched her dress. He winked at Tish and passionately kissed her ruby red lips that complimented her red and white blouse.

"Better now," she responded in a whispered voice, lingering onto his hug. "I got sick on the plane. That's never happened before."

"Sick? Really?" Tom looked at her face and saw that she looked rather pale. "How are you feeling now?"

"Not so good. The flight was real bumpy and it made me get sick to my stomach. I threw up." She laid her head on his shoulder. "I've never thrown up on a plane before. It was so embarrassing."

"And that's why they have those sick bags on the back of the chairs...they know it can happen. So don't feel bad about it. You're human and it's only normal."

"I know...and it's over now. I'm ready to get to my room and lie down for a while. Let's get our luggage."

Tom took Sheila from her arms and wrapped his arm around Tish's waist as they silently walked toward the baggage claim area.

I wish I'd picked up some roses for her on my way to the airport. She looks like she really needs some pampering right now.

He leaned over and kissed Tish's forehead and squeezed her tighter.

As soon as they entered their timeshare suite, Tish ran into the bathroom and closed the door. Tom heard her gagging as she threw up again. "Baby, can I come in?" he asked with a concerned tone.

"I'll be okay. But thanks," she answered, just above a whisper.

Her weak response held him at the door, his hand on the knob, ready to enter anyway. "Sure? Can I get you anything?"

"Yeah, ask Dee to come here, please."

"Okay, be right back." He went to the kitchen where Dee was slicing a hot pizza while Aaron and the children watched "Mrs. Doubtfire."

"Dee, can you go to our bathroom and see Tish for a minute? She's sick and asked for you. I'll finish the pizza."

"Sure, no problem." She wiped her hands off with the damp towel and went directly to their bedroom suite. "Tish?" Dee tapped on the bathroom door and waited.

"Hey…" she responded and slowly opened the door. She sat back on the floor by the toilet with her arms across her stomach.

"Soror, what's wrong?" She entered and sat beside her friend.

"I feel like I have morning sickness…and it ain't morning." She looked up at Dee and took a deep breath. "I know this feeling and it's not the flu."

"Oh, my… are you pregnant?" Dee smiled and kicked the door closed.

"Not sure, but I think this might be an indication. I remember getting sick the moment I conceived Melanie and Simon. I stayed sick for weeks each time, too. I haven't had my period this month and it's overdue."

"Have you told Tom?"

"I don't know what to tell him—not yet anyway. Sure, I haven't been able to keep anything down all day. I thought it might be from all the stress, but heck, I've had worse days and never got sick over it."

Dee pushed Tish's hair behind her ears then placed her arm around her shoulder. "Well, I think you should tell him that you might be pregnant. He's so worried and you look so weak, girl. Don't you need some water or something?"

"I suppose so…water, juice—just no food. Not yet."

"I'll send Tom in with some apple juice for you. Talk to him, please." She squeezed Tish. "It's going to be all right. He loves you, girl and besides, you guys want a baby. So I hope what's going on with you right now is that child snuggling down in your womb." She stood and left the bathroom.

Dee met Tom in the kitchen leaning against the stove, eating pizza. "She's not feeling much better. Would you take her a glass of juice?"

"Sure…" He grabbed a glass from the cabinet and opened the refrigerator. "What's going on? What'd she say?"

"She needs fluids right now." She picked up her purse and the car keys. "I'm going to run out to the store for a couple things." She walked toward the family room and tapped Aaron on the shoulder to get his attention. "Baby, I'll be right back. You need anything from the store?"

"I'm good."

Melanie sat up from her position on the floor and swung her head toward the front door. "Auntie Dee, can I go with you?"

"Sure, come on."

"Dad," Melanie turned to Tom with a sweet smile. "Is it okay?"

"It's okay." He felt charmed by how nicely "Dad" sounded coming from his stepdaughter. "I'll let your mom know you've gone with Auntie Dee. See you in a bit." He walked into the bedroom and found Tish lying on the bed fully dressed and curled up in a fetal position. He sat beside her and rubbed her shoulder. "Hey, I have some juice for you."

She sat up slowly and took the glass. "Thanks."

"Dee and Melanie just left to go to the store."

"Okay." She drank the juice and handed the glass to Tom.

"Want some pizza? I saved you a couple slices." He kissed her cheek.

"Oh no…no pizza for now. Juice is fine." Tish fell back on the pillow and curled up. "I want to take a nap. I'll get up in a little bit, okay?"

"You rest as long as you need to." He rubbed her shoulder. "I'll go check on the kids to see if they've had enough to eat and then I'll come lie down with you."

"K," she whispered and shut her eyes.

Tom thought she looked like she felt better already.

The next morning, Dee tapped on Tish's bedroom door. "Soror, can I come in?"

"Sure." She tied her robe and stepped out of the bathroom. "Come on in."

"Tom and Aaron are cooking breakfast following Melanie's directions. Can you believe that?" Dee grinned. "They're as excited as the children about going to Epcot today. How you feeling?"

"Oh, I'm doing better, but I don't think I'll be hanging out with you guys today, though." She glanced at the plastic bag Dee had placed on the bed. "What's that?"

"I went out last night and got you a home pregnancy test. The pharmacist said it's the best one on the market." She picked the bag up and handed it to Tish. "Go pee and do this. I want to know if you're having a baby."

"Oh see…you ain't right." Tish chuckled and headed into the bathroom with the bag.

"It's a beautiful day, it'd be a shame to miss being out with us 'cause you're sick." Dee spoke behind the bathroom door. "What would you like for breakfast? I got some oatmeal, just in case you wanted something bland."

"That actually sounds pretty good… with some honey."

"Okay, I'll get it going. Be right back for the results."

Tish followed the directions for the test. She sat on the bed and waited, staring at the strip to change colors.

Someone tapped on the door. "Yes?"

Tom poked his head in and smiled. "Hey, there. I'm glad to see you're up." He walked in and sat beside her. "What'cha doing?"

"Thanks to Dee, I have news to share with you." She nodded at the strip in her hand. "It looks like we're pregnant. Can you believe this?"

"Oh, wow!" Tom's heart pounded and he jumped to his feet. He took her by the hands and pulled her into his arms, hugging her with all the passion he could share. "This is a blessed day! I'm so sorry you're sick, but I'm so happy you're going to have our baby."

"Yes, this is nearly a miracle. I really didn't expect to ever be able to do this again. I'm glad that this baby is with you. We're going to have a beautiful, healthy child!"

Seventy-Nine

Six Months Later

This journey will end
The time, no one really knows
Prepare for this fate.

Tom awakened from a deep sleep with Tish's hair, pressed against his nose, smelling like fresh vanilla, and his arm wrapped around her torso. He loved that she preferred to sleep in the nude and enjoyed having her warm body next to his, especially waking up finding her backed into his arms.

He kissed her head and caressed her enlarged belly that incubated their unborn child. He took a deep breath, smiled and felt great joy basking in yet another tender moment of love he'd longed to experience.

Life with Tish had been so easy, almost too easy. They'd never argued or had any major disagreements. They'd worked as a team on family issues, financial decisions, and work problems.

When Sable had her son, Jake, she learned very quickly that she couldn't handle parenting two children on her own. She gave up custody of their daughter and Sheila came to live with them seven weeks after Jake was born. David agreed to pay her child support but hadn't stepped up to the plate to do anything more. It proved too much for her to figure out, trying to work and take care of two children, she'd told Tom.

He gently kissed Tish's shoulder, appreciating her understanding nature. She'd happily converted the guestroom into a little girl's dream bedroom for Sheila. Her children had welcomed their stepsister as a fulltime member of the family as if she was supposed to be there all along. *How blessed could any man ever be?*

"Good morning, sweetie," Tish whispered as she took his hand and kissed it. "You sleep okay?"

"Never better…good morning, gorgeous." He pulled her closer to his chest. "How you feeling this morning?"

"Good. I'm glad the morning sickness has passed." She yawned and stretched. "I have a taste for strawberry pancakes and sausage. How about you?"

"Sounds yummy. Shall I go down and get it started or do you want to run out to Denny's?"

She rolled over and faced him with a sleepy smile. "You're so thoughtful…I love so much, you know that?"

"Absolutely, and I love you with all my heart. I want to spend the rest of my life waking up with you just like this."

"Well, in about three months, our waking up will be a lot different with a newborn in the house, you know."

"True, but we'll work through that. It'll be temporary – the baby won't be a newborn always. I'm looking forward to it."

"Really?"

"Yes, really. Now, I'm going to clean up and start breakfast for my pregnant queen." He kissed her lips. "We can continue to enjoy our quiet weekend together while the children are with their other parents."

"For sure, 'cause we don't get these that often; when all of them have a visitation weekend at the same time. The house is almost too quiet."

"You rest," Tom said, as he pulled away from her and threw the covers back. "I'll bring you breakfast in bed in just a few minutes."

"Oh, my…I get royal treatment. How very nice."

"You deserve it. Be back in a bit."

Tom left and Tish went to the bathroom and freshened up. She stepped back into the bedroom in her robe, turned on her stereo then sat at her desk as the morning sun beamed into the window. She pulled out her journal and as she listened to Kyle Turner's soft jazz she wrote the following words.

I Have Known You for Ages

I have known you for ages. We are in unison with the universe. Our love compliments the beauty of a rose bud as it opens in the warmth of the sun and the flight of two fireflies dancing together on air. Our love is as smooth as the flow of a slow moving forest brook and as powerful as rushing water from the highest falls.

When you make love to me, my body remembers you. It remembers how you were there to love and touch me for the very first time. It remembers how you made it feel then and how it feels now; my body remembers you. It remembers how you shook me and tantalized my nerves and made joyful tears flow from my eyes. My body remembers how you were there for me the first time, and many times through the ages. It has always been you. You have been my only true love. No one else has made me feel the fire-like spark that comes when you touch my body. No one else meets my energy with energy we both understand and welcome.

I have known you in Ancient times when great pyramids were under construction. I have known you when buffalo roamed as freely as the Native people and we depended on them for shelter and food. My body remembers you, as you loved me along many great rivers, in sand dunes as camel watched in awe, in piles of fallen autumn leaves, and in the middle of cotton fields when our picking was done. Our love survives millenniums of full moons, brilliant sunrises and winter storms.

When we look at each other and cannot speak, it is a reflection of the incredible source from which we were created and for which there are no words. When we cannot speak, it is because we remember, but have forgotten how to interpret what we know. It is awesome to now know, to remember you, and to understand that it has been you all along. You have returned into my life and now I am free to love you unconditionally because you have been and will always be there for me.

We are in unison with the universe. I share myself with you again, and with joy, I remember and I understand.

Just as she closed the book and placed the pen on the desk, Tom entered with their breakfast on a tray. She followed him to the bed and sat on her side with her legs stretched out. He placed the tray across her lap and then pulled up a chair and sat beside her.

He took her hand and offered the blessing. “Father, thank you for this beautiful morning, our good health, our devoted love for each other and the wonderful children you’ve entrusted into our care. Help us to be the best parents and loyal friends we are capable of being. Bless us with the wisdom, patience, and faithfulness we will need to face the changes and challenges life will undoubtedly bring. Thank you for this food we are about to eat. May it nourish and strengthen our bodies and minds. Amen.”

“Amen.” She kissed his cheek. “That was beautiful. I think you may have missed your calling.”

“What?” He had no idea what she meant.

“I’m just kidding. But have you ever thought about going into the ministry?”

“Not at all. Now enjoy your breakfast.” He shook his head and gave her a smirk.

“This is delicious,” she said after tasting a bite of everything on her plate. “The pancakes are hot and fluffy with lots of fresh strawberries, the sausage nicely browned to perfection, and the milk is cold just like I like it.” She took a deep breath. “Thank you sweetie, you take good care of me.”

“That’s my job. I do it with pleasure, too.” He sat back in the chair and glanced at the desk. “So did you get some writing done this morning already?”

“Sure did. I woke up feeling like we’re actually reliving our love story all over again. I was thinking about what Madame LaSay and Dr. Chung told us and wrote what came to mind that kinda’ summarizes all that. I’ll let you read it once I go back and edit it some. It’s still a rough draft.”

“Cool, I can’t wait to read it, or have you read it to me.” He put a chunk of sausage in his mouth and chewed.

“Tom, there’s something I want to talk with you about. It just needs to be said and understood, you know just in case…”

“In case of what?”

“Well, it’s not really just in case, it’s actually for when it happens…” She took a sip of milk and continued. “We’ve never talked about what happens when we die. We did our wills, but what about what we want done with our bodies? That stuff.”

“I never thought about the body thing. What do you mean?”

"After my father died, I decided to be an organ donor and then be cremated. It's crazy to spend a whole lota' money on the coffin and trappings that go along with the traditional burial."

She took his hand and continued. "I've already planned it all out and paid for my cremation. If I leave before you do, please carry out my instructions. You can do whatever you want with my ashes. Just don't spend unnecessary money on a funeral. Promise me?"

"And why are we talking about this right now?" He sat back and placed his hands on his lap. "You aren't going anywhere anytime soon. We have plenty of time to have this discussion."

"I'm sure we do, honey. But I've already thought about it and want you to know my wishes, that's all. Everything is in the bottom desk file drawer."

She paused. "There never is a best time to talk about this stuff, Tom. And it's better to plan for it while you're healthy rather than when you're sick and frightened."

"I suppose you're right. But, I don't know if I can let them cremate you, though. That's a very hard thing for you to ask of me. Hopefully, I'll go first and I won't have to deal with that."

"Either way, that's what I want. You should give some thought to your final arrangements, too. Whatever you decide, that's what I'll do if you go first." She smiled and placed her palm on his face. "The bottom line is we're in this together until death do us part. So we need to know what to do when that happens. It's not a what-if question you know."

"Sure. Enough of that for now." He stood and stretched. "Do you feel up to taking a walk? It's a beautiful September morning." He took the tray from the bed.

"Sounds good. Thanks again for breakfast. I feel energized and ready to enjoy my entire Saturday with you." Tish moved from the bed. "Isn't the Omega party tonight?"

"Yep," he answered as he walked toward the door. "Wanna go?"

"Why not? Dancing should be good exercise for me." She swayed her hips and snapped her fingers.

He glanced over his shoulder at her and laughed. "You're too much."

Eighty

To be here always
Dedicated to our love
Means the world to me.

"Can you believe that it was three years ago when we first met?" Tom drove through the gate at Fort Sam Houston and headed toward the NCO Club. He glanced over at Tish and admired the glow she projected when she smiled back at him.

"That's right, and here at this very place!" She reached for his hand. "And look at us now, married and pregnant. Who would've ever guessed this outcome, then?"

"No kidding." He grinned and squeezed her hand. "But it's the best one yet."

"I agree," she replied. "There's a parking space over there."

Tom parked and helped Tish out of the car. "Look, we don't have to stay long. I don't want to tire you out. Whenever you're ready to go, just let me know, okay?"

"No problem. I feel fine. It's good to get out and hang with our friends for a change. And there's nothing like an Omega party!"

Tom opened the door to the club and as Tish entered, he heard the blast of music coming from the ballroom. Iceman's selection of Barry White's "You're the First, the Last, My Everything," had attracted one couple to the dance floor. Most of the party-goers were in line at the buffet table or ordering drinks at the bar.

"I smell smoked ribs," Tish said, smacking her lips. "And I just got hungry, too."

"Then let's get a plate before we sit down. There're plenty of empty tables and chairs so far." He scanned the room and waved at his fraternity brothers as they walked by, food and drinks in hand. "Aaron and Dee are supposed to be here. Do you see them?"

"No, not yet." She looked up at Tom and added, "I need to make a bathroom run. The baby just sat on my bladder. Hold my place in line, be right back."

He kept his eyes on her as she left the room then turned his attention to the people standing in front of him. He saw David approach the buffet table and pick up a plate. He handed it to a beautiful, young woman who stood in line behind him. Tom watched him flash his playa smile at her and lick his lips. He shook his head. *Man, grow up…*

Then he looked toward the doorway and saw a group of women walk in together. One of them was Sable, sporting a short, black, spandex dress and four-inch heels. She'd gotten her pre-pregnancy body back since Jake was born and she looked sexy as hell with her hair pulled up in a ponytail and bangs down to her eyes. He watched her as she spotted David and strutted across the dance floor toward her target.

She extended her hand to him and Tom heard her say, "Baby, thanks for saving my place in line," as she stepped in front of the woman who'd captured David's attention and picked up a plate from the table.

"Sable…" David mumbled. "I didn't know you were coming tonight."

"Of course you did, sugar, we talked about it this morning." She grinned and looked at the woman, then rolled her eyes to David.

"Whatever, Sable." He turned his back to her and filled his plate with ribs, potato salad, red beans, and coleslaw without speaking to her again.

Tom glanced at the door for Tish to return and saw Dee and Aaron walk in. He waved them over to him.

"Hey, there. Where's Tish?" Dee asked, greeting Tom with a warm hug.

"What's up, man?" Aaron gave him a handshake and looked ahead at the buffet table. "Sho' smells good in here."

"She's in the bathroom. She should be back any minute." Tom's eyes were still focused on the door. "And the food should be pretty good tonight. Ribs smell like they're done right, that's for sure."

"I'll go check on Tish. Hold my place in line." Dee said to Aaron. "I'll be mad if all the food's gone when I get back. So if it's looking slim when you get your plate, go ahead and make ours, too." She walked toward the ladies room.

Dee found Tish sitting on the lounge chair crying. "What the hell's going on?"

"Oh, nothing really…it's just stupid women who don't care about what they say about people."

"Who said what to you to make you cry?"

"I was just washing my hands when Sable and her posse came in and one of them looked at me and said, 'So when did they start inviting *white girls* to the Omega party?'" Tish blew her nose.

"Did she say that to you?"

"No, she directed her comment to Sable," she replied, then looked down at her lap. "Before I could say anything, Sable looked at me all surprised when I turned around and she said, 'Oh child, they'll let anybody in here, husband-stealing bitches and all.' They laughed and left the bathroom together."

"Oh, damn." Dee took Tish's hand. "That hurt, huh?"

"It did hit that last nerve. Any other time I'd be mad enough to kick butt over something like that." She dried her eyes. "I can't believe I fell apart like this. It must be the hormones."

"Well, let's get out of here and go see what our men are doing. They should have our plates made by now." Dee stood and helped Tish to her feet. "You ready to get our grub on?" She smiled and gave her friend a hug.

"Yeah, but do I look all right?"

"Girl, yes. Don't let them huzzies get you down. They just mad 'cause they can't get a man and keep one when they do, that's all. Let's go party."

They returned to the ballroom together. "Look, Aaron and Tom are heading toward that table over there with our food. Great, we don't have to wait in line."

The two couples enjoyed their food silently listening to Sade's song, "Somebody Already Broke My Heart." When the song ended, Iceman picked up the tempo of the music. "All right, nah—let's get this party started!" he announced as Michael Jackson's "Thriller" blared from his speakers.

Dee wiped her mouth with a napkin and looked at Tom. "Speaking of scary, we need to keep an eye on Sable tonight. She's up to no good with her gang over there. I think she's trying to show out for them or something." Dee nodded to have Tom look at the dance floor where Sable and three of her girlfriends danced together.

Tom watched Sable approach David with her arms extended inviting him to join her. He raised his hand to her and walked away in the opposite direction. She laughed, flipped him the finger and continued to dance with her friends.

"Wow, I see what you're saying. Look, Tish, we can go now. I don't trust her."

"I'd like to get one dance in before we leave, okay?"

"Sure, baby, but something slow. I want to hold you close." He kissed the back of her hand.

While they danced to Patti LaBelle's "If You Ask Me To," Sable went to their table and tipped over a glass of water so that it spilled on the chair and floor where Tish had been sitting. With a devilish grin, she whispered, "Bitch" and continued walking out of the ballroom.

Tom escorted Tish back to the table and pulled her chair out facing the dance floor. "I'm going to the bathroom real quick and then we can go home."

Tish sat in her chair. "*Damn it*!" She stood quickly after he walked away and lost her balance. She slipped on the wet floor and fell flat on her bottom. "Ahhh!" she yelled.

Tom ran back to her and stooped down. "What happened? You okay?"

The look she gave him could have ripped his heart out. "Someone spilled water or something on my chair and I sat in it. I couldn't keep from falling when I stood up."

"Are you hurt? Can you stand?" His heart was pounding with fear that this was worse than just a slip and fall.

"Help me up. Then let's just go home."

Dee and Aaron left the dance floor and met them at the table. "Are you okay, Soror?" Dee asked giving Tish a hug. "I saw you fall."

"I'm a little shaken still, we're leaving now."

"I think you should run by the emergency room for a check to make sure you and the baby are okay, girl." Dee's voice was soft and reassuring. "The Brook Army Medical Center is less than five minutes from here. Just do it."

"I'm taking her over there before we go home." Tom responded before Tish had a chance to object. "You guys want to meet us?"

"Oh come on, it's not that serious, guys," Tish protested. "I'll go get checked but you don't have to leave the party just 'cause I fell. Stay and enjoy your time out tonight."

Dee grabbed her purse and took Aaron's arm. "We're right behind you Tom, let's go."

After the physician examined Tish and reviewed the test results, he called Tom into the examination room. "I have good news and I have bad news."

Tom sat on the bed beside her and took her hand.

"You're having a boy and he's fine. But I'm not comfortable letting you go home tonight. I want to keep you overnight for observation and more tests. Your blood pressure is elevated and I want to make sure you don't start spotting blood."

"Oh my." Tish exhaled. "Sure, that's a good idea. I can stay overnight." She looked at Tom. "Will you call Cathy and let her know? I want you here with me tonight. Ask her if she can stay with the children until the morning."

"No problem. Be right back" He kissed her forehead and left to give Aaron and Dee the update.

"Mrs. Manning," Dr. Mills said. "There's one more thing. Your fibroids may complicate things for your pregnancy and delivery. We want to take all precautions."

"I understand, doctor. I'll do whatever you say."

Eighty-One

Time is not a friend
It has no loyal measure.
Live in it wisely.

"Guys, thanks for coming by," Tish said as Aaron and Dee prepared to leave her bedroom. "I appreciate your company. It's great having Mrs. Manning here to help with the kids and everything, but I'm about to lose my mind with this required bed rest until the baby's born."

"Girl, you've done well to stay put for almost thirty days. I know I couldn't have lasted this long." Dee leaned over and kissed her cheek. "We've got everything at the job covered, the boss man is cool, so you can chill and take advantage of this quiet time."

"I guess…but you know I still have a couple months to go, yet." Tish stretched under the covers. "I feel like I'm just getting fat and my muscles are sagging. This is absolutely no fun."

Aaron kissed her forehead. "I can come by tomorrow and bring you some more movie videos if you like. Have you read the books we brought you already?"

"Sure did." She laughed and pointed to her laptop. "I'm organizing the poetry I've written to create my own book, too. Tom's leaving tomorrow morning for a training assignment in Dallas until next Friday. I plan to have it finished by the time he gets back."

"Cool, do you have a title for it yet?" Dee asked.

"No, not yet. I'll come up with something, I guess after I put it all together." Tish pulled the covers away from her and stood. "In the morning I'll e-mail what I have to you so you can print it out for me. It's easier to edit when it's in hard copy."

"Sure, I plan to come back over tomorrow with some lasagna for dinner, anyway. I'll bring the printout to you then." Dee helped her with her slippers. "Where do you think you're going?"

"I gotta pee, okay? I *can* go to the bathroom!"

"Well, just be careful. We don't want another slip and fall. That's what got you in this mess anyway." Aaron said, walking cautiously behind her until she entered and closed the bathroom door.

After Tish got back in bed, her friends said their goodbyes and left. She turned her attention to the laptop and read her e-mail until Tom came in to check on her.

"Hey baby, you doing all right?" He had that wide, sexy smile that still made her heart beat faster. He sat beside her on the bed and gave her a romantic kiss. "I love you so much."

"I'm glad you do, 'cause I love you, too so much." She stroked his face and leaned into his arms. "I'm doing as well as can be expected. This is the hardest thing I think I've ever had to do, though. Wish you didn't have to leave me tomorrow. It's going to make it even lonelier not having you around."

"I know, but the Army calls and I have to respond." He kissed her fingers. "I'll talk to you every chance I get and I'll make sure you have the emergency number where they can locate me immediately just in case you need me."

"Everything will be fine. Your mother is taking really good care of us and the kids love having her around. You'll be back before we know it."

"That's right. Now hand me that computer so you can go to sleep. I'll be there in a few minutes and you can curl up in my arms all night just like you always do."

"Before you go shower, can we decide on a name for our son? We haven't even talked about it yet and I have a request."

"Sure, baby. What's on your mind?" He brushed the hair from her face and smiled.

"I'd like to name him James Edward after my mother's husband." She spoke softly with her eyes lowered. "He should've been my father, but wasn't because of how everything happened. I'd like to symbolically give him his life back."

"That's a great idea. Have you talked to your mother about it yet? How will she react to this?"

"Knowing her, she won't like it. But it's our decision not hers." Tish took a deep breath and continued. "She named my brother and I after people in her family. Carl's named after her favorite uncle, his middle name is McDonald, her maiden name." Tish giggled. "She was so mad when his friends nicknamed him Hamburger Joint."

"What?" Tom looked puzzled. "Oh, I get it. Carl's and McDonald's hamburgers. That's just cold." He laughed.

"I'm named after my mother's mother Trista and her sister Ruth." She began to feel better about her decision. "So she's established a pattern already. I'm just following her lead."

"Well, I like the name and the reason." He hugged her shoulders. "We agree and that's all that matters. So go to sleep, now. We have that settled."

The next morning, Tish opened her eyes as sunrays brightened her room and made it feel warm and cozy. She reached behind her for Tom and realized he wasn't there. She rolled over and found a big brown teddy bear propped on his pillow wearing Tom's green beret and holding a note card. She opened it and read his handwritten message.

> "Teddy here has been assigned to watch over you until I get back. He's got all authority to take whatever means necessary to protect you from harm and to accept as many hugs you need to share in the middle of the night.
>
> You were sleeping so soundly that I just couldn't wake you so early. I want you to take care of yourself and our baby boy, James Edward Manning.
>
> I can't wait to meet and hold him in my arms.
>
> I love you, Tom."

Tish sat up and wiped a tear from her eye. She took a deep breath when she saw a vase full of at least two dozen red roses and babies' breath on the end table by the recliner facing the television. It was wrapped with a huge red ribbon and beside it was a small blue teddy bear. She went over to it and saw another note from Tom. It read, "This one's for James. Love, Dad."

*He's the sweetest man...*she thought as more tears fell down her cheeks. She heard a tap on the door. "Yes?"

"Tish, you up? I have your breakfast," Mrs. Manning's kind voice responded.

"Yes ma'am, come on in. I'll be in the bathroom."

"The children left for school already and so we have the house to ourselves, now." She placed the tray of food on the bed and waited for Tish to return. "How you doing this morning?"

Tish stood from using the toilet and felt water gushing between her legs. "*Oh my God!* My water just broke!"

"You sure? It's too soon to be having that baby, now." She went to the bathroom door and pushed it open. "You're passing blood too. That's not good at all. I'm calling 911."

Dee and Aaron joined Mrs. Manning at the hospital and waited for the doctor to give them an update on Tish's condition. Dee's cell phone rang.

"Hello?"

"Dee, it's Tom. I got your message to call. What's going on?"

"It's Tish. She's in labor and it's not looking good. You need to get here."

"What? She was fine this morning. What happened?"

"Her water broke this morning and she also passed a lot of blood before EMS got to the house. They've been working on her the past hour or so. How fast can you get here?"

"I'm on my way out the door right now. It's going to take five hours to drive back and that's if the traffic's not crazy. You know how it can get in Austin. Damn, I wish I hadn't left."

"Call Southwest and see if you can catch the next thing out of Love Field. That might be quicker," Dee offered.

"Will do. I'll let you know what I can work out." Tom ran to his car. "Tell Tish I'm on my way and that I love her."

"No problem. Now be careful." Dee took Aaron's hand when she hung up. "Let's pray for this family," she whispered.

An hour passed and Tish saw her son for the first time. "Hello, James," she whispered into his ear as the nurse held him close to her face. "He's so small, but he's crying so I guess that means he's all right?"

"He's going to be fine, Tish. He's a little premature, but he's got all his parts and his lungs are nice and healthy." The nurse took James to the pediatrician and they huddled around him. Tish couldn't feel a thing. She heard voices talking about her and getting blood replaced.

"Is your husband here?" someone asked.

"No, he left for Dallas very early this morning. He should be on his way back. I'm sure my girlfriend has talked to him by now."

She felt so tired, so weak that she closed her eyes and drifted off.

"Tish?" Tom's voice seemed to beckon her from a distant place. She felt his warm hands holding hers and hoped she wasn't dreaming.

"Tish baby, I'm right here." She heard him again, this time he sounded closer.

She opened her eyes and saw him sitting on her bed, leaning toward her and smiling through the look of fear. His bottom lip trembled.

"Hey…" She swallowed and tried to say more, but couldn't.

"Want some water?" He reached for a cup and placed the straw in her mouth. "You've had a rough time of it, sweetie."

"I guess I have." She glanced at her surroundings. "I don't remember them moving me into this room."

"They can't bring the baby to you yet. He needs to be in the nursery for a while. I haven't held him to see him up close, but I hear he's beautiful."

"Yeah, he looks just like his daddy." She tried to touch Tom's face but her arm felt like lead. "I can't lift my arm… What's going on?"

"You're still weak, baby. You lost a lot of blood." He kissed her cheek. "They're working on it and you'll be a lot better soon."

"Tom," she didn't believe that and wanted to prepare him for what she felt was more like the truth, "I want you to do something for me."

"Sure, anything, just name it."

"Give my poetry to Dee so she can have it published for me. Tell her the title of the book is *Maybe the Next Time*." She paused and took another sip of water. "I want you to write a poem by that title and include it in the book, okay?"

"You want *me* to write a poem?" He smirked and then frowned at her. "Why do you want Dee to publish your book for you?"

"Because I'm not going to be able to do it." She felt a sharp pain in her side and paused. "Before I heard your voice I heard my father's telling me he'd be back to guide me when I cross over. I don't think it was a dream."

"Oh baby, it's just the medication they're giving you. You're not crossing over any time soon, trust me." He squeezed her hands. "Just hang in there and don't give up. We have a long life ahead of us."

"Tom," she looked over his shoulder to the back of the room. "He's here."

"Who's here? There's no one else in the room but us."

"My father's waiting for me. This is real, I feel my body getting weaker and weaker. My time is very short now," she said just above a whisper.

"Oh no, you can't leave me..." He pulled her into his arms. "Women don't die in childbirth anymore...Tish, tell him, you can't leave, not now. What am I supposed to do without you?"

"Remember, Tom," she felt so cold against his warm body, "our love is eternal. We'll come back and find each other again. Always look for me...know me by my hands, my eyes and my touch."

"If you leave me now, it's not fair...it's just not fair," he whimpered.

"The next time," she paused as she felt the room fade away, "know me right away and let's get it right."

"Baby, I just want to hold you, please let me hold you again," he whispered.

"I love you." She took her last breath and her life energy passed through him before going to the dark, nowhere place.

Eighty-Two

The finality
of death brings not joy but pain
Rebirth comes again.

Five days later, Aaron and Dee hosted a memorial service in honor of Tish's life at the Fort Sam Houston Chapel. They arrived early and positioned her portrait in front of the pulpit and moved several red and white floral arrangements around it. A recording of Native American songs with flute and drums played softly in the background.

Chaplain Scott entered, dressed in a black suit, and embraced Dee, then shook Aaron's hand. "I haven't heard from Tom. Is he doing all right?"

"He's been pretty torn up as you can imagine," Dee responded. "I talked to him this morning and he sounded a lot better. Aaron's been helping him with the arrangements Tish requested."

"Yes, it's been really tough, though, Sir. I mean, she wanted her organs donated then to have her body cremated. How you do that to your wife?" Aaron shook his head. "He didn't have a choice—man, it had to be hard."

"So will he have her ashes here today?" Chaplain Scott asked.

"No, Tom's having them interned in the morning at the National Cemetery here on Post. He wants to be very private about that."

"Of course."

Dee smiled and added, "I went online and helped him find a white, heart-shaped wooden urn. We had it lined with red velvet. It's very nice."

"Yeah, then yesterday I took it to a friend's shop who's painting her name and dates of her birth and death on the lid." Aaron scratched his head. "The words 'Tom's Queen' will be there too. I'll go by and pick it up this evening after the service."

The chaplain looked at Tish's portraít. "She was a very beautiful woman and Tom loved her dearly. I'm sure he's feeling rather numb right now. He's blessed to have friends like you to be close and care for him the way you do. Keep up with him, he's going to need your love and support for a while."

"No doubt, Sir." Aaron lowered his head and wiped a tear. "He's my best friend and that numb feeling you just mentioned, well, he's not the only one who's got it. We all miss Tish and wish this had never happened."

"I'm sure, son. But you have to be strong for him now."

"We're doing our best, Sir," Dee said. "Right now we have *to do this* and move on to the next phase of life. And we have guests arriving."

Tom awakened just before dawn the next morning and quietly dressed in his Army uniform. Just as the morning light signaled the street lights off, he backed out of the driveway and headed toward the cemetery alone. In the passenger seat was the urn that held Tish's ashes that he'd carefully poured to rest next to the soft velvet lining.

He turned down the sound on his radio and drove for thirty minutes in total silence. He was on a mission, and it took all the strength and concentration he had to keep his composure.

When he arrived at his destination, he parked, took the urn into his arms and then walked to the gravesite with a dignified military stride. He looked for the plot where she'd be the first to be laid to rest. He saw two attendants, older Mexican-American men, standing beside the grave they'd dug, with shovels in hand, waiting for him.

"Good morning," Tom said in a hushed voice, smelling the earthiness of the freshly turned dirt. "Thanks for meeting me so early."

"Good morning, Sir," they answered in unison.

Tom handed the urn to one of the men who lowered it into a small, cement tomb-like casing and placed a lid on top. Together, the men guided the casing into the grave using a small crane with ropes and pulleys.

He waited as they completed their tasks and covered the grave with dirt. He thanked them and as he watched them leave, he listened to a mockingbird sing its morning song.

The sun began to warm the air and the dew-covered lawn glimmered like tiny stars that had fallen to the ground. The beauty of the moment was lost in the depth of his pain. Tom took a deep breath and forced himself to look once more at her grave.

"Tish, I miss you so much. My heart aches each moment I realize I won't see you again. I know you're in a better place and probably looking down at me right now. Before I leave I want to tell you that everything you asked was done and I even wrote that poem for your book. I did my best to come up with something that you'd be happy with, you know, since you're the real poet. So here goes, I hope you like it."

He unfolded a sheet of paper and read the poem aloud.

"Maybe when we meet again
the next time for the first time
maybe then we will get it right
Maybe the next time we will know
right away what has taken us too long
to figure out this time
Maybe we will recognize something special
and maybe we will get it right
Maybe the next life will be the one
that holds new promise for a whole life
together – not just bits and pieces
Maybe the next time when we meet again
for the first time we will not waste time
like we have before and we will
know what it is we are supposed to do
and we will just do it rather than
wait to be sure and until everything
is perfect – which it will never be…
Maybe the next time we meet again
we will have paid our dues and
planted our seeds and said our last goodbye
Maybe the next time
our first hello will be the beginning of
our new and improved eternity together."

Tom cleared his throat and folded the paper twice. He placed the poem next to her headstone and whispered, "You'll be near my side forever and ever."

He stared at her grave silently wishing he could hear her voice, feel her touch or smell her hair just one more time. He slid his hands into the pockets of his trousers and walked back to his car.

As he drove out of the cemetery he turned up the sound on his radio and heard Peabo Bryson's song, "If Ever You're in My Arms Again."

The words were more than he could bear. Tom pulled over, parked his car and he cried.

Epilogue

Love that is ancient
does not ever fade away
it can never die.

Tom drove through the gate at Fort Sam Houston and tried to push away the memories clouding his heart, which were in direct contrast to the bright, warm September day. He parked his shiny new gold Lexus beside the pastor's black Seville, the only other car in view. As he sat facing the white limestone chapel, he knew it would take great effort for him to enter the door, even for his son's wedding. Not since Tish, the love of his life died and was memorialized here, had he stepped into the building.

Today, he had good reason to come back. Their son, James would marry his high school sweetheart in the same spot he'd married Tish. Though it didn't make it any less painful, Tom knew he had to face his longing for her all over again. His story with Tish had begun at Fort Sam Houston and, when fate intervened, Fort Sam had also been the place where it ended.

As he slowly opened the car door and forced himself to step out to the pavement, he wiped a tear from his eye. Then he took a deep breath, reluctant to have his feelings show, especially to James. This would hopefully be the happiest day of his son's life and he deserved to remain oblivious to Tom's pain.

He climbed the limestone steps toward the front door of the chapel. The hum of an engine made him turn. A black limo slowed and stopped just behind him. He lingered curiously with one foot on the step. A small breeze lifted the tail of his tuxedo, and dried the last signs of any tears on his face.

"Hey, Dad!" His son climbed out from the backseat. His ear-to-ear smile warmed Tom's heart. Though James was a few inches taller than Tom, he looked very much like his father—milk chocolate skin and dark hazel eyes, and curly, almost black hair. But that smile was definitely just like Tish's. The excitement in his son's voice swept away any remnants of sad memories.

Josh, the best man, stood behind James. Both were dressed in their formal navy blue Army uniforms and looked sharp and serious.

"Hi, son. Don't you men look great!" he replied, smiling proudly and holding out a hand to his son. He pulled James into his arms for a big hug. "I'm so proud of you. I know your mother is telling the angels how proud she is, too."

James pulled away to gaze in his father's eyes. "You know, you and grandma did a great job raising me, so she's as proud of you as she is of me. I certainly didn't do anything without your guidance. You've loved me unconditionally and I'm sure my mother would be happy about that." Smiling like a child at Christmas, he turned toward the handsome, tall young man next to him and continued, "You remember Josh, don't you? He was the caption of our college basketball team. Josh, this is my dad, Mr. Manning. You met him when he came up for our graduation."

"Hello, Mr. Manning." Josh responded, smiling broadly and looking like a younger version of Denzel Washington. He shook Tom's hand with a very firm grip. "It's good seeing you again."

Another black limo pulled up and parked behind the first one. The two young men craned their necks to get a first peek at the occupants.

"That must be your beautiful bride and her attendants." Tom stepped in front of his son to block the view. "They say it's bad luck for the groom to see the bride before the wedding. You guys had better run on into the chapel and get with the pastor."

The men didn't move still hoping to catch a glimpse of Anna and her friends. Tom placed his hand on his son's back and said, "I'll help the ladies in and make sure they have everything they need. I want you to have a long, happy marriage." He gave James a slight push in the chapel's direction. "So let's start this day off right."

Watching the two young men stroll up the stairs, Tom nearly laughed out loud as he saw James take a quick look behind him before they entered the chapel. *He's so happy.*

Tom turned toward the limo just in time to see the driver open the rear door. Anna Trevino, his future daughter-in-law, stepped out prepared for the warm day dressed in a sleeveless, white linen dress and matching high-heeled sandals. Her hair was wrapped in a white scarf, which barely covered the hair rollers poking out from under the edges.

He stood there for a moment gazing at the golden beauty. Tom had known her since she came to Churchill High School as a sophomore. James was a junior then. The two had been inseparable since the evening they met at a Spanish Club meeting. Anna accelerated her high school courses so they could graduate together. At her request, Tom had talked her parents into letting her attend Howard University with James. It was a major feat for him to convince the Mexican-American couple that the desire for the young lovebirds to remain together was not just a passing fancy. In return, Anna promised she'd return to San Antonio and attend law school at her parents' alma mater, St. Mary's University, while James attended the dental school at the University of Texas Health Science Center.

The sound of the six bridesmaids' chatter pierced the air when they exited the limo and stood on the sidewalk waiting for the driver to hand them their dresses from the trunk.

Ana turned to him and smiled. "Hi, Mr. Manning. You sure look nice today."

He reached for her and placed a gentle kiss on her smooth forehead. The sent of Red perfume enveloped him in another rush of memories. "Thanks, Ana. I clean up pretty good, huh?" He admired her vibrant makeup, unlike the soft neutral tones she normally wore, which complimented her rich brown skin and heart-shaped face.

The bridesmaids, some now holding their dresses, continued to laugh and talk all at one time. Tom glanced over to them and to see if anyone was actually listening to anyone else.

He then looked at Ana with admiring eyes. "I'm so pleased that you and James are getting married."

She grinned, "Thanks, I'm happy," she replied while juggling to keep her purse from falling to the ground, catching it by the bright red scarf tied to the handle.

"Anna, the scarf. What's that about?" He asked, trying to keep her steady. "You're wearing so much white, it really stands out."

"It's a gift from my grandmother. When she visited the United States the last time, she went to New Orleans and a street vendor insisted she purchase it. That night she dreamed that she should give it to me and tell me it was a symbol from my past."

Where have I heard that before? Tom tore his eyes away from Anna's fearing that he had just seen someone more familiar to him than he had ever expected.

Anna smiled shyly and took a deep breath as he offered his arm to escort her into the chapel.

Against his wishes, tears began to form in Tom's eyes as he realized how much she reminded him of Tish. He'd never thought about it before but Anna looked something like Tish and today, she even smelled like her. With all that sensory input, the memories tried to break forth, but Tom held them at bay. Today was all about celebrating.

Once the ladies were safely behind the closed door of the Bride's Room to dress for the wedding and take pictures, Tom walked to the back of the chapel admiring the newly constructed courtyard while allowing time for his memories to replay in his mind. Removing his tuxedo jacket, he sat on a concrete bench shaded by an old sycamore tree. A mockingbird, singing his medley of stolen songs, kept him company.

Taking deep breaths to fight off tears, Tom sat reliving that time in his life, many years before, when he met and married his queen. A time when the same happiness on his son's face had been ever present in his life.

It had all happened in this very place.

Quietly, words that spanned millennia of time echoed from her lips to his ears…*"I will come back to you. Remember, our love is eternal."*

The moral of this story is…

When you find your soulmate…
hold on, don't let go, don't waste time –
no matter what.

About the Author

Since 1990, Linda Everett Moyé, JD has owned and operated the successful, small-press publishing company, LEJ Poetic Expressions. She authored and published four books of poetry: *From A Delta's Heart, The Courage to Say It, Imagine This...* and *Where Spirits Dance.* As the managing editor and publisher of the book, *Delta Girls Stories of Sisterhood*, she published the personal stories of sisterhood written by thirty-nine members of her sorority. A contributing poet in the book, *Violets,* Linda also has a recipe included in the cookbook, *Occasions to Savor*. Her short story, "Wild Game" was published in the premiere issue of *Afra Victoria Magazine.*

Linda's work has received several awards and appears on www.poetry.com. She was inducted into the San Antonio Women's Hall of Fame in recognition of her writing accomplishments. The International Society of Poetry awarded Linda the 2004 Outstanding Achievement in Poetry Award and included her in their 2006 National Poetry Month Poetry Ambassador Online Directory. She is a member of Writers' League of Texas.

With an extensive career as a trainer, human resources professional, mediator and adjunct college professor, Linda is sought after as a keynote speaker and lecturer on cruise ships, at universities, churches, and business sponsored cultural and literary events. With a BS Degree in psychology from Virginia State University and a Law Degree from St. Mary's University, she has traveled throughout the country leading workshops and training sessions on human resources and problem solving topics.

Contact: Lindamoye@aol.com